Toxic

Jackie McLean

TP

ThunderPoint Publishing Limited

D1344528

First Published in Great Britain in 2014 by
ThunderPoint Publishing Limited
Summit House
4-5 Mitchell Street
Edinburgh
Scotland EH6 7BD

Copyright © Jackie McLean 2014
The moral right of the author has been asserted.
All rights reserved.

Without limiting the rights under copyright reserved
above, no part of this publication may be reproduced,
stored in or introduced into a retrieval system, or
transmitted in any form or by any means (electronic,
mechanical, photocopying, recording or otherwise),
without the prior written permission of both the
copyright owner and the above publisher of the work.

This book is a work of fiction.
Names, places, characters and locations are used
fictitiously and any resemblance to actual persons,
living or dead, is purely coincidental and a product of
the authors creativity.

ISBN (Paperback): 978-0-9575689-9-0
ISBN (eBook): 978-0-9575689-8-3

www.thunderpoint.scot

Cover Image: © Eky Studio / Shutterstock.com

Acknowledgments

While the events and characters in this book are fictional, the 1984 Bhopal disaster really did happen. Many thousands of people died or were injured as a result, and many still live with its consequences. Legal wrangling over accountability for what happened continues to this day. This book is dedicated to those who campaign for justice for the victims of Bhopal, the world's biggest industrial accident. The Bhopal Medical Appeal, a UK-based charity, supports two clinics in Bhopal and their web site is well worth a visit for ways to help – www.bhopal.org. Part of my own proceeds from this book will be donated to them.

Arbroath is my home town, and much development has taken place in it over the time span it took to complete Toxic. Therefore some of the places in the book have altered. For example, the harbour area has been completely revamped, and it now has a lovely visitor centre, which wasn't there when I started writing. The abbey, however, stands as magnificent as it has done for centuries, as do the cliffs.

Toxic was a work in progress for many years, and my thanks go to friends and family who patiently bore with me and remained encouraging, even when there seemed no end to it. Their genuine pleasure at finally seeing the book published is heartwarming. Thanks to my father-in-law, Ian, for reading an early draft and suggesting improvements to it before it got sent out to fend for itself.

Special thanks go to my partner Ally, without whom the storyline would have remained dull as ditchwater. From the evening we sat with hot chocolates at Bean Scene in Shawlands and worked out a plot, she has been my constant encourager and much needed critical eye. It is due to her that Toxic was finally written. And named – she came up with the title.

My nephew, Chris Wragg, pointed me in the direction of MIC, and my thanks go to him for answering lots of chemistry-related questions. He doesn't have to hide from his emails any more.

Special thanks, too, to my dear friend (she knows who she is) for patiently answering a stream of silly policing questions.

During the writing of Toxic, I enrolled on the Writers Bureau's comprehensive writing course, which provided me with much needed discipline to sit and write, as well as positive feedback from tutors. I'd recommend it, and I'm not on commission!

And, of course, I would like to thank the team at ThunderPoint Publishing Ltd for taking the book on, and putting in all the effort that it takes to drag a draft manuscript through the stages to publication. They have made a dream come true.

December 3, 1984
Bhopal, India

The sudden screaming and the commotion outside awoke the dying.

It was still dark and muggy as the panicked youth scrambled from his bunk and switched on the lamp. Above the everyday stench that lingered even at this hour, his nostrils were immediately assaulted by a sharp, pungent smell that knifed into his lungs and set him coughing so that he could barely stand up.

He looked around the room. Mo was gone. He clawed open the shack door. Immediately the smell and his choking grew worse, his grey eyes burning red and beginning to water. A heavy punch landed on his chest, and he found himself propelled back into the room.

"Quick, get this on!" He heard Mo's voice, muffled and strange, but he failed to understand what she was saying.

His head was grabbed. His arms flailed in terror. His face was squeezed into something tight. He caught his breath. He was panting like a cornered animal.

"Are you ok? Can you breathe?" Panic in her voice, muffled through the gas mask.

The masks had been a source of ridicule when he and Mo had first arrived here, when the overly enthusiastic curator of the planned 16th Punjab Regiment museum had brought them the crate of wartime relics to document.

Now the sight of the mask made him cry out in alarm, but when he focused on what was beyond the door, he recoiled in horror and had to force down the bile that came to his throat.

The shanty suburb that lined the walls of the Union Carbide plant was enveloped in a massive plume of smoke, and through the haze he heard clearly the shrieks and the stampeding that had broken into his sleep. There were thousands of people on the street, and they were all running, crying, wailing.

He pressed himself against the shack wall, breathing hard inside his gas mask.

"There's been a gas leak from the plant," said Mo. "Come on." She tugged at his arm. Had she come back to help him because she cared about him, he wondered, or did she just need somebody to do her dirty work for her? When they'd set out together on their gap year travels, things had been good between them. But she'd grown cold towards him. Bossy. He didn't like it. What kind of man was he turning into, jumping to her beck and call?

Then the smoke was all around him.

A surge of adrenalin sent him towards the road. Arms and shoulders barged into him through the fog. He began to run alongside them, fighting to keep his balance in all the jostling. Then his foot caught on something large and he sprawled, face-first into the dust. From the level of the ground he examined the road surface. It was littered with dead and dying people and animals. Bare feet, sandals and sandshoes were pounding all around him. He'd tripped over a *bakra*, a huge, ugly goat. Its eyes were fixed wide, its tongue protruding and already covered in dust.

He slowly stood up, appalled.

Stumbling through the toxic gas cloud, his own breathing loud in the mask, he scrambled over still bodies and writhing ones.

Patches of the chaos around him emerged through the mist, and he saw the futile attempts of a street beggar to hold onto the bare threads of life. He stared, transfixed, as the man's last breaths were exhaled and life extinguished. Then the fog rolled past again and hid the terrible sight, as the running crowds set him along the road once more. He breathed into the mask deeply. Easily. Powerfully.

He twisted away in disgust from the grasping hands of a woman whose eyes were opaque and weeping, her gaping mouth uttering silent screams of agony from lungs torn by the poisonous air.

The woman reached out, grasping desperately.

He stumbled on, looking back at her with revulsion. The stampeding and the shouting, the screaming, terrified chaos in the blinding fog continued amok. He stopped.

Nobody was going to help her.

He turned back and looked at the woman again.

She heard his footsteps approach and she reached up for him, her rasping breath uttering incoherent pleas.

He saw her dirty fingernails, like those that constantly jabbed and picked at his clothing, those women in bare feet and filthy rags and their ceaseless laughing at him and his skinny, pale frame.

Well, they wouldn't be laughing at him now, he thought, as he felt the rush of blood in his veins.

With the first stirrings of arousal, he dragged the blinded woman behind an oil drum. Testosterone flooded his head at her shocked expression as he kicked her legs apart.

He would teach these bitches a lesson, and then he would return home, a man.

*On the morning of December 4th 1984,
municipal workers in Bhopal, India, were clearing
some 4,000 dead bodies and thousands of animal
carcasses from the streets following the world's
worst industrial accident.
The toxic cloud that caused the massive death toll
formed when water poured into a tank of
improperly stored methyl isocyanate (MIC).
It doesn't look dangerous. And you can't smell it
until it's too late.
You can only hope it's not sitting around anywhere
near you . . .*

The present day,
Dundee, Scotland

Monday

Chapter One

"Oh, she's in trouble this time."

"Do you really think it was her?"

"Who else could it have been? I wouldn't want to be in her shoes today – Ross is on the warpath."

"God, you're right there, Ted. I've never seen him so angry."

Sergeant Alice Moone stopped abruptly at the sound of boots clumping along the corridor towards them. She and Sergeant Ted Granger pressed themselves into the doorway by which they'd been standing, and watched as Detective Chief Inspector Angus Ross passed them. Ross's face was as red as his hair, and he walked on, his expression grim, without acknowledging the officers. They stared after him, watched him go into his office, and blinked when he slammed the door behind him.

"Well, good morning to you, too, *Sir*," said Alice.

"She's in big trouble."

"Oh, I don't know; she got out of that whole school liaison thing unscathed."

"Only Donna, eh?" said Ted, as the two officers snorted in laughter.

A door whined open at the end of the corridor, and a cloud of cigarette smoke appeared.

"Talk of the devil," said Ted.

Detective Inspector Donna Davenport walked towards them, puffing furiously on a cigarette. As she reached Ted and Alice she stubbed it out into a bottle of water, and pitched it into a bin. Her face was pale.

"Got any chewing gum?" she asked.

Ted laughed. "Here you go, lass. Covering up your habit's going to be the least of your worries today."

"Wish me luck," said Donna.

"Do whatever grovelling you have to do," said Alice. "We bloody need you." Her voice began to break, and she coughed to cover her embarrassment.

"Thanks," said Donna. She smiled meekly at her colleagues, saluted with two fingers to her forehead, and set off towards Ross's office.

DCI Angus Ross let the newspaper drop onto his desk when the knock came to his door. He rested his head in the palm of his hand, and didn't look up while Donna slunk into a chair opposite him. His fiery red eyebrows were furrowed, creating a knot of tension. But he knew that any resulting headache wouldn't cause him half as much grief as the problem he had to deal with here. He felt drained already.

He reached for the newspaper again and flashed it at Donna. She rolled her eyes to the ceiling. Ross ignored the gesture, recognising it for the false display of bravado that it was; her rapid jaw movements as she chewed the gum told him she was agitated.

"You're giving evidence in this trial, Davenport," he said. "Don't treat it like a joke."

Davenport? thought Donna, anger threatening to spill over at the uncharacteristic formality of using her surname. Her boss he may be, but they were old friends, going way back. How could he fail to see what was going on here?

"Well, I'm sorry," she said, leaning forward in a way that made Ross retreat further from his side of the desk. "But I don't see anybody laughing. And you, of all people . . . " She let the words trail away, and shook her head, saddened by her thoughts. Ross immediately felt like he'd failed some test.

"You're putting this case in jeopardy," he said. "Your own career, even. A police officer cannot behave like that in a court of law."

He threw the newspaper back down on his desk. Donna's picture glared out of the front page.

Ross closed his eyes for a moment, trying to steady his breath. Yes, he knew her stance on this matter, but how could she have put him in this position? After all they'd been through together?

The female gang that had been targeting wealthy men across the region, posing as prostitutes and leaving them penniless and mortified – and one of them dead – had been tracked down and brought to justice only as a result of Donna's persistent digging, uncanny intuition, and her enviable knack of getting the most unlikely characters to give her the information she needed. And while she'd opined loudly and frequently over the resources being poured into this case, she'd done her job diligently and followed procedure throughout. Or at least, she'd managed to avoid being caught doing otherwise.

But the victory for law enforcement, it seemed, had come at a price, and Donna's uninhibited tendency to admire the work of the gang had handed the media an ace as she dished out the sound bites that were likely to turn these women into popular heroes. And that hadn't proved to be very difficult, with Donna now exposing the comparison in resources that tended to be deployed on cases where the genders were reversed.

He opened his eyes again and studied her. She looked the same as always, but that didn't hide the fact that something about her had changed. Ross couldn't quite put his finger on it. She hadn't been herself these past few weeks, a timescale that Ross couldn't correlate with anything he knew of. The normally affable and sparky DI seemed to have been possessed by this new angry person, and now she had become even more of a loose cannon than before.

What the hell is wrong with you these days? he wanted to yell at her.

Only last week, in an episode that Ross would prefer not to have been associated with his team, he'd had to pull her from the community liaison rota for telling youngsters, "*Don't mess with us, you wee shites,*" on her first school visit. The seven complaints he'd received about the episode were all a little unsure they'd heard quite right. They didn't want to get that nice lady into trouble, but . . .

The department's bigwigs had heard all the excuses under the sun from Ross on her behalf, but they could never shake free of the fact that she got results. Results that nobody else ever managed to get. And so, exasperated as they often got, they knew they needed her, and enough had been swept under the carpet to create quite a mound. Ross, for one, would do whatever it took to hang onto her. Except this time. He was out of rope. He'd thought the school liaison thing was a step too far, but now this. He could never have predicted this one. For the first time, he found himself nervous of what she might do next.

So instead he said, "Donna, I can't make excuses for you this time. I'm going to have to suspend you until the impact of your statements to the media on this case can be assessed."

Donna sprang to her feet, her eyes blazing fury. Ross tried not to flinch.

"You know I'd give my life for this Force!" she yelled at him. "I can't do this any more! I quit."

And she turned on her heel and marched out of his office.

Ross heard the waver in her voice and saw her eyes begin to well, before he jumped with the rattle of the office walls at the force of her slamming the door behind her.

Ross took several deep breaths. With a heavy heart he reached for the paperwork that would have to be completed to action Donna's suspension, when he heard his fax machine begin to whir.

Mildly surprised that the fax machine still even worked, and alarmed to think he might be receiving information too sensitive to be trusted to email, he watched until the last page emerged from it. He read the contents before sitting back down and reading it again.

A handwritten memo from the Assistant Chief Constable. Ross felt goose bumps form across his arms at the irregularity and the seriousness it suggested.

In stunned silence he read about the volatile toxin MIC. He read about its potential for disaster, how its exposure to water produced a deadly vapour. The last thing he'd want in his area would be a vat of this stuff not being properly stored. But here it was in the memo, confirmation that trace samples had been found here in Tayside following an anonymous tip-off two weeks ago. No information about where it had come from or where it was being kept, far less about the state of its storage.

Two weeks ago, and I'm just hearing about this now?

He was unnerved, particularly at the reference to evacuation plans in the event . . . Ross couldn't contemplate it.

The ACC's memo didn't say as much, but he was certain the initial investigation would have gone to bloody Chief Superintendent Lawson and his ego. No doubt Lawson had been handed some line of inquiry he couldn't be bothered with, or that was beneath his so-called special task force. Well, if Ross had got that job last year, he'd have applied proper police work instead of creating some special band of arse-lickers and calling it a task force.

He looked again at the detail in the memo, and the awful statistics soon took his mind off Lawson. He was left in no doubt about the gravity of the situation, and this was probably no time for resentment. This toxin, MIC, was being stored on his patch, and one wrong move could blow Dundee right off the map.

He read about the covert government investigation being pulled together by the MP Bob Skinner and a visiting expert, Professor David Chisholm, and with his jaw dropping open he read approximately twelve times the Assistant Chief's order to attend a briefing on the matter along with Detective Inspector Jonas Evanton, due to his experience at Aberdeen, as well as the only person in the department who would work with him, the Force's sharpest wit, one DI Donna Davenport.

"Oh, God," said Ross out loud, the palms of his hands beginning to sweat.

Chapter Two

The punch caught Iksan square on the chin, and the force of it knocked him onto the sand.

The impact of the fall sent his breath gushing from his chest, and stunned him just long enough to break his hysteria. Lurching up onto one elbow he stared at Gorak, who was now standing rubbing his sore fist.

Iksan opened his mouth wide to yell, to sob, but his voice was no match against the thunderous waves and the tearing wind. He had never seen a dead body before. Over and over his mind replayed it, tormenting him.

The boat had been fighting its way into the bay, when Iksan heard the deep baritone of the rocks slicing through the hull. He'd lost his footing and sprawled ungracefully onto the deck, and he remembered thinking Gorak was shouting at him again.

"Head into the waves!" he'd heard Mehmet yell at Gorak.

"The waters are too shallow," Gorak yelled back.

"You're going to get us killed."

"Just do what you're told."

"No, we do this my way now," Mehmet had growled in Gorak's face.

Iksan had scrambled to his feet, grasping for the lifebelt as the tug lurched too far into the water. He stared at the two men, who were arguing frantically now, his eyes burning with salt water.

Paralysed by fear as the tiny vessel pitched uncontrollably, he'd stared as Gorak lashed out and pushed Mehmet. Mehmet had grabbed back at Gorak, almost losing his balance but managing to keep upright.

The noise of the rocks on the hull and the frantic arguing between Gorak and Mehmet were the terrible sounds pounding in Iksan's head as he'd clung to the lifebelt, and suddenly seen Mehmet's hands grasping at the air and disappearing over the side of the boat.

Iksan had desperately sought out Gorak. The old sailor was gripping the side of the boat where Mehmet had fallen and was staring down into the water.

Iksan clambered to the spot, and heard his own voice calling out, "Mehmet!"

Gorak turned towards Iksan, who stopped at the expression on the older man's face.

"Did you . . . ?" Iksan couldn't believe what he was seeing. The lifebelt lay useless – and un-thrown – at Gorak's feet. He stared at it, then back into the water, where he could see no sign of Mehmet.

Then a lifeless form, its face forever frozen in silent shock, exploded from the waves for a second, only to be swallowed into the deep again, leaving a wake of froth that revealed nothing.

At that moment, water had rushed across the deck and swept Gorak and Iksan off the tug.

Now lying on the sand in the secluded bay, towered over by a sheer cliff-face, Iksan tried to comprehend Gorak's orders. It wasn't Mehmet's body they were to retrieve from the boat's wreckage. It was the canisters.

My God, Iksan thought. *What is in those containers?*

"Sun rises in the east," Donna muttered to herself, squinting with fond appreciation across the choppy Firth of Tay. The Fife coastline faded almost to white through the rain in the distance. With each step that pounded onto the tarmac under her trainers, her breath came laboured, and a plume of smoke flew from every other exhalation. She eased the pace as she neared her spot, her place of solace, and threw the cigarette butt ahead of her, stamping it out as she drew to a brisk walking pace.

She still felt the prick of tears threatening to sprout from her eyes, and a tumultuous swell of anger and fear added to her rapid heartbeat. But there was no doubt the six-mile jog and eight cigarettes along the way had helped to calm her.

As she'd run through the winding alleyways of the city's modest but pretty centre and out towards the shoreline, she'd ignored the stares and the wolf-whistles, although she had quickly checked several times that her clothes were actually on. Just to be sure. She'd recognised at least half of her audience as punters she'd nicked at one time or another, and hers wasn't a face they'd forget in a hurry.

What a start to a bloody Monday, she thought, and felt her mood dip suddenly. She lit another cigarette quickly, cupping the flame from her lighter with her free hand, shielding it from the breeze coming off the water. Mercifully she was alone now.

Slowing to a stop, gazing out across the firth, her mind's eye returned to the confrontation she'd had with Ross that morning. As the bitter words of their exchange replayed in her head, she was quite unaware of the black Skoda that approached from behind her, dropping to second gear on the road as it slowed.

The first thing she'd noticed about Ross was his intense sadness. Because of her. She understood the conflict their longstanding friendship presented him at times like these. Lots of times lately. If only she could have just told him.

She threw the cigarette stub under her toe and lit another, still unaware of the Skoda that had now stopped just a stone's throw from her back.

She took several steps down onto the grassy bank by the water and sat down.

"You're giving evidence in this trial, Davenport," Ross's words came back to her. "What, now I can't trust my own officers in a court of law?"

Even Ross can't trust me now, Donna thought, taking the cigarette from her mouth.

When he'd said that, she'd predicted what was coming, but she'd still felt herself go numb with shock. If only she'd sat there and lowered her head as it was now. She bit her lip in frustration. If only she'd told Ross the truth, deep in her heart she knew he'd have understood. But instead, she'd leapt to her feet, shouting her mouth off. Her only shred of hope was that if she'd seen him start at her fury, then he must surely have caught a glimpse beneath her melodramatic performance.

Lost in thought, Donna failed to note the subtle change as the black Skoda's engine was turned off.

Chapter Three

It came back to him, like it always did, the screaming and the commotion in the disorienting fog...the lingering stench... knifing into his lungs...his grey eyes burning red...resting on the choking, the dying...

Then he heard a siren, piercing. That was new. When had he heard that? He tried to place it, but it was tearing his attention from the gasping last breaths, taking them out of his reach...

Feeling as though he was being propelled backwards through a vortex, he sprang upright, panting, sweating and aroused, and found himself in his quiet, tidy room.

He felt bewildered until he realised it had been that dream. Again. Taking him back to that night.

He gulped at the clean air. Breathing hard, he looked around his room cautiously, then re-set the alarm. He wasn't going to be scared off by threats of being found out. He could take care of this. Get things back under control, the way they should be.

He swung his legs out of the bed, and sat for a moment to steady his heart rate. Time to shower, to rid himself of the grime and the filth that clung to him even now, three decades since it had happened. Time to clothe himself in fine tailoring and expensive scent, to push the memory far behind him. He had things to get on with today.

Professor David Chisholm took his time, newly aware of creeping middle age in the ache through his knees and his fingers. Carefully, he set out his slides in order on the plush chairs that lined this little room behind the podium. He'd been impressed by the facilities at the conference centre, satisfyingly so, since he'd arrived here yesterday. He'd spoken at many venues across the globe, and this one in Edinburgh compared with the best of them.

The tall slender academic rehearsed his opening lines, his soft grey eyes running ahead to pick out the landmarks in his notes that would jog his memory in the event of going blank in front of the audience.

In a well-tailored dark suit and with still only a little grey finding its way through his short honey-blond hair, Chisholm cut a handsome and confident figure. But confident was not how he was feeling right now. This was his first time in the UK in over twelve years. He blew on his hands, although it wasn't cold, and paced a little back and forth.

Sure, he was nervous about getting tongue-tied in front of an audience. That was always nerve-racking, and something he had never really gotten used to. Speaking on an issue he felt so passionately about meant he was anxious for his audience to warm to his message.

But the phone calls, more than anything else, were distracting him and setting him on edge today. He had refused so many requests to speak at UK conferences over the years, afraid of returning here and having to face up to what he had done, fearful of the floodgates that would fly open if he were to be found out. He felt sick, because now it was clear that somebody did know. The phone calls had been menacing and direct, beginning almost as soon as he'd accepted this speaking engagement, but he had tried to convince himself that the caller wouldn't ever actually carry out his threat, was calling his bluff. Chisholm was nonetheless unnerved, and with no idea who was behind the calls, he found himself constantly looking over his shoulder with the feeling he was being watched.

The rap on the door made him jump. A sweat broke out across his forehead.

"Time, now." It was the conference organiser, Tom Daniels, who started at the professor's uncharacteristic disposition. "Uh, are you ok?"

"Yes . . . yes," Chisholm offered a weak smile and scooped up his papers. "Thanks, Tom. I was miles away."

Standing at the podium, giving the appearance of being at ease at his full height, Chisholm allowed his eyes to roam across his audience, taking in the variety of faces in this collection of two-hundred or so. A great diversity of age groups, he noted, no doubt reflecting their student and boardroom backgrounds. He reminded himself that they were here to take up a common cause, if he could persuade them.

An expectant buzz emanated from them and their faces, all turned towards him, showed an eagerness that his presence had come to generate at such gatherings. Chisholm prompted himself that he owed it to the victims of one of the world's most awful chemical disasters to concentrate on his message now and to forget about the phone calls. He had a job to do.

He cleared his throat, made as to begin his opening remarks, and suddenly cried out, clutching at this throat. Eyes bulging in terror, his full weight fell against the podium, his mouth wide open, gasping for a breath that would not come.

Panic took hold of the audience, and several in the front row leaped to their feet and rushed to the choking professor.

As the first few shocked delegates reached him, Professor Chisholm suddenly regained his composure, stood again to his full height, and smiled at the bewildered looks on their faces. With a kindly gesture he ushered them back to their seats.

"Picture the moments before dawn," he began. "You're tucked up in bed. It's that inky-blue silence when even the birds haven't stirred. You're warm, you're cosy, and you know you don't have to get up just yet.

"You slip into a dream where there's a glove clamped over your nose and mouth. There's a searing burning in your lungs, but you can't get a breath. Your nightmare gets worse when you realise you're awake. You fall onto the floor, gasping for breath. Imagine your terror, the burning, and the suffocation. And the last sounds you hear are the piercing screams and the thrashing struggle from the apartments above you.

"Ladies and gentlemen, this is what happened to some four thousand people – four thousand – in Bhopal one night in December 1984, and to a further eight thousand since then. Though, to a shame we should all bear, we'll never know the true number. It happened in a city about one and a half times the size of Edinburgh here."

Yes, save the world, professor, after what you did, thought the woman in the back row.

"I understand we have toxicology, chemistry and chemical engineering disciplines represented here today," Chisholm continued, unaware of the woman's accusing stare. "And we even have some bogey men from industry."

He had won them over, their relieved murmur of laughter confirmed. He was focused now.

"Methyl isocyanate, ladies and gentlemen," Chisholm went on. "Otherwise known as MIC. It's a helluva substance. But don't get me wrong, I've never campaigned against the substance itself. It works wonders in cheap pesticide production, and there are compelling economic arguments for using it across a range of product types. The world would be a more affordable place if we used it more. But it would also be a more dangerous place. To date we haven't found a fail-safe method of storing it, although we have new evidence about geological storage to consider during this conference. As things stand, MIC causes havoc and untold tragedy when its storage is breached."

He paused briefly, wondering whether he should tell them about the news that MIC was being stored under the radar here in their own country. And then what? Alert them to the possibility that some act of carelessness might expose the liquid to water and envelop them in a toxic cloud and another Bhopal? No, he'd been asked to respect confidentiality on that matter, paradoxically asked by a politician who was known for his strong stance against cover-ups.

Chisholm took a sip of water and went on following his notes.

"You're all here because you have an interest in finding new ways to store MIC safely. But when you study it, when you conduct tests, when you debate it, never ever forget or marginalise the human cost. When you analyse case studies of toxic chemical spills, never skip over the experiences of the people who suffered their effects."

At that, a young gentleman from the middle rows sprang to his feet, clapping his hands, setting off a standing ovation for the professor. In the clamour that followed, with the shuffling of chairs, the raising of hands, and the stream of questions, caught up in the exhilaration of their cause, Chisholm forgot all about the phone calls. And he failed to notice the one person in the room who remained seated, with her eyes narrowed in anger. Her mouth was set in a frown, and she clasped her red leather-encased iPad to her chest as she rose and left the conference room.

Chapter Four

Chief Superintendent Lawson strode into Ross's office, rapping his knuckles on the door after the event.

"Sir," said Ross automatically, avoiding eye contact.

Lawson nodded to the sheaf of fax papers still in Ross's hand, as he sat himself down unbidden.

"What do you make of this business, then?" he said. His voice carried a jovial note to it.

"Do you mean the presence of a volatile and highly toxic substance that appears to be illegally stored in our area? The same substance that killed and maimed thousands of people the last time it was carelessly stored? That we need to be preparing for a potential national disaster? *That* business?" said Ross, this time levelling his gaze into Lawson's startled eyes.

"Look, I'm sorry you were kept out of the loop," said Lawson. He scooped a pill into his mouth quickly. "Damned angina tablets," he muttered.

"Out of the loop?" Ross felt his neck grow red as his voice began to rise. "Look at what this stuff does!" He shook the fax papers in front of Lawson's face. "We need every scrap of resource available to find it. And you saw fit to keep most of our Force out of it?"

"There are, ah, other things going on at higher levels that you will be brought in on in due course."

Don't give him the satisfaction of asking, thought Ross. "The ACC wants to hold a briefing. Is that why you're here?"

Lawson made a display of arranging himself comfortably in his chair. It groaned like a cow in labour as he shuffled his large frame.

"Obviously a lot has happened behind the scenes in the last two weeks, to verify the details phoned anonymously to one of our plods up in Arbroath."

"Police Constable Aiden Moore," said Ross, again holding up the fax. "Please don't refer to our officers as plods."

"Look, Ross, did somebody get on your goat today?"

Ross held his breath. His eye caught the documents on his desk that were to be filed for Donna's suspension. "No. Sir." He quickly set down the fax sheets on top of them.

"Well, good," said Lawson. "I actually came here to offer my support." He paused to allow a response from Ross, but got none. "The Evanton thing?"

Ross let out a heavy sigh. Yes, Detective Inspector Jonas Evanton.

"I know you were landed with him, Ross," said Lawson. "But he saved our necks over that botched petrochemical thing that went on in Aberdeen."

"Getting a confession by beating the crap out of the witnesses?" said Ross. "*That's* going to stand up in court."

"We'd be having our arses hauled over the coals for Abram Kozel's death if it wasn't for him. You'd do well to remember that, Ross," said Lawson. "Anyway, Evanton has the expertise we need on this case, and I'll do what I can to help you manage him."

"He got sent here from Grampian into a demoted post," said Ross. "He's a very angry man. I don't trust him."

"Granted, he has a colourful history," said Lawson. "Bit of a player with the ladies, though, eh?" His leering grin vanished as quickly as it had appeared when he saw the expression on Ross's face.

"Divorced three times is not what I would call a player with the ladies. Sir." Ross wanted to stand up and throw his chair in Lawson's pompous face. "I would say he has a serious problem with women, and I don't feel my female staff are particularly safe around him. What with his reputation with his fists, and all."

"Those allegations were all made by male prisoners."

"He certainly isn't going to take kindly to being paired with Donna Davenport," said Ross. "Or by any woman in possession of an IQ." *But especially Donna*, he thought, as his brow creased in concern. Suddenly he yearned to have her here in the room with him. She'd make mince meat out of the Chief Superintendent, and she'd get away with it.

"I would have thought you'd have more concerns about Davenport's role in all of this," said Lawson. "The ACC insists on having her in, but quite frankly she's off her trolley."

Ross opened his mouth to argue, but found himself having to agree. Something wasn't right with Donna just now. What was it she wasn't telling him? What could she possibly not trust him with, after all they'd been through together?

"And don't think I didn't hear about the school liaison thing," Lawson went on. "But orders are orders. Bad toxin. Two volatile senior officers. We've got a serious problem on our hands, Ross. What say we set aside the petty stuff and help each other get this right?"

Ross closed his eyes and nodded his head. Lawson was right. Finding the MIC was paramount. The other stuff could wait.

"I don't mind telling you, Ross," said Lawson with his head lowered. "The COBRA meeting last week was one of the scariest things I've ever attended. We had to spell out our estimates of the number of casualties. In front of the Prime Minister! The Leader of the Council had to present a detailed account of how we would evacuate the area." He shook his head slowly.

"I'll have my full team here at four," said Ross.

Lawson nodded approval and relief in equal measure. "One more thing," he said as he rose from his chair. "The world expert on all of this, Professor David Chisholm, just happens to be making a rare appearance in the UK this week. Bit of a coincidence, don't you think?"

Ross cocked his head. *A coincidence and a half,* he thought.

Ross sat in silence for a long ten minutes once Lawson was gone.

He took Donna's suspension paperwork to the shredder, all the while fretting.

He checked the clock, and reached a decision. There would still be time before the four o'clock briefing.

It wasn't going to go down well, but he was willing to try anything.

He looked up Anna's number, and hoped with all his might that she was free.

"An hour? Are you kidding me?"

"Please, Anna, run with me on this one. We've just received some intel and I need these two working together. Time really isn't on our side here."

Anna heard the wheeze in Ross's breathing. She'd known him long enough now to know this wasn't good.

"Then I'll pull out my magic wand," she said.

Chapter Five

Donna sat on the grassy bank, gazing out across the Firth of Tay, her eye falling upon the bridge. Her doctor had been right to suggest she find somewhere like this. It was a place that gave her space in her head to think. To get things into perspective.

It was still a little breezy, even in this sheltered nook, but the blood pounding in her head was making her feel dizzy. She took off her running top and let the cool air form goose bumps on her arms.

The driver of the black Skoda slowly eased himself from the car and stood watching Donna's back. He could tell from the tremor in her shoulders that she was upset. Crying or fuming, he wasn't sure. He watched as she swallowed two lithium pills, a sure sign that something had happened.

Donna hated the pills, but she'd learned to read the signs now, and she'd been ignoring them for too long. She could see that here, in this quiet place. She could see how the mood roller coaster had begun to affect her decisions and her behaviour again during the six weeks since breaking up with Libby. She was arguing with Angus Ross nearly all the time now, and he'd been such a good friend to her in the past. But she just couldn't talk to him about this. She was sure others had begun to notice at work, and feared it would only be a matter of time before they figured it out if she didn't get a grip on her life and take control, even if that meant taking these damned pills.

The stumps of the old Tay Bridge followed the new one like an eerie stalker, popping above the waterline no matter when you looked, refusing to let go of the memories of the seventy-five souls drowned there in the 1879 disaster.

This always worked for Donna. Taking a deep breath, she squinted across the span of water whose bobbing ripples reflected dazzling sunlight straight back at her, and allowed her imagination to replay the noise of that hurricane force storm on the night of the famous bridge disaster. Those huge waves thundering against the bridge. The petticoats, top hats and sturdy luggage being bundled onto the train. Their faces, the colour of their hair and their eyes, the cries of alarm as the train pulled its way across the raging Firth.

She always tried to see their faces.

Donna held her head in her hands as she listened for the ghastly creaking of tearing metal as the winds ripped through the ironwork and wrenched the bridge from its castors, pitching the train and its screaming, terrified passengers to a terrible, storm-ravaged grave, the train lights disappearing into the waves.

Silent today. But these waters still held the thirty or so who were never recovered.

Donna took out a new packet of cigarettes and lit one. Yes, it put this day into perspective, she told herself. The ghosts of the wreckage told her that things would never get that bad.

But she'd had enough, and she had to make a decision.

"A cop," she said, flicking cigarette ash onto the grass beside her.

"Not a cop," with the next flick.

She withdrew her warrant card from her jacket pocket, glanced at it and wondered if it would float or sink if she pitched it into the bobbing water right now. She held it out, as if offering it to the lost passengers.

Flick with the ash. "A cop."

Flick. "Not a cop."

Was it such a bad thing to have admired that gang? Was it really them that deserved the book of the law to be thrown at them, instead of the sleazy lowlifes that had told their wives they were working late, when they'd been buying favours from some poor junked-up creature that had no worth of her own?

And what about the Abram Kozel cock-up? Not that Donna was sorry to hear about the gangster's death, but there were rumours about how the police had handled it, and the efficiency with which it got swept under the carpet hadn't escaped her notice. There were double standards, all right. What was justice all about, she wondered. Whose right and whose wrong was it that counted? Who was the victim? It wasn't always obvious.

Flick. "A cop."

Flick. Last flick left. "Not a cop."

Donna stubbed the cigarette out on the grass and stood up.

There it was, then, decision made.

The driver watched Donna stand up and stretch. Something about the stretch. What was she doing? He craned his neck to see

21

better, and as Donna exhaled the last mouthful of smoke, he saw and made a dash towards her, but it was too late. She threw her warrant card into the water, a javelin thrower's pitch, where it hit with hardly a ripple and vanished.

"Hey, Donna, stop!"

Donna spun towards him, and despite the red rims around her eyes, a smile came instinctively to her lips.

"Natesh, how come you always turn up just when I'm having a bad day?" she said, and took another cigarette out of her pocket.

Natesh brought his pace to failed saunter, and put his hand on her arm.

"Another bad day? Man, I need to start taking better care of you. What's up?" He forced himself to remove his hand.

"I'm suspended from duty."

"You got the sack?"

"No, I've been suspended. Pending an investigation into my *inappropriate behaviour*." She faked a voice. "But I suppose I'm going to end up getting the sack."

"Because of the newspaper thing?" he said, steadying his breath as she tugged on his arm, beckoning him to sit with her.

"Yeah. Top brass don't like it when cops discuss high profile cases in the media. God, what an idiot. What have I done?"

They both stared out over the water.

"Can't you talk to Ross?" said Natesh.

Donna snorted. "It was Ross who suspended me. He's furious." Then she lowered her head. "I don't blame him. I'm biting his head off all the time these days. Now even he doesn't want to know me. I just can't handle this any more."

"The job, or the . . ?"

"Yeah, that," said Donna. "It's coming every day now. I can't stop it. Some wee corner in my head is going *take the pills and it'll go away*, but it won't, will it? And every time I go on a high, I get this birds-eye view of what I'm acting like, and I think *what an arse*, but I can't stop myself."

"Take some slow breaths," said Natesh, guiding her breathing with his hands, like an orchestra conductor.

He studied her profile. The darling of the sports field in their youth, she'd surprised everyone by deciding to go to university to study chemical engineering. And she'd excelled there every bit as much as she had done in the track and field, finding a superhuman energy that had left Natesh star-struck as she blazed her way to a first class honours. And then, as surprisingly as the up had appeared, the down came crashing and burning around her, leaving a wreckage of Donna in its wake. It had been Natesh who'd persuaded her to seek medical advice.

"How come you're fighting so much with Ross?"

"Why do you think?"

"Still moping over Libby?" he said. "Man, it's been a while now."

"Six weeks, two days, four hours."

"Time you got back out there, then."

Donna's mobile rang. "Saved by the bell," she said, giving him a weak smile. The smile vanished when she saw who was calling. Angus Ross.

She answered, snapping, "I'm suspended, remember?" Then bit hard on her lip, immediately regretting her words.

"Donna," Ross said rapidly. "Something big's come in, and I need you on it right away."

She heard a wheeze in his breath. It made the hairs on the back of her neck prickle. Ross only got that wheeze when he was scared. He'd told her about it once, the time they were both stuck on the other side of a plasterboard partition from an armed lunatic with only their batons for protection while waiting for back-up to arrive. She felt a sudden rush of loyalty to him and her anger dissipated into the grass.

"I'll be right there."

"Good. You've got a meeting with Anna in Room 2.25 in half an hour."

She sprinted to the top of the grass verge, getting herself into a knot in her haste to put her running top back on. Natesh sprang to his feet, a rush of excitement rising to his chest as he ran after her.

"Can you take me to Bell Street, please?" said Donna, letting herself into his taxi.

"Cool," said Natesh. He returned Donna's grin, his teeth white against olive skin.

"Natesh," Donna said, picking up his ID tag and reading from it. "That's a terrible photo, it looks like a bad impersonation of Che Guevara. I thought you were getting a new one? Mind if I smoke?"

23

She was already lighting up.

"As long as I get to break the speed limit."

"Knock yourself out."

Natesh grinned.

"So, is this some top secret mission?" he asked, all hopeful and eager.

"I think you can go a bit faster than this," said Donna.

"Aw, but you never tell me anything!"

Donna raised an eyebrow and blew smoke out of the window. Natesh jammed his foot down to the floor and hooted in delight. He might never get juicy gossip from Donna, but having a cop for a friend still had its plusses. He glanced at her briefly, but her gaze was far away.

Her thoughts had returned to Ross. What was it that had made him so scared? And why was he asking her to meet with Anna, the psychologist? Her stomach lurched at the possibility that somehow he'd found out about her bipolar disorder. If he had, she was finished, for sure.

Chapter Six

"At least there's a phone signal up here," said Sally, hoping her light tone would be enough to end Colin's sulk. She stepped aside as the Man with a Van that she'd hired clambered in with a large box and crossed the bare living room. She watched as he placed the box carefully on the floor, rubbed his hands together, and then went back outside for more.

"Well, that's something, at least," Colin's voice came across the line.

Damn, he still sounds pissed at me.

"It's not the far end of the world," she said. "And the summer break is only a matter of weeks away."

Colin's huffed snort made her press her lips together in annoyance. She heard the man coming back up the stairs to the flat, and decided to try again. One more time.

"I still haven't worked out what language they speak here," she said, keeping her voice casual and chatty. "It certainly isn't English."

The man stared at her as he passed, and said, "Speakforyersel."

Sally smiled what she hoped was a polite smile. The Man with a Van put down the box and rolled his eyes.

"It's just as well we emailed all the details," she said into the phone, lowering her voice to conspiratorial. "We haven't been able to understand each other face to face at all."

"Well, good for you," said Colin. "Maybe you could drop me the odd email as well when I figure in your life again." And he ended the call. Sally listened to the sudden dial tone and squeezed the phone in her hand, imagining it was Colin's throat crushed in her grip.

Breathing deeply, she thought of the day she'd received the letter. It seemed like a lifetime ago now.

Back then, she'd been woken out of a troubled sleep by next door's dog going berserk at the postman. She had crept past her mother's room, hoping against hope that the racket hadn't roused her. They'd had a terrible night with her, and Sally could hardly bear the thought of an early start to her day.

Then she'd seen the letter. She remembered staring at the university's familiar crest on the envelope – familiar because she'd received so many polite rejections in response to her submissions to the prolific researcher and editor of *Environmental Toxicology*, Dr. Libby Quinn. Another rejection letter would have been nothing out of the ordinary, except Sally hadn't sent any articles that she was awaiting news of.

With a mixture of curiosity and fear that it might be a rebuke along the lines of *please stop pestering Dr. Quinn*, her trembling fingers had sliced the envelope open. What she hadn't expected was the invitation to take up a year's study placement with Libby Quinn at the university in Dundee.

She had held her breath for longer than she'd believed possible, and had let the tide of excitement steadily rise up through her body.

Without bothering to dress, she'd thrown on an overcoat and had rushed along the street to Colin's flat. He'd been up already, showered, fed and ready for morning lectures. A range of expressions, none of them positive, had crossed his face at her news.

"She's fine, don't worry," said Sally's sister on the phone.

"I still feel terrible about leaving it all to you," Sally said.

"We're fine. Anyway, is it cold up there in bonny Scotland?"

"It's freezing. And I can't understand a word anyone says."

"Therryarhen," said the Man with a Van as he came back into the room with another box.

It had seemed like a getaway dream to her, the offer of a study placement that came with this flat with its glimpse of the sea from the front window and next to the magnificent Arbroath Abbey.

Suddenly, Colin's mantra, *You're not responsible for her drinking*, had turned into, *But what about your mother?* And Sally had gained a dreary insight into her own life. She had supported Colin through his studies these past four years, even when she was struggling herself. He had taken for granted that she would always be there for him, would always provide that safety net for him, while he got to concern himself only with his ambition and not with the day to day dramas Sally had to contend with, keeping a lid on her alcoholic mother, all the while eking a living from her sampling business and firing off the academic articles.

Be there for Colin, look after mum. But who was Sally? The letter had allowed her to begin to wonder what she should make of her own life.

"So, I take it the engagement's off?" her sister said on the phone.

"It was never on," said Sally. "He never got round to asking." It was good to hear her sister laugh.

"So, would this be a good time to say, thank God for that?"

Sally was about to protest in response, but then found herself laughing along with her sister.

"He's not that bad," Sally said.

"Sister, get yourself a life."

The Man with a Van moved a mini sofa into the living room, and Sally waited until he was out of the room before sitting down on it. Her feet ached.

She let her mind drift back. Twelve years ago, her father had gathered her, her two sisters and their mother together to show them the letter inviting him to take up a temporary professorship in California. It was a once-in-a-lifetime opportunity, he had told them.

Sally remembered the tears, the pleadings, the blazing rows, as her parents had been unable to agree on common ground. Move the family to California for two years then home again? Be apart for two years then reunite? Give up the opportunity?

In the end, the now Emeritus Professor David Chisholm had left on his own.

During the first year the letters and phone calls were frequent. Then his temporary professorship was extended for a further year, during which time the communications had gradually dried up, and Sally's mother struggled on her own with her three daughters. Occasionally they saw his name referred to during evidence in various enquiries into toxic leaks that made it onto the national news, but other than that, they heard nothing of him.

Until, shortly after she'd received the letter, she saw the flyer advertising his speech in Edinburgh. It had appeared in her inbox, as if she should be proud of his achievements.

Wanting her anger and resentment to stop her from reading the details, Sally had felt the floodgates open as her yearning to see her father after all this time won over. It had felt like a betrayal of all she'd been through with her mother since he'd gone, but she hadn't been able to help it.

The flyer displayed a photo of her father, smiling and a little older looking than she had remembered him. Her eyes had sought out the bio line, and she had suddenly felt sick to her stomach to learn that in the years since he had forsaken her, her sisters and her mother, he had re-married and had two more children. She had closed the email, and resolved to go to the conference and make him face up to what he'd done.

And, on her way north, she'd stopped in Edinburgh and gone to the conference. But she'd been unable to make herself known to him, and had slunk away at the end, angry and ashamed. Ashamed that, in the end, she was running away, just as he had done.

She ended the call with her sister, deciding not to tell her about their father's return to the UK, and in silence she waited until her belongings were unloaded from the van and sitting in piles around the flat. When the man had gone, she slumped back onto the sofa, a cloud gathering across her brow as she made up her mind who she was going to be. She was going to use this placement with Libby Quinn as the stepping stone to overshadow her father's career. She was going to make him look up to her; she was going to knock him off his pedestal.

Chapter Seven

Anna sat facing the two detectives. Animosity stalked the room, palpable as the smoke swirling from the cigarette that Donna had insisted on lighting. It was a large room, and from the whiteboard at the far end, it seemed it had last been used for some brain-storming session that involved the buzzwords *positive action*, *community focus* and *capturing best practice*, with lots of arrows and other crap for the management hopefuls. A collection of about a dozen chairs sat facing it, although Anna and her small audience occupied only the coffee table near the door.

Anna sighed and was skimming the notes she had jotted down, when Donna lunged forward in her seat.

"He's an arse," she declared. She'd been astonished to find both Anna and Evanton here when she'd arrived, but relieved that it must mean Ross hadn't figured out her secret.

Anna looked directly at her. How she would dearly have loved to see something as honest as this on the whiteboard at the back. But she had to try and make headway here as quickly as possible.

"Now Donna," she said, "Try to remember what we just spoke about."

"OK," said Donna, waving her cigarette in the air as she sat back again. "*In my opinion*, he's an arse."

Before Anna could salvage the situation, Evanton jabbed a perfectly manicured finger in Donna's face.

"And she's a fucking freak," he said. He patted down his designer tie and ran his hand through his hair.

"Listen, could we go back to our focus on positive qualities?" said Anna. She was beginning to wonder whether Ross shouldn't just pair these two with new partners. For the first time in her career, she felt out of her depth and unable to reconcile the differences between the two officers. And if she was honest, she felt more than a little inadequate in their company.

"Are we done here?" Donna asked, stubbing out her cigarette in her makeshift ashtray, the bottle top from an Oasis.

"You've only been here ten minutes," said Anna. "I'm sure we can make some kind of progress in the remainder of our hour together?"

She said it, but she didn't believe it.

If only each of them could sit where she was sitting, she thought, and look at themselves. They were so very similar to each other, in the way that love and hate were so thinly divided. Obsessive intellectual giants. It was the only phrase she could find for it. They looked like they'd just walked the red carpet, and Anna, like so many others, found herself having to make an effort to stop staring at them.

But there was nothing glamorous about the impenetrable wall of ice between them. And while Anna had the distinct feeling that Donna's recalcitrance came from low self esteem, she didn't really want to find herself digging too deeply into Evanton's psyche. She knew his reputation for brutality, and she knew he'd been sent here from Grampian, from a higher rank, because of what he'd done with his fists in the Kozel case. An already angry man made worse with the demotion and, no doubt, pissed off at having to work with a woman – the department's brightest yet most difficult woman at that.

"So," she tried to rescue the session. "Donna, would you like to go first?"

Anna felt the first glimmer of hope, a mini triumph, as Donna's body language appeared to soften. She sat back in her chair and paused for a moment, her eyes faraway as she considered Anna's question.

"I know," she said. "I like that he's very logical on a case. I like logic." She looked up for approval and Anna nodded it. She shifted her attention to Evanton.

His eyebrows grew together and he began to roll his thumbs around one another. It took several moments, almost to the point where Anna thought it wasn't going to happen, until he spoke.

"She's good at getting people into her confidence," he said. It was almost a mumble. "I think she's good at reading people." He sat back and let out a short sigh, as though relieved to have passed some test.

"Well, that's great," said Anna. "Now we have something positive to build on. Now, tell me quickly, Donna, why did you want to join the police?"

The question caught Donna off guard.

"Quick," Anna snapped her fingers.

"Uh, for the excitement, I suppose," said Donna. She seemed to be taken by surprise at her own revelation. "I was good at sport, and had a bit of a craving for the adrenaline rush. It was either the Army or the police."

She stopped short of saying why she couldn't join the Army, and brushed her hand for reassurance against the tub of lithium in her pocket. She gave a little nervous laugh, passing the ball back to Anna.

"The excitement," said Anna. "That's as valid a reason as any. And you, Jonas?"

Evanton's head snapped up, but he retained a sombre expression.

"My father was in the Force," he said. "Lothian and Borders."

"When did he retire?" asked Anna.

"He didn't retire," said Evanton flatly. "He was killed on duty."

Donna spun in her chair suddenly to face him. She was surprised as much by the admission as by the fact that he wasn't, after all, spawned by the devil.

"A speeding lorry lost control on a bend and ploughed head-on into the patrol car," said Evanton. "Best of it was, it turned out to be a fucking hoax call. Lost his life for nothing."

"I'm sorry to hear that," said Anna. "How old were you when it happened?"

"It doesn't matter how old I was," said Evanton, his attention returning to the here and now. "Do we have stuff to do here, or can we go now?"

"DCI Ross wants to see you both at four," said Anna. "I don't know what it's about, but he impressed upon me the importance of you two working together and co-operating with each other."

"We always do," said Donna. "We just don't like each other." She was beginning to get twitchy about Anna's ability to spring unexpected questions on them.

But Anna knew where to draw the line. Another thirty minutes of this was not likely to take them any further forward, and Donna was right. They didn't have to like each other to work well together. She felt confident enough about handing them on to Ross, to task them with whatever was freaking him out.

Chapter Eight

Iksan let his body be pulled under by the force of the current. Under the water, everything became instantly calm. All the noise turned into canned rumbling somewhere far off, and the cold vanished. Now he wasn't trembling. He had the ludicrous sensation of dancing gracefully across the surface of the moon, when he was suddenly thrown back up and into the brick wall of cold air.

He'd been shocked by the strength of the waves, even waist-deep in the secluded bay. The wind had dropped, but the water effervesced a loathsome soup of debris, hurling flotsam against the shore's rocks.

"Over there! Over there!" he heard Gorak's voice, frantic yet exhausted. He felt the captain grasp him beneath his arms and heave him from the water. As soon as his head hit the surface, he vomited with the force of choking on the salt water.

"Over there." Gorak ignored the young sailor's predicament, and pushed him in the direction of a looming steel canister, its corner breaching the waves. "Bring it in. Quickly."

Afraid now to think for himself, Iksan pushed towards the canister, only faintly aware of Gorak's cursing as he, too, went in to retrieve what he could.

Donna and Evanton walked the corridor to the briefing room. They remained silent, and they were careful to avoid any physical contact while they walked side by side, neither one willing to give way to the other.

As they neared the room, Donna could hear the sounds of joviality and clinking coffee cups coming from inside. The door wasn't wide enough for them both to go through together, and so there was an awkward moment of stand-off. Donna drew her shoulders upright and turned a stare on Evanton. He sighed in annoyance, folded his arms, and stood aside.

"Donna," she heard several voices call as she entered the room, and instantly she found herself flocked by her colleagues.

There was the newbie, DC Dom Hilton, who glided into Donna's orbit, in awe at the fact that nobody dared challenge her as she lit up her cigarette.

Ted Granger nodded a greeting to her, his bagged eyes gleaming beneath bushy eyebrows. The near-retired sergeant generally managed to avoid briefings these days, so the fact that he was here today signalled to Donna that this was indeed something big.

"Well, where have you been?" said Sergeant Alice Moone, a smile igniting her battle-weary features. As always, Alice's uniform gleamed, and Donna momentarily regretted the loss of regalia at moving over to CID. She had to catch herself, feeling her hand ready to reach out and touch the fabric of Alice's uniform. It gave her a moment of panic that her actions might start running ahead of her brain again.

"Oh, Romeo was trying to get me to run away with him," said Donna, rolling her eyes to Evanton. "But I said, *get a grip, there's a team briefing to get to.*"

They laughed in unison. Evanton's brows furrowed together, casting a shadow over his eyes.

DCI Ross took a step towards her, caught her eye, and they exchanged sheepish smiles.

By the window at the far end of the room stood three officers she didn't know. Lawson's task force specials, she speculated, and she watched with some curiosity as Evanton walked towards them.

A brouhaha of voices approaching the door ushered in further personnel, then, into the humdrum of small talk came the stomping of important boots along the corridor, and the door crashed open as Chief Superintendent Lawson, chest puffed out, strode into the room.

Donna rolled her eyes when she saw his three stooges straighten up at Lawson's entrance. Ross's team, as one, folded their arms across their chests and watched him with barely disguised contempt.

"Afternoon," barked Lawson.

"Mhuhmn," came a low level jumble of responses from the officers in the room.

Lawson, oblivious to the lack of jumping to attention, marched over to the whiteboard at the far end of the room, and turned to face them, forcing them all to shuffle across the room towards him.

"I must insist on absolute confidentiality," he began with no pleasantries. "We have been alerted to a situation. An unusual and very serious one. Can I have a scribe, please?"

To the amusement of Ross, and to the visible dismay of Lawson, Donna sprang forward and picked up the black marker pen. The expression on her face unnerved Lawson, making him feel intellectually the weaker, and his air of superiority slipped for a moment, before he squared his shoulders and reasserted his authority.

Rank beats smart, he reminded himself.

"So, the story from the beginning," he said, while unknown to him Donna scribbled *once upon a time* on the whiteboard, eliciting at least two sniggers. Ross flashed her a warning look. *Don't piss him off.*

Lawson went on.

"Two weeks ago, Arbroath police received an anonymous phone call making claims that methyl isocyanate was being smuggled into the area. The caller provided details of where to locate traces of contamination." He began to hand out sheets of paper to the group. "You can read at your leisure just how nasty this stuff is. The information was given to SEPA, who sanctioned the creation of an expert working group to oversee testing, and in the event of positive findings, to take an investigative role in tracing where the MIC is being stored. Early this morning, the SEPA senior investigating officer was able to confirm positive sampling for MIC in the areas given by our anonymous caller. A number of lines of inquiry have been immediately opened. These are relatively straightforward: how is the MIC getting in? Who is bringing it in and why? Where is it being stored? And the matter I want you to handle, Angus, who made the anonymous phone call?"

Yes, the one you can't be bothered with, Ross thought irritably.

Lawson caught Ross's mood. It was time to let him in on the other matter, and he resolved to have a word in private at the end of the briefing. He paused and looked back to see what Donna had recorded on the whiteboard. To his immense relief it was a concise and accurate list of the points he'd just made.

"I attended a meeting last week with the Chief Constable and the First Minister. A second meeting of the UK's COBRA committee is scheduled for tomorrow afternoon . . . "

Ross, studying his feet, zoned out whilst Lawson spent some time impressing his importance and seniority upon the group.

"One more thing," Lawson went on. "Given the potential for public panic, there is a news blackout on this matter. We have briefed senior editors, and they have instructions should we enter an evacuation scenario. In the meantime, the media are co-operating with the blackout."

Chapter Nine

He found his thoughts dwelling on it again. That shanty suburb lining the walls of the corporation plant. He thought about the massive plume of smoke enveloping it, and the shrieks coming through its haze...the noise, the noise just wouldn't stop.

His hands went involuntarily to his ears, to try to shut it out. Shouting, running, crying, wailing . . . dead and dying people and animals. The dead were no good to him. But the dying . . . Oh, the sound and the smell of the dying; his heart quickened at it.

That's not right! he told himself. *Not normal!* Keep everything under control, and the past would stay under control, too. But back it came. The toxic vapour that swirled and clouded into every crevice and every hiding place moved ahead towards the city. There, it would grasp thousands more in its clutches, choking them and burning them. Now he was choking, too, getting trapped. He would have to fight his way out.

Suddenly aware again of the present, he caught his breath, and looked around to make sure nobody had seen him slip into the nightmare trance.

Feeling aroused, yet ashamed, he shook his head.

This was no time to be losing it. He had work to take care of. No slipping up.

Being able to switch it off at will pleased him.

Graeme Hunter sat down and looked with smug satisfaction around the tidy desk in front of him. He crumpled up the handwritten note left for him to phone his wife, and threw it skilfully into the recycling box that sat next to him. They had nothing to say to each other these days that mattered much to him.

The huge glass-topped rose mahogany desk had been imported especially for him upon taking the role of Dean at the Engineering Faculty. The University Board had raised a few eyebrows at his extravagance in the early days, but his success in wooing first rate investors into their eager departments had silenced them. And the less they asked about those investors the better, Hunter thought.

He had painstakingly worked his way up the academic ladder while building one of the country's most lucrative engineering outfits, and he knew a few shortcuts to the money that would have curled their hair.

If you were to get anywhere in this life, he believed, your moral code had to be a little . . . *flexible.*

His office was suitably spacious to accommodate his lavish furnishings. Large potted palms added to the sense of opulence and luxury, and a round conference table with padded seating around it sat by his door. Facing it, mounted on the wall, was a state of the art plasma screen with wireless connection to discreetly placed laptop and Mac hardware facilities. Behind him, a substantial window looked out onto pleasantly landscaped parkland, and the sun was beginning its descent over the city. It cast shafts of light that disappeared into the deep plush carpet of his office, and picked up dust motes hanging in its beams.

The tranquillity of the office pleased him. It was a contrast with the noisy, dusty environment of Hunter's Quarries, where he had made his fortune.

Yes, he thought. Life was good.

Hunter was about to pick up the steaming mug of coffee that had been left there for his arrival, when his phone rang. It was his direct line, not a call routed through the office, and he experienced a stab of alarm. The corner of his eye twitched.

"Yes?" he said into the receiver.

"I hope you're sitting comfortably."

Hunter's hand began to tremble, and a bead of sweat broke free of his forehead and ran down to the corner of his eye. It didn't sound like the delivery was off. Hunter had already tried to have that discussion, and he winced as his hand instinctively touched the bruising on his ribs that was his reminder of the lengths this maniac would go to, to get what he wanted.

"What are you talking about?"

"We've got a problem," said the caller.

Hunter's dam burst.

"What, again? What did I tell you, it was suicide to take another consignment after the last time."

The dry chuckle on the end of the line made him stop.

"Not that kind of problem," said the caller. "You're still picking up from the usual place."

"No," Hunter cut in. "No more of this. I'm out. I've had it with your problems."

"We've been grassed up."

Hunter's tirade stuck in his throat, and he found himself unable to utter a word in response. The tremble in his hand turned into uncontrollable shaking. Lately his nerves had begun to get the better of him, and he'd proffered various excuses to get out of this increasingly demanding arrangement. He finally seemed to have found the ideal get-out when the careless carriage of the last consignment left traces of the MIC spilled all over the road to his quarry. Not so much that it would have been noticed unless anyone was looking for it, but if they had been, it wouldn't have taken Sherlock to lead them to Hunter's doorstep.

"We've been grassed up," the caller repeated. "And now the government is all over it like a fucking rash."

Oh my God, thought Hunter, aghast, the phone call from Bob Skinner last week suddenly coming to mind. His old friend, the MP for the town further up the coast, had phoned, all cloak and dagger, quite unlike himself, confiding in him that he'd been asked to pull together a working group, away from the prying eyes of the media, to quietly investigate the source of various toxic chemical readings that had been picked up in the region. Skinner, against his well known stance on openness, had refused to divulge more, but said he needed a research facility and a safe pair of hands to provide data for his working group, and so he had turned to Hunter. Hunter, ever sensitive to the threat of being discovered, was initially convinced it was a set-up, though he'd quickly rebuked his paranoia. Squeaky-clean Skinner wasn't the deceptive type. And his faculty did take care of environmental toxicology, under the auspices of that irritating woman, Dr. Libby Quinn. It was a reasonable request. He'd pass this one on to her, he'd thought. But now Hunter retreated to his original caution over Skinner's call.

"The government investigation is being led by your mate, Bob Skinner, and some visiting professor by the name of Chisholm. I'll persuade Chisholm to drop the case. You do the same with Skinner."

Chisholm's involved? thought Hunter nervously.

"I'm an engineer, damn it, not a gangster," he snapped.

He was desperate to play for time and to find some way of getting out of this without drawing close again to this thug's short fuse, but his thoughts were all jumbled and he found himself unable to form a coherent objection.

"This investigation isn't going to go away by itself, Hunter. It's only a matter of time before they trace the MIC to your quarry. And if you're hauled over the coals for that, who knows when they might stumble across the details of your dirty little indiscretion?"

Hunter closed his eyes tightly against the flash of anger at the hold over him. He tried to think faster than his palpitations. This situation was rapidly moving out of his control.

"I can't," Hunter said, a little too quickly.

"*Can't?* Oh, I don't think so," said the caller. Hunter could almost feel the steely-grey eyes piercing him as he spoke.

"You don't know Bob Skinner." Hunter really didn't know if there was a price high enough to corrupt goody-Skinner-two-shoes, but if the investigation went ahead, he simply could not contemplate the consequences. He was left in no doubt that it would be he alone, and not the other man, that would be placed fully in the frame. He would be finished.

"He's a politician," said the caller. "They can all be bought, believe me. Make him an offer he can't refuse, and do it today. And if he doesn't take the bait . . . "

Hunter slumped onto one elbow, the colour draining from his face as he listened, growing nauseous, while the plan of action in the event of Skinner's failure to accept more reasonable terms for silence was outlined.

"And don't forget," said the caller. "The usual place. Make sure you're there."

There really was no way out of this.

"All right," Hunter said. "But I'll need a bit more than the usual payment this time."

Chapter Ten

Danny rubbed his hands together nervously, but was unable to hide his delight. His youthful frame and his boyish smile were a contrast to the experience he could now claim. It had taken seven long months of hard graft and wrangling to get *The Bampot* open, and now seventeen of the available twenty-one seats were booked for its first night tonight. All full dinners.

Seventeen dinners, he pondered. Manageable for one person, he hoped, as he was the only chef. He'd invited his parents and two sets of friends the previous week for a free meal trial run, and that had gone well, give or take the odd oversight. He had spent the following five days ironing out any little snags, and drafted in his two friends, Drew and Gavin, as waiters for this evening. Drew and Gavin had talked of little else that week, miraculously keeping them off their usual topics of booze, sex and booze. Their best mate had his own restaurant!

Danny was anxiously studying the hands on his watch as they crawled towards opening time, but they had a while to go yet. He took a deep breath, strode towards the doors of his little restaurant, unlocked them, and held them open to the brief glimpses of Arbroath's late afternoon sunshine that managed to break through the dissipating cloud that was gradually taking the rain with it.

He breathed in the salt air as he glanced along the old cobbled street that led down to the fish-houses and the harbour. It was nice to be back in his home town, Danny realised with a sense of quiet achievement. He'd been sharing a house in Dundee with his sister for the past seven years, having left home at seventeen, and it had never occurred to him that returning to the small town might not be so bad. And there was a definite buzz in the air. The little town's team had made it to its first ever quarter final, and there was no doubt in Danny's mind that this was a good week to have opened, his being one of the few available eateries to cater for visiting supporters.

Noisy gulls were scrimmaging and shrieking, never far away, while Danny turned to examine the restaurant, set for its first night's wining and dining.

To his immediate left, in front of the window, sat the only table not taken for tonight, laid only with simple cutlery and the ripple of sunlight catching the tabletop. Beyond that was a large round table set for eight people. This was an eightieth birthday. The daughter, Marion, had been in earlier that day to deliver the cake, complete with candles, to the kitchen. Danny had spent half an hour blowing up balloons for her while she'd regaled him with anecdotes from her father's eighty long years. Marion's cheer had lifted him out of his increasing dejection at having taken on this seemingly hopeless business venture, but following her departure, the phone had rung three times, each to make a booking for this evening, adding to his relief.

Having re-trained as a chef following a career in serial redundancy, Danny had applied himself heart and soul to making this little restaurant in the ageing harbour town the one they would all talk about.

But for now Danny's ambition was that *The Bampot* would serve the finest quality food to be sourced only locally, whether from his own back garden, from the North Sea on *The Bampot's* front door, or from the dairy, beef and berry farms that surrounded it in abundance.

Keen with new ideas, and desperate for his big break, Danny was determined to become the country's top chef, preferably a celebrity one. Being *The Bampot's* chef, catering to a tiny seaside town (for now), was as important to him as being a chef at the Ritz in London.

Danny took a step towards the birthday table and adjusted the balloons to hold them better in place, and wondered about the others who would be dining here tonight.

In the centre of the restaurant was a smaller round table set for four. To the far right was a small two-seated table, and he knew this was to host the local MP. Bob Skinner had spoken on Danny's behalf a fair few times during the course of charting his various plans and permissions through council bureaucracy. Skinner was one politician Danny had respect for amongst what was, in his view, a despicable bunch. Danny wondered if it would be a political dinner. Would the local press mention it? Or was Bob Skinner simply taking some time out with his lawyer wife to support a new local business?

To his right, in front of the restaurant's other window, was a round table that would be seating three. Each table was polished oak, with heavy polished oak chairs, all commissioned and carved locally.

Danny had applied blood and sweat to this venture. His sister, Libby, had applied her life savings.

A sharp knock on the window made him turn around.

"Donna," he called, grinning at the sight of her.

"Well, look at you," she said, as she took her cue that it was safe to go in. Any doubt in her mind about how welcome she might be here was dispelled when Danny hugged her enthusiastically.

Danny ignored his guilt at feeling so pleased to see her, guilt because she'd left Libby stricken, even now, six weeks since their break-up. Donna's warning that nobody could live with a cop except another cop had been no consolation, especially as it'd had nothing to do with her odd shifts that she'd decided to shag some tart at a works do. But it was impossible not to love Donna, and Danny missed her.

"Off duty?" he asked.

"On call," she said. "Except my warrant card is somewhere between here and Brent Alpha, so I hope I don't have to arrest anyone today."

"What?"

Danny's eyes grew wide with amusement as Donna told him about her day.

"Obviously it'd be kind of awkward for me to be here later on," she said. "So I thought, no time like the present. I'm at your disposal – where's my pinnie?"

Danny pointed her towards the kitchen as his mobile started to vibrate. It was Libby. He sighed. Now he'd have to be a shoulder to cry on, whilst Donna was hovering around him.

Chapter Eleven

The details were coming back to him clearer now, and more frequent.

He remembered the futile attempts of street beggars to hold onto bare threads of life . . . burning, last breaths exhaled, lives extinguished.

He remembered her frothing mouth gaping at him mutely.

He felt a sudden rush of excitement and needed to be alone with the memory. *Why won't it go away?*

The woman had stopped screaming, he remembered, but not whether she was alive or dead by the time he'd finished with her. He tried to scrape the memory out of his head. The shame. But his mind returned to the toxic cloud. He remembered it heading towards the city. The apartment dwellers; he had to get to them before their lives were cut short. He had to get to them while they were still in the throes of dying.

His hand moved quickly in time with his heart beat as he remembered. This was his secret. His to keep, and his to hide. To savour.

He zipped his trousers back up, and felt disgust at the clammy sweat he'd produced. What the hell was happening to him? These feelings were meant to be gone. Hadn't he kept control all of these years? Made up for his youthful mistake?

The 1930s terraced stone houses stood huddled in a row, attempting to fend off the biting cold wind that swept up off the North Sea. Crisp packets and empty cans skirmished around exposed corners with each irregular gust. The rain was slowing to a drizzle now, and although a hint of sunshine appeared in brief bursts, the skies were still grey. Yet the street didn't look as miserable today as it generally did. A rumble in the distance heralded the extra refuse collections that were on duty in a bid to tart up the town for its TV appearance in the historic quarter final. Maroon football scarves were appearing along window sills, and the promise of cheer seemed to be coming just around the corner.

If only they knew, thought Bob Skinner inside number twelve, where he'd lived since he was at school. Returning to the attic, he carefully coupled the new engine onto the Hornby wagons, and stood back to admire the complete effect, taking a puff from his inhaler and loosening his tie from his collar. He had spent all of his spare time during the past seven months – which hadn't amounted to much, really – painting the waiting room on the Lilliputian platform, cultivating a miniature forest on the trackside hills, placing cows that mooed around a pint-sized dairy farm, and laying the tracks in four different formations before settling on their route around his loft conversion. During all this time he held off running the engine, waiting for it to be just right.

Mo, his wife of twenty-four years, was perched on the edge of her desk that sat in a corner of the loft conversion. She had to compete for space on the desk, which was suffering under the strain of many years' worth of legal caseload. She worried briefly that the sight in her good eye was also beginning to strain. The other eye, opaque and scarred, acted as her impetus to keep working. But the years had now stretched into decades, with little hope of progress.

She clapped her hands in glee as Bob stood back to admire his masterpiece.

He turned to her, with a boyish grin on his face that she hadn't seen in so long, pushing his heavy-rimmed glasses back to the top of his nose.

"Do you want to throw the switch?"

"Oh, you go on," said Mo, enjoying the pleasure beaming from his face. For too long it had shown strain and despair. This loft conversion, and particularly its capacity to house the impressive model railway circuit, had saved Bob from the worst depths of his depression, and provided him with a healthy outlet when the stresses of fighting constant uphill battles on behalf of demanding and ungrateful constituents threatened to overcome him.

Bob threw the switch, and with a breath-stopping stutter then a delicious purr the Hornby engine and wagons began to pull their way along the tracks. Mo came and stood beside him, and together they watched the set, mesmerised by it. Bob's gaze became faraway and his expression wistful. Where was he going on his miniature train ride, Mo wondered?

"Is it that phone call?" she said, breaking into his thoughts.

Bob frowned.

"I can't stop thinking about it," he said. "What should I do?"

Mo turned to face him, concerned that this spell of contentment was now broken, and that Bob was hurtling along the worry lines again.

"You have to talk to the police," she said.

"But why did he phone me?" Bob demanded. "Nobody knows about the working group. And he told me to beware of the police. What does that mean? What if someone high up is involved in this whole thing? Something could happen to us . . . to you."

Bob sighed heavily.

He had been flattered when he'd first been asked to pull together a team to investigate the suspected illegal storage of MIC in his area. He was well aware that the invitation was at least in part due to Mo's famed relentless pursuit of the company executives responsible for Bhopal. But he'd still been flattered. It was frustrating that the tip-off was anonymous, but he'd seen this as the pinnacle of his career, recognition for his years of fighting and campaigning for his town to be put on the political map.

Then the need to avoid public panic on the matter had been explained to him, an excuse, he initially argued, for secrecy. He had fought his whole political life for openness and against secrecy and cover-ups; he had seen too many tragic cases brought to Mo's legal files for keeping the truth under wraps to sit easily with him.

Skinner had his own insight into this substance MIC, and what it had done to so many thousands of people in Bhopal – its highest profile casualty – and to his own wife. He had quickly understood the need for confidentiality, but had then just as quickly found himself in turmoil.

Still, he had, after much agonising and extra tinkering with the Hornby, agreed to take on the role, consoling himself with the notion that he hadn't yet decided whether to keep the public in the dark about the investigation. Until he made that decision, he was going to put his very best efforts into the task of bringing together the correct team of experts who would be able to accurately get to the truth. One of those experts, a coup for Bob Skinner, happened to be visiting the UK at the moment and had agreed to join the group. It was near impossible to perform even the scantest research on toxic chemical spills anywhere in the world without coming across the name Professor David Chisholm.

If his home town was at risk of a serious toxic leak, Bob Skinner was going to do the best damned job of getting to the bottom of it, bringing the perpetrators to justice, and making sure of a no-mess clean-up operation.

And now, this afternoon, he'd received the phone call. The one who'd tipped off the authorities in the first place. Except Bob recognised the voice. The farmer, Bill Geddes, and he'd pleaded with Bob to keep quiet and to not trust the police. Then he'd hung up, and Bob hadn't known what to do. There had been no mistaking it, Geddes had sounded terrified – and out of his depth.

Professor Chisholm was speaking in Edinburgh again this evening. Maybe he should seek his advice, Skinner mused.

"Well, you know what I think about him," said Mo. "He's one of the reasons there was never any punishment for Bhopal."

"He's an independent expert," said Bob. "He was never in a position to take sides."

"He was in an ideal position to take sides, and he chose the industry. He's not to be trusted."

Deep in thought, Bob only noticed Mo's absence from his side when she called to him from below the loft hatch.

"Phone for you." She sounded less than impressed. "The charming and delightful Graeme Hunter."

Hunter, thought Bob. *Of course. He's the one to talk to; he'll know what I should do.*

Chapter Twelve

Sally let herself fall limply onto the rolled up rug, and caught her breath. She'd worked solidly since the Man with a Van had left, and now the flat resembled something that could be turned into something habitable.

She'd resisted several urges to phone Colin, and to her surprise, she found herself growing content on her own.

She sighed as someone knocked at the door, and groaned as she got to her feet.

A large woman, who could have been anywhere between thirty and fifty, stood there in a bright red top. She held out a tray holding a steaming mug of tea and a plate of sandwiches. She smiled, ready to introduce herself, when a movement at her side made her turn and roar, "Craig!"

A young boy darted in front of her and ran down the stairs.

The woman looked back at Sally and resumed her smile.

"I'm Marion," she boomed. "Welcome to Walker Place. You'll like it here. It's quiet. Well, except for my four bairns." She let out a hearty laugh.

"Oh, thank you so much," said Sally, taking the tray. She couldn't take her eyes off the sandwiches.

"Honestly, they'd do your head in," Marion went on. At that, Craig rushed back up the stairs bouncing a ball. He tripped over it, and landed at Marion's feet with an earth-shattering wail.

"Oh, for fuck's sake," Marion muttered in Sally's direction, before scooping her son up and heading back to the stairs. "It is actually a quiet street. Honestly."

"Waaahhh!" yelled Craig.

Sally couldn't help but smile, and she thanked Marion with genuine gratitude. It took an effort to understand the accent, but she'd never had a neighbour turn up on her doorstep before with tea and sandwiches.

Holding the mug of tea in both hands, Sally stepped over the rug and picked her way amongst boxes across the room to the window. There were no curtains yet, not even any netting. So she stood behind the mug of tea and gazed at the view outside. The wind and rain had eased now.

The flat she had come to live in was one of six in a block, with only three other blocks nearby. She was on the middle floor. This particular window looked out over a grassy area with a swing park in it; to the right of that were the incredible east walls of Arbroath Abbey. From here you could see the Abbey's famous stone ring, which in days gone by would blaze with fire as a warning to approaching ships. Sally's head began to calm as she immersed herself in the image that must have presented. Far to the west of the abbey walls, the sun was beginning to set, and it was now that Sally felt how far from home she was. The sun would have set there an hour ago.

But as she gazed out, she began to realise that she wasn't looking into the back of another row of flats, and she wasn't looking at a busy main road. There were no hurrying commuters, no sirens or flashing lights trying to weave their way through piles of traffic.

Compared with Putney there was so much space here, so much fresh air and tranquillity.

Her brief moment of home sickness passed, and she breathed in deeply, slowly beginning to relax. She finally allowed herself to think that maybe life would be better here without Colin. It wasn't just the overcrowding of Putney that had made it feel so claustrophobic.

Only a short walk, but out of view from here to the east, was the shore with its impressive red sandstone cliffs. What Sally, enjoying her tea and her peaceful view from Walker Place, could not see was a relay tug smashed on the rocks, its cargo of stainless steel canisters fallen overboard and bobbing about among the wreckage, looking no more sinister than toys floating in a baby's bath.

Nor could she see the two surviving crew members frantically thrashing their way through waist-deep ice-cold water, desperately trying to grasp and gather the canisters in the choppy waters and the dimming light.

The new shipment was lacking style in its arrival.

Gorak had already presided over damage to the previous delivery of MIC canisters. He was well aware that any damage to these ones would risk their running foul of the client's notorious short fuse, and neither of the two seamen would be likely to survive it.

"You did well," said Gorak, his breathing heavy with effort. He could see the boy was shivering badly, close perhaps to hypothermia. He counted the canisters they'd brought ashore. All there. He turned his attention back to Iksan.

"Come on, up here," he said, motioning to the vertical cliff face. "We have a shelter here."

Sally saw none of this, as she finished her tea and watched the light fade from the sky

Two hours later, some of the right boxes were in the right rooms. She glanced at her watch and raised her eyebrows in surprise.

"I'd better go and eat, it's gone nine," she said aloud, and worried briefly that living on her own might make her talk to herself. Perhaps she should get a cat.

Sally wiped a hand across her damp brow, and putting the other hand to the arch of her aching back, sought out her jacket.

Chapter Thirteen

Danny took a moment to look through the hatch from his kitchen and watch his diners in the main restaurant. Libby had arrived thirty minutes before to give him a hand, and he'd needed it more than he had realised. He watched the birthday table, where Marion held court, catching up with gossip at this, the family's first get-together in too long. Her father was working his way steadily through the generous helping that had just been served by Drew in his waiter's garb, enjoyment obvious on his face.

"Craig!" Marion hissed a warning.

Danny caught Drew's eye and smiled broadly. His two friends were doing him proud tonight, delighting the customers with their comic banter and, more importantly, getting the orders right.

"Maybe I'll give up my day job and come and work here," said Libby, warmed to see her brother's contentment at how the opening night was going. This was what he had worked so hard for, what Danny had dreamed of and sweated over all these months since they'd acquired the lease to the restaurant. And he was right, Libby realised. There was something nice about being in their home town again, and not just to see the excitement created by the quarter final that was almost upon them. It was good to be among familiar faces.

Gavin appeared at the hatch with a slip of paper.

"Table Two," he said, handing over the order with a flourish and flashing a smile at Libby. Danny looked it over, took another glance across the restaurant, and darted over to the cold area to begin preparation of the meals for Table Two.

"That's the rest of Table Four ready," said Libby, fetching the hot grills from the oven.

"Thanks, Sis," said Danny. "Could you chip these potatoes for me and I'll plate up the hot food?"

They swapped places, and Danny began to dish up and present the food decoratively on the remaining plates for Table Four, the birthday table. Once he'd done that, he pressed a buzzer, and Gavin appeared at the hatch again to take the plates to the table.

Danny felt his chest swell with pride and satisfaction when he saw the expressions of appreciation on the diners' faces.

He took another look at Table One. The politician, Bob Skinner, was still seated alone, pushing his glasses back up to the top of his nose as he perused the menu.

Bob Skinner was a slender man of medium height, not unlike his own father in looks, Danny thought. As always, the MP wore a dark suit and tie, and held the appearance of a man ready to roll up his sleeves and put in a day's hard work. Danny wondered again who his guest would be tonight, then he turned and went back to the cold area to prepare Table Two's meals.

Outside *The Bampot*, sitting in his BMW's plush interior with the engine switched off and the driver window down, Graeme Hunter wrestled with a mixture of self preservation and guilt. He knew the self preservation would win over in the end – it always did – but he decided to let the palpitations calm down before he made his next move. Squat and overweight as he was, the palpitations added to his already perspiring face, and he continually mopped his forehead with a tissue.

Sitting near the open door of the restaurant, Hunter could hear the mingled sounds of loud chatter, hushed conversations, and bouncing birthday babble added to cutlery scraping on porcelain. The first stirrings of restlessness were appearing among the children, with a girn and a stomping chair leg. Damn that there were kids here tonight, Hunter cursed. The weight of guilt almost threatened to take over.

Almost, but not quite.

When he'd phoned Bob Skinner earlier to arrange this dinner, he'd been taken by surprise at Bob's revelation that he had the identity of their anonymous grass and wanted to talk *in confidence*. Not only was he going to buy Skinner's co-operation in putting the working group to rest, then, but there was an added bonus. It made Hunter smirk.

He reached into the glove compartment and lifted out the glass vial of clear liquid. It could be vinegar or water, he thought, as he stared at it and marvelled at the power it gave him.

Methyl isocyanate, he intoned, emphasising the M, the I and the

C. He'd never been too concerned about its reputation when he'd agreed to store it at his quarry. As long as the money changed hands. But when he'd been instructed to move to Plan B tonight in the event of Skinner refusing the bribe, for old time's sake he had looked up some video footage of the original news reports from Bhopal. Dated and chaotic they may have been, but they didn't soften the blow of seeing what this stuff was capable of doing. He recalled the screams caught on camera, the blistered skin and the oozing eyes replayed countless times, to the backdrop of the chatter and the children's happy voices inside *The Bampot*.

He stared at the liquid for quite some time, and made himself rehearse the plan in his head. He was going to try the conservative approach first. Surely Bob Skinner would bow to pressure and he wouldn't have to resort to using this vial? What politician would turn down the offer he was going to make? But with the seed of doubt sown in his mind, he feared Bob Skinner would be the one.

Turning the car engine back on, he touched a button and the window swished closed. He moved the car around the corner. A little less conspicuous, he thought. He placed the vial of MIC inside his jacket pocket, nervous now at its proximity to his own skin. Then Graeme Hunter stepped out of his car and made his way inside *The Bampot* for a night to remember.

Libby was standing at the hatch when she saw Graeme Hunter walk into the restaurant. Her nose wrinkled involuntarily, her dislike for her arrogant boss overwhelming her.

She kept herself out of view. The last thing she needed was to meet Graeme Hunter at a social event. There was no love lost between the two of them, and Libby reckoned Hunter would be just as pleased to not see her as she would be to not see him.

She turned back toward Danny. He seemed on a roll now, everything under control and running smoothly. She thought about the twelve student essays she still had to read and mark tonight.

"Can you cope without me for the rest of the night?" she said to Danny. Danny enveloped her in his lanky arms.

"I owe you big time," he said, kissing her on the cheek. "Yet again. I'll see you back at the house. Have the kettle on for me."

Seeing Hunter entering the restaurant, Bob Skinner stood and welcomed his dinner guest enthusiastically. Hunter and he went back a long way. All the way back to school days, in fact. In their youthful days they had sometimes joined ranks to keep themselves amused in relatively harmless ways while bunking off the odd class. They hadn't been the closest of friends, but they'd always kept in touch, and generally made an effort to socialise periodically, although less so in recent times. And as Hunter's enterprise grew into a local then a national success story, business interests had brought him into contact with Skinner's political ones from time to time over the years.

Hunter was beginning to look like his weight could become a problem for him before long, Skinner thought as he studied his old friend. All that *networking* was starting to show.

Hunter, for his part, thought Skinner looked old before his time. He remembered Skinner as an asthmatic, sickly boy, and if school yearbooks had been a thing in their day, Skinner would surely have been voted most likely to die young. *Maybe even tonight*, Hunter thought, a bitter veneer toughening his purpose. Now he was here, he couldn't go back.

"Good to see you, Bob," he said through a feigned smile as they shook hands and he took his seat.

Libby gathered her bag and her jacket, and pulling the hood up, she slipped out of the kitchen and out of the restaurant, all the while with Hunter's back to her. It wasn't until she was outside in the cool evening air that she let herself relax, sure that she'd avoided contact with him.

Taking a short cut around the corner to where her own car was parked, she saw his BMW parked there, and felt a sudden childish urge to scrape a coin along its paintwork. It must be the influence of spending the evening with Danny's old schoolmates in their home town, she thought. She smiled at the thought, and walked on, letting a group of boisterous visiting football supporters pass on their way to the small pubs around *The Bampot*.

Drew handed Danny the order for Skinner and Hunter. Curious to know who was with Skinner, Danny stuck his head through the hatch, but he didn't recognise the other man. Just some pompous businessman by the look of it, he thought as he returned to his meal preparation.

"So, this MIC investigation," Hunter said to Skinner. "What are your thoughts?"

"Oh, early days," said Skinner, pushing his glasses back up to the top of his nose. He took a sip of water. "Like I said, some traces were picked up in and around Tayside, so it looks like we've been able to confirm the tip-off. Problem is working out where it's being stored, though. Needle in a haystack, but we need to find it and get it moved to a licensed facility."

"And you say you know the identity of the anonymous caller?" said Hunter, hoping to sound casual. It was the best way of getting Skinner to open up and reveal what he knew.

Skinner nodded his head. Hunter held his breath and his tongue.

"I must say," said Skinner, "I'm not happy with all the secrecy. I do understand, of course. Public panic and all that. But it doesn't seem proper, do you know what I mean?" He pushed his glasses back up from the end of his nose again, and looked to Hunter for a response.

Who is the fucking grass? Hunter wanted to say. In his imagination he had Skinner by the throat. He mopped his brow and forced himself to breathe slowly.

"As long as you're open with the police about anything you know, you can let them decide what's to get kept secret," he said. "I mean, you won't have the full picture the way they do, and you could end up painting yourself into a corner. Take this anonymous caller, for example. I take it you've informed the police?"

Skinner shifted in his seat. "Actually, no. I was hoping to have a word with you about that, if you don't mind keeping it just between the two of us?"

It took all of Hunter's effort to look relaxed.

"Of course," he said. "Any way I can help with this sorry business, before someone gets hurt, eh?" Bob Skinner's stare made him think he'd seen through the phoney smile. His collar began to feel uncomfortably tight.

"Ok," said Skinner, leaning forward and dropping his voice to a whisper. "So, the police get this anonymous call saying there's MIC being smuggled in, they're given details that check out, and now there's a confidential investigation on the go. This afternoon I get a phone call from somebody claiming to be the informer, begging me to stop the investigation and warning me not to trust the police."

Who? Who? Who?

"Now, in the first place," Skinner went on, "how would he have known about the investigation, unless he got that from the police? It must mean he's right for me not to trust them. Graeme, I don't know what to do."

"Would you like me to have a quiet word with . . . who did you say it was? He might feel safer talking to someone like me, I mean, me being a step removed from the authorities in this matter?"

Skinner shook his head. "You wouldn't know him. A farmer out by Marywell . . . "

The rest of Skinner's words formed a jumbled background as light dawned in Hunter's mind. Bill Geddes was the grass. The farmer who provided the safe house when the MIC shipments came in. A discreet pick-up point, from where Hunter's trucks could take the consignments along the back roads to his quarry. Now, it seemed, Geddes had broken ranks.

Skinner paused as Drew came to the table and set down their starters. Digging his fork into a goat's cheese salad, he said, "Bon apétit."

Bon apétit indeed, thought Hunter smugly. So far so good.

"But I don't mind telling you, Graeme," Skinner went on after a while. "The drugs squad are taking a close interest in this as well. It seems that drugs are still coming in from Estonia. Abram Kozel is barely in the ground and some other thug has taken his place. They might have moved their entry point from Aberdeen to here, though. Less monitoring, so they think. But you'd be surprised how much surveillance there really is. The drugs squad think there's a connection with the MIC."

Hunter's fork stopped midway to his mouth, as something sharp jabbed inside his chest.

"A connection?"

"Illegal substances," Skinner said, articulating with his fork. Hunter raised an interested eyebrow, but his mind was racing.

If Skinner had picked up on the Estonian connection this early on, then Hunter really did have to put a stop to this investigation tonight. Otherwise, it wouldn't be long before the trail leading to Hunter's Quarries was uncovered. And then he'd be finished. He couldn't let that happen, he'd worked too damned hard to get where he was today. He took a tissue to his forehead.

"What if I could tell you something about where this MIC might be?" Hunter ventured.

Skinner's head snapped up, his glasses bumping to the end of his nose.

"One condition," said Hunter, raising a finger to halt Skinner's outpouring of surprise. "You have to call off the investigation."

"What?"

"Call off the investigation, Bob. I can't have the authorities crawling through my hair."

"But, how . . . ? What's . . . ?" Skinner's fork clattered onto his plate.

"For God's sake," said Hunter. "Don't draw attention to us."

"What are you saying? The MIC has something to do with *you*? You're involved?"

"You always were the smart one, weren't you? Well, if you're smart about this, I'll make it worth your while."

Skinner stared at Hunter, words of astonishment traced across his lips. Hunter leaned towards him.

"Here's the deal," he said. "You find a way to call off the MIC investigation. The operation's worth too much to let it end now. I'm willing to cut you in, if you keep quiet. You'll be richer than you ever dreamed of. Take Mo on that cruise she's been harping on about for years. Oh, and I won't let slip that I know about Bill Geddes. After all, we don't need any bloodshed, do we? Like I said, this is a lucrative venture. Do we have a deal?"

"No, we do not!"

Danny stole a glance at Skinner's table, and saw the businessman leaning forward in his chair with a satisfied smirk, while Skinner sat back, his glasses displaced at the end of his nose, and his face turned ashen. A stirring of concern caught in Danny's throat, causing him to hold his breath. He shivered as the businessman turned his head and momentarily caught his eye.

"You'd better sit up and look relaxed," Hunter murmured to Skinner as he noticed the young chef watching them. "If you draw attention, it'll only be worse."

Skinner straightened himself and his glasses, but could not bring the colour back to his cheeks.

"What happened to you, Graeme?" he whispered.

Incredulous, Skinner sat across from his old friend. Not only was there, indeed, the illegal storage of MIC nearby, but Hunter was in it up to his neck. Skinner's stare confirmed to Hunter that the MP was not about to give in to his demand.

Hunter repeated his instruction.

"Find a way to get the MIC investigation stopped. I can transfer the money into your account and you'll never have to work another day in your life. It'll blow your pitiful pension out of the water."

"You think you can buy your way out of this?" Skinner said, contempt rising in his voice. "I'll make sure they throw away the key."

Pathetic, thought Hunter. Well, he'd tried. And, as he'd feared, Skinner was not going to go with the easy option. He felt the weight of the vial in his jacket pocket. This was plan B. The video footage of the burning bodies played again on his mind. A pang of guilt made him glance around the restaurant. Although the little vial would be enough to take care of Skinner, and its vapour was unlikely to travel much further than this table, it would be enough to close the business. Hunter admired enterprise, and it would be a shame for the young chef. But there was a bigger picture here, and he couldn't take back what he'd told Bob Skinner. He knew Skinner well enough to know he would go straight to the authorities. This was the moment.

"Then you do whatever you have to," Hunter said, standing up. "Just remember, I know where the MIC is stored. And if you breathe one word about this, it'll be your last."

Careful to make sure nobody was paying any attention to him, he opened one palm in a mock gesture of defeat, while the other hand removed the vial's cap and tipped its contents into the water jug on the table. Skinner's eyes predictably followed the open palm, and he sat unaware, while Hunter excused himself to go to the gents'.

Locked inside a cubicle there, Hunter calmly brought a gas mask out of his briefcase, fitted it securely as he'd been shown, and waited. There was little chance of being affected in here, but he hadn't made his fortune by being careless with chance.

In the jug on Skinner's table, the water reacted with the MIC, silently producing its toxic vapour.

Bob Skinner sat staring blankly at the dark night, torn by feelings of fury and disbelief. He felt his chest constrict with the warning signs of asthma, undoubtedly brought on by the stress of his meeting with Hunter. He reached for his inhaler, his hand fumbling as his breath caught, and he fell, choking, across the table.

"Waaahhh!" Craig dropped the cutlery he'd been playing with under the table.

"Feck!" roared Marion, "You're worse than the . . . My God!" She jumped to her feet at the sight of her young child rubbing his very red eyes.

Danny looked into the restaurant, and immediately put down the tray he was holding. He looked from Bob Skinner slumped across his table to Marion with the struggling boy, before he heard two diners, who'd hurried to help Skinner, begin to cough and choke.

A clamour of confused and worried voices joined the scraping of chairs across the floor as the restaurant exploded into coughing and cries of alarm.

"Call an ambulance," Danny said to Drew as he ran into the centre of the restaurant.

"What's going on in here?" called a voice as the restaurant door crashed open. A group of drunken revelers fell inside, four young men in football scarves who stopped short, kicked into sobriety at the chaotic scene before them.

Their panicked shouting brought running footsteps from the neighbouring pubs.

Hunter remained stock still in his cubicle, breathing noisily into the gas mask, desperately hoping he wouldn't be found there. This was necessary, he told himself, flinching at the commotion outside. There was no way the government investigation could be allowed to go ahead.

He waited until he was sure that the mayhem was at its peak and, assured that the gas must have evaporated to harmless levels, he unlocked the cubicle door, shoved the gas mask back into his briefcase, and swiftly made his way outside.

Chapter Fourteen

Donna threw herself flat back onto her bed, having drained the last drop from her wine glass. Really, she wanted to drain the whole bottle, as she often did of an evening, but tonight she was on call.

She eyed her pager suspiciously. It sat silently on her dressing table, mocking her.

Go on, it was saying, *down the lot*.

But Donna believed in sod's law.

She left the wine bottle unfinished.

She'd spent the last half hour chatting online with Natesh, where he'd tried in vain to get out of her what her dash to Bell Street had been about that afternoon. But now he was off to collect a fare, and Donna felt alone again.

She was at a loose end. She couldn't concentrate on her book. Denise Mina, the final book in the *Garnethill* trilogy. Donna loved the main character, the luckless and rough-around-the-edges Maureen. She could be Maureen, she felt, except maybe for the accent. And for having bipolar disorder. And, of course, for getting paid to solve crimes. No, she wasn't in the mood for reading tonight.

She glanced at the time. *Out* would be opening in a couple of hours, where she would be able to walk in and with her show-stopping good looks turn all the girls' heads and find herself some company for the night. It was over six weeks now since it had all ended with Libby. She'd done her lamenting, and she was beginning to feel the need again for affection. She had very nearly convinced herself to go, when the pager whispered to her. She wanted to spit on it.

A night in with the pager, then, Donna resigned herself. Or, if the pager did sound, an evening (and probably several if an unexplained death was involved) with Jonas Evanton.

But she really needed to get away from this grotty bedsit and its claustrophobic walls. *Emergency accommodation*, she'd termed it at the time, when it was on offer from Natesh's friend of a friend after Libby had kicked her out. Now the weeks were going by too quickly for her liking. Too much overtime was making it difficult to get any flat hunting done, and although Natesh had done plenty to help by coming up with an endless stream of flats she should look at, no doubt trying to redeem himself for landing her in this awful place, she just hadn't had the time. She resolved to ease off a bit at work for the next week and sort that one out. She couldn't bear it here any longer.

The nicotine-stained walls were the bedsit's most attractive feature. Donna had done what she could to disguise them under posters of anything she could find at the station, telling herself it was only for a few days...or maybe a couple of weeks...until she got herself somewhere decent. Or, as she really hoped, until Libby let her come back home. But unless that happened, she was stuck here with the walls declaring war on drugs. Her and Foxy, the lop-eared rabbit that she'd shared with Libby. Donna reached down and stroked his face, smiling as she found her mind wandering back to the day Libby had arrived home with a surprise for her. Donna had been delighted. She'd always wanted a pet rabbit, and they'd treated him like a baby.

She watched absent mindedly as Foxy nibbled a hole in the sleeve of a sweater she had left lying on the floor. He was all she had left in the world. That's what it felt like to her at that moment. Her mind lingered on Libby, and she cursed her own stupidity of having that one drink too many and gallously flirting with the office tart, who had only slept with her *to see what it would be like*. She had decided to play the honesty card with Libby, and Libby had put her swiftly out on her ear.

Living with Libby had been like sweet nectar poured on her tormented soul, bringing her to a place where she'd begun to feel at ease with who she was; she'd been able to stop hiding and begin to believe she was as good as anybody else. And it had given her four years' wonderful relief from the mood swings. Now the nectar had turned bitter, and the mood swings were back with a vengeance.

Donna picked up the wine bottle again. Put it back down. Paced the horrible room. She felt her nerves begin to jangle, and recognised it for what it was, though she'd already taken her quota of pills for the day. More than that, if she was honest. But hadn't she turned a corner earlier on today? Hadn't she answered the ghosts of the old bridge disaster by deciding to get a grip on her life? She was not going to sit back and let it take over her life this time. This time, she was in charge. She pulled on her running shoes, then stood holding onto the headboard of her bed and slowly began to stretch her calf muscles.

What were the chances of getting a call-out now?

Her pager buzzed. She rolled her eyes and dialled Ross's number. He picked up immediately.

"We've got a CBRN, report to Arbroath High Street immediately. Chief Superintendent Lawson is Bronze Command," he barked. "This is not an exercise, repeat, this is NOT an exercise."

"I'm on my way," Donna heard her own voice respond like an automaton. Like a calm person, while her head spun in all directions.

CBRN? she thought, stunned. After the briefing today, it could only mean one thing, surely? This was chemical, not biological, radioactive or nuclear. But, from what she'd learned, it might as well be. Her heart in her mouth, she threw on her jacket and ran out the door of the grubby flat. When she got to her car, she realised she'd left the keys behind, and cursed long and loud while she ran back to get them.

Sticking her blues and twos on top of her car would let her drive like a maniac and reach the scene within ten minutes. She flicked on her radio and asked for what details there were.

As she listened to the bones of information that were trickling through, her mouth flew open.

Shit, she realised with a sense of horror, *that's Danny's place!*

Sally went out in search of an eatery. After a few wrong turns she found herself on East Abbey Street, a wide street with a health centre on the corner and the abbey at her back. She followed it until it became Hill Place, winding downhill. She squinted at the sign on the gates to a large red building that she passed.

"Library," she read aloud, and made a mental note to go there in the morning to see what they had of local interest. She could do that before heading into Dundee for her meeting with Dr. Quinn.

Happy that she had some kind of plan for the next day, she continued on down the narrowing road towards the sound of surf breaking on rocks. In the distance she could hear sirens, and she found her senses tuning in to them. Sirens were a familiar sound to her in Putney, but there seemed to be a lot of them here.

She passed a row of fishermen's cottages just as the road turned into a sandy way and she faced a choice of going left or right. She turned right and all at once found herself at the foot of High Street, with shops shuttered up against the night, and a few bars.

Up ahead she saw what was the only restaurant on High Street; outside it were three ambulances, four police cars and several fire appliances, all with blue lights ablaze.

A small but growing crowd had gathered outside *The Bampot*. Some had clearly run to the scene and were out of breath. Others were shouting to people inside the restaurant. As one of the ambulances slowly pulled away onto the main road, more sirens could be heard approaching fast, and a further two ambulances arrived in swift succession. From these two vehicles, personnel dressed in white protective clothing and gas masks descended and began to move people out of the vicinity, creating a cordon by securing police tape around the area of the restaurant. The restaurant's doorway saw an array of distressed people hurrying back and forth. People were pushing and shoving, some trying to leave, some trying to get in. All of them shouting.

"Move back! Move back!" The order came in muffled shouts as the masked personnel widened the exclusion zone around *The Bampot*.

Through the din of the engines could be heard rasping coughing and screaming children from inside the restaurant. Men's voices shouted in desperation. Above it all, the heart-rending wail of a woman, ceaseless in its agony.

Sally wrapped her arms tightly across her chest and watched a woman being led out, an oxygen mask held over her face, alongside a young boy who was writhing in agony on a stretcher. Sally's eye caught the woman's red top, and she realized with a start that it was her neighbour, the one who'd brought her tea and sandwiches.

Sally found herself being ushered by rough hands pushing her backwards away from the taped zone. She covered her mouth with her hand, unable to take in what she was seeing and hearing. From what she could tell, what she was witnessing was some kind of gas leak. Protective clothing, gas masks, police tape, flashing blue lights, coughing, shouting, people running to and fro, stretchers, panic and chaos.

Among all this, Sally watched, astonished, as a squat middle aged man simply walked away from the scene, his head bowed into his coat collar.

Five gears were entirely inadequate for the speed at which Donna raced along the dual carriageway, and the brake pads suffered enormously as she pulled up near *The Bampot*. The scene before her was chaotic, and more blue lights than she thought existed in this part of the country flashed the length of the small town's main street. Darkness had descended an hour ago, bringing with it a biting cold, and the blue lights added to the morgue-like chill in the air.

She could see police tape marking an inner cordon already, and there were personnel in chemical suits beginning their work inside it. Also just inside the cordon, where they definitely should not have been, she could see a rabble of casually clothed people – the press pack. A large number of civilians, inadequately wrapped against the cold, were staggering into one another around the cordon, kept at bay by angry shouts from the uniformed officers assigned to bring control to the area.

She ran along the street towards the epicentre, and spotted Ross standing talking with the Chief Fire Officer and Chief Superintendent Lawson beside the cordon. A sizeable crowd of onlookers had gathered by now, jostling each other in their anxiety to know what was going on.

Ross had already seen her, and made his way towards her, his face grim.

"An ambulance was called at 20.15," he said, drawing close to her ear. "People in the restaurant were choking. The paramedics felt it was no ordinary A and E matter. They called in Fire and Rescue, who made a preliminary assessment of the premises, but there's no gas leak, so the Chief Fire Officer made it a CBRN. SEPA investigating officers are on their way up. There's a chance this could be related to the MIC matter, but we can't confirm yet, so let's not jump the gun. Some substance has caused the choking, and we need to find out what it is. That's all we've got." He threw his hands up in the air. "The Press are here already."

"How did they get here before me?" Donna said, incredulous.

"It doesn't matter," Ross said, "But the first thing I need you to do is get them out of our hair. They won't get out of the cordon. Then I need you to collate the information about casualties."

"Have you called Evanton?" Donna asked.

"On his way up from Edinburgh."

"Where's Martha?" Donna swiftly moved on, looking for their media manager.

"I'm here," came Martha's voice at her side. "They're all over the place. I can't get them reigned in; they scent blood." She held Donna's arm as the DI made her move towards the cameras that were being set up. "Whatever you do, make them think it's just a gas leak."

Donna nodded agreement, and presented herself before a group of a dozen or so reporters and camera crew.

Hubba-hubba, she heard one of them mutter. She looked him in the eye.

"You scrub up well, yourself," she said to him, and although her voice was level and humourless, it triggered hearty sniggers from the rest of the pack. "Now, can I ask that you stay behind the cordon here until we assess the area for safety? As soon as we can, we'll arrange escorted access to the building for you." Even as she spoke, more vans with media teams were turning up.

"Is this a terrorist attack?" called one of the reporters.

"At this stage we have reason to believe there's been a gas leak," Donna said in a low, calming voice. "But as you can see, we're taking every precaution until we know the area is safe."

The camera technicians put down their equipment, and the reporters grew quiet, vying with one another to squeeze themselves into the palm of Donna's hand. They shuffled backwards, like a group of awed children in front of the teacher, until they stood outside of the cordon.

"I'm Lindsey Forsyth with *The Courier*," a petite petulant looking young journalist said, stepping towards Donna. She was heavily wrapped in woollen scarf, hat and gloves, clearly setting up camp for the night. "You're treating this as a major incident?"

Donna leaned in close to the girl. "We're taking it *very* seriously," she murmured, drawing the others in close. "As soon as it's safe, you can come with me for a de-briefing."

The reporter blushed at Donna's wink, then in a sudden clamour when they realised they had been managed, all the other reporters began firing questions again, clicking cameras and issuing orders to their crews. But they remained safely outside the cordon.

"How did you do that?" said Martha, impressed, taking the press pack back from Donna.

"I'm rent-a-gob, remember?" said Donna. "They never know when I might say something career-wrecking."

There was a queue of fretful personnel waiting to see Donna as she approached the front door of *The Bampot*. As they waited, they exchanged information with one another, confirming roles and duties that they'd practiced months ago.

"I'm Detective Inspector Davenport," she announced to the assembled personnel. "Please report on casualties."

There was a pause during which she heard *woman in charge?* muttered from the back.

"Just pay attention to my words, not my tits," she said. "Casualties."

She watched as a young paramedic stepped from the line, nervously chewing his lip.

"Two casualties required urgent hospital treatment," said the paramedic, reading from his scrambled head, scratching at his mop of red hair. "One adult male, one juvenile male. The youngster's mother went with him in the ambulance. From what we can tell, there were seventeen diners and three members of staff in the restaurant, but the initial commotion brought a whole lot of spectators in, so we've no idea how many in all could have been affected. We've taken thirty-eight people so far up to the casualty clearing station to get medical assessment."

He paused, checking that he'd covered everything, then took a step back.

"Thank you," said Donna. "Where is the casualty clearing station?"

The paramedic pointed to a large white tent that had been erected in a side street facing the restaurant.

"And we have a casualty bureau?" Donna prompted.

"Your team are setting it up now in the library, it's to be used as the reception and rest centre," said the paramedic.

Donna nodded, satisfied.

"Who's gone with the casualties to hospital?"

A uniformed police officer stood forward, bringing out a notepad and reading from it.

"PC Jane Eadie and PC Jonathan Batley, Ma'am."

Donna thought for a moment, bringing their faces to mind.

"Good. I'd like you to accompany me this evening and keep records. What's your name?" He looked about twelve, she thought, how could he be old enough to have finished school and gone through police training?

"Aiden Moore," he said, stumbling in his haste to get himself to Donna's side, his cheeks flushed pink. Here was somebody taking charge, he thought, and bringing a glimmer of order to the wailing mayhem of the night.

Donna turned around to find the Chief Fire Officer at her shoulder. He nodded her aside.

"Something you should know," he told Donna, standing eye to eye with her. "On the surface this looks like a deliberate chemical leak. We'll have to do more tests, of course, but I've never seen the likes. Your main casualty is the area's MP, don't know if you'd think that relevant?"

Donna pondered the information. The local MP, Bob Skinner, was a familiar figure around the town. To her knowledge he majored in leaky roofs, bin collections and dog shit on the pavements, not the sort of stuff that got you mixed up in a terrorist effort. She made a mental note to ask Ross about Skinner's recent activities.

A white-suited woman approached her and Aiden, passing them each a bundle. Emma from forensics.

"You'll need these on," Emma said, "I don't want you messing up my tidy crime scene."

Donna remained silent as she took off her jacket. Laying it at her feet, she began to step into the white suit.

"Oh, for God's sake," she heard beside her, and looked up sharply to see DCI Ross scolding her. She heard Aiden Moore snigger.

"What?" she asked, quite unaware of her tee-shirt declaring to the world, *Mine's a Slow Comfortable Screw*. Now caught on camera by an eager Lindsey Forsyth, her scarf flowing Biggles-style in the breeze.

"Keep back, please," Donna told her as she zipped up the coverall. "We don't know how safe the area is yet."

She turned to a uniformed officer who was writing details into his notebook.

"I want you to liaise with Traffic," she said to him. "Let me know the road diversions."

Pointing at another police officer, she said to a paramedic who entered the cordon, "Give him the details of relatives who need to be informed."

A queue formed once more in front of Donna, and she barked orders at each one in turn.

"Get the coastguard down here."

"I want a second opinion from the gas engineers."

"Go and meet the SEPA chemists, they'll be here any time."

"Contact the Marine Base. We're going to need a hand with all these folk."

Then she took a deep breath and faced up to what she now had to do – go and find Danny.

Chapter Fifteen

Another venue, another appreciative audience. Professor David Chisholm accepted the rapturous applause given at the end of his speech. The delegates were animated and enthused, he could see, and a number of them had already made their way towards the podium in order to speak with him personally. If he could get one message through to them, he believed, then it had to be the urgent need to find safe methods of storing MIC, and until then to press for its use to be banned.

Powerful interests would always work against him on this, he knew. MIC made pesticide production cheap in monetary terms, though often costly in human terms. Throughout his career, and more lately as it had developed to focus on this particular matter, Chisholm had been at pains to express his wish to co-operate with industrialists to find a guaranteed safe way of storing MIC and its by-products. His message and theirs need not be in conflict. Particularly if the industrialists put up the research cash, but so far that had remained on the wish list.

He gathered his papers, stepped down from behind the podium, and reached out to shake hands with the collection of eager young minds that stood patiently awaiting their chance to speak with him. A well-dressed man with an expensive watch and carefully tended hair stepped in front of him.

"Professor Chisholm," said the man politely but assertively. "If you wouldn't mind accompanying me next door, please."

Chisholm was surprised, and took the man to be perhaps a security agent. In any case, he accepted the man's air of authority, made brief excuses to his audience, and stepped aside with the stranger into the room behind the podium.

"Is there a problem, sir?" Chisholm asked, his London accent mixed with more than a little Californian drawl.

The man grimaced.

"I thought we should speak in person. David."

Chisholm's stomach turned to ice. He stared into the man's watchful grey eyes. His was the voice that had been making the phone calls threatening to wreck his marriage if he accepted the

Scottish Government's invitation to join Bob Skinner's working group. In disbelief he studied the man behind the intimidation.

"I'm not giving in to your threats." Chisholm tried to keep his voice steady, but his heart was flipping and he broke out in a cold sweat.

"I think you will," said the blackmailer. He poured himself a glass of water. "Care for one?"

"What are you doing here?"

The man paused a moment, looking Chisholm up and down. He didn't seem impressed with what he saw.

"I'm going to give you one more chance," he said. "Give you the benefit of the doubt, see if we can sort this thing out in a civilised way."

"*This thing*?" Chisholm was getting angry. He was cornered and he knew it. The flight response was no longer open to him; it had to be fight.

Without warning the man's face grew dark, and something about it scared Chisholm more than he'd been scared of anyone else in his life.

"Tell me what you've done with the invitation from Bob Skinner," the man said.

Chisholm swallowed.

"I accepted. I'm meeting with him tomorrow to assess how to take the investigation forward."

"I'm getting really fucking fed up, Professor," the man said casually. "Turn down the invitation and return to your ivory tower, or your dirty little secret gets discussed with your wife. Or, should I say, with both of your wives?"

Chisholm felt himself grow purple in the face, and felt his fists clench.

"I don't give in to blackmail."

He hoped beyond hope that he was calling the man's bluff. When he'd left the UK twelve years ago, he'd left behind his wife Laura and their three daughters. The intensity of his studies, the romance of being the expert who was sought-after the world over, meant that communication between them had gradually dried up. They'd had nothing left in common, and each had built their own new life.

But he had never divorced.

And when he met hotel heiress Nicola Dabrinski, there had never come an opportune moment in the early days, over their whirlwind courtship and marriage, to discuss it. She had from the beginning assumed he was divorced. He had neither confirmed nor contradicted it, and at some point along the way, things had progressed too far for him to find a way to tell her. And so he had married Dabrinski, become the golden boy of the charity lunch set, found that his work was attracting more funding and more attention, and during the course of the past six years had given Dabrinski two wonderful children.

Over the years he had received numerous invitations from UK institutions and he had declined them all. Because he knew. And now this man standing in front of him knew as well.

This was it. The moment that he had dreaded for years was here now. He tried to push away images of Nicola's shocked face. Or would it be furious? And what about Laura after all this time? What would his daughters think of him?

"I don't give in to blackmail," he said again, feeling his voice waver.

The man shook his head. "Don't piss with me, Chisholm. I've arranged a video conference with Nicola at 2 a.m. our time. Get the investigation stopped, or we're having a talk."

Chisholm's courage drained away.

The man's phone began to ring in his pocket. He turned away partially as he took the call.

"Any fatalities?" he said into the phone. Chisholm became alert. The man's mood had changed; a flash of anger shot across his face. "None? Are you sure?"

When he ended the call he stood silent for a moment, as if weighing up his options.

Then he turned to Chisholm. As he turned, he drew a pistol from his jacket pocket, and pressed it into Chisholm's gut. Chisholm coughed at the assault.

"I don't think you're going to be meeting Mr. Skinner tomorrow," he said. "He's in intensive care. *He* didn't do as he was told."

And he turned and left.

Tuesday

Chapter Sixteen

Dr. Libby Quinn pulled into her driveway and let out an exhausted sigh of relief. By the time she'd reached Claypotts Castle she'd been almost crying with the effort of driving, she'd been so tired, and she hadn't registered Donna's car whizzing past in the opposite direction with its blue lights flashing. The sight of the round towers on the beautifully preserved stronghold had meant she was nearly home, and hanging onto her concentration for a few minutes more while she pulled round to Claypotts Place was just about bearable.

Now, tired as she was, she sat for a moment before getting out of her car, allowing herself to feel satisfied that her brother's big night had gone so well. Maybe this time, she thought, he would get the break he had worked so hard for. It had been painfully difficult over the years to watch him crash and burn as each job he'd had turned into a P45 victim of recession. Always a hard worker, putting his soul into his labour, Danny had taken the list of job losses increasingly badly, and she'd been worried at one point that she was going to lose him to the oblivion of drink. She chuckled out loud at an early memory of Donna grabbing a bottle of vodka out of his hands and launching it through a closed window (not before taking a good few slugs from it herself). He'd sat there, stunned, had listened to her advice, and, after fixing the window, had started on his road to becoming a chef.

Donna, she thought, with a sad mixture of anger and regret, locking her car and running her hands roughly through her short dark hair. She shook her head – she needed coffee. She had work to do. No time for moping.

Sitting down with a cup of coffee, Libby eyed the pile of student essays that were awaiting her scrutiny. She steeled herself, and picked the first one up.

She'd gotten through four of the student essays, when she began to feel her eyelids drifting closed. She fought the sensation for several heroic minutes, then gave in to that glorious apathy and nodded off to sleep on the sofa.

At four in the morning she was still slumped there, in a deep sleep, when her phone rang. She peered blearily at Danny's number.

"Come on, Danny, do you realise what time . . . "

"Libby?"

Oh, for God's sake, thought Libby. It was Donna on the phone, not Danny. She must be on the sauce. That was usually when she phoned, especially these days when her mood swings managed to get the better of her. But she felt a moment of guilt, and reminded herself that Donna wasn't able to control them without the right help. And as it turned out, she had jumped to the wrong conclusion.

"Libby," Donna said again, her voice strong and serious. "You'd better come and get Danny. We're at the station. I'll explain when you get here."

Donna only spoke like that when she was working. Libby sat up, her bleary head beginning to clear.

"What's happened? Is Danny ok?"

"Just get here and I'll explain. But you need to come and get Danny."

Donna's tone was uncompromising, an order. Libby, wide awake now, grabbed her jacket and hurried to the car.

Dundee at four in the morning was dark and drizzly, and there was not a soul to be seen anywhere.

When Libby arrived at the police station, with its rows of narrow windows giving the perfectly-angled building a 1970s-style hotel-like appearance, Donna was standing on the entrance steps having a smoke. She stubbed out her cigarette when she saw Libby's car pull up, and went to open the driver's side door, causing Libby almost to fall out. Taken by surprise, Libby felt a chasm open in her heart, and all of the getting over Donna that she had managed to achieve tumbled into it, as their eyes briefly met.

Donna broke the eye contact first, and folded her arms in front of her.

"I need to talk to you first," Donna said, leaning into the car, her face almost touching Libby's. There was no warmth in her tone.

"OK," Libby said carefully. She felt suddenly self conscious, catching the scent of Donna's familiar perfume, while she had rushed out straight from a deep sleep, not even washed. "What's going on?"

"I'm not sure what's going on," Donna said. It came out harshly. "There's been some kind of chemical gas leak at *The Bampot* . . ."

Libby's eyebrows rose.

"People are in hospital," Donna continued. "Danny has been arrested on suspicion of storing dangerous chemicals on the premises . . ."

"*What?*"

"Something really fucked up is going on," Donna said, almost to herself. Even at this unearthly hour she managed to look amazing, Libby thought. Donna, however, was on a mission, and Libby was relieved to see that her attentions went unnoticed. "I will get to the bottom of what's happened and I will get Danny cleared. But just now you need to keep him under wraps."

None of this was making any sense to Libby. Too many things were assaulting her mind all at once, not least Donna's aloofness towards her. Surely, at a time like this, she'd show some compassion and lay aside their personal estrangement? Her cold manner made Libby set her own heart back to stone.

"Fine," she said. "Where is he?"

"I'm releasing him from custody," Donna said. "But the media are going to get themselves in a frenzy over this. They're going to be crawling about everywhere, and they'll try every trick in the book to get you to talk. Then they'll print stuff you didn't say."

Donna took a long, hard look at Libby. Her heart yearned to hold her tight, to shut out this nightmare for her. She looked shocked. But the last thing she would be wanting right now, Donna reckoned, would be to open up old wounds. And Donna wasn't prepared to trust her own emotions if she were to let them loose. No way was she going to make a fool of herself in front of Libby.

"Take Danny home, and keep him in. For his own good." And she stepped aside to let Libby out of the car.

Donna led Libby through the dark car park and into the main entrance to Tayside Police HQ. At this unreal hour of the morning, cold and trying to understand what Donna had said, Libby shivered, and her eyes stung as she stared ahead waiting for Danny.

The sound of a door banging open made her jump; for the briefest moment she thought she was at home having a bad dream. But then she saw Danny shuffling into the waiting room, closely followed by Donna, and she stood up, making an effort not to react to his appearance. His eyes were bloodshot and red-rimmed, and stubble had formed across his face. His clothes were in a state, and his shirt was damp with sweat. He stood as if suspended by invisible threads from the ceiling, looking as though these could snap at any moment, to let him plummet to the ground in a heap. He didn't say a word, but simply stood and let Libby fuss over him.

"Go," Donna ordered. "Take him home, and remember what I said. An officer will be round later on today to take more statements."

Libby had a sudden sense that time was turned upside down. *Later on today* sounded odd when it was the middle of the night. She was reminded of the odd hours Donna worked, and felt herself join the twilight world of the things that went on while she would once have waited for Donna to come home and creep into bed beside her.

Danny remained silent on their journey home, refusing to engage with Libby, staring vacantly ahead with an expression that scared her because of its despair. She'd never seen him so withdrawn. When they got home, he slumped onto his bed, pulling the duvet over his head, and Libby curled up next to him, watching until she, too, finally fell into a fitful sleep at around five-thirty.

At seven in the morning the telephone rang. It was their mother. She had heard something on the news, was it Danny's restaurant? And shortly afterwards, both parents arrived at the door.

Chapter Seventeen

It was almost nine o'clock in the morning. It was March, so it was cold here anyway, but now the heating system at Bell Street had conked out. There were grumblings from the civvy staff in the building, who gathered for longer than necessary around their coffee machines, remarking on their discomfort. For the team due to assemble in Room 2.25, however, there were other matters to attend to. As Donna crushed her fourth cigarette stub into a saucer in the empty room, temperature was simply inversely related to the number of layers of clothing that must be deployed, and she'd kept on her overcoat.

I can do this, she thought. *I can clear Danny.* But she found the creeping tendrils of paranoia slowly grasping at her reasoning. She tried to shake it off. Surely she was just too closely involved to be objective about it. Yet she'd handled things well with Libby, she reassured herself. *I can do this.*

A racket of footsteps and chatter came along the corridor, and Donna quickly lit another cigarette.

"Good God," said Ted Granger as he entered the room, waving his hand across his face. "I'd like to retire before I die from passive smoking, lass."

"Oh, it's freezing in here," said Alice Moone.

"Just doing my bit to provide a bit of warmth," said Donna, waving her cigarette in the air.

She watched as Ted faked a coughing fit, saw that the laughter lines didn't fade from around his eyes when he stopped, and suddenly felt the weight of responsibility of her job. She had a headlong glimpse of the prospect of another twenty years' uphill struggle battling crime in this city. *I can do this.* She stifled a yawn.

Young DC Dom Hilton nodded a shy greeting to her. All three went to remove their outdoor jackets as they entered the room, then, like Donna, decided it was better to keep them on for now.

Angus Ross walked in, grunting good mornings to his team, while blowing on his hands.

"Could you have picked a venue just a little bit colder?" asked Alice Moone.

Ted Granger responded with a hearty laugh, while Dom Hilton remained quiet and self-conscious. He glanced from one officer to another, smiling whenever he made eye contact, wishing he could think of something witty to say. Wishing he could exude the kind of charisma that Donna had.

Then Lawson and four of his specials spewed into the room, breaking the uneasy silence.

Close behind followed Evanton, who slid in nodding a general greeting and eying each officer in turn.

"Good morning," said Lawson, "I appreciate you haven't had much of a break during the night, but I think you'll agree matters have cranked up a notch."

Without pause, he then recounted the details of the poisoning at *The Bampot*, and added a further four lines of inquiry: to find out who was dining with Bob Skinner; to dig into Danny Quinn's background with a view to assessing whether he was victim or perpetrator; to confirm the toxin involved and trace its chemical process in the restaurant; and to establish if this incident was linked to the MIC investigation or if it was some ghastly coincidence.

"Because," he added, "what you haven't been party to until now is the fact that Bob Skinner was heading up the government investigation into the MIC traces." He allowed himself a moment to bask in the surprised oohs and aahs from the officers assembled before him. It was seldom enough that he was able to do that. "This information is still classified, and under no circumstances have the media to report on his involvement in any of this. Even to name him as a casualty. We have to assume he was targeted because of his role in the MIC working group. In which case, we must also assume that the other members of the working group could be targets."

He handed out notes to the officers.

"Are the media really ok with that?" asked Alice.

"I'm assured of their full co-operation on this matter," said Lawson. "Of course, they don't have to comply, so it's important that we play ball and help them with any legitimate information they ask for. Is that clear?"

All eyes were busy scanning the notes he'd handed out. Lawson decided against repeating the point. Another silence would be humiliating. He cleared his throat, cast a sideways glance at Ross, and continued.

"DI Evanton, I'd like you to assume the protective role for the working group's highest profile member, Professor David Chisholm. He's visiting from the States at the moment, and you'll find his details in your paperwork there."

Evanton, as usual, accepted the assignment with the barest nod of his head.

Chapter Eighteen

Jonas Evanton frowned as he flipped through the pages of Lawson's briefing notes. He sat down in the small audio visual room, and savoured the silence it offered in this busy complex of police activity. Evanton loved the hustle and bustle of a busy station, the purpose and the discipline, everyone knowing their tasks and their roles. But the humiliation of his demotion burned deep, and he'd been unable to muster up the good grace necessary to integrate himself within Ross's team. They all looked at him as though he was some sort of monster, as if none of them would break the rule book, given the chance. They had no idea what he'd been up against, what he'd saved them from, dealing with Kozel's gang the way he had.

And that bloody woman, Davenport. He'd heard all about her, even in Grampian. A head-case. What was Ross playing at, pairing him with her?

Patronising bastard, thought Evanton. *He doesn't know the half of it*. Then he checked himself.

Slowed his breathing.

Ran his hand through well tended hair, and brought his temper under control.

He pushed back in his chair, and looked again at the briefing notes. The Chief Superintendent really must have his knickers in a twist. He'd clearly been up all night putting this stuff together. Evanton picked out the main details, and had to concede that he was impressed by what Lawson had collated; there was stuff in here that even he hadn't seen before.

He switched on the monitor in front of him, and keyed in the first video link provided in the notes. Dated and chaotic pictures appeared on the screen, and Evanton watched impassively as original news footage of the Bhopal disaster began to play. A reporter in rolled up sleeves stood in front of a hospital, and had to shout to make himself heard above the din of tragedy and calamity. A distressed doctor frantically relayed his story of admitting piles of victims, unable to help more than a handful of choking, burning people. The news item stopped abruptly, and there followed a montage of headlines from across the globe, capturing the enormity of what had happened.

Evanton grew pale as he watched, anger simmering just below the surface. What business of theirs was it? None of them had been there when it had actually happened. By the time the first TV cameras had arrived, the noxious gas had already worked its way through the population, grabbing lives and tossing them aside as it raced on and left no trace of itself but the human misery, the bodies and the carcasses.

Evanton snapped the monitor back off. He better not watch any more. He quickly scanned the remaining notes. Evacuation plans. Hospital capacities. Professor Chisholm's resume. No leads on the anonymous caller. No clues as to where the MIC was being stored.

He wiped sweat from his lip, checked the time and hurried from the room.

Chapter Nineteen

Donna stopped for one more cigarette, oblivious to the stares she was receiving from the group of pyjama-wearing patients who were gathered at the hospital's tardis-like entrance capsule. It was chilly up here on the side of the hill, but she knew when to stop pushing her luck – try lighting up inside the hospital, and she knew what would happen.

She and the patients were huddled against the biting wind that whipped around the huge sprawling white metropolis, where it felt a little too exposed to the nearby airport's flight path. The patients were speculating about the news reporters who were arranged like infantry before them. It was clear to Donna that the waiting pack of press reporters and TV crews were torn between huddling together so as to keep warm and to overhear each others' titbits of gossip, versus keeping far apart from each other to protect any exclusive pieces of information they managed to pick up. As a result, the fairly small group managed to look like a beehive of activity.

"I'm sure I've seen her in something," Donna heard one of the patients whisper to the others, as they glanced furtively at her.

Donna smiled to herself as she ground out her stub, took another look at the assembly of news reporters, and waved to the petite blonde one that she recognised from the night before. They must be as exhausted as she was, she thought. The journalist in a woollen hat and scarf, hopping around eagerly, desperate to be the one with the scoop, caught Donna's wave, and blushed in response. But Donna had turned now and was heading into the hospital foyer.

Remarkably little activity was going on inside the main lobby of the hospital. Checking the briefing note from Lawson, Donna presented herself at the information desk, where a flash of her new warrant card got her the information she wanted with no hesitation.

Following the instructions to Bob Skinner's room, she found a uniformed officer standing watch outside it.

"Aiden Moore, isn't it?" she said, recognising the young officer who'd spent the previous night assisting her around *The Bampot*.

"Ma'am," responded Moore, jumping to attention. She saw him stifle a yawn by trying to keep his mouth closed.

"I can take over here for a while," Donna said, and she smiled to see Moore gratefully speed off in the direction of the canteen before she could change her mind.

I can do this she told herself again, as she knocked on Skinner's hospital door and stuck her head into the room. Immediately her senses were assaulted by dazzling white, heat, and beeping.

Inside the room she saw a woman in her fifties sitting beside the hospital bed. This she took to be Skinner's wife, Mo.

At the sound of the door opening, Mo Skinner looked up, and after only the briefest moment, her expression of expectancy turned to one of question. This was no doctor.

"Good morning. Mrs. Skinner?" said Donna politely. She held out her warrant card for Mo to examine.

"He's not conscious yet," Mo replied tartly. "So you're wasting your time here."

"Sorry," said Donna, opening her palm in a peace gesture. She hadn't been expecting a welcome with open arms – not from a lawyer. But she recognised the defensiveness that came from fear. What Mo feared most now, she could tell, was that her husband might not pull through, and that she'd never know why.

Mo's eyes were heavy set behind dark circles of fatigue and anxiety. She bit her lip, aware that the officer coming into the room had done nothing wrong and hadn't deserved to be spoken to that way.

"No, I'm sorry," she said. "It's just . . . "

"You don't have to explain," said Donna. "I know you've had a terrible shock. And I'm here to try and help in any way I can." *And, by the way, it wasn't Danny's fault*, her head screamed. She blinked, and checked Mo's expression for confirmation that she hadn't said it aloud. *Time for more pills*, she thought.

She watched Mo sit back, no fight in her. Donna took the cue, and sat down in a chair on the other side of Skinner's bed. She looked at him, and watched his chest rise and fall with his breathing.

"So, how are you holding up?" she asked Mo.

Mo cocked her head, looking surprised to be getting asked about herself. It took a moment for her to form an answer.

"I'm, uh, numb," she said. "Just numb. He went out for dinner last night; now he's in a coma. I don't know if he's going to . . . "

"He's in good hands," said Donna. She quickly motioned to her ear. *Coma patients can hear what you're saying.* "I'm sure he'll make

81

a speedy recovery."

Mo followed her lead. "Yes, yes, of course he will. It's so tiring in here. I just want him back home." She returned Donna's smile.

"Obviously we have to look at any connection this incident might have with the working group Mr. Skinner is leading," said Donna. She studied the conflict going on in Mo's body language. Her leaning toward Donna, yet her arms folding quickly across her chest. Her eyes darting around the room, then settling on Donna's steady gaze.

"I'm not sure I can talk to you about that."

"Look, I know the working group is off the record," said Donna. "But you're his wife. I'm assuming he talked to you about it. And it must have crossed your mind."

"Of course it did," said Mo. "But it seems so far fetched. I mean, surely this was just a terrible accident? Nobody knew about Bob's involvement."

Donna sensed the hesitation in Mo's voice, the sudden recall of a relevant detail.

"But?"

Mo looked at her, then at Bob as if to check whether he was listening, then back at Donna.

"Bob got a phone call," she said. She began to pluck at the sleeve of her jumper.

Donna sat back in her chair. She knew when a person felt they'd said too much, and she knew how quickly they could retract.

"Whatever's going on with the MIC storage," said Donna, "we know one of the party has broken ranks."

"Yes," said Mo. "That's who phoned Bob. The one who tipped off the police."

Donna nodded her head and said nothing. Best to let Mo keep talking.

"He said the caller warned him to be wary of the police." Mo quickly turned her gaze away from Donna. "Begged him to kill off the investigation."

"Are you saying Bob received a direct threat?"

"Not as such," said Mo. "Bob said the caller sounded terrified. It was a warning, though. But that can't have had anything to do with last night?"

"It's beginning to sound like a plausible line of inquiry to me," said Donna. "Which means the other members of the working group may be at risk of similar scare tactics."

Mo nodded her understanding, though her eyes widened slightly.

"It would be helpful if you told me what you know about Bob's work on the investigation," said Donna. "From the beginning."

Mo thought for a minute.

"About two weeks ago," she began, "Bob got a call from the Cabinet Office. He had to go down to London, where they told him about the anonymous call about there being MIC in the area."

Something habitual about the way she said it caught Donna's attention. "You're familiar with MIC?"

"Yes," said Mo. "I've been providing free legal representation for Victims of Bhopal, a group who've been seeking justice for what happened there in 1984. I was a student there when it happened." Involuntarily, she touched her scarred eye. "I was one of the lucky ones, I got airlifted out straight away."

"Wow," said Donna. "I watched the original news footage. You were lucky, right enough. Is your legal work for Victims of Bhopal widely known?"

"I suppose," said Mo. "It's never had the profile it should have had, but it's never been kept quiet, either."

"Was that why Bob was asked to chair the investigation?" said Donna.

"It's at least part of the reason," said Mo. "I guess there are other politicians in the area who could have been asked. Where are you going with this?"

Always the lawyer, thought Donna. "I'm a detective," she said. "I'm following my nose. No concrete thoughts yet – I'd tell you, believe me."

"Sorry," said Mo.

"How did Bob come to recruit Professor Chisholm onto the group?" Donna asked. "I mean, he's quite a scoop, by all accounts."

A flicker of annoyance on Mo's face made Donna stop.

"What is it?" she asked. "What did you just think of there?"

"David Chisholm has consistently provided expert witness for the company responsible for Bhopal," said Mo. "He has an agenda, and he's not on our side."

Donna sat back in her chair. She could murder a cigarette right now. *Concentrate.* Could David Chisholm have something to do with all of this? The timing of his arrival in the UK did seem to be too much of a coincidence.

"You and Chisholm have bad history?"

"He has a vested interest. In the industry. They pay his exorbitant fees."

"Do you think he'd have an interest in getting this investigation stopped?" said Donna.

"I wouldn't put it past him."

Hmm, thought Donna. *Evanton needs to know about this.*

"Thank you, Mo," she said, standing up from her chair. Her hands had begun to jitter. Nicotine or lithium, she wasn't sure which one it was she needed first. "You've been very helpful. Myself or my colleague, Detective Inspector Jonas Evanton, will call back in on you later . . . " She trailed off as Mo's face blanched.

"Jonas Evanton?" said Mo. "What the hell is he doing here? I thought he was in Grampian?"

Donna shrugged apologetically. No doubt all the lawyers were aware of his fisty-cuff habits. Probably had kept them going in Legal Aid quite nicely. And she left the hospital room in a hurry, contemplating her next move, and already searching her pocket for her lighter.

Chapter Twenty

He found his mind travelling back there more and more, now that he was stuck here in this hellish place.

Cramped, contained.

Like the coal shed his father used to lock him in, for hours on end, where he played the game to help him survive, pretending his father was dying out there and that he was safe in his hiding place, the little boy in the coal shed, feeling alive and invincible while the monster outside was dying. It made him feel good. Excited, sometimes.

That excitement had come back, unexpectedly, when he'd worn the gas mask. Except it had become more than that, mixed up with his confused adolescent feelings and his simmering anger at the scornful women who teased him, and at Mo's belittling of him.

Then he remembered how it had felt when the surge of adrenalin had sent him out and onto the road, when his foot had caught on the *bakra* and he'd sprawled, face-first into the dust. Lying in the dust seeing the road littered with dead and dying people and animals. They were all failing to live. He'd been the strong one then, breathing easily, moving freely. A man, like his father had wanted him to be.

And now?

His face grew red in anger. He'd kept control all these years. Paid the price.

Now he was stuck here.

In this fucking mess, getting backed into a corner. Like being shoved back into the coal shed.

"Is there any suggestion of this being a terrorist attack?" asked the newsreader.

Sally had stayed up most of the night watching the endless repeats of the events she'd walked into the previous night. While the details remained broadly the same – eight admitted to hospital, three of them now home – new information emerged from time to time. Now the reporting had moved onto speculation about a terrorist attack, which the police seemed to be struggling to keep under control.

She'd learned from the news it was her neighbour's young boy –
little blond Craig who'd tripped over the ball he was playing with
outside her door – that she had seen on the stretcher, and that his
condition was not hopeful. So far all morning there had been
footsteps up and down to and from her neighbour's flat, and a TV
crew, which had planned to cover the quarter final, was now
stationed outside the six-in-a-block.

Sally was growing agitated. Today she was to meet Libby Quinn
in Dundee, but her bleary eyes kept lifting from her academic
papers to the news coverage on the TV. She could hardly believe
all this coverage was for an incident that she'd walked into here in
her new home town. But she had to concentrate, prepare for this
meeting. She was not going to botch this opportunity. And now
she hated that she reminded herself of her father.

The phone rang, making her jump.

"I saw that restaurant in the news – the one in Scotland. You
weren't cooking dinner last night, were you?" her sister's cheery
voice cackled over the line. "Sally? Are you there?"

It didn't take Sally long to tell her sister what she'd seen. It came
out faltering at first, then she found she couldn't stop talking.

"God," said her sister, "I'm so sorry, I had no idea. What are the
chances?"

A moment of static underscored their silence.

"How's mum been?" asked Sally, in an attempt to change the
subject.

"You only left yesterday," said her sister. "We're surviving. By the
sound of it, better than you are."

"Well, that's not the worst of it," said Sally. "You won't believe
who else is in the area at the moment."

"Who?"

"Dad."

"What?"

Sally bit hard on her lip and closed her eyes tightly. She hadn't
intended to say it. But now her sister was pressing for details.

"Is that why you left?" her sister asked.

"No, of course not." It came out sounding angry. "I found out
he was at a conference in Edinburgh, and I . . . uh, I . . . "

"You went to see him?" Now it was her sister who was sounding angry.

There he was, upsetting them again.

By the end of the call, Sally was so wound up she had to get out of the flat for fresh air to clear her head. There was no way she was going to be able to concentrate on the papers for her meeting now. She decided on a walk to the library to have a look at geological maps of the nearby cliffs.

Heading downstairs, Sally nodded an inadequate greeting to the huddle of three tearful people standing smoking outside her neighbour's door, and then found herself outside the block's entrance door and standing in front of a TV camera.

"Don't worry, love," said the man who was dismantling the camera from its stand with one hand, while balancing a cigarette and a polystyrene cup of coffee in his other hand. "It's not switched on."

Sally took in the small white tarpaulin shelter where two people were sitting and drinking coffee, a short man in a suit who looked like a reporter, pacing back and forth, two uniformed police officers standing close to the entrance door, and an array of lighting equipment carefully covered against the drizzling rain. The reporter snapped his attention on Sally as she emerged from the building.

"Are you a relative?" he asked her, quickly clipping his microphone to his jacket and placing another one at Sally's mouth.

"No, just a neighbour," she said uncertainly. She saw another camera as its operator brought it swiftly round to place Sally squarely in its frame.

"What can you tell us about the events of last night?" the reporter asked.

Sally shrugged her shoulders.

"Sorry, I don't know anything." And she brought up the hood of her red and cream Trespass jacket, turned away, and began walking as quickly as she could.

The rain eased off as she walked along the street towards the library. But she saw, to her dismay, that its entrance was cordoned off by a large white tent and police tape, guarded by three police vans and two Army trucks. She was unnerved to see Army personnel wandering to and fro within the tented area. Towards one end of the cordon she saw another set of TV cameras and reporters.

Feeling intrusive, she walked quickly on and decided to make her way to the cliffs themselves. She could pour over their mapped geological features another time.

The shore was surprisingly calm after yesterday's storm. Thick cloud settled low overhead, hugging the sky in a claustrophobic embrace while it gathered the threat of heavy rain. Sally could see the swell of the sea further out as evidence of strong winds, but the curve of the cliffs around the sea-front here, and the buttress of the harbour walls that she could make out in the distance in the opposite direction formed a buffer that absorbed the worst of the turbulent air before it reached inland.

She made directly for the cliff top walk, a grassy track that despite its perilous proximity to the edge of the sheer drop was a popular route for dog walkers and as a shortcut to the neighbouring village. Up there on the track, she could admire the height and the depth of the cliffs. From here she could see what was less obvious from ground level, that the cliffs sprawled northwards in a series of finger-like mini peninsulas, providing sheltered coves, any one of which you could sail into in a small boat and be quite hidden from view. Whenever she looked over the edge, Sally invariably found rough tracks and make-do stepping stone circuits running their way zigzag fashion downwards among the rocks towards the shoreline. She imagined generations of intrepid venturers hewing out these rough courses, and wondered what made them stop at this point or that point in attempting their descent.

She took her time, walking slowly and taking in all the details of her surroundings, her mind calming as she focused on the wonderful geology.

Some thirty meters below Sally's feet, but still above the high tide line, a cave burrowed well into the rock face. As far as Gorak and Iksan could tell, huddled in the cave, cold and exhausted, all of the canisters had been accounted for. None of them appeared to be damaged this time. Just the boat. Losing that to the rocks was not only an additional expense, but it left Gorak and Iksan without a means to re-join their ship for home. At least the wreckage of the boat was well hidden in one of the many natural bays at the foot of the cliffs.

Iksan moved his head incrementally, inwardly grimacing at the sharp pain in his neck. His eyes felt huge and dry, and even his mouth ached. A heavy cough echoed in the cave and made him jump, jarring his neck. It was Gorak, rousing from a fitful sleep by the entrance to the cave. Iksan peered past him, through the opening to a white sky. He could hear the lapping of waves far out and some way below, and heard the clamour of gulls circling in a spiralling pattern all around. The only source of comfort was the fact that he had been able to change into a dry boiler suit that was hoarded among other provisions in the cave.

A scuffle alerted him to Gorak's awakening. The older man looked not much better than the ragged rocks among which he had lain. He nodded at Iksan.

"You still here?"

Iksan nodded back, remembering the way Gorak had sought out warm blankets for him during the night when he'd whimpered with the cold.

Gorak sat up, taking time to stretch each limb one after the other, to slowly circle his head and arch his back. He rubbed his hands roughly over his face.

"What is in the canisters?" Iksan asked.

Gorak studied the youth. "All you need to know," he said, "is that this stuff forms a very poisonous gas if it mixes with water. The canisters need to be intact."

"And we just carried it across the sea?" Iksan asked incredulously. His head started to pound.

"The pay is good," said Gorak. "Stop asking questions. We'll be home soon."

The two Estonians exchanged little conversation during the rest of the morning. All they could do was to sit tight and wait for their contact to come for them.

The white sky changed through various shades of pale gray, and the sea continued to lap against the cliff face some way below the cave. The gulls never ceased their circling and cawing.

And still they sat, waiting.

Iksan's eyes adjusted to the darkness of the cave, but never fully, allowing him to study its main features while the details remained hidden. From what he could see, this cave was well used. For one, the store of basic provisions that included the dry boiler suits was a cleverly hewed pantry disguised behind a light boulder. This sat to his left and behind him. Behind him on the other side was another carved out hollow containing two rows of about twelve silver canisters, each one about three feet high. Each one identical to the cargo they'd recovered from the boat the night before. As far as he could see into the back of the cave were littered various papers, rolled up tarpaulin sheets, coils of rope. Curious as to what this cargo was, Iksan quickly returned his focus to the silver canisters. The sun unexpectedly appearing from behind the cloud made him wince as the light suddenly reflected back off them.

He drew his knees up to his chest and hugged them, listening to the endless cawing of the gulls.

Up on the cliff top walk, Sally watched the gulls for a while, picking out the first hints of their summer plumage emerging. She checked the time, and took another glance along the footholds that led down the rock face. She decided it wouldn't do any harm to take a quick look. If she made it to the bottom, she noted, she would be able to make her way safely back to dry land, as the tide was on the way out.

Gingerly placing her foot in the first crevice, and holding on to a clump of grass, she tested the track. To her surprise, she found the way relatively easy, and she made her way to the foot of the cliffs in good time. She found herself in a sheltered cove, gulls flapping angrily at her intrusion. Standing there, it would be possible to be completely unaware of the existence of the rest of the coastline beyond these rocks. And to be completely hidden from the rest of the world.

Sally knelt down, running her hand across the various rock layers, naming them to herself and marvelling at their beauty as they caught the light from the rising sun. She meandered across the rocks, savouring the smell of salt on the air and enjoying the antics of the flustered gulls. Shielding her eyes against the sun she studied the horizon for signs of boats out there, before remembering to check the time. She was going to have to run.

Looking for a route back from the shore, she noticed a large amount of floating debris lapping in and out of the bay's northern edge. Such a shame that pollution always seemed to find its way to beautiful places. Then a cave situated about six feet above her head caught her eye, and although she couldn't be sure, she had the unnerving feeling that she'd seen something moving inside it. The hairs on the back of her neck stood on end, sending goose bumps crawling over her skin. Sally took heed of her sudden unease, and began to pick her way across the rocks as quickly as she could, back towards Victoria Park, where she would find the foot of the road leading up to the library. In her haste, she took no note of the speedboat skimming the water along the cliff-line.

Gorak sprang to the cave entrance at the approaching drone of the small boat engine. He looked out and down to the water, and flicked his hand in acknowledgement. He then scuttled back into the cave to where the canisters were stacked, and began to put them into a nearby crate.

"Come on," he said to Iksan, "help me lift this over the edge."

Iksan looked uncertainly at the lip of the cave entrance, but quickly jumped to Gorak's side and did as he was told.

"It's ok," Gorak called as he levered himself backwards out of the cave, dragging his end of the crate. His breathing was heavy with the effort of manoeuvring his large frame in the small space. "You just hold on here, and you can use the holes in the rocks like steps."

Several more gasps of effort.

"It's easy." And he sank from view, leaving the crate looking precarious.

Iksan held on tight to his end of the crate and shuffled toward the mouth of the cave. At once he saw an easy trail of foot holes and rock edges for holding onto, and he scrambled after Gorak, the canisters sitting quietly between them.

A small motor boat bobbed at the foot of the rocks, held steady by a tall man who was well-wrapped against the elements. The man offered no assistance as the two Estonians wrestled the crate of canisters into the boat.

"There'd better be no damage this time," said the man, casting them a look that made Iksan shiver.

Gorak grunted.

The tall man ushered them to the back seat of the boat, the expression on his face grim.

"Right then, let's get you to the farm. You've wasted enough time already."

With that, he revved the boat's engine and they took off, skimming the now peaceful surface of the water past a rocky outcrop, quickly leaving the cliffs behind them. They entered the walls of the town's small harbour in time to see two four-by-fours pulling away, leaving a dark green Audi parked there alone. Iksan could see delivery vans being unloaded by the harbour-side pubs, but nobody was paying any attention to them. Blending into the busy tasks of the morning, the three men loaded their canisters onto the trailer attached to the Audi.

The man paid little heed to the two Estonians as he turned the car onto the main road out of the marina.

Entering the town, they passed by a bus station on their left. Commuters were gathering around buses headed for either Dundee or Aberdeen, too preoccupied to notice a car with a trailer speeding by.

The road went on between two supermarket sites, each one still empty of customers, before it ended at a roundabout. The car slowed then took a right, bringing the structures of the town's famous abbey into view ahead of them. An old lady was walking through its archway, pulling a shopping trolley behind her. Iksan stared at her blankly as they drove by, and on through a short street of terraced and detached housing that quickly gave way onto a country road flanked by hedgerows and berry fields. Several large lorries passed in the other direction, but the Audi remained the only vehicle on this side of the road.

Barely ten minutes since leaving the harbour, they pulled into a track leading up to two farm houses. An oversized quarry truck sat beside the furthest one; a tall, lean man appeared, frowning, at the doorway. He folded his arms as the Audi drew up alongside him and Gorak and Iksan were ushered out.

"Two guests for you, Mr. Geddes."

"OK." Geddes acknowledged them, nervously glancing along the track behind them. "You'd better get the truck loaded up quickly."

Gorak didn't need telling twice. He'd done this several times before, but he'd never had to remain at the farm house once the canisters were on the truck. He motioned, expressionless, to the fat man at the wheel of the truck, indicating the cargo was good to go. The engine revved, and dust flew high into the air as the heavy vehicle moved off slowly down the narrow road.

The farm house was well heated, and a radio was playing quietly in the over-furnished kitchen. Looking into the shadows at the back of the room, Iksan saw a number of familiar canisters stored there.

By the way Geddes was pacing and wringing his hands, Iksan could tell that the farmer was agitated, and was not happy at receiving the two Estonians. He listened, trying to make sense of the conversation he was having with their contact.

"My wife is due back with the kids on Thursday," said Geddes. "They'll be gone by then."

Iksan could tell the words were not friendly, and he felt the trusted knot of fear in his stomach.

Chapter Twenty-one

Libby remained transfixed in front of the the TV, horrified at every word of the news coverage of the tragedy at her brother's restaurant. Surreal images of *The Bampot* provided the backdrop to a chaotic performance. The cast comprising reporters with their TV crews, fire appliances with uniformed personnel, soldiers, an ambulance with its blue lights flashing, several figures dressed in white protective coveralls, more police officers than Arbroath station actually contained, and plenty of police tape flapping in the wind to keep *The Bampot* set apart like a naughty child.

"And do we know any more about the condition of the people who were rushed to hospital?" the newscaster asked.

A windswept reporter with an oversized microphone stood in front of the police tape, holding her jacket closed while her long hair danced around her face.

"Well, as I said, initial reports suggest eight people were taken to Ninewells Hospital in Dundee last night, but three of them were released in the early hours of this morning. Two of the five people still in Ninewells we understand to be in a critical but stable condition, and one of them is a boy of four. Details at this stage are patchy, though, Frances."

"Is there any suggestion of this being a terrorist attack?" asked the newsreader.

The reporter stared into the camera for a moment, the technical link delaying transmission from the studio.

"Arbroath is a small harbour town with no known links to any extreme groups or activities. It sits in between Aberdeen and Dundee, which would be much more likely targets if there were to be a terrorist strike coming via the North Sea. So at the moment, this is being treated as a terrible tragedy in a small town that was all set to celebrate its part-time team's historic place in the cup quarter final. Police aren't confirming this, but we understand the restaurant's owner has been arrested. Whether that's for criminal negligence or a deliberate act, we can't speculate just now."

"Bullshit," muttered Libby. She was angry that Danny was being blamed for this, and angry at herself for letting Donna get inside her head again.

"I think you should switch that off now, love," Libby's mother Bernadette said, pursing her lips against her daughter's language. "They've just been saying the same things all morning."

Libby handed the TV remote to her mother without saying a word.

This was the first time in over seven years that Libby's parents had set foot over her threshold. She'd bought the neat bungalow near Claypotts Castle back then, and Danny had moved in with her not long after, disgusted at their parents' refusal to accept Libby's admission to them that she was gay. Incredulously, they'd maintained that Libby's sexuality was somehow a matter of her own choosing; and presumably she had chosen the hatred and discrimination that being openly gay brought with it. They argued that she was living contrary to their religious beliefs, yet Libby shared those beliefs without the conflict. Had he asked around his own congregation, the Reverend Norman Quinn would have found most of them to be baffled at his stance. But he hadn't, and had thus for the past seven years refused to acknowledge his daughter in any way.

So their presence now in the house was not without its discomfort. Bernadette, who had been unable to cut her ties with her daughter, and regularly phoned her when Norman was out of earshot, remained in the living room now with Libby. Norman had briefly met her eye at the door, but had then made his way to the kitchen where he had sat since with the broken and dishevelled Danny.

Gradually throughout the morning, salvos of communication had begun to emerge between the kitchen and the living room, like the soldiers on the Somme popping their heads above the parapet, slowly emerging that famous Christmas day to form their football game. And like a Christmas day, the small shoots of new beginnings began to take root as Norman, a little more comfortable for knowing Donna was no longer living here, felt enough shame for how he had treated his daughter to begin a tentative dialogue.

But, like that day on the Somme, the war wasn't over. Seven years was a long time, and Libby was in no mood for a truce.

When Bernadette came back from her latest excursion to the kitchen this time bearing four cups of tea, Libby braced herself.

Then Norman appeared at the living room door, his hair greyer around the temples than before, and his eyes studying the floor. Libby stood, daring him to meet her eye. If this was going to happen, then it would be on her terms. An apology from him would be a good start.

"I, uh . . . I've done a terrible thing, turning my back on you all this time," he said.

Libby folded her arms and bit her lip. She couldn't let him grovel. It made her uncomfortable.

"Let's just focus on how we're going to help Danny," she said, beckoning him to a seat. He brushed past her, and sat down, grateful for the instruction.

"We will," said Norman. "But first tell me how you are."

Libby shrugged her shoulders, but relaxed them at Bernadette's sharp glance.

"I've been better," she said. "How are you?"

They stuck to safe territory over the next hour, talking chiefly about Libby's work at the university. Her meteoric rise to head of research in the environmental toxicology department astounded and delighted Norman.

"And what happened at Danny's restaurant?" Norman wanted to know. "What could possibly have caused those people to get so sick? Do you think it could have been sabotage?"

Libby paused for a moment to reflect again on Donna's words. She spoke carefully.

"I think there's a lot more to what happened than we realise," she said. "We're going to have to trust the police to do a thorough investigation."

Norman shook his head in agreement with his daughter. Perhaps he had judged her too harshly, and he felt a glimmer of hope that now this Donna character was out of the picture, Libby might at last return to the fold.

When the doorbell rang, Libby said, "It'll be the police. We're expecting them."

"I'll go," Norman offered, standing up and going to the door. He could see, through the window, a large van that had pulled up outside the house being unloaded with what looked like TV cameras. He gulped, nervous as he opened the door.

There on the doorstep stood a tall woman looking uncomfortable in a suit. She took in Norman from head to toe in one look.

"Holy crap," said Donna Davenport, blowing a cloud of smoke in his direction.

The Reverend Norman Quinn turned on his heel, leaving Donna standing at the door. He took himself firmly back to the kitchen, in an agitated state. A glance in at the door told his wife that he was far from ready to accept the reality of his daughter's private life, and he was grieving all over again for his perceived loss of her. She went to him, not so much to console him this time as to give him a talking-to. It was time for Norman to hear some home truths.

Libby's heart both sank and skipped a beat when she saw Donna at the door. At this moment she felt relieved that she'd managed to conceal her mixed emotions last night and hadn't given Donna any false hopes.

Donna folded her arms and said, "I'm here to see Danny."

Libby held the door open for her, but could not make eye contact. She was grateful that Donna had been strong for them last night and taken care of Danny, but anger and hurt were bubbling just skin-deep below the surface. Why was Donna being so harsh with her? She feared the tears might start right there and then if she looked in Donna's eyes. Or caught the scent of her perfume as she passed. Or felt the touch of her arm as she brushed against her in the narrow hall. She didn't have the strength this morning to confront her pain.

Suddenly, and seemingly from the doorframe itself, a man appeared and barged into Donna's side.

"What can you tell us about the allegations that you stored drugs in your restaurant?" he demanded. He was immediately joined on the doorstep by a pack of microphone-and-camera-wielding journalists, who all began to shout at once.

"Was this a gangland attack?"

"What else were you smuggling into the country?"

"Was the restaurant a front for your drugs business?"

Momentarily startled, Donna regained her composure. She pushed Libby back from the door, came into the hallway, and closed it firmly behind her. Libby covered her face as the reporters hammered at the door, yelling their senseless questions.

"What's going on?" asked Bernadette, emerging from the kitchen. Libby turned and flew past her, to her room.

"I'm sorry, Mrs. Quinn," said Donna, "but with what happened last night, you're going to get this for a while – news reporters."

"Oh, my!"

"You're going to have to be really careful wherever you go in the next few days," said Donna. "And hope that your friends know how to keep quiet."

"But we've nothing to hide," said Bernadette, almost defiantly. "And what are those horrible things they're saying about drugs?"

"Ignore them." said Donna. "Milk and two sugars, please."

Bernadette relaxed a little at Donna's smile. She gave Donna a brief hug.

"It's good to see you, dear." And she meant it.

Unknown to them all, Bernadette had already discarded the morning's newspaper that bore a front page photo of Donna with her *Mine's a Slow Comfortable Screw* tee-shirt before anyone else in the household could see it. Secretly it had made her laugh. Donna always had done and she had fond feelings for the girl.

Donna let herself into the living room and sat down. Instinctively, she reached into her pocket for her cigarettes, but then let them go again, suddenly feeling conscious that this wasn't her home any more. A cloud of sadness managed to pierce her professional armour as she sat in the familiar room. The settee that she and Libby had bought from IKEA the night they'd gotten so hopelessly lost in Glasgow that they'd ended up checking into a hotel for the night instead of coming home. The wallpaper Donna had spent two years putting up and still hadn't finished. The painting of swirls that Libby had made with children's paints and mounted in an expensive frame to make it look like a real one. And the laugh she'd had at Libby's snotty academic friends fawning over it, believing it to be so.

And there was the calendar still in its place. They'd ordered it from a Christmas catalogue and each month featured a photo of the two of them together. Donna couldn't help herself, and went over to it, reading over the appointments and times scribbled in it, telling of a better life that was now gone. It plunged her mood before she could catch it, and she feared the onset of another roller coaster.

Before she turned her back on the calendar she noticed her name was still on this week's line – *Donna, doc appointment 3pm*. She had an appointment on Thursday, she realised. She'd clean forgotten.

She gathered her thoughts together as Danny walked heavily into the room, sitting himself opposite her like a schoolboy in the head teacher's office, looking miserable and beaten.

"You look like shit," she told him.

"Thanks, so do you," he muttered.

"Listen, you're going to be getting visitors all day," Donna said. "A uniform will be round in a wee while to go over some details." She brushed off his protests that he'd already answered all their questions. "I'm just here to give you a heads-up. By the looks of what's going on outside, you're going to need all the help you can get."

The living room door rattled open, and Bernadette came in with a tray of hot drinks and rolls.

"Oh, I'm fucking ravenous," Donna said when she saw them. "Sorry, Mrs. Quinn, I mean . . . "

"Don't worry dear," Bernadette said. "Just look after him, will you?" And she gave Danny a squeeze of the shoulder as she left them.

Danny stared up at Donna, his eyes pleading with her to make this all go away.

"I could throw another vodka bottle out the window," she said. "That could be good for a broken nose or two." But Danny didn't respond.

Donna leaned close to him.

"You're going to get asked a lot of questions about Bob Skinner," she said. "Either he was poisoned by somebody on purpose, or some chemical was lying around that shouldn't have been. Personally I don't believe anyone is going to be convinced by the carelessness theory. But we are following a lead about why Bob Skinner might have been targeted. I can't go into details about that with you now, obviously, but is there anything you can tell me about him?"

Danny tried to clear his head, to think straight, but a big cloud of panic stole all his thoughts. He shook his head miserably.

"We've been interviewing all the customers," Donna said, flipping back through her notebook. "But nobody knows who it was dining with Bob Skinner." She looked at Danny. "Do you know?"

Danny shook his head. He was drained by the shock of what had happened, and he was clearly struggling to re-live the details, even for Donna. All of his energies were spent.

"Bob Skinner made the reservation," he said. "He booked a table for two under his own name."

"Did you get a look at the person he was with?" Donna asked. "Male or female?"

"Some fat bloke, a businessman maybe," said Danny. "I can't remember."

"Libby was there for a while, wasn't she?" Donna was trying her best to not sound accusing, but the effort of trying so hard made the question loud in her head and it came out harshly. Danny looked up at her, but he knew Donna. He knew this was hurting her, too.

"She, eh, doesn't have to speak to me," Donna blustered, momentarily losing her professional calm. "But she is going to be interviewed."

She fished a card from inside her jacket pocket, scribbled a number on it and gave it to Danny.

"This is my card. Tell Libby she can phone me, or if she'd rather not, I've written my partner's number, Detective Jonas Evanton. Can you ask Libby to phone one of us? It's really important we interview her."

She thought for a moment, as if weighing up a decision. Donna was professional through and through, but Danny was family. Kind of. Her eyes darted around the familiar room, before settling back on Danny's pained state. She needed to give him something.

"Danny, I think something funny's going on. I've got a bad feeling you're being set up. And don't repeat that to anyone outside this house – I'm in enough trouble at work as it is. I need to trust you to keep yourself hidden from view, and you know you can trust me. Nobody's going to pin this on you."

Danny felt his eyes grow hot, and he let his head fall into his hands, and his body shook as he sobbed. This was a living nightmare.

"I need to go," said Donna. She knew this was the point at which he needed to be left alone, but she needed to warn him again. "Don't come to the door. Don't answer it, and don't go out."

Danny stood up and gave her a brief hug, then let her go to the door. As she left, he could hear the clamour of voices raised outside, lots of questions being shouted at Donna as she left the house.

As he stood in the hallway, Donna gone, her words reverberated around in his head. *I think something funny's going on.* Something funny? What the hell was he mixed up in?

He glanced again at Evanton's number scribbled onto Donna's card.

He'd better give this to Libby. The sooner she gave him a call, Danny thought, the better.

Donna felt an emptiness open up within her as she walked away from the house. Wrenched herself from it. The pain in her heart threatened to engulf her, and she walked through the throng of press and cameras with her head down and her eyes dull.

She needed to get away from everybody for a while. She decided to go to her spot by the bridge to see if that helped. At least she had the doctor on Thursday. Maybe a change in medication would help stop the really bad mood swings from coming back. She couldn't bear to think what would happen if they did. Her colleagues already thought she was unreliable. What would they think if they really knew? She'd lose her job for sure, she was convinced.

No, she needed to make a monumental effort to get past this. She owed it to Danny to stay with it and solve this case. Taking the cigarettes from her pocket this time, she set her path towards the Dundee waterfront.

Chapter Twenty-two

David Chisholm ordered room service. He didn't normally do this, but he'd slept badly and he just didn't want to see anyone right now. Meeting the blackmailer face to face last night had shot his nerves to pieces, particularly when he'd been told that Bob Skinner was now in intensive care because *he didn't do as he was told*.

Returning to the UK had proven to be much harder on his emotions than he'd initially believed, he thought self-pityingly. In California and in travelling the world, he'd never had to confront what he'd done by leaving Laura and his daughters behind in Putney. He had been able to push them to the far recesses of his mind, safe in the knowledge he wasn't going to come face to face with the guilt of deserting them. But here, the weather, the roads, the buildings, the TV channels . . . there was so much familiarity rushing at him, bringing with it long buried memories. When he looked in the mirror, they were there in his reflection, incriminating him for the swine that he was. And for the first time in all these years, instead of feeling the need to hide what he'd done, he began to feel contrition and sorrow for the loss he had caused.

But how could he tell Nicola? What would she do if she knew he still had a wife and children here in the UK? And would his daughters, now grown up, maybe even the eldest having children of her own, want to know him when he'd abandoned them so?

He switched on the news channel, seeking some distraction from this torment.

"Is there any suggestion of this being a terrorist attack?" asked the newsreader.

The news item caught Chisholm's attention; he noted the breaking news strap line crossing the bottom of the TV screen that told of a number of casualties from a suspected gas leak at a restaurant nearby. *Suspected gas leak*. How many times during his career had he offered his expert opinion on those? Chisholm sat up straight, his intuition suddenly alerted. Or his paranoia running ahead of him? The news item didn't have details of who'd been taken to hospital, but the blackmailer's reference to Skinner was fresh in Chisholm's mind.

The TV camera panned across an Abroath block of flats. The figure of a young woman could be seen leaving the block, pulling up a hood, and walking away from the cameras. Chisholm stared at the screen, then rubbed his tired eyes. Something about the posture and the profile of the young woman brought his older daughter Sally to mind and his heart leaped. She'd not quite reached her teens when he'd last seen her, but he must be missing her now if someone of her age and build could startle him like this.

"Breaking news just reaching us," the news reporter outside the block of flats was saying. "We've just heard from a hospital spokesperson that a four year old boy poisoned in last night's incident, has lost his fight for life. We join our correspondent at Ninewells . . . "

The newsreader's voice trailed off into the background as Chisholm buried his face in his hands, trying to make sense of what was troubling him most about the news report.

Like a serpent silently creeping up on its prey, the coils of unease slowly wound their way around his neck. He was being blackmailed to make him stop an investigation into a possible leakage of MIC. Last night he'd been told that Bob Skinner was lying in hospital seriously unwell.

David Chisholm didn't believe in coincidence. Not like this.

He turned his full attention back to the news report. His unease grew as he began to wonder about the links between this restaurant incident and his MIC investigation. If the two were indeed linked, it meant his tormentor was not working alone – he'd been speaking with him at the very time this horrendous attack was happening.

Chisholm was going to have to go to unthinkable lengths to make sure the investigation did go ahead. He'd seen the effects of badly stored MIC too many times to allow himself to become part of a conspiracy that allowed it to happen here.

He decided he was going to go to the police. He would tell them about his concerns and give them a full description of the blackmailer. Even though he knew bigamy was a criminal offence, and he'd be arrested for that.

But first, he swallowed hard and picked up his phone.

"Nicola?" he said. "There's something very important I need to discuss with you."

There was a sharp knock on the door. Chisholm opened it to an attractive woman chewing gum. She held up a card with her photo on it for him to examine. It took a moment before he realised that she was from the police.

"Professor David Chisholm?"

"Yes." He sounded wary.

"I'm Detective Inspector Donna Davenport," the woman said. "Do you mind if I come in and ask you a few questions?"

Chisholm felt the blood drain from his head. That was quick, he thought. He raised his hands in a submissive gesture, and let her in.

The hotel room was dark, with the curtains drawn against what would have been a pleasant view over the Firth of Tay, maybe even to the spot where she'd been sitting during the last hour and come up with the idea of making this visit.

A briefcase lay open beside the bed, and Donna could see that it was stuffed full of papers. The bed was strewn with clothes, and one corner had the covers pulled back as if it had just been slept in.

"Sorry, did I wake you?" Donna asked, suddenly aware of the professor's dishevelled appearance.

"No, don't worry," said Chisholm. "Jetlag just catching up with me."

He could barely believe they had come for him so soon.

He watched in silence for a moment as Donna scanned the room, taking her time to return her attention to him.

"So…" she said, turning to face Chisholm.

"I'm sorry," said Chisholm. "What must you think of me? It's all my fault. I never meant for any of it to happen."

Donna's eyebrow rose as she sensed mischief. "Not any of it?"

She watched, with her arms folded, as Chisholm sat on the edge of the bed and put his head in his hands.

"I know it sounds pathetic," he said. "And I'm not going to make excuses for myself. So I guess it's best to just get this over with. Do you have to arrest me?"

"Well, that all depends," said Donna.

"I'll co-operate fully, of course," said Chisholm. He stopped abruptly, as if a thought had occurred to him, and he looked at Donna. "It all depends on what, exactly?"

"You go first," said Donna. "Why do you think I'm here?"

Chisholm kept his mouth closed and continued to stare at her. Donna rolled her eyes. Whatever was bothering the professor could wait until later; time wasn't on her side if she wanted to avoid the hassle of being found intruding on Evanton's call. She sat down beside Chisholm. She smelled delicious, a subtle hint of fresh citrus. He felt self conscious, like a teenager.

"I came to ask you some questions about your work with Bob Skinner."

Donna marvelled at the sudden change in demeanour as Chisholm blew out a huge huff of relief, and pulled himself up straighter. He looked as though he might burst into laughter.

"I'm so sorry," he said. "We were at cross purposes. I thought you were here about, uh, another matter. Sorry. Do continue, please. Bob Skinner?"

"Aye," said Donna. *I've got a right one here*, she thought. But her instinct was telling her she'd been right to break protocol and come here. "Am I correct in thinking you were to join a working group convened by Mr. Skinner?"

"That's right, yes," said Chisholm. "He's leading an investigation into . . . "

"Yes, I know," said Donna. "Or rather, he was. He's in hospital now, in intensive care."

"I heard about that," said Chisholm, his eyes downcast.

"Can I ask how you knew about that?"

As far as Donna was aware, Skinner's details hadn't been released yet to the media. There was a press conference being held this afternoon, but until then it wouldn't be common knowledge. As she asked the question, she noticed the way Chisholm bristled and began to fluster.

"Eh, there was a report on the news channel," he said.

"Mr. Skinner's name hasn't been released to the media yet," said Donna. "Let me ask you again. How did you know about Mr. Skinner being in hospital?"

Chisholm looked away from Donna searching frantically for a way to answer her, but he couldn't escape her stare.

"It's complicated," he said. "Rather a long story."

"I'll put the kettle on, then," said Donna. "Or do you get room service here?"

Chisholm looked at her, not quite sure whether she was being serious or not.

"Tell you what," said Donna, getting to her feet and popping her chewing gum into the bin. "I won't ask about your 'other matter' if you just cut the bullshit and tell me what you know about Bob Skinner. Somebody tried to kill him last night, and I need to find out who that was. If it was you, that would make it easy. But my hunch is it wasn't."

"I'm relieved to hear it," said Chisholm. And he slapped his forehead. "Er, that you don't suspect me, not that Mr. Skinner was . . . oh, how terrible."

He felt disarmed by her forward manner. But there was also something very warming about her.

"It's not that I trust you," said Donna. "I happen to know you were in Edinburgh last night when it happened. So, unless your *other matter* is an evil twin brother, you're not in the frame there. But you do know something, right?"

Her tone had softened, but it was obvious to Chisholm that she wasn't about to tolerate any nonsense. She was clearly in charge of this discussion, and he began to feel the burden of his earlier confession too heavy to bear on his own. He'd been left silent and alone after Nicola had slammed down the phone on him. And now, with the news report, he really needed to share his fears about his blackmailer and the poisoning at the restaurant.

"Let's have that coffee," he said.

Donna had begun to pick up items around the room, pretending to inspect them, giving him time. Now she turned and looked at him. Waiting. Expecting the truth.

Suddenly Chisholm felt he wanted to tell her everything.

"It's a long story," he said. "Let me start at the beginning."

Donna stood outside the hotel foyer and lit a cigarette, the better to gather her shaken thoughts. Chisholm was being blackmailed by someone who was paranoid about Skinner's MIC investigation, and damn it if Chisholm's description of the blackmailer hadn't sounded a lot like DI Jonas Evanton. And Evanton had been in Edinburgh last night.

It was inconceivable, and yet . . .

I am not going mad. Am I?

Donna took several drags while she tumbled the information around. It was circumstantial, but she had learned to trust her gut, and her gut was telling her now that Chisholm's confession marked a horrible turn of events. But then again, she was aware of her mind playing tricks on her these days, tossing her emotions around like spray in a storm. It must be this business with Danny, bringing out the worst in her that she'd tried to suppress since the break-up with Libby. She couldn't hide her fragile state of mind forever, she realised. Sooner or later, and it seemed to be happening sooner, she was going to have to tell Ross and risk being sacked.

A car horn beeping wildly shook Donna from her reflection. There was a black Skoda, and the driver was waving his hand out of the window. Donna only realised how tense and unnerved she'd become, when the sight of her friend drew a grateful smile to her lips. Overreacting, that's what she'd been doing.

"Natesh," said Donna. "Are you stalking me?"

"Of course," said Natesh. "You hungry?"

"Sure."

Crighton's was a bright, spacious, airy pub in the town centre, and it was busy as usual this lunchtime. As Donna walked inside with Natesh, she was still shaking her head in amazement that he'd found a space to park right next door, in a nifty little space she hadn't even known existed.

"Tell you," said Natesh, "us taxi drivers know the city better than you cops do."

"You're not wrong," Donna had to agree. "Bet you can tell me a few stories. By the way, what's with the cut at your eye?"

Natesh instinctively touched the cut, seeming self conscious about it. They sat down together at a booth.

"Harry Potter got me," he said.

Donna laid flat the menu she'd picked up, and laughed out loud. A couple of heads turned to look at her.

"Got me a good one. My mum hates him. Had to have two stitches."

He touched the cut again.

"That cat's an animal," said Donna, drawing a cigarette from her pocket and ignoring the looks from other diners.

"Yes." He shrugged his shoulders. "The only person my mum hates more than him is my girlfriend. It's a problem."

"A new girlfriend?" said Donna, lighting up. She avoided eye contact with the customers who were tutting. "Tell."

"Yeah, two weeks now," he said casually.

"Bloody hell, Natesh, you should be a professional poker player."

He tapped the side of his nose and grinned.

"I'm going to ask her to marry me."

"You always want to ask them to marry you. So, what's her name?"

"Nancy."

"Uh huh. And this one knows you've never set foot outside Scotland?" She blew out a blissful stream of smoke, and ignored the angry stares from other diners.

"Ha, I learned my lesson. Man, it was hard work keeping up the Latino accent with Natalie. Worth it, though." He grinned.

They ordered their food, Donna saluting the waiter with her forbidden cigarette, and chattered amiably as they ate.

"So, you coming to the wedding?" Natesh asked.

"Cool," said Donna, "count me in."

"I know a good hairdresser," said Natesh.

"What's wrong with my hair?"

Natesh made a squeaky noise before he answered. "Just a little . . . Eighties, maybe."

"Eighties? So you know about hair now?" Donna had never really paid attention to the way her hair looked. It just kind of grew on.

"I'll drop you at Swanky Lanky's," said Natesh. "Get something funky. For the wedding."

Donna considered for a moment, then shrugged. She could do with a bit of time out this afternoon to get her thoughts in order. After all, she needed some head space to digest what she'd just heard from Chisholm.

"Trip to the hairdresser's it is, then," she said.

Natesh pulled away from Swanky Lanky's, and seeing that the traffic on the main road was heavy and slow going, swung into a lane that looked narrower than the Skoda. Natesh sucked in his stomach and drove in. At the end of the lane was a man speaking into a mobile, with his back to the car. Natesh had drawn up pretty close before he realised that the man hadn't heard him. It looked like the guy was yelling in anger down his phone. Natesh pressed the horn. The man jumped, and as he spun round to face the car Natesh could see that his face was purple with fury. Natesh felt his skin crawl at the expression on the man's face, and just to be on the safe side he locked the car doors. He did so just in time, as the man sprang forward and with a roar that scared the crap out of Natesh – as he put it later – hammered his fist on the bonnet. Then the man turned and headed off round the corner and out of sight. Alone in the lane, Natesh flipped his middle finger at the space where the man had been, then wiped the dampness from his forehead.

Chapter Twenty-three

It happened again.

Hunter's private line in his plush university office rang.

His eye twitched. His nerves were frayed. Palpitations throughout the day had left him feeling clammy and dizzy. And his ribs ached whenever he moved. Now he'd just heard on the news that a youngster was dead, following his release of the MIC at *The Bampot*. While he'd been prepared to see Skinner off as the price for getting this investigation stopped, this latest development would surely mean there would now be an even more thorough investigation by the police. He was sorry the kid was dead, of course. But there was a lot at stake here.

He cleared his throat and picked up the phone. "Yes?" he answered.

"Time to roll up your sleeves, Hunter," said the caller without introduction. Hunter's nerves tightened at the tone of Evanton's voice. "Things are about to get messy, and if this government investigation goes ahead, your head's on the block."

"What do you mean?" *How can things get any more messy than they already are?*

"Chisholm," said Evanton, a hard edge evident in his voice, and Hunter had to suppress a feeling of nausea as he sensed Evanton's mood change. Until now he had accepted the orders, taken the money – and the odd beating – and ignored Evanton's violent and sociopathic reputation. His hand shook. He was not cut out for this.

Evanton pressed on. "He told his fucking wife everything."

Hunter took several deep breaths to regain control and clear thinking.

"How do you know? How can you be sure he hasn't just told you that to get you off his back?" he asked, trying for an authoritative tone.

"He told her," Evanton repeated. "We need to stop him. At least Bob Skinner isn't going to be blabbing any time soon. But we've got another problem."

Hunter heard the strain in Evanton's voice. He hoped he wasn't going to lose it. He really didn't want to be around if that happened.

"Another problem?"

"My partner, Davenport," said Evanton. "She's gone and interviewed Chisholm. Which means she's going behind my back. I'm going to have to deal with her. You'll need to put a stop to Chisholm. And you'd better pray he didn't give the game away to Davenport."

Hunter thought frantically, searching for a way out of this. He let Evanton rant while he desperately tried to reign in the morsel of promise that niggled at the back of his mind. He knew there was something he could use. Then he remembered.

"Listen," Hunter cut in on Evanton's outburst of rage against Chisholm and Donna. "I think I may have something of use to you."

Evanton's ranting stopped immediately. Suddenly bold, Hunter felt renewed vigour flow through his veins. Now he had something to bargain with. A smile crept across his lips at the beauty of it.

Then over the phone he heard a car horn, a clatter, and sounds of rage coming from Evanton as if he'd dropped his mobile. Moments later, Evanton came back on the line.

"I'm listening, and I don't have much time," said Evanton.

"It'll look suspicious if the government investigation suddenly ends, just as the police investigation begins."

He could almost feel Evanton concentrating, trying to second guess his line of thinking.

"We need to make it look as though the working group has looked at the evidence and come to the conclusion that there was never any MIC. Do you agree?" There was no response from Evanton, so Hunter continued. "I can have a false report prepared, which will allow the working group to meet and conclude its deliberations in our favour."

"Is that it?" Evanton exploded over the line. "A fucking falsified report?"

"Well, here's the thing," said Hunter, most pleased with himself and unable to hide it in his voice. "I know exactly how we can persuade Professor Chisholm to go along with it. I made a bit of a speculative investment."

And he told Evanton about how he'd stumbled across the connection between Sally and David Chisholm. How, when Sally had repeatedly written to Libby Quinn, he had noticed her

Chisholm Sampling letterhead. That after investigating further into what this connection might be worth to his departments, Hunter had decided to test the waters and told Libby to offer her a study placement here in Dundee. He had known full well that Sally would not refuse the offer if she believed the initiative had come from Libby Quinn. He also hoped her arrival would result in some Chisholm funding and a boost to his reputation, though he didn't mention that to Evanton.

Now he felt his speculative investment had paid off, albeit not as he had originally intended.

"If Chisholm knows his daughter is here," Hunter told Evanton, "and you are the one to tell him, I think you'll have all the leverage with him that you'll need. Don't you agree?"

There was a long pause on the line.

"Nice one, Hunter," said Evanton, with a trace of admiration. "Give me her details and I'll sort something out. You get that report ready."

Hunter's cheeks flushed at the praise and his palpitations became a little kinder with Evanton's change in tone.

"And you'll be pleased to know I've picked up some other information you might find useful." He couldn't help himself. "It was Geddes who grassed us up."

There was another long pause on the line then, "You're a dark horse."

Not my problem now, thought Hunter as he replaced the phone. A smirk strained at the corner of his mouth. Perhaps he was going to get away with murder, after all.

Chapter Twenty-four

Don't send a boy to do a man's job, he muttered to himself.

His mind suddenly took him back to Bhopal, quick as a flash when he hadn't even been thinking about it. There he was, a naïve young student. A fish out of water. And how they'd laughed at him, those women. When he'd realised nobody was going to help that woman in the midst of the stampeding mayhem of the toxic cloud, he'd become overwhelmed – possessed, even, by that feeling. That excitement at being alive, mixed up with his other adolescent feelings that had nowhere else to go.

Evanton shook his head.

He was getting distracted.

The memory of her, the memory of all of them that night so long ago, was causing him a level of arousal that hurt. He knew it was wrong.

But it kept coming back to him.

Kept getting inside his head, when he should be getting on with the here and now. God knows, there was enough for him to be doing in the here and now, and he didn't have room for making mistakes. Somebody was going to have to pay, to make this go away.

Iksan awoke with a headache, thick from a fitful afternoon slumber. He sat up on the single bed he had taken in the small, pleasantly furnished room on the upstairs of the farm house. On the opposite side of the room lay Gorak, snoring, on an identical single bed. Both men had thrown themselves down and fallen asleep fully clothed. Gorak smelled bad, Iksan noted, although he was sure he must smell just the same.

Miserably, he pondered his situation. He had no money, no passport, no phone, no contacts here. Not even a knowledge of the area.

Rising from the bed silently, he crept out of the room and closed the door quietly behind him. He stepped into the hallway, then stopped and listened carefully. There was no sound other than the drone of machinery from the fields. Careful to step lightly, he made his way along the hallway to the top of a flight of stairs. Looking down them, he saw no sign of anyone else being nearby. He continued past the stairs and stopped outside the next door.

He pressed his ear to the door.

There was no sound.

He silently opened the door just enough to let him look inside. He saw what appeared to be an adult's bedroom, which contained a TV set but no other electrical equipment. He left that door ajar and continued on to the next room along the hallway. Again he pressed his ear to the door. Again there was no sound. He looked inside at the bathroom.

He went on to the next room, a kids' room. Their names, *Jennifer* and *Amy* mounted on a plaque on the door. He looked inside. Plenty of electronic equipment in there.

Iksan slipped inside, located the computer, and moved the mouse over its pad. The computer had been left switched on, its broadband connection live, and Iksan almost shouted out in joy. In his haste to key in Google maps, he had to correct his keypad errors several times.

The location finder told him he was on the UK's north eastern coast, just outside a small harbour town called Arbroath. Iksan puzzled at how the name should be pronounced, but he felt a deep sense of relief at making sense of the geography at least. He could now picture where on the planet he actually was, noting that the closest city was called Dundee, some twenty kilometres along one main road, going south west along the coast.

Dundee, he thought, running the name around in his head several times. There was something vaguely familiar sounding about it. Maybe he'd watched them play some friendly against his own team, Flora Tallinn, and suddenly the ghost of a memory filled him with an indescribable sadness for home.

He turned just as Evanton lifted the gun butt above his head. Everything went black.

Evanton made his way to the bedroom where Gorak was still sleeping.

"Get up," he said loudly, and got a mouthful of muttering from Gorak in response.

Evanton slapped him on the back of the head, and stood back while the sailor roused from his sleep.

"Change of plan," Evanton went on. "I need some business taken care of before you get to go home."

At this, Gorak woke fully, and seemed ready to spring his anger on Evanton, but he quickly checked himself, grunted and settled himself on the edge of the bed, ready to listen.

Watching Gorak carefully, Evanton removed a photograph from his jacket pocket and gave it to him. It showed a young woman, pretty, mid twenties, with shoulder length blonde hair and a broad smile lighting a heart-shaped face.

"Her name is Sally Chisholm," said Evanton. "Memorise the face. I need you to find her for me."

"What?" Gorak sounded incredulous. "Are you out of your mind? Just get us out of here and back home like you promised."

"Things have changed now." Evanton remained outwardly calm, but Gorak noticed the tell-tale pulse in the detective's temple. "You will go home, but the errand first. She won't be hard to find. She lives here in the town, which isn't large. Here's her address. I want you to find her at ten tonight, whether she's at home or not – it's your problem how to find out where she is. Give her this phone number, and tell her to phone it. Understood?"

"Tell her to phone that number?" Gorak responded. "Tell her your fucking self." And he threw both the photo and the paper with the phone number on the floor at Evanton's feet.

"You really can't afford to piss me off," said Evanton, pulling the gun from his jacket and holding it against Gorak's forehead. Gorak turned pale.

"Woah, man!"

"Please," Iksan whispered, appearing in the doorway, his lip cut and swollen. His eyes pleaded with Gorak.

"Pick them up," said Evanton, kicking the photo and the paper towards Gorak. Gorak, trembling now, gritted his teeth, and took them. Evanton returned the gun to his jacket pocket.

"And if the girl doesn't phone?" Gorak asked.

"Do what it takes to persuade her," said Evanton. "But don't kill her. I'm going to need her. When you're done, bring her and meet me on the bridge heading out of the town going south. It's not safe for you to be staying here any longer. The bridge, got it?"

And he turned and left the room.

Gorak punched the headboard of his bed, and it echoed loudly through the upstairs of the house.

Chapter Twenty-five

"Family problems?" said Sally.

"I'm afraid so," said the woman on the line who'd introduced herself as Dr. Quinn's secretary, Janice. "But Dr. Quinn has asked me to re-arrange your meeting for tomorrow, if that's convenient for you?"

Sally felt the heavy weight of disappointment. She was keen to get started, to get her name out there while her father was still in the UK.

"Yes, of course, tomorrow will be fine," she said, hoping that she didn't sound the way she felt.

Sally let her train ticket fall onto her coffee table, gazing out of the window, wondering what to do now. She felt a sudden pang of need for familiar surroundings. But she steeled herself. This was where her career was going to begin. Being homesick wasn't going to help any. She would go back outside. She could finish looking at the cliffs, and brush off her irritation at Dr. Quinn for postponing their meeting.

The afternoon air was fresh, with a soft but cool breeze coming from the sea. Sally held her jacket closed tight around her as she walked at a brisk pace towards the beach. She wanted to feel the sand, to listen to the gulls, and to watch the waves.

She passed by the library, which was still cordoned off to the public and surrounded by police and Army vehicles, and took the road that narrowed and wound downhill. The way became sandy even before the beach came into view. But when it did, Sally threw open her arms, and took in deep breaths of sea air, smiling broadly at the glistening water spread before her. The sight of the seaside thrilled her now as it did when she was a child. She ran onto the pebbly beach, and kicked sand high into the air. There was one car parked close to the beach, but nobody was in it, and she couldn't see anyone around. She felt free.

To her left rose the turf-topped cliffs potted with caves. She could see someone walking a dog along the dirt track up there, where she'd been just a short time ago. Behind her, in the same direction, opened a large expanse of parkland, which rose uphill where she could make out the tops of caravans – a holiday park overlooking the sea. Along to her right stretched the beach. She decided not to go back to the cliffs for now. She wanted to walk on the beach.

It was part sandy and part shingle, and towards the water's edge Sally could make out several species of plover grubbing around in the wet sand. Watching them, fascinated, she stumbled on the rocks, and with a painful twist, fell awkwardly.

She sat on the shingle, holding her ankle, annoyed with herself.

"Are you ok?" The call made her look round in surprise. She'd thought she was the only person on the beach. Edging towards her, looking unsure of himself, was a young man about her own age, with closely cropped dark hair. His face was unshaven; he looked like he hadn't slept the night before, and his eyes looked raw with a lack of sleep. All at once she felt vulnerable. The pain in her ankle meant she couldn't get up, far less run away, if this man turned out to be dangerous.

"I'm fine," she lied, hoping to brush him off.

The man stopped and took a long look at her. "Let me see you get up, then."

"Excuse me?"

"Well, if you're ok, you can get up. It's starting to rain."

It was.

Sally shifted uncomfortably. The man took a step closer to her and held out his hand to help her up.

"No, really, I'm fine," said Sally. "Thanks anyway."

Next she heard a soft crunch as the man sat himself down beside her. Alarm took hold of her.

"I'm Danny," said the man, "and you look like you could do with a bit of help here."

She turned to look at him. He was exhausted, she could see, and she saw in him no threat after all.

"I'm Sally," she said finally. "I think it's twisted." She motioned towards her ankle.

"My sister has the car just up there," said Danny, pointing to the one car Sally had seen when she had gotten to the beach. "I'll give her a phone. She can run you home. You're nearby?"

"Yes, but really, don't go to any trouble, I'll be ok."

Danny raised a quizzical eyebrow as he dug in his pocket for his phone.

"Just a minute," he said to Sally as he dialled a number. "Libby? Can you give me a hand here on the beach . . . a twisted ankle . . . yes, I know, but could you give us a hand? She'll need a lift home."

Libby? Surely to goodness not, Sally thought. If this turned out to be the self same Dr. Libby Quinn coming to her rescue, she just could not bear it. Their first meeting was supposed to be all about impressing her with the Chisholm charm and academic prowess. Not *this*. With brute determination, she tried with all her might to get up on her own two feet. She got a stab of pain in her ankle and another raised eyebrow from Danny. No, she decided, there must be lots of Libbies here; it couldn't be the same one.

"She's just coming," said Danny. "We'll get you home. You need to get an ice pack on that right away. So, what brings you to this neck of the woods? Your accent doesn't come from here." Something in his manner told Sally he was as unsure of her as she'd been of him. It felt like an odd reversal of roles.

"I just got here yesterday, I drove up from Putney in London. I'm due to be starting work at the university in Dundee."

"Actually that's a coincidence," said Danny, suddenly hopeful that here was somebody in the town who didn't know his face. "My sister works at the university too, bit of an egghead."

Sally's heart sank. It was going to be her, wasn't it?

"Not Libby Quinn?" she heard coming out of her mouth. Danny looked surprised and then alarmed.

"How did you know that?"

"Oh, just a hunch," said Sally miserably.

"Talk of the devil," said Danny, standing up and nodding towards a petite woman with short dark hair who'd appeared at the edge of the shingle. Sally studied the woman carefully as she approached. She had a pretty face, but it was frowning. She had the same exhausted look about her that Danny had. Sally was reminded then about the reason for her meeting being called off – family problems. Suddenly she felt guilty that she had encroached on something that this brother and sister were going through.

"What's happened here?" Libby Quinn's voice was surprisingly soft and lyrical, and she looked genuinely concerned.

"She's got a twisted ankle," said Danny. "She's too heavy for me to lift myself." He'd said it without smiling, making his intent ambiguous, but Sally heard herself laugh out loud. Although she'd seen pain in his eyes, she could also see a kind and funny side to him that wasn't far behind whatever was hurting him.

"Let me see," said Libby, crouching down to get a look at Sally's ankle.

Good God, thought Sally, *Wonder Woman is also a paramedic.*

"Mm, it's really swollen," said Libby. "But it doesn't look broken. Do you think you could stand up if you hold onto us?"

And with much huffing and puffing, with one arm around each of Danny's and Libby's shoulders, Sally got to her feet, and they slowly made their way to Libby's car.

"Oh, and you should know," Danny said to Libby once they were sitting in the car. "Sally here is starting at the university."

For the rest of that afternoon, Sally sat in the flat with her ankle wrapped in a tea towel she'd filled with ice cubes, reliving in her mind every detail of her encounter with Danny and Libby Quinn on the beach. She was almost hyperventilating with excitement at the thought of their planned visit that evening. Frustrated at her inability to throw herself into tidying the flat, she found herself looking forward to seeing Danny again. Although she could tell something had been wrong, he was funny and kind. And she was looking forward to meeting Libby again, too, despite feeling more than a little guilt that the ropes binding her to home were beginning to loosen.

Chapter Twenty-six

Sally hopped from one foot onto the other, and muffled a cry at the shooting pain. She'd alternated between ice packs and hot compresses all afternoon, and she could only console herself with the belief now that her ankle would have been even worse than this if she hadn't. She cursed the shingle on the beach, and she cursed the rash invitation she'd extended to Danny and Libby to visit her tonight. How on earth was she going to get the place in a fit condition for visitors? She couldn't even go out for a pint of milk. Or a box of painkillers.

The only thing that stopped her from screaming at the walls was the warm glow of having made new friends. Danny had texted her soon after she'd arrived home, asking after her twisted ankle. And her phone beeped again now, Danny letting her know that he and Libby had just parked around the corner.

Despite her anxiety, she felt a buzz of excitement when the entry phone sounded. They were here.

Danny still had dark circles around his eyes, Sally noticed, although he'd shaved and his hair looked freshly washed. He came into the room, brandishing a pack of lager cans, and stood to the side to let Libby in. She looked a little more relaxed now, minus the frown she'd had earlier, and cradled a bottle of red wine.

"Nice flat," Danny said. Sally watched Libby as she, too, took in the pleasant flat, and allowed herself to feel a little pride.

"I'm really sorry I had to cancel earlier," said Libby, as she smiled shyly, and kissed Sally lightly on the cheek. "But I hope I can make up for it now. Ankle all better?"

Catching the delicate scent of Libby's perfume, Sally found a blush creeping across her face, and was glad of the dim lighting.

"On the mend," she said.

"Just as well I didn't listen to your nonsense on the beach, then," said Danny, also kissing her on the cheek. She felt a warm glow light a smile on her face.

"Well, come in and have a seat," she said, waving them in. "What can I get you to drink?"

"You sit down, and let me get the drinks," said Danny, making a point of nodding to her ankle. "Let you two boffins get to know each other."

And before she had a chance to argue otherwise, Danny had a hold of her elbow and was leading her to the sofa. She could tell he'd already had a few. The alcohol was on his breath and he was slightly clumsy. He swayed a little on his feet, and Sally found the blush coming back to her cheek as they smiled shyly at one another.

Donna spilled out the door of the pub not far from the flat. Literally. She lost her balance and found herself upright only as a result of having slumped against the wall. She'd been drinking steadily here since four this afternoon, when she'd finished interviewing the family whose little boy had died in *The Bampot* poisoning. Donna had had to let it wash over her when the family had vented their anger at Danny, blaming him for what happened and believing what they'd read in the papers. She'd understood. But it had been a difficult visit, and Donna had headed straight here to the pub to help calm herself. Over and over until the publican suggested that she'd maybe had enough.

Now she made her way unsteadily along Arbroath High Street, and turned off towards the car park at the abbey.

Fuck it, she thought, in her hazed state feeling invincible, *I'm fit enough to drive*. And she fished her car key from her pocket.

One round of drinks became a second. And then a third. After some initial reserve from Libby, she and Sally had discussed the study placement in a way that only science geeks could. Danny had finally got them off a subject he couldn't understand with a flow of jokes that made Sally laugh. Gradually the formality and the strangeness between them eased off, and the discussion took on a more intimate nature.

"They're trying to say I was storing illegal substances in the restaurant," said Danny, his head slumped miserably in his hands. "Making up stuff about drugs. I've never seen anybody choke like that before."

"It's just horrible," Libby said gently. "A nightmare. You know the press, though, they're looking for a scapegoat, and they're after my brother."

"It's awful," said Sally, "I saw all the emergency services there last night. What do you think happened?"

"I haven't a clue," said Danny. "But Donna said something weird is going on. We need to trust her."

"Who's Donna?" asked Sally.

"She's a friend," said Danny.

"CID," said Libby at the same time.

"Friends in high places," said Danny, and Libby shot him a look. An awkward moment of silence followed, something going on between the brother and sister that Sally was not party to.

"I know one thing," said Libby. "There is no way I am going to let them pin this on you." And she held Danny's hand firm.

Sally felt that Danny and Libby needed a moment together, so she excused herself, on the grounds of clearing her head, and hobbled outside.

Even Gorak was blowing on his hands to try and warm them up. They'd found the right address, it seemed, but the block of flats had a controlled entry system, and they'd had to wait outside until somebody entered the building before they could get in and verify this. The man and woman, carrying beer and wine, had been oblivious to their allowing the two Estonians to slip into the building. Gorak and Iksan had waited until the visitors were safely indoors, before stealing up the stairs and taking a discreet peek through the letterbox. Gorak had confirmed their target was inside, then they made their way back outdoors to wait.

There was a north easterly wind coming in, bringing with it some numbing cold blasts. Iksan's teeth chattered uncontrollably as they waited in the dark.

"What if she doesn't come out?" he asked.

They didn't have a plan B. Going into the flat wasn't an option, they'd decided, when it had become clear that Sally wasn't alone in there. They could hardly go up to the door, and with her visitors looking on, demand that she go with them. And they certainly couldn't meet Evanton without her. Gorak refused to contemplate that outcome. No, they were going to have to wait it out here in the cold and the dark, even until the morning if need be, to capture their prey alone.

Just when Iksan felt he could bear the cold no longer, he was jolted from his wallowing by the sound of footsteps and the main door clicking open.

There she was, the girl in the photograph.

Iksan's heart quickened, and he felt a little sick all of a sudden. But Gorak was quick as he stepped from the shadows.

The raw air came as a surprise to Sally as the door closed behind her. She hadn't thought to bring a jacket, but at least she was only going outside for a brief moment. She took a few steps away from the door, stretching her arms and testing her ankle, when from nowhere she felt a weight slam into her side, and a fist clamp over her mouth. Trying in terror to yell out, her muffled voice was gagged by an enormous hand as she was dragged into the lane by the side of the flats.

Painfully regaining her feet, she could see two men. One was holding her; the other, younger looking than herself, was nervously hopping from one foot to the other.

They stopped against the wall, and the man holding her spoke.

"If you scream when I take my hand away, I will hurt you. Do you understand?" The voice was coarse, and thick with an Eastern European accent.

Sally nodded. She was trembling so much her head hurt.

The man took his hand from her mouth, and she put her own arms up to cover her face.

"I want you to phone this number now," said the man, handing her a phone already primed with the number. Sally looked at him blankly.

"Phone it. Now!" he demanded.

"And say what?"

"Just do what I tell you."

Sally took the phone from him and threw it back at him as hard as she could. Gorak slapped her hard across the face, and she reeled with the pain.

He thrust the phone back into her shaking hand.

"Next time I won't be so understanding," said Gorak. "Now call the number."

Sally gritted her teeth and pressed the call button. While she listened to the line ring she surreptitiously glanced around, trying to spot some way of getting away from these thugs.

"Hello?" an American voice on the end of the phone enquired.

Suddenly her full attention honed in on the voice.

"Hello? Who's calling?"

She couldn't believe what she was hearing. She stared at the phone, and all she could say was, "Dad! Help!" before the Eastern European man snatched it from her again.

Just then, the younger man, much slighter than the one that had been holding her, pushed the older man with all his might, and yelled to Sally.

"Run! Go, quickly!"

The older man regained his balance surprisingly quickly but appeared stunned by the intervention, and his eyes darted in indecision from Sally to the younger man.

Seizing her chance, Sally ran back around the corner, her ankle blazing in agony. Desperately fumbling with the electronic key, hearing the two men begin to argue, she fell through the entry door, her heart beating wildly, terrified and confused by what had just happened.

Panting from fear, pain and exertion, she limped up the stairs, back to the flat.

"Oh my God!" Libby cried out when she saw Sally. Her eye, where Gorak had slapped her, was bruising quickly and was already beginning to swell.

Chapter Twenty-seven

David Chisholm loosened his tie, poured himself another Southern Comfort and fell back in the armchair, listening to the sounds of traffic going by his hotel room. His suitcase lay unpacked beside the bed, he was too exhausted to open it. Jetlag was catching up with him, and the alcohol was beginning to blur the mental gymnastics he'd had to perform during the past twenty-four hours since his encounter with his blackmailer.

He'd intended to visit the MP, Bob Skinner, in hospital today. But instead, he'd holed himself up in his hotel room with the Southern Comfort. He had done the unthinkable. He'd told Nicola about the blackmail and admitted to her that he had never divorced. That their marriage was void. His mind replayed the ferocious argument that had ensued. The bitter recriminations. The insults traded. The raw shock of true feelings unearthed when they were simply two people no longer surrounded by the glitz and the followers.

But there had been no tears. And, to his initial astonishment, Nicola had instructed him to remain silent about the matter. His astonishment soon turned to revulsion, however, when he began to realize she was concerned first and foremost with her own reputation, and that their sham marriage had really only ever been about reputation. She would be consulting lawyers and press consultants alike. But Chisholm knew he was in no position to take the moral high ground. The marriage had served his career well, too. Perhaps it was no more than he deserved, he mused, that Nicola's public image took precedence over the particulars of their so-called relationship. And there it was, like a pack of cards, collapsed, and Chisholm found himself reeling in its aftermath. Left to figure out how he would keep contact with his children *this* time.

Still, he took some comfort from knowing he had spoken to the police earlier. That woman officer had seemed more than capable, and he was sure he could at least leave the matter of the blackmailer in her hands. She'd certainly taken a keen interest in that.

So here sat Chisholm, with his Southern Comfort, thousands of miles from home, trying to read his toxicology papers, his mind turning time and again to the family he'd abandoned all those years ago. He'd known that returning to the UK would be difficult, but he hadn't reckoned on any of this. Reaching into his wallet, he drew out an old worn photograph showing three happy schoolgirls flanked by himself and Laura, just another ordinary family caught in a 1990s street shot. The girls would be all grown up now, and for the first time in so many years, he began to feel a yearning to be in their lives and a wretchedness for the way he had put his own interests first.

He hadn't heard from the blackmailer all day. Since calling this morning and finding out that Chisholm had called his bluff, the man had remained silent. Ominously so. But Chisholm wasn't naïve enough to think this was the end of the matter. He'd gone to too much trouble already, and obviously had too much at stake to let the MIC investigation go ahead. Chisholm was under no illusion that there was more to come. Just what this monster would do now, he could only wait and see. Unless, of course, DI Davenport had been able to put a stop to him.

As he poured himself another glass, the shrill ring of his phone startled him and some of the liquid missed the glass. He cursed under his breath.

"Hello?" he answered, wary at receiving a call this late in the evening.

Sounds of scuffling came across the line.

"Hello? Who's calling?"

The hairs on the back of Chisholm's neck stood on end as he heard a muffled cry. The voice of his daughter, unmistakable even after so long since he'd heard it, shouted, "Dad! Help!" before the line went dead.

Chapter Twenty-eight

Evanton barely registered the pain in his shoulder as he barged through the farm house door. He flung it wide with such force, it rattled in its frame, sending shock waves into the late night air. He saw Geddes spin round in surprise, then shrink back in fear.

Coward, he thought. *Fucking, grassing coward.*

Before Geddes could react, Evanton crossed the kitchen and had his hand around the farmer's throat.

"Want to phone your mates down at the station now?" he sneered, sending spittle flying into Geddes's face. Geddes flailed and gurgled in terror, but a sound from the hallway caught Evanton's attention, and he released his grip, leaving Geddes heaving for breath.

There, looking at him from the door leading deeper into the house, was the sailor, Gorak, with the kid snivelling over his shoulder. Evanton was on them in an instant.

"I gave you one fucking simple thing to do!" he yelled, his voice cracking in rage. He jabbed Gorak in the chest, and a red haze rose in him when the older man squared up for a fight.

"Where is the girl?"

"She got away," said Gorak, and Evanton caught his attempt to usher Iksan further back.

"Away?" Evanton's voice rose to a shriek. His eyes bulged and he felt as though the veins in his neck would burst.

"She made the phone call," Gorak said loudly.

Evanton broke into a peel of wild laughter.

"Oh, she made the phone call, that's all right then."

He turned on Geddes and struck out viciously with his boot. Geddes gasped and collapsed to the floor, clutching his groin.

"Well, don't worry," said Evanton, turning back to Gorak. "I have a way for you to redeem yourself. You see, I have another problem. Geddes here has phoned the police and told them about our enterprise."

He noted the expressions of disgust and anger on Gorak's face, as they all turned to focus on Geddes. The farmer scrambled to a sitting position and whimpered, pleading as Evanton beckoned Gorak and Iksan nearer to him.

"Fortunately I can handle things from the police end," said Evanton. "But I won't have a traitor in the ranks." He heard his own heart beating wildly, as the moment drew nearer. He turned to the Estonians. Slowly, he reached inside his jacket and drew out a pistol. He stepped back, teasing, at Gorak's gesture towards taking the pistol from him.

"No, no, no, that's not what I had in mind." He almost laughed at the pitiful sigh of relief that came from Geddes.

Ha! If only you knew, you grassing bastard!

There was a large vegetable knife sitting on the kitchen table. He motioned Gorak towards it.

"Pick it up," he said.

Gorak faltered at the mad gleam in his eye. Evanton released the safety catch on the pistol. At the loud click, Gorak moved forward and reluctantly picked up the knife from the table.

"Stand up," Evanton ordered a shaking Geddes. "I said, get up!" Evanton's voice was hoarse with the force of the shout.

Geddes scrambled to his feet, but his knees buckled and he lurched forward, grabbing on to the back of a chair for support.

This is it, thought Evanton, the imminent death causing arousal to course around his body almost painfully.

"Cut his throat."

He knew Gorak wouldn't act on this instruction. Not without some persuasion. He grabbed Iksan by the hair, and standing behind the quaking youth, pressed the pistol to his temple.

"Cut his throat."

Gorak emitted a grunt of anguish, seeing his young charge held at gunpoint. He looked at the farmer, the one who had betrayed them. He could see that their informer was paralysed by fear. Gorak caught a glimpse of a photograph on the wall behind Geddes – a smiling family. And he recalled the names on the children's bedroom door – *Jennifer* and *Amy*. This guy wasn't cut out for all of this; he'd been lured by the money, enough to pay off some debts, then he'd gotten scared. Nobody deserved to die because they were scared, Gorak thought. But Iksan. He had to get the lad home safely. Iksan, caught like a cornered rabbit at the wrong end of a gun. With faltering steps Gorak made his way slowly towards Geddes.

Fight back, he thought. *Run. Do something!* But the whites of

Geddes's eyes told him there would be no fight, no attempt to run. Paralysed by fear, Geddes simply howled in terror as the Estonian advanced on him with the knife.

Evanton watched the turmoil play out on Gorak's face, and breathed hard as the moment of killing was on him. Soon the dying would begin. That was the part he needed to watch. Killing was a messy business, beneath him. But the spectacle of dying, that was another matter. It was what fulfilled his desire to feel invincible, vibrant and truly alive.

Iksan yelped in pain under Evanton's grip on his hair. Evanton tried to focus on the feel of the gun in his hand while he watched Gorak take the knife to Geddes, but the memories came flooding back, unbidden, and blurring his focus.

The brute power of fighting for life.

The rasp of a last breath.

...Gorak slashing with the knife . . .

...Bleeding...

...Life ebbing away...

The life slipping away from those street beggars in the toxic fog. How they pleaded with him, sought his strength, as he breathed deeply through it all.

He shook his head to clear it. He couldn't let those memories cloud this new, fresh moment of dying . . .

. . . The vapour, stealing from him those last gasps . . . snatching away the satisfaction of his arousal . . . Geddes leaving a trail of blood on the wall, issuing one final gurgle from a flooded trachea . . . The woman with the dirty fingernails clawing at him . . .

"Bitch!" he yelled at the memory, angered at its intrusion into this moment. Frantic, he rammed Iksan's head against the wall, and turned towards Gorak.

Gorak stood over Geddes's bloodied body, shock registering on his face as he watched Evanton's gun take aim at him.

With a howl of frustration, Evanton pulled the trigger. Gorak's body barely made a sound as it fell back onto the bloodied and lifeless form of Geddes.

Wednesday

Chapter Twenty-nine

Donna's eyes dragged open. She looked in confusion at a room that didn't seem familiar in any way. Cautiously she sat up and noted, with some relief, that she was fully dressed. The strange bed that she found herself in creaked as she leaned on to her elbow. A pair of eyes appeared in front of her; she shot out her fist on impulse.

"Ow! What the . . . " And a clatter.

"Who's there?" asked Donna, startled at how loud her voice sounded in the semi darkness.

"It's me," came the voice of Natesh, though he sounded as if he was holding his nose. "Damn, but you've got some right hook!"

"Sorry," said Donna, quieter this time. She felt a piercing pain on one side of her head, and a wave of nausea rose to her throat.

Her pager buzzed.

"You going to get that?" asked Natesh. "It's been going for ages."

"Is this your house?" Donna asked. She couldn't remember coming here, she just couldn't figure out how it could have happened. She heard a miaow.

"You crashed your car in a lay-by," said Natesh. "Good job I was working tonight. Any weirdo could have picked you up."

"Thanks," Donna mumbled. Fragments of her evening were trooping back to her mind, and she was beginning to feel appalled at herself for drinking so much and then driving. The consequences really didn't bear thinking about if Natesh hadn't come by whenever he had. "I really owe you. Any chance of a coffee while I make this call?"

"I'm on it," said Natesh. She saw his shadow head off through a doorway. As he went, a soft light body landed on the bed next to Donna, and a cat rubbed itself against her. She stroked its back while she dialled Ross.

When Ross answered, he sounded as if he was out of doors. She had no idea what time it was, only that it was still dark.

"Donna, about bloody time. There's been a double murder at a farm house just outside of Arbroath. Neighbour called it in, poor

130

sod. I need you over here right away. I'm here with the forensic examiner, and Evanton's on his way. The rest of the crew are suiting up. Where the hell have you been?"

"I'll be there in, er, as soon as I can," said Donna. She had no idea where her car was, and she was pretty sure she was still over the limit for driving. It would be a bit of a big ask to expect Natesh to drive her to the scene at this hour.

Oh, what a mess, she thought in despair, and tried to wake herself by rubbing her cheeks vigorously.

The blinding pain in her eyes felt like a hot poker going straight to the back of her head when the room lights suddenly went on. She cried out in protest.

"Shush," said Natesh. "You'll wake the whole house."

"Fuck," Donna said sharply. "You could have told me the light was going on."

"Coffee," said Natesh, putting the cup down on a bedside cabinet next to her. He stepped back to assess her. "Oh, you've woken Harry Potter."

Donna looked at the cat, who was weaving round and about her arm.

She slurped at the coffee. Natesh sat down beside her. He was wearing jeans and a vest and he was in his bare feet.

"You need to go into work?" he asked. Donna nodded her head, then winced at the pain.

"You're not fit to drive," he said. "And your car is ten miles away with a busted headlight."

"Are you offering?" asked Donna. Through the slit in one eye she could see Natesh's grin beaming back at her.

"What are you waiting for?" he asked. He was already pulling on his socks and shoes.

Donna finished her coffee in two more gulps, then got to her feet. Her head was a little clearer but she still felt nauseous. She got a brief shock when she ran her hands through her hair, before remembering the funky new do.

"What time is it?" she asked as they stepped outside. She felt the chill air smack her between the eyes and on the back of her newly exposed neck.

"Half past five," said Natesh, full of bounce and cheer.

"Mm, well it's a bad start to the day for somebody," said Donna.

Natesh chattered all the way through Dundee, while Donna held her aching head. When they were just a few miles from Arbroath, like a tour guide Natesh pointed out Donna's sorry-looking car that was sitting in a lay-by on the other side of the road. She made a note to have it towed home later in the day.

As they approached the railway bridge through which they would arrive in the small seaside town, Donna saw the McDonalds all lit up.

"I need food," she said, and the words were barely out of her mouth before Natesh slammed on the brakes and swung the car round to the drive-thru.

Donna lined her stomach as they drove through Arbroath, passing only one other vehicle on the road, and came onto the road that would bring them to the farm house. There were no streetlights on this stretch, which made the crop of police lights at the entrance to the farmstead all the more startling. Natesh could barely contain himself.

"You can say I'm your assistant," he pleaded.

"Sorry, Natesh," said Donna. "But you're going to have to stay this side of the tape."

"Can I wait here, then, and watch?" he asked. "Pleeeeease?"

He pulled the car into the verge, at the end of a line of police and other cars.

"No further than this," Donna put up a warning finger. "If you behave, I'll tell you all about it later on."

"Ok, scout's honour," said Natesh. "I'll be right here. I'll wait for you."

"No, don't do that," said Donna. "There's no telling how long I might be. You get yourself back home."

"You kidding? This is the most exciting thing that's happened to me since Harry Potter attacked me."

Donna smiled as she left the car, but her mood was grim.

She walked towards the farm gate, where she saw Evanton standing talking to Emma from forensics. She regarded him for a moment, and thought back to Chisholm's description of the blackmailer from the previous afternoon. But she shook her aching head. Her hatred for Evanton must be making her imagine things. And yet, and yet, the little voice at the back of her mind nagged her.

At the gate, a uniformed officer was standing watching Donna approach. His attention alerted Evanton and Emma to the new arrival, and she noticed Evanton's double take. He then covered up by making a point of looking beyond her to where Natesh was parked.

"Did you get a taxi here?" he asked.

"My car's fucked," said Donna; it was about as civil as they were going to be to one another.

She looked along the lane and saw two farm houses. The first sat quietly, its soft lights betraying the trauma that must be going on inside, with its residents reeling from their grisly discovery. The second house was lit up like a beacon, surrounded by the harsh glare that screamed *crime scene*. Just short of two miles to the south she saw the street lights of Arbroath, while some half a mile north was the outline of a huddle of cottages. Otherwise, the countryside sat silent and dark all around.

Donna smiled in Emma's direction, and the forensic scene examiner held out a pale blue bundle.

"There you go," said Emma, "You'll look fetching in this gear. Getting to be a bit of a habit, eh?"

"You're telling me," said Donna, taking the paper suit and bootees that would cut down any contamination of the crime scene. "Arbroath is beginning to get interesting."

"Well, brace yourself, it's pretty gruesome in there," said Emma. "By the way, your hair is amazing. How do you manage to look so damned good at this hour?"

Donna laughed as she pulled on the coveralls. Then she caught Evanton's eye lingering on her and it made her squirm.

"I'll come with you," said Emma, "Got a few more snaps to take." She slung her camera bag over her shoulder, and walked towards the officer at the farm gate.

"Only two of you can go in," said the officer, almost embarrassed at having to say it.

"It's ok," said Evanton, "I'm going to wait here for a bit." He seemed distracted, and Donna was only vaguely aware that he was peering at the line of cars, paying particular attention to Natesh's taxi.

She waited patiently as the officer wrote down her details, in keeping with his role as crime scene manager at the outer cordon.

Once he'd done that, he gave them a nod, and Emma led the way through the farm gate, holding a huge flashlight out in front of her.

They trudged along the farm track in single file, and about half way along towards the house, Donna stopped suddenly and knelt down to examine something on the ground.

"Found a clue?" said Emma brightly, bringing her camera out.

"Maybe," said Donna. She pointed to a spot on the stony verge. "See the tyre tracks here?"

Emma looked in closely.

"Oh, yeah. And?"

"They don't look right," said Donna. She looked up at Emma's chuckle. "No, really, something about them doesn't seem right."

Emma dutifully took a set of snaps, then reached for her measuring tape and recorded details of the tyre tracks.

"Anything you can put your finger on?" she asked.

Donna shrugged her shoulders, somewhat puzzled. "This is a berry farm, right?"

Emma nodded in agreement.

"So, these tracks just look a bit . . . fucking enormous."

Both women stared for a moment at the tracks, then Emma sighed.

"I'll send off the pictures and measurements, see what we can find out about them."

"Actually, Emma, can I ask you not to do that?" said Donna. "I mean, could you see what you can make of it, without, er, going through the usual channels?"

There was a long pause, and another sigh from Emma.

"You'd better come up with a good story to get me off the hook if I get found out, then," she said. Donna nodded solemnly. Her instinct was telling her to keep some information back from this investigation, just for the meantime.

An owl swooped past them, and Emma shrieked, then laughed in embarrassment. Suddenly Donna felt her mood plummet; she wanted to cry. Holding it in made her chest feel tight, and she faltered and stopped by a boulder at the side of the track to sit down. She longed, more than anything else at that moment, to hold Libby.

"Are you ok?" said Emma, swinging the flashlight round.

Donna sighed, and with it came the first of the tears that she'd been dreading. She tried to wipe them away, but Emma had her in the spotlight.

"Hey, what is it? What's the matter?"

Donna rummaged in her pocket for a tissue, and her tub of lithium pills fell from her pocket. Emma was on it in an instant.

"Lithium?" She knelt beside Donna and placed an arm around her. Donna wept silently for a moment then cleared her throat.

"Sorry," she said. "Not dealing too well with a break-up. Great timing, eh?"

"And bipolar disorder?" said Emma gently. "An emotional upset like that can cause problems."

"Don't tell anyone," said Donna, suddenly alarmed. "Please don't say anything."

"Do you mean your boss doesn't know?" said Emma.

Donna shook her head.

"But you'll get help from occupational health."

Donna let out a bitter laugh. "Are you kidding? They'll have me out on my arse if they find out. They'll think I'm a nutter."

"That's not true," said Emma, "but I'll not say anything anyway. Are you having your meds reviewed regularly?"

"Yeah, well, sort of. I've got the doctor's tomorrow."

Emma gave her a quick hug. "Just stick with me in there then, ok? I'll keep an eye on you." And she stood up, and beckoned Donna on towards the farm house.

"I'll let Ross fill you in," she said. "He's up there with Lawson and two of his special cronies."

Donna took several deep breaths as they approached the house, to gather herself together.

Standing outside the farm house front door was the young PC Aiden Moore, looking pale and clammy as if he'd just been sick.

"Ma'am," he said weakly, glad to see Donna. She smiled at him and instinctively squeezed his shoulder as he opened the door for her and Emma.

Chapter Thirty

It was approaching eight-thirty in the morning. Libby listened to the traffic going by outside her office. The mesmeric swish of wheels on a wet road surface, that snaking swarm working its way warily through the city, only served to encourage her zombie-like mental capacity following her monumental effort to resume some sense of normal life. But as she sat, she felt so terribly detached from that normal life, that she found it hard to grasp that the everyday things were continuing to go on as they always had done. As if nothing had happened.

She noted the ordinary sounds of the new working day that began to warm up the department, but she remained impervious to them. She was still hurting from the argument she'd had with her father before he'd left her house the previous afternoon. He had only stayed on after Donna's visit for Danny's sake, but her appearance had been enough to set him off again on a blinkered, narrow-minded rant that had little to do with his faith and more to do with his own pride. Libby wondered miserably if it would be another seven years before he visited her again. She forced her rising temper to settle back down. Heaven knows, there was enough to deal with in the here and now. She was going to have to function through each day and be strong for Danny until this whole mess was sorted. And then . . . oh, how she just wanted Donna to walk through the door right now and make everything all right. Libby shook her head and reminded herself of the frustration Donna had caused by hinting that something untoward was going on behind the scenes, yet refusing to elaborate. She took a deep breath, and opened her inbox. The emails there asked much the same of her as they generally did. And that went for the queue of phone messages sitting on her answering machine. Attend this meeting. Peer review that article. Provide a reference for a graduate student. Submit a proposal for the new research grant. Libby looked at them all, and she thought about the routine and the sameness of it all. If she had just been dropped into this morning, skipping the last couple of days, she would simply have continued in her usual manner.

But the last couple of days had happened. For Libby, the world was different now. She had made her way to the university, nodded hello to the parking attendant, said good morning to Janice and several others en route to her office, and none of them knew that it was her own brother that this thing hung over.

A little boy had died after being at Danny's restaurant. A man was still in a coma in hospital. And the police were champing at the bit to have Danny put behind bars. She had only the hope that Donna was on top of things to cling on to, but, well, how much of a hope was that? She felt time was running out for Danny, especially with the media and their outrageous headlines hot on his heels. At least the journalists hadn't yet made the connection with her, and for now she could slip away from the nightmare and take part in normal life.

Then there was this business with Sally. Her story had been muddled and, at times, contradictory, and she'd refused to go to the police about her attack. She'd insisted on being left alone, and in the end Libby and Danny had had to respect her wish. But muggers hanging around a quiet street late at night? Libby wasn't buying it, unless . . . maybe . . . it had something to do with the little boy. His family lived in that same block, she was aware. But if there was one thing Libby rarely accepted, it was coincidence.

Eight-thirty, thought Libby, as the normal routines of the morning failed to suppress her worry or even to offer her a distraction from it. She wasn't going to respond to the emails or answer the phone messages, far less start any of her own work. There was something else she had to do first. She'd known it when she'd made her way to work this morning. Actually she'd known it since she collected Danny from the police station on Monday night: she was going to have to go and talk to Graeme Hunter. For all she knew, though, he might not even be at work today. She hadn't heard him. Perhaps the shock of what happened in Danny's restaurant had hit him . . . perhaps he was in hospital. Maybe he'd been one of the casualties, Libby thought with a start. With a tremendous effort she heaved herself from her seat and sighed heavily as she crossed the room and walked along the corridor into reception.

Time to find out.

Janice smiled when she saw Libby.

"Are you wanting to see Mr. Hunter?"

"Is he in?"

"Yes," said Janice, sounding surprised at the question. "He has nothing until 2pm today. Did you enjoy your day off yesterday?"

Libby faltered, unsure of how to answer.

"Just some family business needing seeing to," she said. "Well, if Hunter's free just now . . . ?"

Janice smiled at the irreverence in Libby's tone. Her dislike of Hunter was renowned as topping everyone else's dislike of him. And she didn't hide it.

"Go on in," said Janice.

Hunter was sitting at his desk reading the morning newspaper, amused at the bad press Danny Quinn was getting. Evanton had worked a stroke of genius there, he had to admit. Sipping his coffee and engrossed in the news coverage, he was slightly startled to find himself aware of a presence at his door. He looked up, and seeing it was Libby, grunted and made a show of being disturbed. He looked away, bracing himself for a confrontation. But then something struck him about Libby's demeanour. She wasn't emitting her spitfire rays of hostility, but entered the office quietly, meekly. That was what made Graeme Hunter put down his newspaper and look at Libby properly, probably for the first time. Without her spark she seemed tender, vulnerable. Little. Hunter couldn't decide if he preferred her this way or whether it unnerved him. He stayed silent, raising his eyebrows, bidding her to speak.

"I think I'd like to clear my diary today," Libby began, her voice almost timorous. She sat down; normally she stood facing him with her arms folded across her chest in defiance. "You know, after what happened at *The Bampot*?" Her voice trailed off, inviting him to concur with her.

He continued to stare at her, his eyebrows raised.

"My brother's restaurant in Arbroath?" Libby prompted.

And then the penny dropped. Libby Quinn. Danny Quinn.

Shit, thought Hunter, this was a bit too close for comfort.

"That restaurant in the news?" he blustered. "That's your brother's?"

He had to think quickly here, work out what she wanted, and stay a step ahead of her. He racked his brain and couldn't recall seeing her there, so she couldn't know he'd been there with Skinner. Could she? What if she did know? His mind began to spin in panic, and he could barely catch a thought from its whirlpool.

"You must be . . . upset. Terrible business. I've just been reading about it here." He raised his newspaper to show her.

That was when Libby saw the headline: *Restaurant killer's drugs secret.*

Libby advanced on Hunter's desk before she knew what she was doing, and grabbed the paper from him.

"Doesn't make for pleasant reading," said Hunter. "If I'd known your brother was a drugs dealer, it might have had a bearing on your position here in the department."

Libby threw the paper aside and rounded on him.

"A drugs dealer?" Her voice was raised, and the fury erupting from it surprised even herself. "Why would they say that? How can you believe a word that's written there? You were there on Monday night."

"I think you must be mistaken," said Hunter. It came out too quickly. He knew it had. But how could she know he'd been there? What else did she know? Who else had she told? He had to throw her off, miles off. He mustn't be connected with the events of Monday night.

Libby stopped mid flow and stared at him.

"You were at *The Bampot*," she said. Her voice had grown dangerously quiet. "And your car was parked outside. I saw you and I saw your car."

"I don't think so," said Hunter. *Think, think, think.* "I was in Edinburgh on Monday evening. At a conference. This is the first I've heard of the tragedy at your brother's restaurant. And, if there's nothing else, I've work to get on with." He raised the newspaper to his eyes, silently praying that she'd go away.

Libby couldn't believe what she was hearing. Why would Hunter pretend he hadn't been at *The Bampot*? She stood up, still facing him, uncertain of her next move. It wasn't as though he could have forgotten he'd been there, or been mixed up about being somewhere else. He was lying, but why?

"If you need the day off . . . " said Hunter dismissively.

"I was off yesterday," said Libby, something of the hard edge returning to her voice. "I just need my appointments cancelled for today, a bit of peace and quiet, to get on with some work."

Hunter shrugged. "So, cancel them."

The discussion was over. Libby had heard the lie, and knew that

Hunter had found no way to backtrack.

Puzzled, she turned around and left his office, all the time wondering why he would choose to lie about this. What was he hiding? Even if he'd been playing away from home, that wasn't something he was generally discreet about. She put her hand in her pocket and felt Donna's card with Evanton's phone number on it. The stirrings of intrigue began to nibble at the corners of her mind, and once again she remembered Donna's words . . . *Something really fucked up is going on.*

The intrigue began to burn, and Libby increasingly felt that maybe she had stumbled on some information that could somehow help Danny. She couldn't think how; all she knew was that she had to report this. The police would know if it made sense with all the other information they must have. With a renewed vigour she hurried back to her office and dialled Evanton's number.

"DI Evanton."

It sounded like an order instead of answering a phone call.

"Sorry to trouble you," said Libby, making sure to emphasise the annoyance in her voice. Evanton went quiet on his end of the phone. "I understand you need information about who was with Bob Skinner at *The Bampot* on Monday night?"

"And you have that information?" Evanton snapped.

Libby grew a little more than annoyed. "Actually I do. Maybe you could direct me to an officer who's a little more comfortable dealing with the public?"

"Who is this?"

Libby put the phone down. Seconds later it rang.

"DI Evanton here. You have information about Bob Skinner?" There were no pleasantries, certainly no apologies, but Libby could tell Evanton was trying to sound less irritable this time.

"He was with Graeme Hunter, Dean of the Engineering Faculty at the university," said Libby.

"And you are?"

"Dr. Libby Quinn, head of the Toxicology Department. Within the Engineering Faculty."

"And how do you know it was Graeme Hunter you saw?"

"He's my boss. He's pretty hard to mistake for somebody else." And she told Evanton how she'd watched from the kitchen with Danny as Hunter had taken his seat at Bob Skinner's table.

"Did Mr. Hunter see you there?" Evanton asked.

The question threw Libby slightly, but she confirmed that no, Hunter hadn't been aware of her there, and no, she didn't know how long he'd stayed as she'd left early to go home and mark some student assessments.

"Hmm," said Evanton, sounding distracted, maybe as if he was writing down the details. "Well, thank you for your assistance."

"He said to me that he was in Edinburgh all evening," she added quickly, sensing that she was being rushed off the phone.

She felt Evanton draw breath on the end of the line.

"What?"

"I spoke to Mr. Hunter about it, and he pretended not to have been there."

Evanton was silent for a moment.

"Leave the investigating to me, Dr. Quinn," he said flatly. "And do not discuss this with anyone else. This is a serious case, and your brother's in a lot of trouble. I'm sure you don't need reminding."

"That sounds like a threat rather than gratitude," said Libby.

"I'm in the middle of a serious investigation," he said. "I just hope your story checks out." And the line clicked off.

Libby sat for a moment, holding her phone, and wondering if she was just imagining things or if Evanton had reacted oddly to her information. Perhaps she should run this past Donna after all, she thought. But not yet. She didn't feel strong enough right now to hear her voice and have to let go again.

Evanton kept his hand on the receiver long after the call was ended. His chest felt tight, and his head was beginning to pound. What was going on? Why were all the balls refusing to stay in the bag? Skinner was taken care of, but Chisholm was still proving problematic. He'd silenced their grass, but now this Libby Quinn was a witness he could do without. Danny Quinn was lying low, but Donna Davenport was all over the joint, poking her nose in where it shouldn't be.

Well, Danny Quinn, he thought, *let's see how quickly you take the fall when I turn the screws on your sister.* He would have fun figuring out how to deal with her. Then he'd need to deal with Chisholm. And then Davenport. There was no way he was going to let himself get backed into a corner now. Trapped, like being locked in the coal bunker and having to invent those games. He shook his head to clear it.

God, why had Hunter been so stupid? He rang the Dean's office.

"What the fuck are you playing at?" he yelled down the line.

Hunter was already shaken, and hadn't come up with a story yet to cover for his discussion with Libby.

"Libby Quinn saw you – and your car – at the restaurant, and you told her you weren't there?"

"How did you know that?" asked Hunter.

"How do you think? She knows you're hiding something, so she phoned the police. Shit! Just as well it was me she phoned, but she's not going to keep this to herself, Hunter."

Hunter thought frantically for some way to redeem himself.

"Can't we frame her along with her brother?" he said. "I mean, she is a toxicologist, a chemist. Surely . . . "

He heard Evanton let out a breath; it sounded like relief.

"Perfect," he said. "Dr. Libby Quinn isn't going to know what hit her." He ended the call.

Chapter Thirty-one

Donna finally accepted there was no going back. That look in Libby's eyes on Monday night had been shock and fear, not longing or even reminiscence. She sat stroking Foxy while she flicked half-heartedly through the property pages. This was what happened when she tried to fight sleep. When she returned home from a late night, early morning murder scene but still had to be at work for nine, her mind wandered back to Libby. Six weeks, going on seven now, since it had all finished with Libby, and Donna had seen it in her eyes yesterday that there would be no second chance. It suddenly hit Donna for the first time that it really was over for good. When it had happened she'd been terrified; and when her worst fear had come true – when Libby threw her out – she'd gone into hope mode. Hoping that Libby would give her a chance to explain – *yeah, explain that!* – and hoping that Libby would forgive her. Hope, even, that Libby would miss her so much she'd ring up one day and say, *hey, fancy moving back in?* That hope mode had sent her soaring into a frenzy of energetic and, quite frankly, reckless activity. That much was obvious to her, sitting here looking back. But the see-saw was now tipped in the opposite direction. The ink on the property pages was as black as her mood.

The recklessness had almost cost her her job. There was every chance this latest downer could, too, as she lacked the will or the energy to care about anything. It drove her, and she was powerless to control it.

Foxy nudged her hand off his head, rousing her from her dreary daydreaming. He began to nibble at the corner of the property paper. Donna didn't move it away from him. Her arms felt like lead. Her whole body felt as though it had to fight through treacle in order to move. But there was a team briefing in thirty minutes and she needed something to help get her going. She picked up her mobile and dialled Natesh. A friendly voice would help.

"The person you are calling is unavailable," said the clipped voice on the other end.

He must be working. Or sleeping, given the night he'd endured because of her.

She put her mobile back down, and regarded Foxy for a moment. His food bowl was still full, and the newspaper was the only thing he seemed to be eating these days. Something wasn't right with him. She was going to have to call the vet. With a heavy sigh, and making a monumental effort to perform a task, she phoned and got an appointment for later in the afternoon.

"Vet today, doctor tomorrow," she said to the rabbit. "Swap you."

She threw down the property paper. The cost of a decent rental terrified her. She was going to have to put in a fair amount of extra overtime if she and Foxy were going to escape this grotty bedsit. But she wasn't going to have time today to view any flats. She had a briefing to get to, and if she left right now she might just make it on time.

She walked along the street, concentrating furiously. Was Danny the obvious suspect for the poisoning? Was she just too close to him to see that? Had Evanton been right to focus the blame on him? Could he be Chisholm's blackmailer? She almost laughed at how outlandish that sounded. But Evanton had been very quick to try and wrap up this investigation, though he wasn't known to jump to conclusions. It wasn't really his style.

Donna's mobile rang.

"Donna? It's Emma. I've got one set of results back for you. The tracks you picked up in the gravel? They were made by an articulated dumper truck, heavy duty."

Donna's attention focused sharply. The tyre tracks that had struck her as odd because of their size. Emma had been dubious about their significance, given this was a farm and there must be heavy vehicles going in and out all the time.

"What's an articulated dumper truck doing on a berry farm?" she asked Emma. "Unless they've got really huge pieces of fruit up there?"

"Construction work? Renovations?" offered Emma.

It was possible, Donna concurred.

"Where are we most likely to find one of these machines?" she asked.

"They're quarry workers, on the whole," said Emma. "But now you mention it, I didn't see a whole pile of boulders anywhere near the Geddes place this morning."

"Me neither."

"Are you going to throw this into your team briefing?" asked Emma.

"I haven't decided," said Donna. "I don't know if I could bear the humiliation of trying to explain a hunch about tyre tracks on a farm road. Ross is already on the verge of having me certified. Can you run with me on this one?"

"For a while," said Emma. "I'll give you twenty-four hours, then I'll have to tell Ross. And I'll try to have something on your boot print this afternoon."

The boot print. Another of Donna's hunches. She'd found it on an upstairs door in the farm house. Something in her gut had told her it wasn't right, and once again she'd confided in Emma. Taking another step towards her own end by hiding information during an investigation. She could feel the fine line she was walking grow gossamer-thin.

"Thanks, Emma, you're a pal."

She tried Natesh again when Emma rang off, but he was still unavailable.

Chapter Thirty-two

Natesh had been shocked to see the angry man again, the one with the mobile and the bad temper from the narrow lane outside of Swanky Lanky's the day before.

When he'd dropped Donna off at the cordon, he'd been so excited that he'd settled himself in for a long wait, on the promise of some juicy tattle and gore. Maybe this time, he'd hoped, Donna would tell him something. Since she'd joined the Force, she'd resolutely refused to bring him into her confidence on police matters. But this time, surely.

Then he'd seen the man. Now clearly a cop, like Donna. The other cop had stared at the taxi and then Donna as she walked towards him. Natesh had watched the body language as Donna dismissed the man with some comment or other. And he'd shivered as the man stared along the row of vehicles and fixed on his.

Donna had disappeared off down the farm track, but the man had remained there by the road side, staring at the taxi.

Natesh had grabbed his Japa Mala beads from around the rear view mirror and worked them frantically as he watched the man approach his car.

Angry man, Natesh had told himself, working himself into a state of anxiety. Then, to calm himself, *Police man*. But he'd witnessed Donna's obvious dislike of the man, and his unease took over.

Evanton had leaned in the driver side window, after motioning for Natesh to lower it, and stared at the apprehensive driver.

"You've no business here, son," said Evanton. He'd reached in and pulled Natesh's ID tag for a look, then told him to turn around and head back to Dundee.

Natesh hadn't needed to be told twice. He'd made the u-turn and hit the accelerator.

Since getting home he'd only managed two hours' sleep, before he got a call to pick up a fare from the airport. A little fuzzy-headed due to his odd sleep pattern that night, he stretched and yawned as he opened the taxi door, but never doubted that he was up to the job.

He pulled out, zipped skilfully through the short streets into the city centre, and to avoid rush hour and snarl-ups, cut along the Perth Road with its huge houses, before careering towards the congested Riverside Drive towards the airport, singing along to the radio as he went.

With the traffic foresight apparently possessed by all taxi drivers, he hit the brakes late as he approached the junction. The taxi kept on going.

"Oh shit!" he said out loud, working the brake frantically.

Swerving furiously as a blaring horn sounded the approach of a white transit van from his left, Natesh glimpsed the driver's V-sign as his taxi veered right towards oncoming traffic.

Two cars coming towards him slewed left onto the Perth Road to avoid hitting him head-on. There was a screech of metal as they collided with each other, crashing through a garden hedge as a biker, caught unawares by the white transit van correcting itself on the opposite carriageway, ploughed into its windscreen.

Desperately using his gears to slow the car, Natesh felt the impact as a minibus clipped the taxi.

"Fuck fuck fuck!" he yelled as the wheel hit the curb, and his taxi tipped over, landing on its side in the middle of Riverside Drive, now the epicentre of an eight-vehicle smash and a two-mile tailback.

Chapter Thirty-three

Donna's eye caught the headline on a newsagent's A-board at the roadside. Despite all the coffees she'd had since getting home from the farm house she was still slightly hungover, so she'd passed the A-board by several steps before its words sunk in; she stopped in her tracks and looked back at it.

Restaurant killer's drugs secret.

A flash of anger ignited her interest, and puffing furiously on her cigarette she marched into the newsagent's shop. With her anger welling to a fearful knot in the pit of her stomach, she bought a copy of *The Courier* and checked for the name of the journalist behind the ridiculous headline.

Lindsey Forsyth.

Donna remembered her, the petite reporter buried under a pile of woollens. Where would she be getting information like that, Donna wondered? She made a snap decision, and flagged down a taxi. She knew that being late for this team briefing would cause all sorts of ructions, and certainly wouldn't win her any brownie points with Ross. But her anger ran ahead of her. She had to find out who was feeding the media these lies about Danny.

"Ninewells Hospital, please," she said to the taxi driver, who seemed unable to stop leering at her in his rear view mirror during the short trip.

When she got out of the taxi, Donna stood for a moment, looking around her. Her hunch had been right – the press pack was still here, and now that the information had been released that a local MP was one of the casualties here, it had grown into a sizeable army.

Poor sods, thought Donna. Here they were, standing in the cold and rain waiting for snippets of news from busy doctors. No doubt most of them were actually sports reporters here to cover the quarter final, but instructed to cover these latest events instead. She didn't envy them their task once the details of the farm house double murder were released, and hoped they didn't connect them to the restaurant poisoning before the police managed to put the lid on it.

Looking intently at the reporters' faces, Donna noticed only one – Lindsey Forsyth – appeared to be relaxed. Everyone else looked miserable. If Donna's gut feeling was correct, she was about to confirm that she had a real problem on her hands. Sure enough, Lindsey's face lit up when she saw Donna, and she waved and trotted towards her. Donna lit a cigarette and stood leaning on a lamp post while Lindsey approached.

"Oh, I love your hair!" the young journalist gushed. "I'm, like, so in the wrong job, Tayside's finest are just so glamorous!"

"Excuse me?" said Donna.

"Well, your colleague I spoke to yesterday looked like a film star, and so do you." She clamped her hand over her mouth, realising she had blurted out too much information. Donna was ready and seized on it at once.

"Yes, about my colleague who spoke to you yesterday," she said. "He's obviously very keen for us to get to the bottom of what happened at the restaurant. He said you were very helpful."

The journalist nodded her head, her eyes wide.

"I'm grateful, too," said Donna, softening her eyes and smiling. Lindsey Forsyth was putty in her hands. "Can you phone me as soon as you hear anything else on the grapevine?"

The young reporter took Donna's card eagerly.

Donna leaned in close to her ear. "I'll make it worth your while."

Lindsey Forsyth blushed and nodded her head, suddenly tongue-tied. Donna smiled and bid farewell, conscious that she was now running twenty minutes late for her team briefing. Finding Natesh's number still unavailable, she hailed another taxi.

She didn't stub out her cigarette as she entered the station, but made her way, unhurried, to the room she shared with Evanton to grab a coffee to take to the briefing. Their office lay at the end of a narrow, shabby corridor, and as she drew closer, she could hear Evanton's raised voice on the phone. Not like him to lose his cool, thought Donna wryly. She stopped behind the door and listened in.

"Dr. Libby Quinn isn't going to know what hit her," said Evanton's voice. Donna's eyes widened; she held her breath. She needed to think, but she knew that she would have to play this one very carefully. She hadn't heard the whole discussion, and she wasn't on her correct medication. Her brain could be running ahead of her ability to reason. Maybe Libby had phoned him and given some muddled information and he was simply expressing annoyance.

Libby giving muddled information? Her rational self scoffed at the near impossibility of that. And it came back again, that nagging dread that Evanton might be Chisholm's blackmailer. Could Libby hold the key to exposing him somehow? Was she at risk? Donna began to feel giddy. She had to make sure Evanton was kept off guard with her. She barged into the office door, doing her best to appear grumpy and in a hurry.

"What are you doing here?" she asked Evanton. "Aren't you meant to be at the team briefing?"

"Ross held it off until you got here," said Evanton, his face a mask of anger. "Do you think we've got nothing better to do?"

"Oh, fuck off and get over yourself." Donna scowled at him, preparing herself a coffee. There, he wouldn't suspect anything out of the ordinary now, she smirked to herself.

"I'll see you in Room 2.25," said Evanton, getting up from behind his desk and smoothing down the sleeves of his elegant, stylish shirt, before leaving the room without further comment.

By the time Donna reached Room 2.25 everyone else was there, including an irate Chief Superintendent Lawson and a flustered DCI Ross. The other officers were listening to Dom Hilton and Ted Granger relate their experience that morning of dealing with a car wreck at rush hour. Anything to avoid talking about the gruesome scene they'd crawled over at the farm house just hours before.

"Here you are, lass," said Ted. "Listen, could we . . . " He took hold gently of Donna's elbow, and began to lead her away from the group, but stopped when he saw Ross flashing them a glare. Lawson made a song and a dance of clearing his throat and calling the room to attention. For an awful moment of silence, Donna wondered if she'd actually said *wanker* out loud, but the lack of response reassured her that she couldn't have done.

Lawson pointed to the series of photographs on the whiteboard that documented the murder of Bill Geddes along with the shooting of an unidentified man in his farm house. Donna studied what could still be seen of the expression on Geddes's face. She took a note of Lawson's remarks that this was a particularly brutal and frenzied attack, one victim's throat slashed, the other with a clean shot through the chest, the killer making no attempt to clear up, leaving it difficult for them to find distinct traces of himself.

Except maybe for one thing, thought Donna, letting her mind's eye cut to the boot print she'd found on the upstairs door. A long shot, she knew. It was most certainly the print of a heavy kick from a man's boot, and not one that matched either of the dead men's shoes. And so the image remained filed away in Donna's mind under a large question mark.

"This is a brutal, confident killer who's not afraid of being caught any time soon," Lawson admitted. "I've asked for input from Dr Teller in Grampian, anything he can tell us about the profile of a killer like this." His speech was faltering, and Donna got the sense that he wasn't used to dealing with this level of violence on his patch. A small flutter of sympathy stirred for him.

"Teller is an asshole," said Evanton suddenly. The obvious contempt in his outburst made everyone in the room turn to stare at him, but he said no more, standing motionless with his hands folded across his chest, his brows drawn in barely controlled ill temper.

"We've asked SEPA to test the canisters found at the farm house," Lawson continued, in an attempt to win back the room's attention. "If they prove positive for MIC, we may have found our anonymous caller. Unfortunately, if that turns out to be the case, we have a serious problem on our hands: a killer on the loose with a highly lethal toxin."

He paused and there was complete silence in the room. Donna decided, in that moment, to leave the information about the tyre track and the boot print for a private discussion with Ross. To avoid stealing Lawson's thunder, or to avoid being laughed out of the room, she wasn't sure which. But she'd let Ross have the details.

"We can't yet confirm a link with the restaurant," Lawson went on. "There wasn't enough trace chemical in Bob Skinner's water jug for SEPA to detect, so it's gone to forensics to see what they can find."

Ross presented the update from his team on tracing the anonymous caller.

"Does Evanton know about me and Libby?" Donna whispered to Alice Moone.

"I don't think so," said Alice, "but don't quote me on it. Why do you ask?"

"Just wondered."

"If you feel you have a conflict of interest, you know you have to tell Ross?"

"I'm fine. I just wondered."

Ross frowned in Donna's direction as he outlined how they would now tie in with the murder investigation. He then invited Donna to tell the group what she had on Danny, and she gave a concise summary. But she omitted any mention of Libby. She turned to Evanton.

"What about the press reports about Danny Quinn's so-called drugs dealing?" she said.

Evanton put on a good show of looking blankly at her.

"What about them?"

Donna shrugged. "Can't be helping any."

"So, what, you want to censor the press or something?" Evanton said.

"Just saying." She tapped her foot, schoolmarm-like. "What about Bob Skinner? Who was he dining with?"

Ross shuffled noisily, his place as maestro for his team's presentations well and truly usurped.

"I've reviewed all the witness statements from the restaurant," Evanton said. "But so far there's nothing on who was dining with Bob Skinner."

"It can't be that hard," said Donna, unable to help herself. "In a town where everybody knows everybody else's business?"

"Well, everybody is saying they know nothing," said Evanton slowly and clearly. They scowled at each other.

Donna chewed the end of her pen.

"Uh huh," she said again.

Evanton glared at her. "You concentrate on doing your homework, and I'll find out who Skinner was with." What was going on in that fucked-up head of hers, he wondered?

"My *homework*?"

"What about Danny Quinn's sister?" Evanton said.

His eyes bored into Donna's.

The room stopped, electric.

Crap, thought Donna.

"An environmental toxicologist," Evanton went on. "Bet she knows a thing or two about MIC. I say we bring her in for a bit of questioning about what went on in her brother's restaurant."

It was one-nil to Evanton and he and Donna both knew it. Ross was beyond furious.

"One final matter," Lawson said loudly. All eyes swivelled towards him. "I want one of you to go along with Family Liaison to talk to Bill Geddes's widow." His gaze rested on Donna.

"Oh no you don't," said Ross, letting his gut react as he pictured the mess over that school liaison rota. He would not risk letting Donna loose in a sensitive situation right now. He had watched her begin to crack at the seams over the past few weeks, and damn it, she was going to tell him what the hell was going on with her, before he let her work a single minute more.

"I want to see you in my office," Ross hissed at Donna as the meeting broke up. "Evanton, bring in Libby Quinn."

Donna was standing outside the building having a smoke, and fuming over Evanton's coup when her phone rang.

"That's your car ready, hen." It was Fenton, the mechanic.

"Thanks, you're the best," said Donna. She turned round at the sound of Ted clearing his throat beside her. He placed his hand on her shoulder.

"Thought you should know, lass," he said. "The RTI on Riverside Drive this morning? One of the vehicles was your friend's taxi. Didn't look too good. You might want to check it out."

"Fuck," said Donna, feeling the cold dread creep across her neck as she recalled Natesh's failure to answer his phone.

"I'll come with you," said Ted.

"No, Ted, it's fine," said Donna. "Really. I'll just go and see if he's been taken to Ninewells. Take him some grapes."

She took off at a run towards Fenton's. Her showdown with Ross was going to have to wait.

Back in her own car, she pulled onto the Kingsway, heading for Ninewells Hospital. She'd simply reassure herself that nothing had happened to Natesh, then she'd return and make herself present at Libby's questioning. She'd have time to do that.

Donna fidgeted and paced back and forth while the nurse went

153

away to get her the information she'd requested, jolted into action upon seeing Donna's warrant card.

When the nurse returned, she read directly from a folder.

"Natesh Chaudrakar?" she confirmed. Donna chewed her fingernail. "He was in a fatal RTI this morning . . . Are you ok?"

The nurse threw down the folder and leapt to Donna's side, gripping her elbow. Donna's face was suddenly drained of all colour, and her legs could no longer support her. She felt a shelf of comfort shatter and break in her heart, and flashes of light at the back of her eyes flickered and turned to blackness as she fainted.

When she came round, Donna found herself lying on a hospital bed in a cubicle; all she could feel was pain in her heart.

"Detective?" said the nurse.

Donna curled herself into a ball.

"I think you misunderstood me," said the nurse. "It wasn't Natesh who died in the accident. That was another driver. But Natesh is badly injured. I'm afraid he's not up to being questioned at the moment."

Donna bounced up from the bed, her eyes wide.

"He's alive?" she shouted. "I thought . . . oh, my God, I thought I'd lost him. I'm not here to question him. He's my friend. Could I just see him?"

She pleaded with her eyes, and the nurse relented.

"Don't tell the charge nurse," she said. "And just for a minute."

Donna followed the nurse along corridors, up and down stairs, until they approached the critical care unit. During the silent walk, the memory of Evanton staring over her shoulder at Natesh's taxi back at the farmhouse invaded her thoughts. She shook her head. *Get a grip*, she thought.

They were stopped outside the unit's double doors to disinfect their hands, when Donna's phone rang, and she flashed an apologetic smile at the nurse while she answered it.

"Donna? It's Janice. I hope you don't mind me phoning, but Detective Inspector Evanton has just been, and he's arrested Dr. Quinn. What the hell is happening?"

Chapter Thirty-four

From his hotel room to the hospital was a five minute taxi ride or a twenty minute walk. Chisholm chose to walk, even though the rain was now coming down heavily. His shoes, more accustomed to the soft carpeting of top academia, became saturated in minutes. It made his feet ache, but he wasn't thinking about his feet.

Sally was in trouble, and he was in no doubt as to who was responsible for the phone call he'd received from her the night before. At least the police knew now about the blackmailer, and it must surely be only a matter of time before they found him. It looked as though this lowlife was going to stop at nothing to make sure the MIC investigation died a death, and Chisholm couldn't decide whether telling the police about Sally would protect her or harm her. The less he said, the less the blackmailer would have to suspect, he reckoned in the end.

But above the fear for Sally's safety hovered Chisholm's mounting guilt at the way he'd left his family behind. Abandoned them for the sake of his own ambition and career. It grated on his conscience that the blackmailer assumed he was still in touch with his daughter. He felt wretched that he'd broken that most sacrosanct of bonds, that even thugs apparently didn't break.

Well, Chisholm decided, if his blackmailer could find Sally then so could he. And Sally had pleaded for his help. If he could do one thing to make amends, he determined, he was going to help her. It was going to mean breaking his promise to Nicola though, as the only way he could think of to end this mess that Sally had been dragged into was to go public. Very public. About everything.

His mobile rang.

He cursed his fingers, numb with cold, as he fumbled to get the phone out of his jacket pocket. It might be Nicola.

"Enjoying the sights, David?"

Chisholm's breath caught in his throat as the blackmailer's voice growled over the line. All of his fury rushed upwards as soon as he heard it. He glanced around and about, but saw nothing out of the ordinary; there was nobody following him. He swallowed several times before answering.

"Where is Sally?"

"You'll only have to worry about her if you don't end the investigation," said the blackmailer.

"Don't you dare touch her," said Chisholm.

"Well, that's up to you. There's a new plan. If you do exactly as I say, I won't have to touch her."

Chisholm's skin crawled. "What do you mean?"

"The working group will meet as planned," said the blackmailer. "It will be presented with a report that provides the evidence that there is no trace of MIC, after all. You will endorse the report, and you will make an announcement that the government was correct to be cautious, but that there is no cause for concern. You will announce the conclusion of the investigation, and if asked you will strenuously deny the possibility of any link between MIC and the poisoning at the restaurant."

Chisholm let the line remain silent while he thought. He looked around him at the well tended lawns, and imagined his blackmailer behind one of the curtained windows, ready to spill his toxin. He pictured the tendrils of death seeping from the door frame and billowing into a deadly cloud, racing uphill towards the hospital. He had spoken to enough Bhopal survivors, read enough of their journals, and watched enough footage for it to make him shudder, and his hand trembled violently as he held the phone to his ear. It really was here. It came as a shock to him to realise that until now, he hadn't truly believed it. How could he allow the devastation he knew it could cause? The blinding, burning and choking as the gas touched human tissue. And more, the crushing of bone and breath in the stampeding frenzy to try and escape it. Just like Bhopal. He could stop it happening again. Except, Sally's life was in danger. That was what Chisholm feared the most at this moment.

"Then you'll leave me and my family alone?" he said at last, defeated.

If the blackmailer sensed he had Chisholm, he didn't express any glee. He continued in the same tone as before.

"You'll receive the report by email this evening. You will have twenty-four hours to publicly endorse it. Twenty-four hours. Or your daughter will go missing. And if you have any last minute thoughts about trying to pull a fast one, just have a read at the evening newspapers."

A chill grew in the pit of Chisholm's stomach. Following on from the news reports of the attack at the restaurant, he'd also heard reports coming through of a particularly violent pair of murders in the same area. Speculation was rife as to the likelihood of the two being linked, given the general lack of newsworthy badness in this part of the country.

Chisholm needed to get this guy out of his life. He would do what he had to. He was going to put his family before his career, like he should have done all those years ago.

He'd given in.

It was a broken Professor Chisholm who walked on towards Ninewells Hospital for early afternoon visiting.

Chapter Thirty-five

DI Jonas Evanton smirked with the smug satisfaction of a man who'd stared into the abyss and fought his way back out. As if he'd kicked down the door of the coal bunker from all those years ago and gotten out by himself. If he could keep himself in the clear, then nobody else would have to suffer.

His boots made a satisfying echo as he marched along the corridor towards the interview room. The heating system had failed again this morning, so he was sure that Libby Quinn would be suitably uncomfortable by now; cooled down, perhaps, after her angry outburst at him for bringing her here.

All his irons were lying neatly by the fireside, everything back under control. The MIC investigation would stop now: David Chisholm had caved in, and Bob Skinner would never know anything about it. By the time he woke up, if he ever did, nobody would be interested any more. The police investigation into an MIC connection would end when Chisholm made his announcement the next day, and Donna Davenport, if she was smart enough, would be frightened into silence by the car crash that had happened to her friend. Or if not frightened, at least distracted. He could easily see to it that the murder investigation got tied in knots. Yes, everything was back under control.

Evanton stuck out his chin and congratulated himself. He would let the rumours rumble on about Danny Quinn's background, he didn't care about that; and, while he'd enjoyed his fiery set-to with Libby Quinn, he really didn't need her any more. But Donna's reaction to his mention of Libby hadn't escaped his notice. Maybe there was some leverage there, he wondered. It was always handy to keep these little nuggets tucked away for future reference.

With a casual gait, he made his way to the interview room where he'd left Libby to stew with her temper.

She glared at him when he entered the room. When he told her she was free to go, he almost thought she was going to try and slap him across the face, but apparently she didn't need telling twice. She left.

Now to get onto matters more important to his pocket – a visit to the quarry to make sure Hunter hadn't ballsed-up the MIC storage this time, and to make sure the Estonian kid was being kept busy and out of trouble.

The racket going on in the quarry meant Iksan couldn't hear himself think, and for that he was grateful. He crept back to his spot in the corner of the Portakabin office after an hour of pacing back and forth. He cowered there for another hour, then got back up to resume his pacing . . . and throwing things . . . and hammering things with his fists . . . and muttering to himself and to the heavens. Gorak was gone. Made to slit a man's throat to order. It was more than he could bear.

On arriving here at the quarry following the killing last night, Iksan had stripped to his skin, thrown his blood-soaked clothes into a pile and put a match to them, before scrubbing himself down under the water pump used for the trucks. Then he emptied the contents of his stomach, and found himself retching painfully and frequently. Trying to block out the horrors he had just witnessed, he had attempted to think rationally about his own survival and escape, and found himself a boiler suit to replace his burnt clothes. Now wearing the all-in-one, pacing and muttering, he looked and sounded like the caricature of an asylum inmate.

There was a lull in the noise from the heavy machinery outside, and Iksan became aware of the sound of men chatting to one another. He peered out of the tiny window, and through the rivulets of rain water clinging to the Perspex, he saw a small group of men in hard hats standing around an articulated dumper. They were stretching, yawning, and generally looking relaxed. Iksan decided at that moment that he had to get out of here. Somebody had to know about him, even if it meant giving himself up to the authorities. He knew, now more than ever before, that he would never see his home again if he didn't run and get help. He straightened himself up, steeled himself for the encounter, then shrank back again in alarm as he saw a dark green Audi approach the quarry along its single track road. Evanton was here. Iksan turned in full circles, agitated, and began to quietly sob as he heard the men outside bid their farewells and heard the slams of their car doors and the revs of their engines as he was left here, alone, to face Evanton.

Nice timing, thought Evanton, as he pulled in to let the convoy of cars by, the quarry men clocking out for the day. Now he could get on undisturbed. How good it felt when the tide was going his way.

Chapter Thirty-six

Ninewells Hospital was pleasant and modern, unlike so many hospitals David Chisholm had seen in the UK. He dutifully waited his turn to get into one of the lifts, and followed a group of gift-wielding visitors going to the main ward off which Bob Skinner had his own room. Outside the room door stood a uniformed police officer. The officer stood straighter upon seeing Chisholm, ready to challenge.

"I'm Professor Chisholm," he said, offering his hand. The officer looked at him, surprised to be shaking hands. He wrote down Chisholm's particulars and his contact details, before asking him to wait a moment. Chisholm heard the officer mention his name to someone inside the room before returning.

"You can go in," said the officer, beckoning him through the door.

Chisholm thanked the officer, and stepped into the room. Bright lights, beeping monitors and stifling heat hit him before he saw a woman seated beside the hospital bed. She was petite, in her fifties, with short grey hair. She was alert, and certainly didn't look like someone Chisholm would want to get into an argument with. He glanced at Bob Skinner lying there – wired up to beeping machines and unconscious to it all – a man he'd never met before, and briefly wondered if they ever would.

The woman's chair scraped on the tiled floor as she stood up.

"I'm Mo, Bob's wife," she said, greeting Chisholm with a firm handshake and a frown. "Bob talked a lot about your visit to the UK. About having you on the working group."

Chisholm was surprised to hear it mentioned, with the investigation being kept so hush-hush. And at the mention of it he felt a flush of shame for knowing he was going to end it in such an unscrupulous way. He shifted uncomfortably under Mo's stare.

"I'm so sorry to hear about what happened," Chisholm told her. Mo nodded, and gestured towards a spare chair by the bed. They sat facing each other across the hospital bed, Bob Skinner oblivious to their presence.

They talked hesitantly and briefly about Skinner's condition, with the ever present beep of the heart monitor. Mo's eyes flicked frequently towards the monitor, and every few minutes or so the trace took a fraction longer to appear on the screen, making her catch her breath. Chisholm soon found himself doing the same, and the visual representation of Bob Skinner's heart rate soon led their own.

"I wasn't happy with Bob inviting you onto the working group," said Mo. Her bluntness made Chisholm start.

"No? Uh, may I ask why?" said Chisholm. He felt a moment of paranoia. She couldn't be working with the blackmailer, could she?

"You won't remember me, but . . . " Mo stopped, froze, then continued as the heart monitor had one of its hiccoughs. "But we've argued against one another in court. Several times, years ago."

"I'm sorry, I don't recall," he said.

"I thought not. I provide free legal advice to Victims of Bhopal."

Mo watched, with ill-disguised contempt, as David Chisholm relaxed into his chair.

"I understand," he said, opening his hands. "I can see how you might be suspicious of my motives." It was supposed to be self-deprecating, to build a bridge with Mo Skinner.

"Lucrative business, isn't it? Storing MIC," she said. She was going for the jugular.

"You surely can't think I have anything to do with this?" Chisholm almost laughed. "For one, we don't even know that there actually is MIC being stored here." He hoped he sounded convincing.

"You would say that, wouldn't you, professor?" said Mo.

"Ma'am, I'm an academic," said Chisholm. "I work on the basis of evidence. As do you. And right now, although there have been confirmed traces of MIC around this area, we have no proof that there is any storage."

Mo's lip curled. "I trust the working group will go ahead and meet tomorrow as originally planned?"

Chisholm felt wretched. The working group was going to meet, all right, and it was going to endorse a bogus report that would put a stop to the investigation. His daughter was in danger because of this investigation, and his marriage was wrecked. It had to end. Hadn't it?

"Professor Chisholm?"

He shook himself from his reverie.

"I'm sorry," he said. "Time zones catching up with me. Yes, the working group . . . "

The monitor flatlined and Chisholm stumbled to a halt mid sentence.

"Oh my God!" cried Mo, leaping to her feet, reaching for the alarm buzzer. The chair crashed to the floor behind her.

Chisholm stood staring at the greyish face on the pillow. He heard footsteps running towards the room, but felt powerless to do anything.

The door opened, two ward nurses rushing in.

The police officer who'd been waiting by the room reeled in alarm, and removed his hat instinctively. When a further two nurses and a doctor hurriedly filed into Skinner's room, he made a phone call, as instructed, to DI Evanton.

Chisholm found himself attempting to console Mo Skinner, patting her aimlessly on the arm, and it was several moments before the nurse's words filtered through.

"It's ok, Mrs. Skinner," she was saying. "The monitor pads have just slipped off your husband's chest."

Chisholm and Mo stared blankly at the nurse.

"Oh my God, I thought I'd lost him. I thought he was gone." She quickly wiped the tears from her eyes and slumped into her chair, holding Bob's hand and making heroic efforts to get her own breathing back under control.

Chisholm himself let out a long breath and wiped away the beads of sweat that had formed on his forehead. He, too, sat down, and watched as the nurse tended to the shaken Mo, and the doctor re-attached Bob. He thought about the threat to Sally. Could he really protect her by calling off the investigation, when he'd already told the police about the blackmailer? Mo was the only person now who could possibly understand the dilemma he faced.

"May I ask you something, Mo?" he said when they were alone again.

Mo focused on him, looking surprised as though she were seeing him for the first time. She glared at him furiously.

"Do you see?" she hissed. "Do you see what your precious MIC does? It kills people. It tears communities apart. Have you any idea of the horrors I've seen because of this toxin? *I* was in Bhopal, professor. I was there, and I'll never forget the smell of that poison burning flesh. I'll never forget the sound of a thousand people heaving their last breath together. I'll never forget the feeling in the air of people desperately willing their loved ones to be all right, killing each other in their rush to find one another. Never. And now, today, I've had the police suggest that my husband is in this condition because of his involvement in the working group. So, what is it, professor? What is it that you want to ask me?"

The room settled back into its previous stillness, with just the steady beeping to break the silence. Mo's breathing came quickly.

"Can you think of anyone who might wish to see the MIC investigation called off?" he asked her.

Mo looked at Chisholm for such a long time, he thought about repeating the question. But he could see in her eyes that she'd been disarmed and was carefully weighing her response.

"What is it that you want to tell me?"

Tentatively, Chisholm told Mo about the blackmail threats he had been receiving ever since he'd been approached to join the MIC investigation. And while she sat taking in every detail, her eyes hawk-like in their all-seeing scrutiny, he went on to tell her about Sally, about the phone call from her the previous night, and the ultimatum he'd been given.

Mo let her head fall into her hands. "I can't handle this any more," she said. "What is going on? Why has this happened to Bob?"

"Mo," Chisholm said quietly, "somebody wants this investigation stopped badly enough they'll do whatever it takes." He thought for a moment, then asked the question that had been lurking at the back of his mind, until now unable to face asking it. "Would you mind telling me what you know about what happened at the restaurant?"

Mo stared at him. "I wasn't there," she said. "The first I knew, Bob had taken a choking fit."

"Choking?" Chisholm chewed at his lip. "And there were others, also choking?"

Mo nodded.

"Clearly, you are well aware of the effects of MIC poisoning," said Chisholm. "Do you think that's what happened to your husband?"

Mo was clearly agitated.

"We need to go to the police," she said.

Chisholm nodded in agreement. "I understand Bob has

164

approached Graeme Hunter at the university here to provide the investigation's research? Is that correct?"

Mo nodded, distractedly.

"It's possible he's in danger, too," said Chisholm. "Look, why don't I go and meet with Mr. Hunter to warn him of our suspicions, and you speak with the police? Then we can meet again later on today?"

Chapter Thirty-seven

Donna was back behind the wheel, hurtling along the Kingsway. Her two hands managed to hold a mobile phone, a cigarette, a quarter bottle of vodka and the steering wheel, all juggled in sequence. She spoke into her phone.

"Can you collect a car for me?"

"What? Not again, hen?"

"It's not mine this time," she told Fenton. "It was involved in an accident this morning, and it's been taken to the pound." Her voice was level, serious.

"How do you want me to get it from there, hen? It'll be all locked away."

"Could you find a way to do it . . . *unofficially* . . . just for me." Donna knew she was calling in a huge favour, but she also knew Fenton had the tax authorities snapping at his heels. If she were to find herself owing him, she was sure he'd find a way for her to help him out in return.

"Oh, I get you, hen," said Fenton. "Come round to my place after four and I'll have the car here for you. What's the number plate?"

He wasn't one for asking too many questions, and right now that suited Donna. Her next call was to Emma.

"Nothing yet on the boot print," said Emma, sounding almost apologetic.

"There's something else," said Donna. "I'm having a car that was involved in a fatal RTI this morning . . . er . . . relocated. From the pound. I need it checked for prints." She raised her voice at the end, pleading.

"Oh, Donna," whispered Emma. "You're running a few risks, are you not? What if you get caught?"

"It's related to the farm house murders . . . oh, shite!"

"Donna? Donna, are you ok?"

There was a stamping noise and several car horns blared across the phone. Emma held it away from her ear, grimacing.

"Sorry, dropped my fag," said Donna.

"Are you driving?"

Donna took a slug from the bottle. "I don't want to put you on the spot," she said. "But the car will be at Fenton's after four this afternoon, and if a set of prints could be taken, I think I might just have a bombshell."

"On one condition," said Emma.

"Anything."

"That you start taking better care of yourself."

"Love you too, Emma," said Donna. Blowing two noisy kisses down the phone before downing more vodka. The pills weren't working any more; the mood swings were coming back with a vengeance, stealing her sanity.

Emma sighed, her concerns for Donna not eased any.

Donna sped along the Kingsway, aware of the driver in the next lane staring in at her because she was on her mobile. She raised the vodka bottle in salute. The driver shook his head, appalled.

Donna's mobile rang and she answered without hesitation. The mania had taken over her nerves, and she felt invincible, like she could do a thousand things at once. That tiny corner of her mind, the one that stayed sane, was terrified at her inability to stop herself careering into disaster. She was plunging ahead, leading her own investigation against Evanton under the radar, and she wasn't stopping to think her way ahead of him. Couldn't stop, because she had to run to catch up with herself. The majority of her mind was racing on, and she had to rush to keep up with it. Tomorrow's appointment with the doctor couldn't come quickly enough.

"Donna?" It was Danny. "What's going on?"

"What do you mean?" she asked.

"Libby told your guy that her boss was with Bob Skinner on Monday night, and next thing he has her under arrest. Then, no explanation, he lets her go. What's going on?"

"Where is Libby now?"

"She went back to her work," said Danny.

"Wait a minute, did you just say she told Evanton that her boss was with Bob Skinner?" Sobriety slapped her between the eyes.

"Yes, she phoned him this morning."

"What time?"

"I don't know, early," said Danny. "Not long after she got to work. She sent me a text, said she'd phoned Evanton but that something was weird. I don't know what she meant, though. Do you know?"

And there it was, thought Donna. Evanton had known, before

the team briefing, and had lied to withhold crucial information from the investigation. Her hunch about him had been correct. She had to go to Ross with this right now.

"Listen Danny, I need to go," she said, and set her course for Bell Street.

Coming to a vending machine on her way to Ross's office, she bought a pie, and had her mouth full with the crust when she knocked on his door and went in.

"Most people address me as *Sir*," said Ross, as Donna took a seat.

Donna muttered something incoherent as she finished the crust, but it wasn't *Sir*.

Ross was still annoyed with her for holding up the team briefing earlier and for then picking a fight with Evanton in front of Lawson's elite. Lawson had gloated in Ross's face for that one.

"I need to talk to you about something," she said. "It's confidential."

This had better be good, he thought, tapping his fingers on his desk. He nodded to her to go on. He was alarmed to smell vodka on her breath, knowing it was out of character for Donna to be drinking on the job. It added to his unease about her downhill path these days; he needed her to be at her sharpest when they were dealing with such a horrendous case. This wasn't going to be an easy one to tackle. It was only two days ago that she'd stormed out of this office and he'd almost initiated her suspension. Surely it couldn't get worse?

"I think Evanton's involved in all this shit that's been going on," she said, and over Ross's sceptical sigh, she began by outlining her concerns that Evanton was contriving the evidence against Danny Quinn.

"It's as if he wants this case brushed under the carpet," she said. "And he told the briefing this morning that he'd found out nothing about who Bob Skinner was with."

"Well, finding nothing isn't unusual," said Ross. "People don't like talking to the police. Unless it's you."

"I have information that a witness phoned Evanton an hour before this morning's briefing," said Donna.

"What do you mean?" Ross's demeanour suddenly snapped to attention.

"He was told that Bob Skinner was dining with Graeme Hunter, of Hunter's Quarries." And she told him about the tyre tracks back at the Geddes farm. They made a bit more sense now. She told him about her meeting with David Chisholm, and about Evanton giving false information about Danny to the press. Clear-headedness catching up with her, she felt a rush of raw emotion as she told Ross about her reason for being late for this meeting – her visit to Natesh in hospital.

"These are very serious allegations," said Ross, alarmed to see Donna so emotional, and not quite sure how to respond to that. He reached across his desk and put his hand clumsily on top of Donna's. He had never been good at this sort of thing. He studied her carefully. He wasn't going to insult her intelligence by giving her warning of what an investigation into her allegations might entail. And he wasn't naïve enough to believe Donna would leave matters in his hands, even if she told him to his face that she would. Especially if she told him that she would. She had picked up a scent and was going to follow it, and now it was personal for her.

"You know the drill I have to follow now," said Ross. "But I want to work on this with you. Let me do what I have to do, trust me, and meet me back here at five, ok?"

Donna wiped her eyes with the back of her hand, and sniffed. She appeared to think it over. In fact, she was calculating what time she'd have to spare to call in on Libby once she took Foxy to his vet appointment.

"Five-thirty," she said eventually, to Ross's bewilderment.

Ross watched the door close behind Donna's back.

He picked up the phone.

"We've got a problem," he said. "Donna Davenport knows."

Chapter Thirty-eight

Sally was sitting up in bed, her arms clasped around her knees, going over in her mind the attack she'd been subjected to the previous night. She had been made to phone her father. Why would someone want to force her to do that? She felt unable to dwell on that question, because a floodgate of emotion over hearing his voice so unexpectedly had been unleashed. She was taken right back to being the frightened girl torn between her warring parents.

The older thug had warned her against going to the police, and she shuddered to think of him hidden somewhere nearby, watching her. She'd been too scared and confused to tell Libby or Danny what had really happened to her, instead talking the incident down to an attempted mugging. And she hadn't dared breathe a word to her sister, who'd phoned a short time ago.

But her sister wasn't the only one who'd phoned her today. Now, she'd just received a phone call inviting her to meet with the Faculty Dean, Libby Quinn's boss, Graeme Hunter.

Libby must have put a good word in for her, she thought.

Her nerves were on edge. She was now thinking about what could have happened if the younger man hadn't stepped in. She had never felt so unsafe, but she was still scared to go to the police. She wanted to be held, and she felt a deep longing, buried for so long, for her father. She had not stopped hearing his voice since the phone call. And she was angry at herself for that.

Just then her text alert sounded. She picked up her phone, and saw the message was from Danny. He wanted to know how she was, following her bad experience. It was the first time since last night that she felt a smile try to form. And she felt an unexpected extra heart beat to see that Danny had ended his text with an *x*.

She needed to focus. To think clearly now. If she was going to beat her father at his own game, she needed to hold it together. She was due to meet Graeme Hunter at three o'clock. If she got herself ready now and caught a bus, she'd have enough time to have a look around Dundee first, try to calm her nerves. Whatever she did, she was going to have to impress the Dean. This might be her one and only shot.

While Sally took a sight-seeing taxi ride around Dundee, she was accompanied by a stream of texts from Danny. She loved the city's proximity to the sea, and was awed at the beautiful ship *Discovery* docked so close to the city centre. Taking a wider tour around the southern edge of the city, she passed the sweet factory, took in the DC Thomson building, then headed back into the centre towards the university. By then, she was beginning to feel a little calmer.

The university itself emerged gracefully from raised planted gardens and swirling sculpted stone steps, to a series of well organised modern buildings around which assorted groups of young and old milled and manoeuvred.

Following her carefully crafted notes, she found her way to Graeme Hunter's offices. Entering through glass doors, she emerged into a luxurious reception oozing calm and order.

"Mr. Hunter will be with you in a moment," said the woman behind the reception desk. A gold name plaque told Sally her name was Janice.

Sally scanned the area, a combination of comfortable seating among exotic plants, and traditional academic notice boards covered in papers of all colours and sizes. She picked a spot on a sofa by a bookcase, intending to browse through whatever material was to hand while she waited to be called in to the meeting.

A buzzer made her look towards a glass door leading to a corridor behind the reception desk. To her surprise, through the glass door came a flustered Libby Quinn. Clutching several folders that only barely managed to contain their paperwork, and with her head cast down, she rushed through the security door, and smiled briefly at Janice. She then glanced toward the corner where Sally was waiting, and did a double-take. She drew a sharp intake of breath, clearly surprised.

"Hello," she said. "Sorry, was I meeting you this afternoon? My head's a bit . . . "

"No, no," said Sally, rising from her seat to greet Libby. "I've been asked to come in and meet Mr. Hunter."

Libby's eyebrows shot to the ceiling. Her step faltered, and the folders almost toppled from her arms.

"Oh?"

At that moment Janice summoned Sally.

"Mr. Hunter's ready to see you now. Just through that door, his office is first on the left."

Sally shrugged apologetically towards Libby. If Libby hadn't arranged this, she wondered, then who had? "Coffee afterwards?"

Libby, still looking puzzled, smiled and nodded. "That would be lovely."

Feeling self-conscious about her swollen eye, Sally sat overawed at the expanse and the extravagance of Graeme Hunter's office. This was how she might see herself one day, she thought. Sitting facing the Dean across the huge mahogany desk, she felt her heart race in anticipation of what she might have been called here for. And she couldn't quite put her finger on it, but she was sure she'd seen him somewhere before.

"I won't waste your time," said Hunter in a lecturing tone. "In a nutshell, I've been asked to provide data for a confidential government investigation."

Sally made no response, but concentrated hard, waiting for Hunter to reveal his intentions.

Hunter rose from his chair and made a show of opening a filing cabinet drawer, pondering over some papers, and drawing out one particular folder. Sally watched his every move.

Holding the folder close to his chest, Hunter made as if to offer it to Sally, then drew it back again in a melodramatic act of agonising over sharing a secret. Still Sally made no outward response. Hunter sat back down, placing the folder on the desk between himself and Sally, and sighed heavily.

"I need a research assistant, someone I can trust," he said sombrely. "Someone who is willing to learn from me and who has ambition."

Sally sat taller in her seat, holding her breath, and beginning to feel giddy.

"Of course," said Hunter, "this is an extremely sensitive matter. I'd be taking a huge risk taking you on board. But I've seen the papers you've submitted to Dr. Quinn during the past year, and I can tell that you plan to work hard to go far in our field, so I'm willing to take that risk. I'd like to set you an initial assignment, to see how you do."

"Yes, of course," said Sally, scarcely able to contain herself. "What would you like me to do?" She worried that her voice was coming out too squeaky.

"Some very senior figures are going to be taking part in this investigation," said Hunter, his carefully rehearsed approach having the desired effect on the desperate young academic. He savoured the irony of the situation. He was setting her up to side-track her own father, and if she failed, well . . . Evanton would take over if that happened. "I need to see how well you handle the data sets we'll be relying on, and how well you can report on their findings at short notice."

Hunter paused for effect, and then opened the folder. He turned it around so that its contents faced Sally.

"This is the raw data from one of the test sites under investigation," he said. "Do you recognise the methodology?"

Sally glanced at the figures, presented in the usual standard format she was familiar with for sampling environmental toxicity levels. She nodded her recognition.

"If you can prepare me a report by this time tomorrow based on these figures, and if I like what you've done, then I'll be looking to take you on as my research assistant for the whole investigation."

"Thank you so much, Mr. Hunter," said Sally. "I will do my very best."

"If you do that," said Hunter, knowing how to work an ego, "there'll be higher profile work for you down the line."

Hunter placed a heavy hand on top of the folder, stopping Sally from snatching it away just yet. He held Sally's eye for a brief moment.

"Remember," he said. "This work is highly confidential. It will all come into the public domain eventually, of course, and you'll find yourself with plenty of material to publish. But for now I need you to make sure nobody knows you're working on this, and you don't discuss anything to do with the investigation. Can I trust you?"

"You can trust me, Mr. Hunter," said Sally, springing from her seat, to pick up the paperwork, which she clutched close to her chest. Then she almost bounded for the door in her eagerness to start work on the project. Just before she left the room she turned and said, "Thank you again, I really appreciate this opportunity."

Hunter smirked to himself, satisfied that at least something was starting to go right with this mess. Then his private line rang.

Sally stopped outside Hunter's office door to draw breath and leant against the door jamb, her head buzzing. She couldn't believe it. This could be her big break. To be invited to prepare a report at this level, with the promise of more to come, the lure of academia's holy grail of prized publication, it was what she had been dreaming about for so long. And right on her father's professional patch. It couldn't be more perfect. She needed that coffee with Libby now. But should she say anything to Libby about this report? How far did the confidentiality go?

While trying to slow down her breath and think more clearly, Sally heard a phone ring inside the Dean's office, and became aware of Hunter's voice. She didn't mean to eavesdrop, but she didn't move away.

"The kid swallowed it hook, line and sinker," she heard Hunter say. "We'll have our report by tomorrow afternoon, and put this whole damned thing to bed."

Chapter Thirty-nine

Donna sat on the wooden bench in the vet's waiting room, with Foxy in a carry box on her knee. The receptionist was busy clacking away on her keyboard and hadn't spoken except to take the appointment details. Beside Donna on the wall hung a wire rack containing leaflets urging her to have her dog vaccinated, her cat wormed, and her rabbit's teeth checked. A fish tank bubbled softly on a cabinet facing her, but this did little to ease her nervousness, as she peeked inside the box frequently at the miserable rabbit. She had arrived early for the appointment, unfortunately giving herself more time to fret. She forced her mind on to work matters and tried to quell the worry she felt over Natesh's injuries. She hadn't allowed herself to fear the worst, for she was certain that her fragile mental state would not be able to sustain the grief that would surely ensue.

Keep a clear head, she told herself. *He's in good hands.*

She had other things to think about. Like, why was Evanton hiding the fact that Libby had phoned with key information? Was that part of the phone call she'd overheard when he'd threatened Libby? Was he Chisholm's blackmailer? Natesh's attacker? Was Libby next? Or was she just being ridiculous, sensational and imagining things because of her history with Danny and Libby?

Donna felt a cold sweat break out, and she began to feel giddy as the questions swirled in her head with no clear answer. Then a flash of anger burst in her chest as she thought of Evanton's efforts to malign Danny's character and to put the frighteners on Libby. She hoped against hope that Ross had taken her fears seriously, and now wished her time until her next meeting with him would pass more quickly.

Donna glanced towards the reception desk. If she didn't do something now, she would burst.

An idea began to flutter mischievously in her head.

The receptionist was still engrossed in her work and had paid Donna no attention while she waited. Every now and then she heard a yelp or a howl emit from deep within the vet's surgery. To all intents and purposes she was alone, and her idea began to take root. She brought out her phone and, concealing her own number, she rang Lindsey Forsyth.

"I don't want to leave my name," Donna said in a low voice to the breathless reporter. "I saw Graeme Hunter, the owner of the quarry, at *The Bampot* on Monday night." And she rang off.

She waited a moment, then phoned Evanton.

"What the fuck are you doing giving my number to the press?" she demanded, putting on such a performance that the vet's receptionist jumped in her chair and looked at her in astonishment.

"What are you talking about?" Evanton sounded shocked. There was a sudden noise of crows cawing in the background. Donna fleetingly pictured him standing in the middle of a field.

"I've just had some journalist on asking why we've not interviewed the owner of Hunter's Quarries about being at *The Bampot* on Monday," she said, sounding so cross she even began to believe herself. She heard the beginnings of a protest come from Evanton, and she cut him short. "That's your patch. If you want to change how we're doing this investigation, fucking talk to me about it first, and don't ever give my number to anyone again."

And she hung up, pleased with herself that she'd gotten the information about Hunter out in the open while putting pressure on Evanton.

Satisfied that she'd set the cat among the pigeons and would have him in a twist, she sat back to watch the fish. Sending Evanton scuttling to the journalist would buy her some time, but boy would she love to be a fly on the wall when those two met!

The doors leading to the surgery burst open, and a huge boxer with a bandage on its front paw came bounding out, all squeals and slobber, pulling a fragile owner along behind it. While the man struggled to pull the boxer to a halt and drag it to the reception desk to pay his bill, a vet nurse followed through the doors.

Donna looked up, and did a double-take. Standing almost as tall as herself, dressed in dark blue scrubs, her black hair cropped short, the nurse looked over at Donna, sending a smile that made her tummy flip.

"Foxy Davenport?"

"That'll be me," said Donna, leaping to her feet and hoping she hadn't actually said *well, hellooo* out loud. Strange how her mood could change so suddenly, all by itself.

Sally stood fidgeting, before she plucked up the courage and knocked on Libby's door.

"Come in," said Libby. Her smile was genuine as she showed Sally in, with a hand on her shoulder. Sally felt her shoulder buzz under Libby's touch, and the buzz travelled all the way down her spine. It made her remember the touch of kindness that she missed so much, and she was gripped by an overwhelming homesickness so brutal it took her by surprise.

Libby's office had a pleasant outlook onto greenery beyond the main road and a landscaped plaza, where students sat around in small groups enjoying some unexpected sunshine that was breaking through the rain. Libby brought a chair from behind her desk, so that she and Sally could sit side by side, looking out. She allowed the conversation to follow the usual banalities for a while, before her concern for Sally got the better of her.

"So, how are you after what happened to you last night? Have you been to the police?" Libby asked, once it became clear that Sally wasn't going to raise the subject.

Sally shifted uncomfortably in her seat, seeming to struggle with her words. When she looked up and saw the concern on Libby's face, she suddenly felt the shock reality of what had happened to her, and her senses became aware of the contrast now, feeling safe. Her chin quivered with the effort of keeping her tears in, but they made her eyes burn, and she let them fall, crying now for the first time since she'd been attacked.

The news for Foxy wasn't so good. His teeth were overgrown and his inability to eat had led to potentially fatal bloat. He had to remain with the vet overnight. But Donna's doldrums were somewhat lifted, in fact thrown out of the window, when the nurse asked her out for a drink.

Donna left the vet's elated and with her hormones flying. It wasn't the best frame of mind for her to be concentrating on work, especially since her next move on the work front would have to be a visit to Libby to find out more about her discussion with Evanton.

The university was relatively quiet, with a lot of the students at home on exam leave. Donna made her way up the steps to Libby's department, feeling suddenly old. She quickly calculated it was ten years since she'd graduated from here, but she didn't remember looking as young as the students that she passed.

She took a deep breath and went inside.

The route to the Engineering Faculty was reassuringly familiar to Donna, and she wound her way up the floors and along the corridors until she reached the Chemical Engineering Department, where the two disciplines met and brought together the unlikely academic alliance of Graeme Hunter and Libby Quinn.

Entering reception, the first thing Donna saw was Graeme Hunter hovering over Janice's desk and barking out a list of demands which Janice was scribbling down, flinching with distaste at each one.

Hunter looked up and recognised her at once. Davenport, he was sure her name was. He hadn't seen her around for a while; she used to be up here all the time, calling in on Libby Quinn. But she was police, too. Momentarily thrown off his stride, Hunter faltered over his list of demands and stared at Donna as she approached. Donna kept her face expressionless as she gave him a head to toe once over.

"I'd like a few moments with Dr. Quinn, please," Donna said to Janice, showing her warrant card.

Janice took in the details of the card and, with lightning efficiency, put a call through to Libby.

"The police here to see you, Dr. Quinn," said Janice, as she pressed a buzzer that released the doors for Donna to go through to the offices.

A nerve twitched near Graeme Hunter's eye, and he felt the palpitations begin as he watched Donna make her way to Libby's office.

Was she here on police business rather than a personal visit?

Flustered now, he dismissed Janice from her note-taking and returned to his office.

He felt the walls close in on him, and his skin turned clammy. All he could picture was damned Libby Quinn telling that cop she'd seen him with Skinner at *The Bampot*. And more to the point, that she'd already told Evanton. Why the hell had he lied to her earlier?

Hunter's nightmare went into freefall.

Donna began to feel nervous, too. The formality of knocking on Libby's door felt odd. Gone were the days when she could let herself in and surprise Libby on a whim.

Libby looked up to see Donna's awkward form appear, pressed as far as it could be into the doorframe. Donna was nervously chewing her lip.

"You can come in," said Libby, averting her gaze and shifting her posture slightly away from her, folding her arms.

"Cheers," said Donna, taking only one step into the office. She saw that Libby had company, a pretty blonde woman who appeared to be upset and had bruising around her eye.

"Sorry, is this a bad time?" Donna asked.

It was Libby's turn to look uncomfortable.

"No, it's ok," she said. "This is my friend, Sally. Sally, this is Donna."

There was an awkward pause while Donna mumbled a greeting to Sally, and Sally nodded in acknowledgement, trying to hold her bruised eye away from Donna's gaze.

Now all three of them shifted uncomfortably.

"What can I do for you, Donna?" Libby asked, rising to meet her half way across the room. She was concentrating hard on keeping her breathing steady, and an involuntary glance into Donna's eyes told her that she was doing the same.

"I need to ask you something," said Donna, suspiciously eyeing Sally. "About *The Bampot.*"

Her stance alerted Sally.

"Actually, I'd better get going," Sally said, standing up.

Donna felt sure she saw disappointment on Libby's face, and her heart lurched as she wondered just who Sally was to her. She allowed herself a moment of regret, then she swallowed to regain her composure, and stepped aside to let Sally pass.

"Phone me," said Libby as Sally left. Turning back to Donna she asked, "What is it you need to know? I told your partner everything." Her voice was accusing.

Donna's mood grew serious as she shifted from one foot to the other.

"That's actually what I wanted to know about."

"What do you mean?" asked Libby.

"When did you talk to Evanton?"

"This morning," said Libby. "Around nine, maybe. I phoned him, but he wasn't particularly grateful for the call."

"Can you tell me what you told him?"

"I told him I saw Hunter at *The Bampot* with Skinner on Monday night," said Libby. "Why? What's wrong?"

"What did Evanton say to you when you told him about Hunter?"

"Donna," said Libby. "What's going on here? Evanton hauled me in for questioning, then left me in some freezing cold room for an hour, then let me go without any explanation."

Donna hesitated and seemed to carefully consider her response.

"I can't really say just now, but can you just tell me what Evanton said when you phoned him this morning?"

Libby knew Donna well enough to tell she was onto something, and she let out a conciliatory sigh. She already had her own concerns about all of this. Hunter had pretended not to have been at *The Bampot*. Sally had been attacked. There was no reason to think the two matters were connected, but things were definitely not adding up. If anyone could get to the bottom of it all, Donna could, and she needed to trust her now.

"He seemed more concerned about whether Hunter knew that I'd seen him," said Libby, a sense of foreboding creeping up on her that Donna had stumbled onto something sinister and that she was investigating alone. She told Donna about her conversation with Evanton, about Hunter's response to her that morning, and for good measure she also told her about the attack on Sally.

"Sally Chisholm?" Donna asked. "Chisholm?"

The tone of Donna's voice made Libby suddenly afraid for Sally.

"Yes. Does that mean something to you?"

"It could be important," Donna said. "Could you ask Sally to phone me?"

"Donna, is this going to be ok?" Libby asked.

"Just do one thing for me," said Donna after a moment. "Trust me. If Evanton contacts you again, act as though I've not been here. Keep me informed if anything else happens, but play the innocent with Evanton. And ask Sally to phone me. Please."

Donna turned to go. Hesitating at the door, she turned around again to Libby.

"By the way, Foxy's not well, he's at the vet's."

Libby looked concerned, the information catching her off guard.

"It's ok, though," Donna said. "He'll be ok. And, erm, I've got a date with the vet nurse tonight. So, you know, if you and Sally . . . you know, I'm ok with that."

Libby stared at her, open-mouthed and speechless as she left.

Chapter Forty

Shit, shit, shit.

Evanton paced back and forth outside the quarry office. He had to get to that reporter at the hospital and find out who'd told her about Hunter. More to the point, he had to find out what she'd done with the information. Even if he had to wring her neck to find out. The thought appealed to him. But what was she doing phoning that bitch Davenport? He felt a growl of frustration rising in his throat.

This wasn't how it was meant to go. Did he have another grass to deal with now? At least Davenport had given the game away to him, he consoled himself. As if he would have expected anything else. What kind of detective was she, swallowing his story about his father, without even checking it out? He scoffed at the sudden memory of Douglas Evanton, and the idea of him as a police officer made him laugh out loud. Mr. Small Man Syndrome, he laughed to himself. The brute who tried to be a big man. The dying monster outside, while the little boy lived in the coal shed.

Who's the big man now, eh? he thought, staring out at the clouds drifting over the slopes of excavated rock.

He stopped pacing and watched Iksan hauling the pump equipment across the yard towards the garage complex on the eastern edge of the quarry. Cleaning the trucks would keep the kid occupied for the rest of the day.

His mind returned to the journalist. Who had tipped her off? With a sudden realisation, Evanton felt a smile cross his lips. There was only one person it could be, he thought. Libby Quinn. He'd finish taking care of things here at the quarry, go and deal with the journalist, then he'd work out a suitable course of action to take with Dr. Quinn.

Oh, this is going to be good.

Unfinished business was his thing.

Chapter Forty-one

David Chisholm was lost in his thoughts. Sitting in the back of a taxi going from Ninewells Hospital to the university, the rainy cityscape passed him by as he went over and over in his mind the phone call he'd received from Sally. Where was she, and what had happened to her? The blackmailer had threatened to harm her if Chisholm refused to step down from the investigation, which must mean she wasn't in his clutches yet. But the phone call, he couldn't figure out what that meant. He felt useless to help her. But she must be somewhere within comfortable travelling distance of Edinburgh, for that was where he had met the blackmailer. Unless, of course, there were others involved, in which case Sally could be anywhere at all.

It was no good; he felt hopeless.

He felt certain that Laura, Sally's mother, would still be living in Putney, and again he felt the burning shame of having left her with three children to cope with on her own. For the very first time, he took in the shock realisation that his leaving them behind must have devastated his daughters, most probably marking them for life.

The taxi drew to a halt outside the university's main entrance as Chisholm thought of the irony that having spent his academic life trying to mitigate the effects of MIC on populations across the globe, it was MIC that was now ruining his own life. Nicola was refusing to answer his calls. He determined that if he could do anything to make amends for what he'd done in the past, one thing would be to fight to remain in his younger children's lives, and the other would be to make sure this investigation went ahead.

With a renewed sense of purpose, Chisholm left the taxi and made for Graeme Hunter's office.

When he'd phoned to arrange the meeting, he'd been surprised to learn that Hunter was free that afternoon and he'd been able to make an appointment with him so soon. He hadn't had time to rehearse exactly what he was going to discuss with Hunter, but introducing himself followed by a warning to Hunter that he may be in danger would no doubt give them plenty to talk about.

"Just go in, Professor Chisholm," the immaculately manicured receptionist told him when he reached the plush office suite. "Mr. Hunter is expecting you."

Chisholm had barely stepped away from the reception desk, when an office door opened and a squat middle-aged man appeared, offering his hand. When Chisholm shook it, the palm was sweaty and he had to suppress the urge to wipe his hand on something.

"Professor Chisholm?" the man said. "I'm Graeme Hunter, pleased to meet you."

The words said it, but the eyes didn't. Hunter looked wary, his focus darting around and beyond Chisholm as both men entered the office. Chisholm wondered if he'd picked a bad moment.

"Can I offer you something to drink?" Hunter said, motioning to a table that hosted a coffee machine and various cold beverages.

"A coffee would be lovely, thank you," said Chisholm, and he was sure he saw disappointment in Hunter's eyes that their meeting might last long enough to drink one.

Chisholm began cautiously with pleasant small talk about his visit to the UK, but it became clear that Hunter was preoccupied.

"So, Mr. Hunter," he said, cutting to the chase. "Bob Skinner is unable to lead the MIC investigation at the moment, for obvious reasons. I'm therefore stepping in to take things forward until he is fit and able, so I'd be grateful if you'd report your findings directly to me."

Hunter's head snapped up and he focused on Chisholm, as if realizing for the first time that he was in the room.

"Stepping in?" he said. "But . . . I thought . . . " Hunter faltered, rubbing his forehead. Evanton was supposed to have had this angle sorted. What was going on?

From what Chisholm understood, Hunter was an old friend of Bob Skinner's, and Skinner had entrusted him with the research responsibility for the investigation. But something in Hunter's manner – his sweating brow, his frequent sips of water, his nervous hands – grated with Chisholm. He felt uneasy, but for Skinner's sake he had to bring this man into his confidence.

Hunter, for his part, was paranoid and getting worse by the minute. What was Chisholm doing wading in like this? For a man being leant on so heavily by a thug like Evanton, he seemed unnaturally positive about his role in this investigation. Perhaps

Evanton hadn't made contact with the Professor's daughter after all. He was working in a black fog, how was he meant to respond when he didn't know what was going on? He made a quick decision. He would offer his trump card. That would be sure to get Chisholm out of his office.

"As it happens," he told Chisholm, "I had a detailed discussion with Bob Skinner before his unfortunate . . . er . . . accident. He asked me to commission environmental sampling from the test areas, and my report of the findings is being prepared as we speak. I have a post-grad student drafting it up and I expect it to be completed by tomorrow morning, in time for your first working group meeting. I'll have it emailed to you as soon as it's ready."

Chisholm's initial reaction, as Hunter had hoped it would be, was one of gratitude and approval, impressed that this initial step had already been progressed.

But Hunter failed to pick up on the hesitation in Chisholm's response.

A thought niggled at Chisholm. The blackmailer, too, had talked of a report. A false report telling a story of no MIC leak, which Chisholm was supposed to endorse. Something wasn't right here. He couldn't put his finger on it, but he did trust his own instinct. He pictured in his mind the possibility that Hunter was working with the blackmailer. And it looked like a pretty perfect cover – the academic, Bob Skinner's friend, providing the working group's evidence. He already knew that his blackmailer couldn't have been directly involved in Skinner's poisoning. Could this man, Hunter, really be part of this?

Hunter avoided Chisholm's intense gaze, pleased with himself for getting out of a tricky situation.

Standing up, he offered his hand in farewell.

"I look forward to hearing what you make of the report tomorrow," he said.

I'm sure you do, thought Chisholm, but he chose only to nod in reply, unsure of how his voice would sound if he were to speak now. It might give away his suspicion that Graeme Hunter was involved in attempts to stop the MIC investigation. More than this, but that Hunter may even have had something to do with Bob Skinner being poisoned.

As he turned to go, Chisholm had an idea. An insurance policy.

"I'm planning to hold a press conference tomorrow afternoon at four," he told Hunter, beaming an innocent smile. "I'd certainly welcome your presence at it."

He knew a press conference would open the investigation wide to public awareness, as Bob Skinner had wanted all along. It might cause panic, but it would protect the investigation team from any more threats. Blackmail only worked if it was carried out in secret.

Chisholm felt triumph; Hunter watched in silence as the professor left his office.

Chapter Forty-two

A press conference! If everybody and his dog heard about the MIC investigation, there was no fucking way it was going to disappear. Hunter slammed another drawer shut. Where the hell was his passport? He was sure it was in here somewhere. He had plans to make now.

At last, he saw the little red passport in another drawer and grabbed it out. A noise made him spin round.

"What are you doing in here?" Hunter gasped, visibly jumping in alarm to see Libby Quinn standing in his office. And she wasn't looking meek now.

"Going somewhere?" she said, looking at the passport in his hand. He shoved it into his pocket, and retrieved a tissue to wipe his forehead.

"It's none of your business," he said.

"No, but lying about your whereabouts on Monday evening is my business." Libby advanced on him, her finger pointing at his chest, and her face red with fury. "And going behind my back about Sally Chisholm's role here is my business."

"You're talking nonsense," he said. His eyes were darting all over the room.

"You instruct me to invite her here on a study placement, then you call her to your office and arrange for her to carry out some piece of work for you without telling me about first."

"How did you know what she's working on?" Hunter sounded taken aback, and his apparent panic was not lost on Libby.

They were standing close to the room's open door, and Hunter was inching his way towards it, forcing Libby to take a series of backward steps. Behind her back, the hustle and bustle of the departmental reception drew still, as ears were discreetly trained on the warring duo.

"And you were lying about Monday night," Libby shouted. "Why was that? What are you hiding? You were there, and you know what happened, don't you? Why the hell are you lying about it?"

"You have no fucking idea what you're talking about," he hissed in her face, and he imagined his hand reaching out to clamp itself across her mouth, to stop her shouting. Aghast, he realised that his hand was doing just that, when he felt a sharp, sickening crunch as Libby's knee hit his crotch at speed.

As he doubled over, winded from the pain, the reception spectators rushed to action, pulling Libby from the room.

One person rushed to Hunter, asking if he was all right, but he found himself being observed rather than aided, and when he managed to stand upright, his face pale, he pushed the spectators out of the door. He wanted out of this department. Out of the country. Anywhere. It was over for him.

Chapter Forty-three

The quarry was located about six miles along a single track road that headed inland from Arbroath. A network of criss-crossing paths meant you had to know where you were going to avoid getting lost out here, and it was almost impossible to see ahead for any distance due to the trees and the sharp turns. Donna drove carefully, scrutinising every turn in the road and checking every break in the tree line for signs of anything unusual, or anything hidden. She would have time for a quick look around the quarry, she reckoned, before her meeting with Ross. If the connection with Hunter turned out to be true, and she managed to find anything of interest, she was sure Ross would be more than happy to cancel their meeting and bring the team out here instead to wrap this MIC matter up. And then she could go home and get ready for her date with Val, the vet nurse.

Val, Val, Val, she sang the name to herself.

Hunky dory, she thought, smiling to herself.

Rounding a bend on the brow of a hill, she saw the small metal sign pointing the way to Hunter's Quarries, and she pulled her car onto the gravel track that led to it. Moving down to second gear, she eased the car slowly towards the quarry gates, where she could see two lorries parked, big, like ones that could have made the tyre tracks she'd found at the farm house. Beyond them she could make out the walls of an office building. Work here had stopped for the day, and the quarry was silent.

Donna pulled up at the gates and stopped the engine. She sat for several moments, just listening, but heard nothing. Quarries freaked her out, the sheer sides of the rock face making her think about those dreams where she was falling into a void. Thankfully, she thought, the office building was at this side of the quarry, so she wouldn't have to go near the precipice.

The sun was low in the sky now, just visible on the ridge of the quarry behind the office, and taking any remnants of warmth there had been in the day with it. A flock of crows erupted nearby, cawing and flapping as they sought their roost before sunset, making Donna jump. She swallowed, realizing she was more uneasy than she'd believed. The image of Evanton standing in the middle of a field popped into her head, the one she'd conjured up when she heard the crows in the background while she was on the phone to him from the vet's. She dug the tub of lithium pills from her pocket and downed a couple as a precaution. She would deal with the consequences of exceeding the dose later. This was no time to get hyped up. She was going to have to hold her nerve, tread carefully and think clearly before she acted in this place.

Just until tomorrow, she told herself, thinking about her doctor's appointment.

She was grateful for the slack security as she slid through a gap in the gate. It looked as though she would have free reign to snoop around without having to invent a cover story to explain herself to anyone. She stopped inside the gate and listened again. Nothing, except the crows off in the distance. She stretched, yawned, and pondered her next move.

Hunter's Quarries, she thought. *What have you got going with Jonas Evanton?*

The office building was a large Portakabin, and Donna's entry through the gate brought her to the rear wall. There were two small windows, too high up for her to look inside, and keeping close to the cabin walls, she carefully made her way round to the front.

As she came round the front corner of the cabin, she stopped short, and an involuntary gasp of shock escaped her. There, parked in front of the office door, was Evanton's dark green Audi.

Donna barely had time to look round, when she felt her neck suddenly crushed, and she was unable to fight the blackness that came over her.

Jonas Evanton couldn't quite believe his luck. Having received the phone call from the officer at the hospital that Bob Skinner's heart had stopped, his next problem – Donna Davenport – had just walked into the quarry and handed herself to him on a plate. She couldn't have told Ross where she was coming, otherwise she wouldn't be here alone. He glanced towards the garage complex. He could hear Iksan working the pressure washers on the trucks. The kid would be oblivious to anything that went on out here. Perfect. He began to feel the familiar rush of blood through his veins.

"Aren't I going to have some fun with you?" Evanton told Donna.

Donna thrashed violently, finding herself seated on a chair inside the Portakabin, her wrist painfully cuffed to a radiator. A rag was stuffed into her mouth, and she had to fight a rising panic at the sight of Evanton's hungry eyes and the erection that was obvious under his trousers. Fragments of the moments after she'd rounded the Portakabin began to come back to her, and as her memory sharpened, so did the pain that gripped her body. The movement at the corner of her eye gave her barely enough time to brace herself for the blow to her shin, and when she managed to stop screaming into the rag, and was able to open her eyes against the sheer pain, she saw the metal bar he held. Her breathing stopped involuntarily when she saw him raise it again, this time bringing it tearing through skin and muscle at her shoulder.

Evanton was working hard to keep himself under control. The bleeding and the bulging eyes and the sickening thud of metal against bone were driving him crazy, but he was determined to enjoy every damned moment of it. He saw Donna bite down hard on the rag and brace herself when he stepped forward and in one swift movement tore open her t-shirt.

He kicked her legs apart and tore at her jeans. The raw marks it left on her thighs when the material shredded from them sent his pulse racing. He leaned into her, grabbing at her breast with one hand while his mouth found the open wound at her shoulder and with the other hand he unzipped his trousers.

Pain fought with terror fought with anger as Donna thrashed helplessly on her chair, Evanton's tongue lapping closer to her mouth, her open legs useless to stop his obvious intent.

Then she heard his mobile ring somewhere at the other end of the room.

It seemed to puzzle him, and he drew back from her for a moment. His lips were smeared red from the blood on her shoulder wound. When the mobile rang again she saw him blink and shake his head, as if coming out of a trance. Suddenly he tore away from her, spun round and fetched his phone.

From her end of the room, and even although Evanton's back was turned to her, she could tell from the tensing of his shoulders that the caller was telling him something he'd rather not hear.

And then he erupted into fury, bellowing obscenities into the phone and upending the desk, sending papers and pens and loose change flying across the frayed linoleum.

But it was when he kicked the wall in a fit of temper, so hard that Donna thought the Portakabin might collapse, that her blood truly ran cold. She could picture clearly the boot print at the farm house. It was Evanton's.

Donna willed herself into as small a figure as she could, and held perfectly still against all the agony raging across her battered body, hoping beyond hope that Evanton would forget she was there.

Chapter Forty-four

All the students were gone. The reception area was deserted, and the lights were dimmed.

Not a sound issued from Hunter's office as Libby hesitated at his door.

She had witnessed his departure soon after their argument, while she'd had to perform in front of her colleagues who'd all wanted to know what had happened before she could escape to her own office. Then she'd waited until Janice had locked up reception and switched off the lights before making her move.

Libby felt drained following her confrontation with Hunter. After the immediate incident, when her adrenaline had fallen, she'd taken the shakes, unable to believe that their argument had turned physical. But she felt calmer now. Something terribly wrong was going on with Hunter. It had something to do with Danny and with Sally, and she was going to find out what it was.

She fished her key ring from her jeans pocket, and found the key to Hunter's office. She had used it many times in the past, mainly to leave draft reports on his desk late at night – woe betide that he should ever work late. This time she was looking for something of his – something that would reveal the truth of why he had met with Sally. And maybe why he had lied about being with Bob Skinner.

She opened the door cautiously, even though she knew nobody was here, and turned the lock behind her when she entered the luxurious office. It was too dark to see anything without switching on a light and risking drawing attention to the office in an otherwise dark building. But the chances of Hunter returning at this time in the evening were so remote, she pressed the switch.

Hunter's desk loomed large by the window, and as she would have expected, sat pristine with no papers on it. Libby made her way behind the desk, and tried the drawers. In his arrogance, Hunter failed to secure them. There were six drawers in all, but a thorough search of them drew nothing of interest to Libby. All through her sifting, she kept a vigil on the car park within view of the office, just in case.

Libby knew there were two phones on Hunter's desk, and now she took the chance to examine them. One was linked to the switchboard, but the other seemed to be a private line. This puzzled her, but she could find no way of getting its number without giving herself away. Even Libby didn't have a number, other than his direct line via the main switchboard. Why did he have a private line? Was he carrying out business from here that wasn't related to the university? Dialling 1471 only told her the last caller had withheld their number.

Next she turned her attention to the filing cabinet standing next to a huge yucca plant. It was one of three filing cabinets arranged around the room. But neither this nor the other two cabinets revealed anything out of the ordinary, nor that Libby had not already seen through the University Board. Some of the grants awarded did make her eyes water, but she was aware of the amounts already. She had debated them, opposed them, and finally given into them. They were all here, stored for posterity.

Frustrated, Libby stood in the middle of the office, with her hands on her hips, wondering what to do now. She had come across no record of Sally's placement, far less the reason for today's meeting with her. A check showed still no movement outside around the car park. Libby was aware of how late it was getting, when she noticed an unimposing cupboard door beside the coffee machine.

Small space to store milk?

Libby didn't think so. She prised it open.

And a piercing alarm shrieked out across the entire corridor.

Libby jumped, terrified, and ran to the door. But she stopped, thinking fast. Bill Taylor was on security this evening; it would take him at least five full minutes to get up here, even supposing he got the right end of the corridor. She ran back to the cupboard, reached inside, and immediately recoiled at what she found there. Momentarily stunned, she brought the object out of the cupboard and stared at it. Now it made sense. She stuffed it into her bag; Donna had to see this.

The piercing alarm brought her back to her own situation. She had to make sure there was no trace of her having broken in. She used her shirt sleeve as a cloth to wipe the cupboard handle clear of her fingerprints then darted to the window. Covering her hand with the end of her sleeve, she opened one window, leaving it set as it would be during the day. And a second window she opened, and pulled inward on the latch until it broke, making it look as though it had been pushed from outside.

Finally, she closed the cupboard door and the piercing alarm stopped instantly. Then she ran from the office, checking that there was no sign of Bill Taylor yet.

Safely out of the way of Hunter's office, Libby pulled her phone from her pocket and dialled Donna's number. It went straight onto voicemail.

Damn it! thought Libby, as she remembered Donna had a date this evening.

Date or no date, though, she knew Donna wouldn't ignore her pager. She left a message for her to call Libby urgently about the case.

Thursday

Chapter Forty-five

Hunter wasn't used to being at work this early, but he wasn't here to stay. If he could just work out which key opened this door, he could be in, pick up the gas mask, and be on his way to the airport before the first of them arrived. It would be Quinn, he just knew. She was always here early. He grunted as he twisted another key that didn't fit.

Damn it!

The next key slotted in and opened the door, much to his relief. He couldn't believe he'd left the mask behind. He didn't need that getting into the wrong hands during all this MIC palaver. Striding through reception towards his office, he pondered where the best place would be to ditch it. He couldn't take it with him on a flight, that was for sure. He decided to stop by some flats on the way to the airport and dispose of it into some communal bin.

Hunter stepped into his office, and immediately knew something wasn't right.

The window was open.

No, on closer inspection, the window was broken in.

He caught his breath as his eyes quickly scanned his office, looking for signs of burglary. His desk looked tidy, as always. None of the top spec equipment in the room was missing or even damaged. With a growing sense of dread, he opened the locker behind the coffee machine, and his worst fear was confirmed. The gas mask was gone.

Think, think, he told himself. *Did I take it with me yesterday?*

But he knew that he hadn't.

He felt faint as he looked at the broken window again, and had to place a hand on the back of a chair to steady himself while his head swam with scenarios. None of them ended well for him.

Then he jumped when he heard a door slam, and the corridor outside his office flooded with light. His stomach turned to water, before he heard a woman's voice call out.

"Hello?"

A breath of relief escaped him. It was Janice. Was she always here this hellishly early? Thinking quickly, he called back to her.

"I'm in here."

In a moment, Janice's face appeared at his door, her eyes wide in surprise.

"Special occasion?" she asked.

"I wouldn't take your coat off," said Hunter, seizing his chance. "My office has been broken into."

Janice gasped, covering her mouth with her hand that still wore a glove.

"They got in through the window," he said, pointing. "They weren't locked last night."

"But I always lock the windows," said Janice. "And I most definitely remember locking them last night. Because I water the plants on a Wednesday, and . . . "

"You didn't lock the windows, and now my office has been burgled," said Hunter. "That's a gross breach of security, and I can't tolerate that."

"Please, Mr. Hunter," Janice was pleading. "I distinctly remember . . . "

"Collect your belongings," he spoke over her. "I'm going to ask security to escort you from the building. I'm suspending you from duty pending an investigation. You'll receive a hearing date from personnel in due course."

With a bit of luck, he thought, that would create enough of a fuss around the department to allow him to slip away.

Chapter Forty-six

Libby was careful to be in her office by 8am as was her usual habit. Nothing could appear to be out of character. It had to be just like any other Thursday morning. She was acutely self conscious, sure that the slightest twitch would give her away, and although nobody was paying her the slightest bit of attention or behaving oddly towards her, she still bit her lip in fear each time she said *hello* on her way from the car park and through the offices.

Her mind was still in a frenzy over finding the gas mask in Hunter's office. Added to her confusion about Hunter lying to her about being at *The Bampot*, the recurring conclusion in Libby's view was that Hunter had released the poison.

As if that wasn't enough to contend with, she still couldn't get a hold of Donna. A little harder than necessary, she punched in the numbers of Donna's mobile yet again, and sighed in exasperation when the automated message came on. Her mood was caught somewhere between fear and fury. She had already left several messages on her pager, and no reply.

Typical of Donna to be putting her own fun first at a time like this.

She briefly thought back to the crazy days at the beginning of her relationship with Donna. Even during the most passionate of moments, Donna's pager never failed to get her attention, and she suddenly felt a stab of jealousy that somebody else was holding her attention now.

In an attempt to clear her head, she went back to the reception area to fetch herself a cup of water. But the scene in reception only made things worse. Two security guards stood apologetically beside Janice, who was sobbing heavily, and Bill Taylor was standing scratching his head.

"Janice, what's . . . ?"

"I'm sorry, Dr. Quinn," said one of the security guards. "There's been a break-in."

"But Janice..." began Libby, then she realised. Leaving Hunter's windows open was a security breach too far, and it would be Janice who took the blame for that.

"I came up here and checked when the alarm went off," Bill Taylor was saying unconvincingly to one of the security guards. "Everything was locked. Well, as far as I could see."

Libby had never felt so wretched.

"I just don't know how it happened," was all Janice could say, while she nervously packed her few personal belongings into a small box. The security guards took turns offering her reassuring smiles, clearly uncomfortable with their role on this occasion.

Libby was genuinely appalled, riled at herself as the tearful Janice, flanked by the security guards, filed past her.

"Janice, I'll speak to personnel today," she said to their backs. Janice turned and looked at her miserably, before leaving with the security guards. Bill Taylor slumped into a chair, looking puzzled.

"The alarm stopped by itself," he said to Libby. "I just thought it was wonky."

Deep in thought and worried about what to do now, Libby returned to her office. Before she sat down, her phone rang.

"Libby?" It was Sally. "Can I come and see you? This morning. Please? I know you must be busy."

"It's ok, Sally," said Libby. "Come right over. What's the matter?"

There was a pause before Sally answered, "I won't be long. And thanks – I know you're busy."

In the little flat that looked on to the east walls of the Abbey, Sally disconnected. She already had her jacket on and her iPod ready. It was an afterthought to phone Libby and ask first before going to see her.

She'd been unnerved ever since overhearing Hunter on the phone.

Hook, line and sinker. That was what she'd heard, and she was left in no doubt that he'd been referring to her.

She'd been so excited by the call to attend Hunter's office, and dizzy as she'd caught a glimpse of the heights her career could reach with an opportunity like that. Now though, she was sure she'd been set up. Was she being paranoid? Had she been engrossed in too many conspiracy theories? She had to admit, things had turned a little crazy since coming here, and her normal terms of reference could not be relied upon.

But one thing she could not forget, she had uprooted herself from her home town, leaving her mother to cope alone with the empty bottles, so she could nourish her appetite for academic honour. And revenge on her father.

Damn it! she thought, *I need to know the truth.*

She had to know if her fears had foundation. Was Hunter setting her up for a fall?

She had opened Hunter's file and studied the contents, recognising them to be figures from site visits collecting toxicology samples. C_2H_3NO, she'd noted. Checking her memory, she'd looked it up, and sure enough it was methyl isocyanate – one of the substances her father obsessed over. Running her eyes to the bottom of the list, she'd also noted the final site readings had the next day's date on them. Meaning the figures related to samples that couldn't yet have been taken, or somebody had made a big mistake when compiling the data. So Hunter had asked her to use fabricated, or dodgy, site figures for this report. Either way, it looked as though she had unwittingly become involved in falsifying research. She was stunned.

She'd tossed and turned all night over her dilemma. Should she admit to this, and burn her bridges, risking the very real possibility that she could forget about her academic career? Or go along with Hunter's plan, and hope that nobody ever found out? And live in fear that her fraud would one day be discovered, and her career would end anyway, a disgrace that her father would not fail to notice?

So, in the clear light of day, Sally decided she needed to talk to the one person she trusted now. Libby.

Libby had her head in her hands trying to make sense of the gas mask and now of Sally's phone call. There had been genuine fear in her voice, and Libby felt a growing dread that she was about to link together a horrible series of events that involved her own boss releasing a poison at her brother's restaurant. But why? What was all this about? With her hands shaking, she fumbled with her phone to dial Donna again, when the hairs on the back of her neck prickled and made her look up. There, in the doorway, with the expression on his face unreadable, stood Evanton.

Libby felt her pulse quicken; a sweat broke out across her brow. She instinctively stuffed her phone back into her bag at her feet, and tried to compose herself.

She'd never noticed before how tall and impeccably dressed he was. He walked confidently to Libby's desk, and without invitation pulled out a chair and sat facing her. She would have done anything to have seen Donna with him right now. But she remembered Donna's advice to play the innocent with him. If ever she needed her playacting skills, it was now.

"Detective Evanton? Has there been a murder?" It took all her energy to keep her voice level.

"A break-in, Dr. Quinn," said Evanton, his eyes grey and cold like a lizard's. "But astute of you to note it's not a routine police matter."

Libby clasped her hands together in front of her on the desk, partly in an attempt to hold herself together, and partly to place an extra barrier between Evanton and herself.

"How can I help you?"

"Just a few standard questions, Dr. Quinn," said Evanton. "About the break-in last night."

Libby nodded, beckoning him to continue, all the quicker to get him out of there.

"What time did you leave the department last night?"

Libby gulped, and paused before giving her answer.

"About 6pm."

Evanton studied her eyes so intensely that she was forced to look away.

He knows, she thought, feeling her palms grow clammy. As if to confirm her fears, Evanton's stare snapped on to her hands, then back up. She felt a cold shiver creep over her.

"Really?" he said, making his scepticism clear. "And did you see anything suspicious around the department as you were leaving?"

"I don't think so. Not that I can remember."

"A serious crime has been committed, Dr. Quinn," said Evanton. "I suggest you sharpen up your memory."

"I'm sorry, but I didn't realize breaking into an academic office was regarded as such a serious crime," said Libby. *Play the innocent.*

Evanton sat back in his chair. His eyes remained expressionless.

"Have you noticed anything missing?"

Only Janice, Libby thought miserably, but she shook her head. She didn't trust her mouth not to tell him about the gas mask. She wasn't to trust him, according to Donna, and questions were now beginning to bombard her mind about why Evanton would be here about the gas mask she'd taken from Hunter's office. Why would he be so interested in it? Unless he, too, suspected Hunter's involvement in *The Bampot* poisoning and believed her to be in on it with him? It would be all the proof he needed to put her away, as he seemed intent on doing.

But as mysteriously as he'd appeared in her doorway, Evanton stood up suddenly from his chair, breaking her thoughts, and strode back across her office. Looking back at her, and with teeth showing in a sneer, he said, "I'll be watching you closely, Dr. Quinn," and he was gone.

Libby succumbed to the shaking that she'd been working so hard to keep under control, and her breathing came out in irregular gasps. She was going to have to find Donna fast, before Evanton managed to get her framed for the poisoning.

She jumped when she heard the knock on her door, but smiled in relief when she saw Sally there. Instinctively, she hurried across the floor and gave Sally a brief hug.

"Thanks for seeing me," Sally mumbled, seeming startled.

"Oh, you have no idea how glad I am to see you," said Libby. "Here, have a seat. Can I get you a coffee?"

"Are you okay?" asked Sally. "You seem a bit jumpy."

"Sorry," said Libby, sitting down and taking a deep breath. "It's been a bit crazy in here this morning. So, how are you?"

Sally shifted in her seat. The words she had rehearsed suddenly seemed to leave her.

"Has something happened?" said Libby.

"Er . . . well, I wanted to talk to you about some work I've been asked to do."

"You mean your meeting with Hunter yesterday?"

Sally nodded.

"What did he ask you to do?" asked Libby. The gas mask and his lies loomed larger than ever in her mind.

Sally placed a document on Libby's desk. "Do you know about this?"

Libby picked it up and briefly flicked through it. "No. What is it?"

"He said this was confidential," said Sally. "He asked me to prepare a report based on these figures, but they can't be right. I think he's asked me to write a report using dodgy data."

Libby flicked through the papers again, looking more closely at the details of the site readings.

"C2H3NO?" she said, already tapping at some keys on her PC. Something about it rang a bell. "Of course, methyl isocyanate . . . " Not something that crossed her desk much these days.

"Exactly," Sally cut in.

"That means something to you?" Libby asked, turning to her just as the phone rang.

"I'm sorry to trouble you, but we have your number to contact about Foxy the rabbit. Is this Libby Quinn?"

"Yes," said Libby. Her voice came out more harshly than she'd intended, as she now experienced a flash of anger. How dare Donna leave this to her, while she flounced around with her new squeeze?

The voice on the line continued. "We can't get hold of Ms. Davenport. She was supposed to collect Foxy this morning, but…"

"Is this the vet nurse?" Libby answered, the sudden thought bringing panic into her head.

"Yes."

"I don't mean to pry," Libby said hurriedly. "But wasn't Donna with you last night?"

There was an awkward pause on the line. The nurse made a few embarrassed sounds.

"It's ok," Libby said. "She told me you were going for a drink, but I can't get hold of her and she'd never leave the rabbit. I think something's happened to her."

She was aware she was babbling now, her mind gone numb with worry.

"Oh my God," said the vet nurse. "Donna didn't turn up last night, but I thought she'd been caught up at work. Should we contact the police?"

"Donna is the police," said Libby dryly.

So Donna hadn't turned up for her date, wasn't responding to her pager, and had left Foxy at the vet's. Now Libby knew for sure something bad had happened.

Hoping against hope that Donna had simply forgotten about Foxy and gone to work, Libby quickly apologised to Sally for the interruption, and phoned the police station. But after two connections and being placed on hold, she was informed that

Detective Davenport wasn't in her office this morning. Libby felt sick. Her heart raced, and she came over all clammy. Should she report Donna missing? Or was there something she should be remembering? Perhaps all the torment of the last few days was taking its toll, and even if it wasn't this, Libby was, for the first time in her life, afraid of the police. It looked like there was a determined effort on their part to frame her and Danny for the poisoning. And the only person who could protect them was missing. Libby felt close to despair.

"What's going on?" Sally's words brought Libby sharply back.

"Donna's missing. I mean, properly missing I think."

Sally opened her mouth in shock.

"You were going to say something about methyl isocyanate," Libby pressed on. "What was it? It's time we compared notes and got everything out in the open. What does it mean to you?"

Sally nodded her head slowly, taking her time to think about what she was going to say.

"This is going to sound crazy," she said. "But I think this report might have something to do with my father. MIC is one of his key issues; he goes all round the world talking about it."

"Yes, but he works on a whole number of topics," said Libby. "He's an expert on toxic chemical waste generally, not just MIC."

"I know," said Sally. "But on Tuesday night, when I said I was mugged, it was two men, they were waiting for me outside the flat. They made me phone him. They made me phone my father. And now I've been asked to do this report. It has to be connected."

Libby was dumbfounded; now she remembered Donna's odd reaction to the mention of Sally's family name.

"Sally, I'm going to tell you about something I found, too," she said. "Before I left Danny's restaurant on Monday evening, I saw Hunter there, at a table with Bob Skinner. When I asked him about it, he completely denied having been there."

"What?"

"More than that, he actually lied and made up some tale about being in Edinburgh. But I definitely saw him, and he knows it. I had to find out what he was hiding, so I . . . er . . . broke into his office last night."

"You what?"

"I found a gas mask, Sally. Why would he be hiding a gas mask, and lying about being at the restaurant?"

Sally's eyes grew wide in astonishment. "Are you saying your boss was the one who carried out the poisoning?"

"It's looking that way," said Libby. "And now it seems as though he wants you to cover something up. Something related to MIC, but why? None of this is making any sense."

"No, it's not," said Sally. "The report doesn't relate to environmental sampling anywhere near the restaurant."

"But it's got to be connected," said Libby

"We need to go to the police," said Sally.

Libby shook her head. "There's something else you should know about," she told Sally. "After you left here yesterday, Donna warned me not to trust one of her colleagues. I think Danny and I are being set up by the police, to take the blame for the poisoning. And now Donna's missing, and . . . " Libby's voice quavered.

"Libby," Sally placed a hand on her arm. "We can't sit here and do nothing. We need to find out more about Hunter's activities. Who could you talk to?"

"Janice," said Libby, blowing her nose. "If anyone knows about Hunter's extra-curricular activities, she will."

"Then let's go and see Janice now," said Sally.

"OK," said Libby. "But we should all be together, you, me and Danny. I've a feeling none of us is very safe at the moment. I'll phone him to join us here. He went to check on *The Bampot*. Can you collect him from the train station?"

"Of course," said Sally. Her face was pale, but she seemed relieved to have some kind of plan. She put on her jacket while Libby rang her brother.

Chapter Forty-seven

Evanton crossed the reception area, noting the empty desk, and let himself into Hunter's office.

He found Hunter looking agitated.

"What did she say?" Hunter began. "How much does she know? I need to get out of here."

"Oh, give it a rest," said Evanton, annoyed. Hunter could see the anger bubbling just below the surface. "At least I've dealt with the others. We won't be having any problems from them."

"You think so?" said Hunter, pacing anxiously around his room.

Something about the conviction with which he spat this out set alarm bells sounding in Evanton's head. He stared at the academic, the squirmy, whining panic sweating out of each grubby pore.

"Did you know Professor Chisholm is calling a press conference this afternoon?" said Hunter.

"What? No!"

"One minute he's all *how efficient* that we have a report due, and the next minute he's going public . . . "

"What do you mean?" said Evanton. "Did you tell him about the report? You told him about the fucking report!"

Hunter shrank back at the sight of Evanton's neck growing purple and his eyes bulging. An alarming show of veins appeared around his temples. Hunter felt his knees buckle.

"You couldn't keep your fucking mouth shut," said Evanton, his voice now almost a whisper.

Hunter stared at him. "What the hell would it matter if I told him about the report?"

"I told him about it yesterday," said Evanton. "And now you've just told him that you're involved in all this."

Despite the remaining bruising to his ribs, Hunter now took a turn to spit a flash of anger.

"You discussed the report with Chisholm, and you didn't tell me?" he said. "Well, now I know where I stand, don't I? We were never in this together, were we?"

He had his answer as Evanton turned and marched out of the office, slamming the door behind him. With the slam echoing in his head, Hunter quickly keyed in the details of his online flight booking.

Evanton passed the reception desk, his mind a rising white fury at the prospect of Chisholm's press conference. What was it going to take to stop this fucking professor? The sound of Libby Quinn's door opening made him turn and look. He saw a young woman coming out, and something familiar about her made him stop and watch her. She looked lost in her thoughts, and she walked on, struggling into her jacket, while a smile crept to Evanton's face. The woman didn't notice him subtly move into the space directly in front of her, and she bumped headlong into him.

"Oh, sorry," she said, startled.

Evanton didn't miss a beat.

"Sally Chisholm, am I correct?" he said, reaching into his pocket.

"Yes," said Sally, the surprise in her voice evident. "How did you . . . ?" Then she saw the gun pointed at her.

"You and I are going for a little ride," said Evanton.

Chapter Forty-eight

Donna felt numb with cold. A distinct nip to the air had arrived during the night, and the temperature inside the Portakabin had plummeted, with Donna having no shield from it. She still sat on the wooden chair with her wrist cuffed to the radiator which had never come on. Throughout the night, no amount of yanking at the cuff or grabbing at the radiator had done anything to bring her towards release. She'd thought about kicking it, but to her alarm had found she was unable to move her legs without inducing the most excruciating pain she'd ever known. Fearing what she might, or might not, find if she were to look at them, she'd studiously avoided bringing her legs into her field of vision.

She was thirsty now. Craving something to drink, in fact, and worse, she'd missed two vital doses of medication. She felt nauseous, partly because of the erratic pill-taking, partly from the thirst, but also from the smell. She'd been forced to urinate where she sat during the night.

As noon approached, sunlight finally reached in through the Portakabin windows behind Donna's chair, and began to warm the room enough for her to stop shivering so badly. But her head ached terribly, and she was still racked with pain, unable to move her legs. The open wound on her shoulder was beginning to fester, and she had to swallow back vomit whenever she thought of Evanton's mouth there.

She'd fought back several panic attacks during the night, and now she began to feel another one approach. She was locked up, badly injured and beginning to dehydrate, and nobody knew where she was. Why hadn't she left a message with Ross to say where she was going? The insanity of her actions mocked her loud and clear. But she was panicking about more than just her own miserable situation. Libby was the witness that could nail Graeme Hunter, and now Evanton knew it. With Evanton gone, Donna found her imagination creating all kinds of awful scenarios involving Libby being silenced so that Hunter and Evanton could continue with their illicit trade.

Stop it! she told herself firmly. A moment of lucid thought allowed her to take back some control of at least how she was reacting to her situation. Dwelling on her injuries and her fears was not going to get her out of here alive or help Libby. She was going to survive this. She was going to survive.

She forced herself to focus on her surroundings. Could she come up with some plan of action? Any way she could attract attention?

Then she heard a noise, like footsteps outside the Portakabin, and she froze. She couldn't shout for help even if she tried. Her voice was hoarse from her yelling through the night and from her thirst. Terrified that Evanton was back to finish the job, she craned to pick up more sounds. Maybe she'd imagined it. She certainly hadn't heard a car approaching, so if what she'd heard was a person, then that person had spent the night at the quarry, too. But that was ridiculous, she thought. *It must be a fox, or something.*

Then the Portakabin door handle turned.

Into the doorway tumbled a young man, maybe still in his teens, dressed in a boiler suit; when he registered Donna sitting at the far end of the room, he issued a cry of alarm and backed out of the doorway again.

No, please, come back! Donna pleaded. But she was unable to produce a sound.

Chapter Forty-nine

Danny checked the time. His train had got in from Arbroath ten minutes ago. Sally should have arrived by now. She'd had plenty of time to get here before him, even if the traffic was awful. But scanning the roads going by the train station on both sides, he could tell that the traffic was flowing just fine. She hadn't rung to say she was going to be late, and she wasn't picking up when he tried her.

Libby had sounded terrified on the phone, insisting he come into Dundee so that the three of them could be together for safety. And now Libby wasn't answering her phone, either. He felt a knot form in his stomach as he set out to walk to the university, on the much shorter pedestrian route.

He kept his head down as he passed a swarm of students who emerged from an exam room, and found his way to Libby's office, passing the empty reception. He was frustrated to find no sign of Libby or Sally anywhere.

He moved the mouse on Libby's computer, and the screen flashed to life, displaying a bland desktop. Nothing of interest there, but his eye caught something sitting behind the keyboard that made his blood run cold.

He picked the item up and felt his heart beat faster. Libby's phone.

He leaned on Libby's desk to stop his hands from shaking as he checked the call history on her phone. His was the last number she'd called. He re-ran her words in his head, and recalled her plan to visit Janice. Working his way through the menu options on Libby's phone, he found Janice's contact details, including her address.

Worth a shot, he told himself, trying hard to fight off a gnawing fear. He pocketed Libby's phone and set out to visit Janice.

Danny had always imagined Janice living in a large townhouse with tidy gardens, leaving for work every morning after kissing a husband off to his office with his sandwiches in his briefcase. Always perfectly groomed and made-up, Janice certainly didn't fit the image that confronted him now. A crowded street of six-in-a-block flats, dog dirt lining the pavement, drab curtains and nicotine-stained netting covering windows behind which all sorts of obscenities and threats were being yelled. The controlled entry door to Janice's flat was smashed in, so Danny let himself into the urine-reeking close, and knocked on Janice's second floor door.

Janice, her eyes rimmed red and her face blotchy without its make-up, looked surprised when she opened the door to Danny.

"Sorry to bother you," said Danny. "Is Libby here?"

"Libby? No," said Janice. "But come in. What's happened now?"

She showed him into her living room, before hurrying to the kitchen to make them tea.

Danny tried to wait, but his nerves were on edge. He followed Janice into the kitchen.

"Libby said she was coming to see you," Danny said quickly. "And I can't find her anywhere. She's not answering her phone, and she asked me to meet her at her office. She was scared that something terrible was going on. She told me she'd seen Hunter at the restaurant on Monday night, but that he lied to her about it. And she thinks the police are trying to frame her for what happened."

Janice gasped, but waited for him to go on.

"She said she found something in Hunter's office that makes her think he carried out the poisoning."

Janice's hand flew to her mouth.

"Oh, my God," she said. "I knew he was involved in some unsavoury business dealings, but do you really think he was the one behind that?"

"I can only tell you what Libby told me," said Danny. "But I was hoping you could tell me something about the unsavoury things he's involved with? Do you know if he has any dealings with the politician, Bob Skinner?"

A small smile of recognition crept across Janice's lips. "Come through and sit down," she said.

In the living room, she reached for a packet of cigarettes and sat back.

"Where would you like me to begin?" she said. "His friendship with Bob Skinner? Or maybe his debt to the police officer Evanton? Oh, and not to forget his odd meeting yesterday with Professor David Chisholm."

"Chisholm?" said Danny. Now the threads were definitely connected. He sat back, keen to hear what Janice had to say.

"You learn things when you're a secretary," said Janice. "No accident that it begins with *secret*. About four or five months ago, Hunter got himself caught in a compromising position with a girl under sixteen. The arresting officer was DI Evanton, and all of a sudden, everything was hushed up. Not even a court hearing. Ever since then, Evanton's been in and out of Hunter's office like a yo-yo. I reckon they have some crooked business going on. One that involves the quarry rather than the university, because believe me, if there was anything to be found in Hunter's office, I'd have found it."

The quarry, thought Danny. *I wonder what's going on at the quarry...*

Chapter Fifty

Emma could never figure out these corridors. Although her lab was in Aberdeen, the nature of her work brought her regularly to Bell Street, but she got lost every time. She was puzzled to have been called in by Ross, but had looked forward to seeing Donna when she got here, even though she'd not managed to get her on the phone to tell her she was coming. She felt more than a little awkward when she knocked on Ross's door.

To her relief, Ross smiled and stood up to welcome her when she came into the spacious room. She found herself joining a subdued team comprised both of members she recognised and some she didn't. There was the young officer, Dom Hilton. Alice Moone, she knew, and Ted Granger. They each nodded a welcome to Emma when she came in, but none of them said anything. Of Ross's regular team, Emma noticed straight away that Donna and Evanton were both absent. She had an uneasy feeling about the nature of this meeting.

Looking around the table, Emma was struck by how depressingly often they had come together these last couple of days. Everyone looked tired. They sat around a meeting table, nobody talking.

"Thank you for coming here, Emma," Ross said, setting aside in a neat pile the papers he'd been leafing through.

Emma sat down, unbidden.

"We have a new problem on our hands," Ross said, bringing everyone to attention. "It looks as though DI Davenport is missing." He allowed the gasps of disbelief, before continuing. "We had a meeting scheduled for five-thirty yesterday afternoon, and she didn't turn up. Now, I'll admit, I thought it was just Donna being Donna, and I let it go until this morning. But she didn't come in for work, and I sent Dom to check on the various addresses we have for her."

Dom nodded his head in acknowledgement. "She hasn't been seen at any of the addresses overnight," he confirmed.

"Now, we're in the middle of this MIC investigation, and we've had the poisoning, and the double murder," said Ross. His words came out clumsily. Ross was struggling with the dilemma of breaking confidence. "Donna came to me yesterday with a number of concerns. Specifically, allegations that DI Evanton has been corrupting our investigation."

Again, Ross paused to allow the commotion that demonstrated their shock and disbelief.

Emma expressed the fear they all felt when she said, "The MIC – do you think Evanton has it?"

Ross lowered his head and steadied his breathing. He was wheezy. "We've had an internal investigation going on for a while into some irregularities around Evanton's activities. But I never imagined he could be the lunatic with the MIC." His face was ashen.

"If he is," said Alice Moone, "then he's been killing any witnesses that find out. We need to find Donna."

"We've just brought in Libby Quinn at his request, sir," said Ted. "Said she was to be charged over the poisoning."

Everyone around the table began to talk at once.

Ross knew he faced an unthinkable disaster. How to stop Evanton and get Donna back to safety? For he simply had to believe that Donna was alive and unharmed somewhere.

"Our team was brought into the MIC investigation on a pretext," he continued. They had to know everything. It was time to stop the secrets. "The ACC had tasked Lawson with looking into Evanton's activities, and Lawson did this by watching us conduct the lines of enquiry he gave us." There was silence now. "He was right, as it turns out, and I have to take my hat off to him. And now I want you all to give Chief Superintendent Lawson your full co-operation. If he says *jump*, you ask *how high?*. And, as of this moment, I need you all here for as long as it takes. All leave is cancelled until further notice. If you have to make domestic arrangements, make them now. Am I clear?"

There were nods of heads around the table. The silence spoke of astonishment.

"There's one thing you might not know about," said Emma slowly. "Donna's ill."

Ross stared at her. "What do you mean? Do I have to be trawling the hospitals?"

"No," said Emma. "Not that kind of ill. But I can't discuss it here. She swore me to secrecy."

"Damn it, Emma," said Ross, raising his voice unintentionally,

"Donna's life could be at risk here. What is it that you know?"

Emma wrestled with her conscience. But Ross was right. She had a bad feeling about Donna's safety, and she'd much rather be the cause of her embarrassment than the cause of her death.

"She suffers from bipolar disorder," said Emma. "She can't control her mood, and it can lead her to taking crazy risks. She was due to go to her doctor today, but obviously she's . . . not able to go."

Ross's face grew purple.

"Why would she keep something like that from me?"

"She's scared she'll get the sack," said Emma, hearing how hollow it sounded now.

Ross's phone rang and he snatched it up.

"What is it?" he barked into the phone.

The officers in the room grew silent as he rose from the table.

"When was this?" they heard him snap into the phone. Then his tone softened. "Is he able to talk? . . . Okay, I'll be right over."

Ross ended the call and faced his team. "I'll action the search for Donna and put out a warrant for Evanton's arrest," he said, reaching for his jacket. "Alice, go and talk to Libby Quinn. If Evanton's been so keen to have her locked up, then she has something that can help us. All of you stay contactable. Bob Skinner's just woken up. I'm hoping to God he can answer some of our questions."

Chapter Fifty-one

Danny let himself back into Libby's office. Hunter was working with Evanton, according to Janice. And Libby was certain that Hunter had something to do with the poisoning. She was also sure that the police were trying to frame him and Libby. Sally's father had come to meet Hunter yesterday. And now all of them were gone. There had to be something here in Libby's office to help him figure out what was going on, and what to do about it. He needed Donna, but she was missing, too.

Danny's breathing was shallow as he ferreted around Libby's desk contents.

Somebody coughed behind him, and he spun round, startled. A man was standing there, propped up against the doorframe, holding out his hands.

"Sorry," said the man. "Didn't mean to startle you. It's Danny, isn't it?"

Danny relaxed.

"You're Natesh, aren't you? Donna's friend?"

"The very one," said Natesh. "And I'm trying to find her. Do you know where she is?"

Danny raised his eyebrows. "You look pretty badly beat up," he said. "Shouldn't you be in the hospital?"

Natesh shrugged his shoulders, and winced in pain. "I should probably be here about as much as you should be," he said.

Danny's face turned red.

"Close the door, will you?" said Danny. "There's something I need to tell you."

"I'm not liking the sound of that," said Natesh, as he gently closed the door and came into the room. He sat down beside Libby's desk, and looked expectantly at Danny.

Danny blew on his hands, and paced back and forth.

"I don't know what's going on here," he said. "But Libby phoned me this morning. She said Donna was missing."

Natesh sprang to his feet, and cursed with pain.

"Missing? What the . . . ?"

"Donna said there was something weird going on with this case," said Danny. "And this morning Libby sounded terrified. She said Donna was missing, but that Donna had warned her not to trust the police. Libby found evidence that her boss was involved in the poisoning. I got here as fast as I could, and now Libby's gone. And I can't get hold of Sally . . . "

"Whoa, slow down," said Natesh. "Go back. Tell me from the start. Donna told Libby something about the police?"

"Yes," said Danny, with an effort to control his breathing. "She told Libby to let her know if the police contacted her, and to play along if they did. She took it that Donna was warning her not to trust them."

"All of the police?" asked Natesh.

Danny stopped pacing, and thought. "Just the one," he said. "Jonas Evanton, do you know him?"

Natesh bobbed his head slowly. "Not sure, but I might have seen him. Tall, blond hair, flashy suit?"

"Sounds like him," said Danny.

"I saw him twice," said Natesh. "He's a real bad piece of work, real temper on him."

"Oh God," said Danny.

"You said other stuff," Natesh prompted him. "Something about Libby's boss?"

"Yeah, she said she had evidence that he was involved in the poisoning."

"What's his name?" said Natesh.

"Graeme Hunter," said Danny. "Libby says she saw him at the restaurant on Monday, but he lied to her about it, like he was trying to cover up. Then she found something in his office, but she didn't say what. She sounded so scared, so I came here as quickly as I could, but I can't find her, and her phone was lying here. Why would she leave her phone?" Danny struggled to control the panic rising in his voice.

"How did she know Donna was missing?" said Natesh. "Couldn't she just be working?"

"No way," said Danny. "She's not at work, she's not answering her pager, and she left Foxy at the vet's."

Natesh nodded grimly. That was proof enough for him that Donna was in serious trouble. But where could she be?

"You know about my crash?" he asked Danny.

Danny nodded his head. "I heard through the grapevine."

"Well, it wasn't an accident," Natesh said. "I had my brakes checked just the day before. There was nothing wrong one day. Then the next day they fail . . . no accident, no way."

"What are you saying?" said Danny anxiously.

"I think it happened to get at Donna," said Natesh. "Maybe this Evanton is going after people she cares about?"

"But I don't think Donna knows Sally," said Danny. "So that wouldn't explain something happening to her."

"Now you're thinking straight," said Natesh. "We can figure this out. Who is Sally?"

"She's here at the university on a study placement with Libby . . . and her boss."

"The one who was at the restaurant?"

They both fell into a silence, each deep in thought, trying to tie the pieces together.

"I'm going to the hospital," said Danny. "See if I can talk to Bob Skinner. The guy who was poisoned."

"No way," said Natesh. "You think they're going to let you near him? They think you tried to kill him. I'll go."

"You're in a bad way as it is," said Danny. "It's best if you keep out of this." He jumped back as Natesh reared towards his head.

"Fucking say that to my face, man," said Natesh. "Donna is my best friend. If she's in trouble, then I'm in. Ouch! Fuck." He rubbed his bruised neck.

"Sorry," said Danny, holding up a pacifying hand.

A moment of sulking passed between them.

"Then I'll go up to the quarry," Danny said. "Libby's boss owns it, and from what I've been told, there could be something there that'll give us some answers."

"All right," said Natesh. "Here, take my number. It's, what, just gone ten. You phone me at eleven, I phone you at twelve. Too much creepy stuff going on, man."

They both walked out of Libby's office.

"Who am I asking for, again?" asked Natesh.

"Bob Skinner," said Danny. "Politician in the papers." He held out his hand. "Well, good luck."

Chapter Fifty-two

"Graeme Hunter?" Mo held her face in her hands.

The backdrop remained the same. The hospital bed, its white tiled walls, the wires, the monitors and the beeping. Bob lying motionless.

Mo's eyes darted from Bob, to the floor, to Chisholm, and back to Bob.

"Graeme Hunter?" she said again.

"I guess that must be a shock to you," said Chisholm. "But it's the only conclusion I can draw."

"Graeme Hunter?"

"The press conference is our best safeguard at the moment," he said.

She seemed incapable of forming a coherent sentence. Before all this had happened, on the night Bob had switched on his model railway set, she could almost have believed Graeme Hunter to be capable of something like this. But now that it had happened, now that Bob was lying here in a coma . . . a coma . . . *Wait a minute!*

Bob's eye was twitching. Now both eyes. And now he was arching his head as if unknotting a stiff neck.

Chisholm stood back against a wall, allowing the medics to rush in as Mo pushed the alarm button at the change of the beeping on the monitors. In what seemed like a remarkably short period of time, Bob Skinner was awake. Looking around himself in bewilderment at first, then reaching for Mo's hand, then dutifully complying with the various demands of the medics and answering their questions in rough monosyllables and head movements.

Chisholm shuffled closer to the door, intending to slip outside and leave Mo and Bob with at least a little privacy.

"No, stay, please," he was surprised to hear Mo tell him. "You and Bob need to talk."

"I don't think the doctors will . . . "

"This isn't a prison," said Mo. "I think Bob will want to talk to you."

Chisholm smiled in return, glad to see relief on Mo's face.

His phone rang, and he answered without checking to see who

it was. When he heard the caller's voice, his smile vanished.

"Press conference, Professor?" The voice was taunting, hysterical almost. This sounded like a man falling over the edge. Chisholm said nothing, simply waiting for what might come next.

"I'd re-think that idea if I were you," the caller said. Over the line Chisholm could hear gulls calling and the sound of waves lapping on the shore. "Because I have Sally with me now. And believe me, if your press conference goes ahead, you'll be arranging her funeral next."

"Sally?" Chisholm said into his phone. "No, you're lying."

"Dad?" came Sally's distressed shout from the caller's phone.

"As I said. You'd better start co-operating, Professor."

The call ended, leaving Chisholm distraught. Mo was busy hovering around Bob, and the medical team was working as one like a machine. Nobody noticed Chisholm's despairing face as he stared at his silent phone.

Evanton pushed his mobile back into his pocket, satisfied now that he'd averted disaster yet again. The fool, Hunter, could go ahead and incriminate himself. But Evanton was not going to go down for any of this. The swirling rain whipped around him and Sally as he marched her over the shingle towards the cave, holding the pistol against the back of her neck. His shirt was soaked, plastered onto his skin, and rain ran into his eyes from his sodden hair. But he took in heavy gulps of the biting air, invigorated and feeling strong. He closed his hearing off from the sounds of Sally's pleading, and concentrated on getting them across the uneven surface.

Sally recognized the cave that she'd stood outside the day before yesterday. The one from which she'd hurried when she'd had the unnerving feeling that she was being watched. She stumbled as she entered the cave, her breathing rapid and shallow as she tried to contain her terror. She could see that Evanton was holding his pistol loosely at his side now, apparently very pleased with himself.

Sally struggled to adjust her vision to the darkness, and found herself astonished to find what appeared to be a well organized storage unit. There was shelving containing crates, tidy piles of rope and clothing, and silver canisters containing who knew what. Trying her best to make her way along the cave wall and give the impression she was looking for somewhere to sit and nurse her wounds, she stilled her breathing and strained for any sounds that might indicate a lapse in Evanton's watch on her. When she was sure she could sense that his concentration was elsewhere, she made a bolt back towards the cave mouth.

"I don't think so," said Evanton. His foot had barely to move before it caught her. She fell heavily, jarring her shin, and she was sure she'd sliced her knee open. Her senses almost went black and she experienced a brief moment of dizziness, before she felt herself being roughly set upright against the cave wall.

She felt burning around her waist as Evanton suddenly and savagely ripped at the band of her jeans, which tore under his brutality. Sally screamed. Not just in terror, but for her life.

"The way I see it," Evanton said as he unzipped his own trousers while grabbing at Sally's neck, "it's been all work and no play."

Desperately, Sally tried to scratch his face, but his grip around her neck grew tighter, and she began to choke.

Chapter Fifty-three

Natesh stopped in front of the sliding glass doors that led into the hospital. Only two hours ago he'd sneaked out, past the nurses' station, and discharged himself. From his experience of the day before, it was unlikely that his presence would be missed yet. Still, he had a nagging worry about getting into trouble should he be discovered here.

But the nagging worry was nothing compared with his fear for Donna's safety. He was convinced this Evanton was behind his car accident, and he was equally as convinced that it was some kind of warning to Donna. If only she'd told him something about what she'd been working on, he might have some clue as to what was going on. He remembered the way she'd looked at Evanton the previous morning, when he had driven her to the farm house outside Arbroath. And he remembered the mask of fury that was Evanton's face the day he'd pulled out from Swanky Lanky's. Natesh was looking for Donna, but he was also looking for answers.

He chewed his lip, wondering nervously if he'd be allowed to see Bob Skinner. News reports were emerging that he'd regained consciousness, but Natesh was aware that he was a stranger to him and his family, and there was no reason why the politician would want to talk to him.

He found it surprisingly easy to get the information he needed to find Bob Skinner's room off the main ward. When he got there, he saw a tall man standing outside, anxiously rubbing at his forehead and pacing back and forth. The man jumped, clearly agitated, when Natesh cleared his throat.

"Excuse me," Natesh said, "But is this Bob Skinner's room?"

"Yes, it is," said the man, making visible attempts to compose himself.

"Would you mind if I . . . ?"

"Oh, pardon me," said the man, stepping aside from the door. "Are you a relative?"

Natesh hesitated. A relative? Was the man blind or something? An awkward moment passed.

"Nah," said Natesh. "I'm his driver." He cringed at his own words.

Did politicians have drivers? But now he had this tall man's attention. He extended his hand to Natesh.

"I'm David Chisholm," he said. "I've come to the UK to work with Bob on a project, but . . . uh . . . events took another course."

"David Chisholm?" Natesh took a step back, and blinked. The girl Sally, the one Danny had mentioned, was called Chisholm.

Chisholm eyed Natesh warily. Who was he? Why had his name elicited such surprise in him?

"I'm Natesh," he said, now extending his own hand. Where should he begin? "I guess I need to talk to you and Mr. Skinner both."

"Myself and Mr. Skinner? Are you a police officer?"

Natesh let slip a guffaw.

Chisholm grasped the hope that this unexpected interruption might help find his daughter, and led Natesh into the hospital room.

Bob Skinner was propped up on pillows. Mo sat by his side, talking animatedly to him. Both looked up to see Chisholm enter the room with Natesh.

"Sorry for intruding, Mr. Skinner," he said, stepping closer to the bed. "My name is Natesh Chaudrakar. I'm kind of a friend of a friend of a friend, if you know what I mean?"

"Who are you? What are you doing here?" Skinner's eyes were wide in alarm.

Natesh's mouth dropped open at Bob Skinner's hostility, and saw that at his response, the two others in the room squared themselves against him.

"Whatever message Graeme Hunter wants you to pass on," Skinner said, "you can tell him I'm not interested."

Mo Skinner stood up, forcing Natesh to step back towards the door.

"No, no, I don't have a message," said Natesh. "My friend has gone missing." He realized how this must look, but he was running out of time to gain their confidence. Donna and Libby needed him to find some answers quickly. "But it might be Graeme Hunter has something to do with it. You know Donna? Or Libby?" He stared at their blank faces in frustration. "Sally?"

"What do you know about Sally?" Chisholm's face drained of all colour. "Where is she?"

222

"I don't know," Natesh said. "I met Libby's brother this morning. He told me Libby and Sally are both missing, too. Can you help?"

Natesh watched a look pass between Chisholm, Skinner and Mo, but he ploughed on through the heavily charged air.

"Libby had information that Graeme Hunter was working with someone else to do with the poisoning, a police officer maybe?"

Chisholm was the first to compose himself.

"You're correct that Graeme Hunter is working with someone else. I've been receiving blackmail threats for some time now, and the blackmailer is now holding Sally captive. But I don't know his identity."

"So, if Sally's being held captive, what about Donna and Libby?" It came out as a shriek, and Natesh coughed self-consciously, clearing his throat.

"I'm sorry," said Chisholm. "Can you tell us about your friends that are missing?"

"I know who Libby is," said Bob Skinner, making everyone in the room turn to face him. "She works with Graeme Hunter. She's Danny Quinn's sister."

"This isn't looking good," said Mo, with an accusing glint in her eye as she looked at Natesh.

"Hey, it's not good," said Natesh. "Libby phoned Danny to say something screwy is going on, and now she's vanished. She said the police are trying to frame her."

"Where is Danny Quinn?" asked Bob.

"He went to Hunter's quarry," said Natesh. "To see if he can find anything there. I need to find Donna. What if the angry man has her?"

"Angry man?"

"Who?"

"Tell us!"

The voices in the room fired back at him in unison.

"This sounds crazy," Natesh said. "But what if the cops are involved in the cover-up? They're not trying to frame Libby, at all. They're covering up for themselves! That's what Donna meant."

There was a knock on the door.

"Detective Chief Inspector Angus Ross, Tayside Police," said the tall red-headed man who entered the room. "I need to ask Mr. Skinner some questions."

This time, Natesh found himself included in the look that passed between Chisholm, Skinner and Mo.

Chapter Fifty-four

Iksan waited, stock-still, in the doorway of the Portakabin. His shock at finding somebody in the room now gave way to curiosity. It was a woman, almost naked, and it was clear to him now that she was badly injured and unable to move. He was in no doubt as to who had left her here in this state, and he found his eyes darting frequently to the roadside and his ears straining for the sounds of an approaching car. Only stillness echoed back at him from around the quarry. The men wouldn't be finished with their deliveries until tonight, he knew. Slowly he took a step inside the Portakabin and shuffled towards the woman, past the debris from the upturned desk. She seemed unable to talk, but appeared to be miming that she needed a drink.

"Water, yes?" he said, and he rushed to the small sink that stood in one corner of the Portakabin.

Carefully cupping Donna's chin with one hand, Iksan held a plastic cup of water to her lips, and let her sip. The hand she'd used to mime hung exhausted by her side. She sipped slowly but steadily, and when she finished the cup, Iksan fetched another. When she drank that, Iksan held up a finger.

"Wait," he said. Donna was in no mood to quip back that she hardly had any other choice, but she nodded her head, watching him go, sure now that the lad was going to help her.

After several painfully long minutes, Iksan returned to the Portakabin carrying a blanket, which he carefully arranged around Donna's shivering body.

"Thank you," she croaked. "Can you find the key?" She used her free hand to feebly mime unlocking the cuff, though the movement caused a fresh wave of pain to shoot through her arm.

Iksan looked at the cuff and shook his head, looking confused.

Then, from the far end of the room, from amongst the heap of items that had lain on the desk, a telephone rang.

"There's a phone?" said Donna. "Quick, phone the police!"

At Iksan's look of alarm at her sudden animation, Donna forced herself to talk calmly.

"Phone," she nodded towards the corner of the room. "Police, yes?" Her voice was failing again, and she only managed to croak.

Iksan followed her gaze, and when the phone stopped ringing, he rummaged amongst the clutter and found it. He lifted it, but found it to be an old fashioned landline phone, well and truly attached to its cord.

"Police number?" he asked Donna. His head was swimming. Maybe there was a chance to escape now. He wasn't on his own any longer. Somehow, Donna's presence gave him courage and determination to try.

"Nine-nine-nine."

He knew that, he remembered now. He punched the keys into the phone, and was answered by an operator.

"Police," he said as clearly as he could. He was then met with a series of questions that he couldn't understand, and he panicked.

"Hunter's Quarries," said Donna, but it came out only as a hiss.

Iksan couldn't understand what either woman was saying.

He froze like a frightened rabbit as he heard a car entering the gates of the quarry, his face twitching with fear. Iksan dropped the phone, and ran from the Portakabin.

Chapter Fifty-five

Ross shuffled impatiently on the spot. He had an officer missing, probably in great danger, if not already dead. He shook his head to stop that train of thought. He had reason to believe Evanton could have something to do with this whole MIC thing, and the very people who could confirm it and fill in the blanks were gathered here together in this hospital room with him. But they weren't talking. Ross had noticed the body language right away. The arms folded across chests. The chins upturned. The drawing nearer to one another. What was this? Unless, he began to wonder with a growing sense of despair in the pit of his stomach, they were all involved with Evanton?

But his doubts and his frustration evaporated when he saw the response to the photograph that he held up.

"Have you seen this man before?"

"Yes," said Chisholm. He sprang to life, and jabbed his finger at the photo. "That's the man who's been blackmailing me! He's got Sally! You've found them?"

"Sally?" said Ross, fearing he was opening up yet another can of worms.

"My daughter," said Chisholm, sounding breathless. "He's holding my daughter captive, to ensure I call an end to the government's MIC investigation."

Ross felt his heart quicken. "Are you sure this is the man?"

"Yes," said Chisholm. His voice had risen an octave. "Is Sally safe?"

"That's the angry man," said Natesh, craning his neck to see the photo.

"Let me see." Now Mo was pushing forward to look. "What's this about, Detective?"

"Who is he?" Chisholm asked. Ross watched the fear and the uncertainty grow on the professor's face.

"His name is Jonas Evanton," said Mo. "He's a police officer."

Ross gave away nothing in his expression when she looked to him for confirmation.

"Yes, Evanton, he's the angry man," said Natesh. "I saw him with

Donna."

"You know Donna?" snapped Ross, unable to hold his tongue any longer.

"Yes," said Natesh. "But I don't know where she is. I'm trying to find her." He saw the crease of concern on Ross's brow, and knew that this was someone who cared about Donna, too.

"Does Evanton have Donna?" Natesh's voice quavered.

"Is Evanton the one who's been working with Graeme Hunter to blackmail the MIC working group?" said Mo.

"How much do you know about this?" Ross asked, trying not to sound as exasperated as he felt.

"David was already receiving blackmail threats," said Mo. "But he met his blackmailer on Monday night, while the restaurant poisoning was happening, so he knew there must be somebody else involved. Then earlier today he went to see Hunter." She looked at Chisholm for corroboration.

"We thought Hunter might be at risk, too, but he let slip information that told me he has actually been involved in the blackmail," said Chisholm. "But I didn't know the identity of my own blackmailer until now." He motioned to the photograph just as his phoned buzzed. "Excuse me, please," he said, before turning abruptly and leaving the room.

"How do you know Evanton?" Ross asked Mo. He saw the curl of distaste on her lip.

"He and I go back a long way," said Mo. She extended a hand to Ross while she decided how much to tell him. "We first met as gap year students in India, and we ended up in Bhopal. We were there when the Union Carbide disaster happened, and we all got shipped home in the aftermath. There were a group of five of us who shared accommodation in Bhopal, and we all kept in touch, a kind of support group after the horrors we'd witnessed there. Jonas was always different, though." She looked at her feet, then glanced at Ross. He nodded to encourage her to go on. "I never managed to figure him out fully, but by all accounts I know him better than most. I do know his father was a brute. Jonas would always go on about wanting to show him who the big man was now, that kind of thing. But something happened to him during the disaster in Bhopal. Something changed, and he kept having these uncontrollable fits of anger. He didn't react the way the rest of us did." She shuddered. "Anyway, we all went our various ways, Jonas eventually joined the police and I went into law. Over the years, I've brought several cases against him. Brutality, mainly."

"You've taken him to court?" asked Ross. *Why the hell wasn't I told about that?* He saw Mo's accusing stare asking him the same thing.

"I have a dossier of allegations," Mo continued, her voice dropping to a whisper. "There were a number of complaints in Bhopal. Rapes. Women lying injured from the accident reported being raped by a young white man. We've never been able to prove it was Jonas, but I've always had my suspicions. Bhopal. It was the same toxin. He has it, hasn't he?"

"Allegations of rape?" Natesh gasped. "My God, he's got Donna. And Libby. And that man's daughter."

"Try not to worry," said Mo. "He's holding Sally captive so he can get the MIC investigation stopped. As long as he has that leverage, he'll stay calm."

"I had to confirm that Evanton has been working with Graeme Hunter," said Ross. "Donna made allegations to that effect, and I suspect she may have gone out to Hunter's quarry to investigate. You mentioned Libby? Is that Libby Quinn? She's been brought into police custody, I'm afraid. But I'm going to despatch officers to Hunter's quarry now. We'll find Donna and Sally. And we'll bring them back safely." Then he leant into his radio and began issuing commands.

Ross felt relief that the resolution was in sight, and even allowed himself a smug reflection on Lawson's reaction to the news that he'd done it. But when he saw Chisholm return to the room his chest tightened. Something was wrong. He felt the unease that precedes disaster.

Chisholm's face was ashen, and his eyes were glazed in shock.

"Professor Chisholm?"

Chisholm struggled to focus on Ross. "He's releasing the MIC."

Ross looked at Chisholm, hardly daring to ask the next question. "What do you mean?"

"Sally got away from him," said Chisholm. "So he said he's going to release a huge quantity of MIC. He sounds insane. He's going to do it."

"Did he say where?" said Ross. He undid the top button of his shirt as he began to sweat.

"No," said Chisholm.

Ross found that his mouth had grown dry and his breathing came with a wheeze as he pictured the clean, pretty streets of Dundee overlaid with images from the Bhopal disaster.

Shaking himself back to the here and now, he turned to Mo.

"You seem to know him well," said Ross. "Will he do it?"

"While he had Sally captive, he was able to get you to do what he wanted," said Mo. "Now that he's lost that, he'll think he's backed into a corner. From what I've seen of him in the past, the less control he has, the less rationally he'll act. So . . . yes, I believe he'll do it."

"He sounded insane," Chisholm said again.

"But we think he has Donna," said Ross. "Won't he use her to make us back down?"

"Maybe," said Mo. "But he's not stupid. He knows his best chance of ending the investigation was to get at Bob and David."

"Will he bargain?" asked Ross.

Mo shook her head slowly. "If my experience of him is anything to go by, once he's lost it, he's lost it. He won't back down. You need to prepare for the worst."

Oh my God, thought Ross, reaching for his radio.

Sally got away, rang in Natesh's head. And Libby was in police custody. He'd better let Danny know. "But what about Donna?" He tugged at Ross's sleeve.

"I'm sorry," Ross said, "But we're looking at a mass evacuation of the area. I'm afraid we might not have the resources to search for Donna now. But I'll do everything I can. I want to find Donna just as much as you do."

But Natesh was gone from the room before Ross managed to finish his sentence. No way was there anyone who wanted to find Donna as much as he did.

Chapter Fifty-six

The phone call had Tay FM's Marcie Philips in shock. She, along with the other news editors, had attended a police briefing and been sworn to a news blackout on the MIC investigation. The briefing session flashed across her mind now . . .

The Chief Constable's plush office filled with polite chatter as they drank coffee and greeted each other. The atmosphere was relaxed, if intrigued, but that rapidly turned to rapt attention as the chief himself, Robert Finch, walked into the room and made his opening remarks.

"Thank you for coming at short notice," he'd said, eyeing them each in turn. "It's my grave duty to inform you of a potential... catastrophe."

The editors had sat in silence, with raised eyebrows, as Finch presented them with the information on MIC and requested their co-operation in a media blackout.

"Don't you think this is a bit of an over-reaction?" Marcie had asked. "I mean, there can't have been that much of the stuff brought in without anyone noticing?"

"Yeah," another voice had added. "This is Dundee, not Bhopal."

"We've discussed evacuation plans with the Cobra emergency committee," Finch's voice had risen above their sceptical reactions.

"Are you serious?"

Suddenly the voices had grown nervous, and the questions more respectful of Finch's rank.

"In the event of codeword Hierapolis *being sent to you,"* Finch had told them, *"you are required to put out messages instigating a mass evacuation."*

Marcie had never thought it would come to that. But now her named contact for the operation, Chief Superintendent Lawson, was on the phone, yelling "Hierapolis! This is not a drill, operate immediate evacuation plans, repeat, Hierapolis!"

Lawson didn't stay on the line long before hanging up, leaving Marcie sitting stunned at her desk for a few moments. Then, with her heart racing, she ran to the sound room and waved her newsreader out of the way. Hurriedly locating the evacuation recording, she sent the transmission. Every radio in the region would be telling the population to get out. Now.

Natesh sat gripping the steering wheel, the windscreen wipers mesmeric in their clockwork rhythm back and forth against the rain. He'd never stolen a car before, and in his panic, all the controls looked the same.

The car felt muggy inside, like it hadn't long been vacated by its lawful driver. Natesh's head felt unreal as he waited for the traffic to move. It was a fifty zone, a dual carriage way crossing the western edge of the city, but nothing was moving. A BMW driver had cut out too soon in front of the oncoming traffic on the double roundabout ahead, and had stopped everybody. A cacophony of horns and angry voices blared out at him.

The Army truck swung onto the roundabout, and the officer who jumped out of it gave the nod to a waiting traffic cop.

"We're putting the diversion here," said the Army officer. "We'll need northbound traffic stopped at the Perth roundabout, and southbound stopped at Montrose."

"Right you are," said the traffic cop, turning and speaking urgently into his radio.

At the Army officer's clipped command, four soldiers removed red and white barriers from the truck and quickly started setting up road blocks.

"You want to get this road moving," shouted a driver from a waiting car. "This is fucking ridiculous."

The Army officer ignored him, standing motionless watching the opposite carriageway as the traffic on that side grew lighter, until it stood eerily empty.

"Okay, now," he said to the traffic cop, who immediately began to direct the waiting vehicles around the roundabout and back the way they'd come, while soldiers completed the road barriers to block the way ahead.

"Road blocks are now in operation, sir," Alice Moone confirmed to Lawson in the control room. She'd brought the news directly from the officer in charge of the Marines who had been set the task of getting traffic heading away from the city.

"Good work, get everybody the hell out of here, there's no telling when this might blow."

Lawson had never been so flustered.

Alice looked into the air above her, fearing that at any moment it might turn toxic. Hearing a helicopter, she peered more closely. The chopper she saw up there wasn't police or Army.

Bloody hell. The media were up there already.

Cars in front of Natesh and some behind took turns at peeping their horns, but he sat gripping the wheel, sick with dread at what might have happened to Donna. He had to keep a level head, and get to the quarry as quickly as possible.

At last a vehicle gave, and the line of cars approaching the roundabout inched forward.

Natesh had just allowed himself a small breath of relief, when he heard the sound of police sirens approaching at speed on the road behind him. He looked in the rear view mirror to see the blue lights coming up too fast for him to pull into the side. But they weren't waiting. Brief panic took hold of him as he thought the emergency vehicles were going to plough into the back of his misappropriated car, but just before any impact, the police cars, four of them he counted, pulled onto the central reservation and whizzed past him, sirens screaming. Looking ahead, he could make out the BMW driver also pulling onto the central reservation up ahead, and he realised that this was who they were after.

"Suspect travelling north on the south-bound carriage, sir," Lawson received in his earpiece. The control room was quickly filling with too many personnel for him to keep track of.

"Ring the bastard's neck when you get him," he responded.

"Affirmative."

The BMW driver cut across oncoming traffic on the opposite carriageway and sped on into the industrial park that lay beyond it. The four police cars did the same, and the blaze of lights and sirens faded. As the line of traffic Natesh was in began to crawl forward once more, more emergency vehicles arrived from other directions, all apparently in pursuit of the BMW. He wondered what the poor sod had done.

He looked out of his window and saw, as if in slow motion, a trickle of pedestrians making their way towards a fire crew stationed at the main junction. The trickle was joined by steady streams of office and factory workers, who began to spill from the many buildings lining the carriageway. Orderly. Shuffling. Some joking, like kids at a fire drill. But on closer examination, it was clear that they were bewildered, wondering if they'd been subjected to some prank, and not knowing how to react. Pissed off and stroppy, wanting to get back on with what they'd been doing when there was nothing obvious to see out here. Unreal how quickly the streets became packed with people walking, all seeking direction. Natesh could barely tear his eyes from them, watching as the first signs of crushing appeared as two key pedestrian routes merged. A loudspeaker pleaded for calm. Blue flashing lights were everywhere now. Sirens could be heard all around.

Natesh glanced at the unfamiliar dashboard, and found the radio.

" . . . Angus and Grampian are subject to emergency evacuation procedures. If you live or work in the following towns and areas, please evacuate now and follow the instructions of emergency personnel. This is not a drill. The population centres along the coastline of Angus and Grampian are subject to emergency evacuation procedures. If you live or work in . . . "

Natesh's attention switched back to the people filling the streets.

Perspiration formed across his top lip.

His car inched forward, and stopped again. He looked to his right, and saw a large group of people gathered around something. An electrical outlet. Were they raiding it? No, he saw, and his mouth dropped open when he saw what was captivating them. Large TV screens inside the shop were broadcasting aerial footage of their city. He glanced upwards, and saw the media helicopter up there. Images of growing lines of evacuees on foot, road blocks turning traffic away from the city, soldiers pouring into the area, flashing blue lights everywhere, flashed across a multitude of screens.

Natesh pressed more buttons on the radio, seeking other channels, but all he got was the same pre-recorded evacuation message.

Back on the TV screens in the electrical outlet, the cameras panned to what appeared to be a school and the chaotic scenes around it. Buses arriving to ship large numbers of kids out. Parents running towards the gates. Confusion. Yelling parents being pushed back out of the school gates, fighting back against the police, buses shuddering to a stop as kids pushed their way back off.

The footage from the school was relayed immediately to Lawson.

"Bloody hell, get them away from there!" he yelled onto the radio command at the closest road block.

"They're panicking about their kids!" came the frantic reply.

"They'll all be gassed to death if they obstruct the evacuation," Lawson said.

"We need help up here. It's turning ugly."

Lawson looked at the footage again. "Just get them out."

Road blocks. Natesh looked up and ahead. At the next roundabout, the way north was closed and the entire dual carriageway had been turned into a four-lane south bound route back out of Dundee.

"No!" Natesh found himself unable to stop shouting out of his window. "I need to get through, please!"

His yells were swallowed up in the mayhem and the rising hysteria. When it came to his turn, the police officer at the road block knocked on the roof of his car and directed him into the south-bound flow.

No eye contact.

No time to explain.

Everyone out.

End of.

Like everyone else, he would drive south towards Perth. At the main roundabout, like everyone else, his car would be loaded hastily with as many pedestrian evacuees as it could contain, and he'd be directed on his way, along roads lined with uniformed personnel. He was stopped and three businessmen and an elderly woman were bundled in. Only one lane ran into the city, and along it came lines as far as the eye could see of ambulances, fire, police, Army and security vehicles, and buses.

Natesh's head was pounding. Donna! How was he to get to Donna? Who would rescue her? He had to get to Hunter's quarry, but there was no way through the city or anywhere in that direction. He had no way to contact Danny. Natesh and his passengers were frantically trying to call on their mobiles, but the networks were overloaded. The whole country was watching the evacuation of

235

north-east Scotland. Refugee centres were being set up well beyond the exclusion zone. There was no way in.

Chapter Fifty-seven

"I hope we get there in time."

"We don't even know for sure that she's there. She could be anywhere."

DC Dom Hilton knew better than to argue back with Ted Granger. He let the sergeant drive on, without further comment. They'd made slow progress out of Dundee, and radio contact with Ross had been shaky. The soldier at the first roadblock had refused to let them through without the necessary permissions, and that had been the moment that the radio reception had cut out. For nine minutes they'd sat there, and Dom had harboured real fears that Ted Granger was going to have a stroke. He'd never seen anyone's face grow so purple before. But the word had finally reached the soldier, and they'd been allowed through to make their way towards Forfar, skirting their way to the quarry from the north and west, a direction that would let them avoid any traffic escaping Arbroath from the east.

Please, let us get there in time, Dom prayed silently.

Danny left Libby's Focus sitting by a farm gate half a mile further on from the quarry, and made his way back to it on foot.

Believing the quarry to be deserted he began to explore. He started to pick his way around the lip of the quarry face to find a vantage point from which to view his surroundings, when he heard an engine gun and voices raised back up at ground level.

He hunkered down, alert to the possibility of danger. This particular slope that he'd stopped on looked like a dumping chute, and he was gripped with a fear that if rubble were to come tumbling down it now he'd be caught in its violent descent and his bones would end up smashed among the rocks at the bottom of the quarry.

The engine sounded like a huge vehicle, and Danny scrambled as quickly as his adrenalin could propel him off the track and into the bushes that sprung out of the rocks beside it. The voices, which he could hear intermittently through the roar of the engine, didn't sound friendly, and Danny decided that it would clearly be in his best interests to stay hidden.

With the self preservation instinct on red alert, Danny picked his mobile phone from his pocket and put it on silent. It would have been just the thing, he thought, for it to ring now, and to give away his whereabouts. At the same time, he so desperately wanted it to ring, and it to be Libby. Or Donna. Or Sally. He was desperate to know where they were.

Then he heard a commotion from up on ground level.

More shouting, and what sounded like a woman groaning.

"Just under five minutes from the quarry now," said Ted Granger. It was the first he'd spoken since they'd left the main road and joined this single track lane. They crossed a narrow ford at a hairpin bend, and Granger dropped into second gear, craning his neck out the window.

Dom wiped away the beads of sweat that had formed on his top lip and sat up straighter, his muscles tensing instinctively. There was a small tin sign post marking the way to the quarry.

With his heart jack-hammering in his chest, Danny scrambled to the top of the slope, and looked over. And there he stayed, motionless and wide-eyed, watching two men dragging a woman towards a huge truck. The woman was bloodied, her body slumped between the two men, her feet trailing, lifeless, in the gravel. There was no mistaking, it was Donna.

When they set her down on the ground, she didn't move.

Danny recoiled when he saw that the taller of the two men was holding a gun; he stuffed his fist into his mouth and watched, horrified, as the younger man opened the cabin door of the truck. Both of them heaved Donna up and slung her onto the floor of the passenger side. Then the younger man jumped into the cabin and sat with his feet resting on her lifeless form.

"Burial at sea," he heard the man with the gun say, before he climbed into the cabin and steered the truck from the quarry gates.

Danny wiped sweat from his brow as he clambered forward from his position. He was clammy all over, and his head wasn't feeling so good.

He scanned the area around the Portakabin, but saw no signs of anyone else there; he hauled himself up onto the gravel track and ran towards the gate. He caught sight of the truck heading in the direction from which he'd come, but he had no idea what he should do. Follow it? Search around the Portakabin? Get the hell out of here? He was a chef, he thought. He wasn't cut out for this Dan Brown stuff.

His fingers were acting ahead of his brain, punching nine-nine-nine into his mobile. But to his confusion, he'd been greeted by a message that told him the network was busy. Then he'd heard the roar of helicopters approaching, and he ran.

At first he'd run in the same direction as the truck, then he remembered Libby's car. He'd left it parked beyond the quarry gates in the opposite direction, and so he turned and ran that way instead.

Danny made a decision. Yanking the Focus round one hundred and eighty degrees, he went after the truck. As he started following the truck along the lane the helicopters swooped past, and for a moment Danny had feared they were following him, but they flew on past him, hurrying to their destination.

Danny was, however, quite unaware of the dark blue van approaching slowly behind him down the twisty road.

Evanton leaned out of the truck window and looked up. The sudden roar of helicopters almost made him duck in alarm. They were getting this evacuation underway more quickly than he'd expected, and although the road blocks hadn't reached these back roads yet, he was sure that his original plan of making his way to the reservoir in Dundee – half an hour's drive from here – would be out of the question. No matter, he thought. He could make it to Arbroath harbour instead. Water was water, and it reacted just the same with MIC.

Though they may have been quick with the evacuation, he thought, they were still fools if they thought he hadn't noticed the unmarked patrol car now attempting to tail him covertly. And in a Focus! Well, Evanton decided, he'd have a little surprise for them before they left this back road. He'd show them what he could do.

He ran briefly through his mind how it would go once he got to Arbroath. He touched the gas mask that sat on top of his head, all set to just pull down over his face at the last minute. The code that would detonate the lid off the huge MIC drum once he got it into the water was keyed into his mobile phone. The truck lift, he thought with a sudden twinge of anxiety, he hadn't tested that. No reason to think it would be faulty, though, this was a fairly new truck. At the press of a button, the drum would be heaved into the sea. Then five numbers. That was all it would take. Laughably simple. Talking of which, he thought irritably, why did that Estonian half-wit keep giggling to himself?

"No sign of anybody here," said Granger standing outside the Portakabin.

The officers had noticed the smell of diesel exhaust fumes when they'd reached the quarry, telling them there had been vehicle activity here immediately before they'd arrived. With tree lines all around obscuring their view, there was no way of telling what it had been, but there was only one direction it could have gone in.

Dom ran from path to path down the quarry sides, scanning frantically for any form that could be Donna. Nothing.

Relieved, he returned to the Portakabin door, from which Ted was emerging cautiously.

"It looks like someone's been here," said Ted. "There's a lot of blood on the floor."

He left the implication hanging in the air, and after a brief pause, the two officers hurried back to their van. They were in pursuit now. They had to catch up with the vehicle they were sure had just left these gates.

There was a flash of the Focus in the rear view mirror, Evanton saw. Still following him, then. And with no back-up, it seemed, as the helicopters had passed onwards towards Dundee. Well, it was about time to get rid of them now, he decided. Time to show them what they were dealing with. Regain the upper hand and get this situation back under control. He eased off the accelerator.

Caught unawares, the Focus found itself in full view and closer to the truck than it wanted to be.

Chapter Fifty-eight

Hunter's palms were clammy, almost to the point of slipping off the steering wheel. The road was unusually busy, and this double roundabout was a nightmare. His impatience began to turn to rage, and throwing caution to the wind he pulled out where he should have given way. Immediately he was bombarded by a hail of peeping horns and angry voices, and he knew he had contributed to further clogging up the road.

He saw the look of disgust on the face of the driver who urged him to overtake himself in order to get the traffic moving again; he drove past him, keeping his eyes firmly ahead.

Then he heard them. Sirens. He knew they were for him.

Looking in his rear view mirror he couldn't make out the number of cars with flashing blue lights, but there were several, and they were in a hurry. Hesitating, he felt sure they could not get through the line of traffic to reach him – there was no room on the road for the vehicles on it to pull aside. But to his horror, he saw them veer onto the central reservation and close the distance to him.

Gulping in fear and alarm, he barely looked before pressing his foot onto the accelerator and swinging the BMW right across to the other side of the road. He ignored the beeping of horns and the insults that flew in his direction. There was a light industrial park over there, he could surely lose his pursuers and buy himself some time.

The engine roared as he failed to change gears, seeking only to get himself into the shelter of the industrial units that lay dark and silent before him.

He veered into the industrial estate and swore. The doors of the nearest unit flew open and a line of workers poured out, heading towards him. The car stalled, and cursing, Hunter leaped from the vehicle and ran towards the building, running against the flow of workers.

A helicopter appeared overhead, drowning out a muffled voice that had begun to call out over a loud speaker, "Please follow the directions of the emergency services personnel."

The parking area filled rapidly with people as more doors burst open, seemingly in all directions; office workers and labourers swarmed together in confusion. Loudspeakers urged them onwards, away from the buildings. It took only moments, from what Hunter could see, for an orderly exit to descend into chaos. It seemed to begin at the gates leading out onto the main street. The first group to reach them had stopped to see what was going on behind them; further groups arrived just as lines of pedestrians hurried past with armed Marine escorts.

"What the fuck's going on?" someone shouted, squaring up to a soldier who was gesturing at him with a gun.

People still inside the buildings began trying to push their way out. Hunter watched them darting in different directions, knocking into one another, throwing punches. It was pandemonium and mayhem.

He pressed himself against a wall, unable to believe what he was seeing. He began to think that maybe there had been a bomb threat in one of these buildings, when he saw a line of uniformed police officers running through the melee towards him. Bomb or no bomb, Hunter ran further inside the building and found the stairwell. Already gasping for breath, he rushed up the stairs, and with his lungs bursting in protest, *Thank God I don't smoke*, he made it to the top floor and scrambled out onto the factory roof.

The cold air hit him like a sledgehammer as the wind whipped across the top of the building. He had to hold on tight to his jacket to stop it flapping wildly. He barely kept his balance as he stumbled towards the roof edge.

He looked behind him. Two uniformed officers emerged onto the roof, but they stopped abruptly, putting out their hands in a submissive gesture.

"Mr. Hunter," shouted one. "We just want to talk to you."

"We've got him," the voice in Lawson's ear piece confirmed.

"Ross, talk him down. Quickly," Lawson ordered.

Hunter took a quick look over the side of the building. It hadn't looked this high from ground level. There was no way he'd survive a jump – he'd barely survived the run up the stairs. He was cornered, yet the officers remained at a distance.

What would they care if he jumped, he wondered? What was he

to them? Then, why didn't they come for him? He wasn't armed. He'd made no attempts to make any threats. He found no clues to help him make a decision, and simply stood, petrified, on the edge of the roof.

Below him, the chaotic running was still going on, but the crowd was growing thinner as people streamed from the complex. From this height, Hunter could now see the wider vicinity. He could see to his right the road along which he'd been driving. It was blocked at the roundabout. There were soldiers, he saw, directing the traffic back around in the opposite direction. All traffic, he could see, was heading out of the city. And there were crowds of people walking. Walking as far as he could see, chaperoned by uniformed personnel, all leaving Dundee.

"Mr. Hunter," he heard again. The voice on the loud speaker caused him to stumble forward, and he found himself on all fours, staring down over the roof at the vertical drop.

"Mr. Hunter, we need your help."

Help? My help?

"Mr. Hunter, we're running out of time. Can you tell us where Jonas Evanton has taken the MIC?"

Evanton? They're asking me about him?

His shoulders slumped as it hit him that they knew about the MIC. And that meant they knew about everything. He was finished. He looked back down over the edge of the roof. Surely he wouldn't feel anything, if he just . . . ?

Wait a minute. Where Evanton has taken the MIC?

He looked along the streets again, and knew now that what he was witnessing was an evacuation. Of the whole city. There was no bomb. That fucking maniac was going to gas the city.

Self-preservation took hold of Hunter, and he made an attempt to run for the stair well, until he saw the two officers and remembered that the way was blocked. He spun back round to the edge of the building.

"Mr. Hunter, please," said the voice on the loud speaker. He knew now why it sounded so frantic. He looked down, and saw that it was a tall, red-haired officer. Softly spoken, a Highland lilt, Hunter noted.

"I don't know," he shouted back. "I'm sorry, I don't know."

His teeth began to chatter. For once, he was telling the truth, and it was useless.

A woman's voice behind him made him turn around. It was one of the officers by the stair well. She hadn't moved, but she was talking to him now.

"Mr. Hunter, we need to find Jonas Evanton," she was saying.

With his teeth still chattering, Hunter sank to his knees, and the officer took a step towards him.

"Who the fuck is that up there with him?" Lawson demanded, seeing the footage of a figure drawing towards Hunter

"I don't know. Just wait," said Ross into his ear piece. He was pretty certain it was Alice Moone. If it was, he was just as certain that she'd do a better job of talking Hunter down than he ever could. He closed his ear to Lawson's frantic yelling.

"Ross, get back onto that loud speaker. That's an order."

When Hunter made no attempt to move, the officer took several hesitant steps more, until she was by his side. She knelt beside him, placing a hand on his back. A light hand, Hunter thought. Gentle.

"I said that's an order, Ross!"

"I'm Sergeant Alice Moone," the woman said. "We've received a threat from Jonas Evanton. He's going to release the MIC, but we don't know where. Is there anything you can tell us? Please? There are thousands of lives at risk. You're the only one who can help us."

A helicopter hovered above the building. Inside it, an excited Lindsey Forsyth sat listening to the pilot on headphones as they recorded the events going on below them.

"You got that?"

"Yep, right on it," she said, scribbling down with all her might all the details she could glean.

"Can you make out what they're saying?"

"Three . . . two . . . one . . . You're on."

"I'm here live . . . " she began, when static broke in on the line, and she heard a broadcast from police or Army radios, she couldn't tell which.

"How the fuck did they get into secured airspace? Get them to a safe distance right now!"

Lindsey looked out of the helicopter door, and found herself staring at the end of a machine gun held by a soldier sitting precariously on the lip of another helicopter that had appeared out of nowhere.

Back on the roof, the woman's voice was soothing. Calming. They weren't after him, Hunter realised. Perhaps if he helped them now, they'd take that into account later, he thought. But it was hopeless.

"I don't know where he is," said Hunter. His thoughts were muddled. All he could see in his mind was the chaotic scene of all those people running everywhere. And the noise of helicopters was getting worse. He held his hands over his head.

"Where did he take the MIC from?" said Alice Moone.

Hunter froze. His own quarry, that's where from. But how could he tell her that?

"We don't have much time," said Alice. "We need to find Jonas. If we know where he took the MIC from, we can work out where he might be now."

"The reservoir," said Hunter suddenly. "I remember he talked about the reservoir. That's where he's going." He stopped talking when he saw her shake her head.

"He can't get into Dundee," she said, "And he can't travel inside the city. We have road blocks at every junction. Where did he leave from with the MIC?"

He edged away from her, trying to think. But the air flow and the sudden noise as a helicopter swooped down caught him. He lost his footing, and heard the police officer cry out as he plummeted from the roof.

"Fuck, fuck, fuck!" Lawson yelled as his ear piece was bombarded with voices.

Talking to him? Talking to each other?

"We've located the suspect, confirm Arbroath."

"Only one helicopter up there? What is this? All resources north, now!"

"We're seeing a number of police and Army helicopters gathering over the coastline, and they seem to be heading north."

Struggling to draw breath, he felt the pain travel down his arm. *Oh shit*, thought Lawson.

Chapter Fifty-nine

"What the fuck?"

"What the . . . ?" Ted Granger slammed on the brakes. Directly in front of them, driving at a snail's pace, was a Focus. In rapid pursuit of the vehicle that had left the quarry, Ted's foot had been pressed hard on the accelerator, while he wound the van around the twists and turns of the country road. The last thing he expected was this. Where had it come from? They had passed no openings from the fields, the only way the Focus could have joined this road and ended up here in front of them. Unless it too had come from the quarry.

Ted's reflexes were quick and the van's brakes were sharp, but even so, they drew uncomfortably close to the Focus's back end before they managed to pull back from collision. Ted glared into the Focus and saw, in its rear view mirror, the frightened eyes of a young man.

"Who's this tosser?" he muttered. And he let a little more distance open between the van and the car.

Dom Hilton was sitting bolt upright now, his queasiness at the winding road giving way to alarm bells.

"Where the fuck did he come from?"

The Focus's brake lights came on, and Ted brought the van's speed down further. They were moving so slowly now that Dom was sure he'd be able to jump from the van and jog up past the Focus. He undid his seatbelt.

"Lone driver," Ted commented. "But he looks scared. And he's doing less than twenty. He can only have come from the quarry. I think there could be somebody in there with him, hiding. Call for back-up." But the words were barely out of his mouth, when he remembered that back-up was not on the menu for today. They were on their own out here. He stole a glance at Dom as he inched the van closer towards the Focus.

Do or die, he thought. They were going to intercept.

Iksan sat perfectly still, his eyes glazed as he stared ahead. The gently rolling countryside, new leaves unfurling into the fresh spring air on trees all around, afforded him very little sense of where he was or what direction he was travelling in. It was impossible to see along the road for more than a tiny distance, what with all the twists and turns. He kept his mind firmly off the fact that his feet were resting on top of the body of a woman that he'd been helpless to save. But his blank mind fog was disturbed by the growing restlessness of Evanton. Something was irking the maniac. Iksan looked into the wing mirror, but saw nothing other than the greenery they were passing. Then, with a painful thud, he found himself thrown against the dash as Evanton pulled the truck to a sudden stop. Nothing was in front of them. Iksan checked the road behind them again, and there, skidding to a halt and barely missing the back of the truck, came a small car.

Iksan flinched at the torrent of fury that erupted from Evanton. He watched, appalled, as Evanton pulled back the safety catch on his gun and leaped from the truck.

Danny cried out loud when he rounded the bend and found himself almost running into the back of the truck. This was the middle of nowhere. Why had it stopped? Then he felt the blood drain from his head as he glanced in his rear view mirror to see a van come to a halt behind him. He hadn't noticed it before, while he'd concentrated on the truck. Instinct took over as he threw himself to the floor and braced his arms over his head.

Dom Hilton felt his heart beat faster in his chest than he'd ever felt it before. Ted had hinted at his fear that the driver of the Focus might not be alone, and that a firearm might be involved. Crouched low so as to keep in the driver's blind spot as much as possible, Dom crept towards the passenger door, while Ted made for the driver side. But the driver wasn't in sight now. Then, from around the corner ahead of them, Dom heard the slam of a large vehicle door. In slow motion, both he and Ted stood up, and watched, helpless and astounded, as their own colleague, Detective Inspector Jonas Evanton, appeared before them and aimed a gun in their direction. Before a single word could be spoken a shot rang out and blew half of Ted's face away. Dom's hands flew up to protect himself and he shouted incoherently at Evanton. He didn't hear the second shot, the one that entered his own chest, before his lifeless body slumped onto the bonnet of the Focus.

Try calling that one in, thought Evanton. Holding his eyes on the two dead officers for a moment, he satisfied himself that their pursuit was over, and returned to the truck. Too bad he had other things to attend to, he thought. But there'd be more dying soon enough. His breath quickened.

Chapter Sixty

PC Aiden Moore found himself afraid, for the first time in his short career, as he tried to talk down an angry crowd of people. The evacuation call had gone out, and most of the resources had gone immediately to Dundee. As far as Aiden could tell, they'd been left to it here in Arbroath, and he was finding that instead of heading north out of the town towards Aberdeen, people were making their way into the town's main street. Because heading north would mean passing the farm house where there had just been a double murder. And so soon after the incident in the town's new restaurant, rumours and conspiracy theories were running high.

Nobody in the station had anticipated this, that so many people would make their way to the harbour, of all places. It wasn't generally a meeting point. Even three nights ago, when the restaurant incident had happened, the harbour had remained empty. People had gathered primarily outside the restaurant that night, of course, but also in the town square and outside the library. Not here at the harbour. So Aiden had been sent to scout out the harbour alone, what with resources being so thinly spread, never imagining a crowd like this gathering. As he faced them, he noticed another large group approaching from the direction of the football pitch.

Of course, he realised, the visiting supporters for the cup game had come here, seeing the harbour as a natural meeting place, and the crowd was growing larger by the minute. He quickly radioed for help that was unlikely to arrive any time soon.

"Calm down, calm down," he yelled, sounding anything but calm himself. There were too many people in this small space.

"Is it true there's a madman on the loose with the gas?"

"We're not leaving our town!"

"How long have the police known about this?"

"Is this a military experiment gone wrong?"

Aiden was facing a mob of seventy, maybe ninety, that now blocked the end of the main street and hemmed the harbour in.

The harbour was surrounded on three sides by a narrow footpath. Opening out on the east, it gave directly on to the choppy North

Sea. The harbour itself was filled with a variety of moored yachts and tugs, and the southern footpath sat level with the tops of yacht rigging. From there, it was an easy jump on board some of the majestically expensive vessels. But the western and northern footpaths topped a perilous thirty-foot drop into black water. For such an awful precipice, it was a wonder there were almost never any accidents here, especially when there was no safety fence. For Aiden Moore, finding himself trapped by the angry crowd, this was little comfort. He was terrified of heights. Above the shouting from the mob, Aiden thought he heard a faint rumbling drawing closer.

"Move back, please," he shouted into the din. "Move back!" *Where the hell is my back-up?* He quickly wiped the sweat from his top lip and made another call, this time less polite, to the station.

The rumbling noise grew louder. It sounded like a very large vehicle moving through the town. Aiden stretched his head up, but couldn't see beyond the crowd. However, he could see some of them turning around in response to the noise heading towards them, and hear shouting from the far end of the crowd.

He tried to take a step forward, to push his way through, but a wall of people pressed tightly together, pinning him where he was. He gulped as he glanced at the drop behind him, and his head swam a little. As the rumbling turned into a roar, the gleaming hood of a massive truck loomed in front of him.

"Jesus Christ," he said, as the truck ploughed into the people standing in front of him.

Like skittles, they were thrown back, into the water, and under the huge wheels. Panicked voices filled the air, and the sickening ferrous smell of blood rose with it. Huge brakes squealed and hissed savagely as the articulated dumper truck came to an abrupt stop alongside the walkway, and the press of people pitched Aiden Moore backward over the harbour wall.

From her hiding place among the rocks at the cliffs, Sally began to sense that something was going on nearby. She could hear a commotion coming from the direction of the harbour, but she was too scared to come out of hiding. This den was one she'd found only a couple of days ago, when she'd sauntered around these cliffs admiring their geology, and knowing about it now had saved her life. Evanton had scoured the cliffs back and forth, furious at having lost her, but she'd managed to stay hidden. And she wasn't ready to come out yet. Although she was sure it was a number of hours since she'd seen him drive off in his Audi, she was terrified that he might still be here.

She still couldn't quite believe that she'd managed to escape. One minute he'd had her pinned against a wall, with his intent terrifyingly clear, and the next minute he'd been looking down at himself, stalling at his unexpected lack of erection, and in this momentary lapse, Sally's knee had acted almost of its own will and struck him hard in the groin, making him double over in pain. She had taken her chance and bolted. Her feet had easily found their way to the hideout where she now sat, and in only moments she had been out of Evanton's sight.

But where was he now? Gingerly, she crawled from her hiding place. Her knee hurt badly from where she'd fallen in the cave. Her shoulder hurt, too, from her forcible collision with the rock wall, and her ankle was aching again. But this was survival. Sally had heard the gunshots – blending into the afternoon sounds of the seashore and countryside, she knew they were gunshots; she'd seen the gun – fired in Evanton's frustration as he'd searched for her, and she was under no illusion as to the narrowness of her escape today. But she was going to make it. Her mother and her sisters needed her. And if she had a chance now to see her father again, she wanted to take it. She'd learned that life was too short and too precious. So she'd be the bigger person, and make amends with him.

Danny dragged himself from his trance and looked around to find himself driving down Arbroath's main street. He'd followed the truck at a distance for some seven miles from the quarry, never taking his eyes from it, and with no idea what he would do when it stopped. He had repeatedly tried to shake from his mind's eye the awful sight of the young police officer sprawled dead across the bonnet of his car the last time the truck had stopped.

Now that he was in the town, he brought the Focus's speed down. He knew this road led to the harbour, and ultimately into the sea. The truck was going to have to stop.

He brought the Focus to a stop, horrified as the truck ploughed ahead at speed. It made the hairs stand up on the back of his neck.

There were people, he saw, standing around the harbour. A lot of people. The truck was speeding towards them, but none of them were trying to get out of the way, intent on shouting at something up ahead. Finally some of them turned around and noticed the approaching vehicle.

Danny hurled himself out of the car door.

"Move!" he screamed. "Fucking move!" The truck careered into the crowd, pitching people into the air like rag dolls. Then it screeched and shuddered to a halt.

There was a split second of silence, then mayhem erupted. Danny staggered for several steps along the road, and when he saw people come running from side streets towards the desperate calls for help coming from the carnage at the harbour, he stumbled after them until he felt the nausea rising up his throat and he dropped to his knees, vomiting in the street.

Iksan had watched the farmer being knifed to death, Gorak being shot, and now Evanton was about to tip poison into the water. He couldn't take any more. He began to giggle. And he was shivering uncontrollably.

This is where it all ends, he thought. He only hoped they would manage to take Evanton alive. He didn't deserve the release of death, when they could make him suffer so much more. With another giggle, Iksan slid his eyes to his tormentor.

The element of surprise, he thought. Evanton's plan hadn't been difficult for him to work out, and he'd stolen some moments at the quarry to make sure it couldn't happen. *He has no idea.*

When the truck sickeningly hit human bodies, and Iksan heard the shocked screams and the horrific thuds against the huge vehicle, he threw up into his own lap.

"Out," ordered Evanton, as he backed the truck onto the harbour footpath. The engine was still running, the metallic smell of blood rising above the diesel, and the harbour walls seemed to reverberate with the noise of it. Without so much as a second thought, or a moment to survey the carnage spread around the truck, Evanton set the truck's lift until its angle made the huge drum filled with MIC begin to roll slowly.

It won't happen, Iksan told himself confidently.

With a deafening rush, the drum gained momentum and rolled

from the truck and into the water.

Iksan almost threw up. What if he hadn't got it right? All these people would die. He'd never managed to do much right in his life so far.

Evanton brought out his gun, and clambered on to the top of the truck cabin.

"Get up here," he said to Iksan. Iksan climbed up. He looked at Evanton, saw the smirk on his face and his eyes wild with power. Iksan leaned over, saw the drum plunge below the water level, and flinched back.

Inside the truck cabin, Donna's body lay, battered, bloodied and unresponsive to the clamour that filled the air outside. Her skin was pale and cold, her hair matted and congealed. She showed no visible sign of life.

The circle of frantic and shouting people widened around the truck. People were jostling and shoving, trying to get back, yet still craning to see what was going on.

A faint hum hinted at a helicopter approaching from the distance.

"This is the part where you all die," said Evanton, his voice carrying surprisingly far in the immense din. Iksan experienced a sudden moment of clarity, and it was filled with despair and fear. A huge vat of toxic chemical had just been dumped into the water. He stared at the crowd of people gathered around the truck, and was surprised to see two of them aiming phones at him, filming it all.

Evanton took out his mobile phone.

"Say goodbye to your loved ones," he shouted. He pulled the gas mask from the top of his head down over his face. The yelling and the jostling panic in the crowd grew worse at the sight of the gas mask, and several people spontaneously rushed at the truck to stop him. But with barely a glance in their direction, he fired his pistol and felled one of them, sending the others scuttling onto all fours in terror. Iksan heard cries of "*Davie!*" and saw two men in football scarves scrambling towards the man who'd just been shot.

Evanton ignored them. He keyed a series of numbers into his phone; the code that would blow the vat open, releasing the MIC to form a massive toxic cloud that none of these people had a chance of surviving.

Mad scrambling broke out among the crowd, as people attempted to flee the man in the gas mask. But it would be futile, thought Evanton. The gas would reach them faster than they could run. He had seen that happen in Bhopal. They'd drop like flies, gasping and burning. Blinded and dying. Just like they had done back then. All these people dying. His breath quickened.

But something was wrong.

Evanton looked down into the water. The vat hadn't blown.

Confused, he looked at his phone, and keyed in the trigger code again.

Nothing.

Slowly he turned and looked at Iksan, alerted to the youth's defiant grin.

Iksan had watched Evanton work on the mobile phone back at the quarry. He knew enough schoolboy electronics to recognise a makeshift trigger when he saw one, and he'd misspent enough of his adolescent hours to be able to reconfigure a code.

"No half-wit now, eh?" he challenged.

"You? You changed the code?"

He looked at the useless device then back at Iksan.

He levelled the gun at Iksan's temple. "What did you re-code it to?"

Iksan let out a wild peel of laughter.

"Tell me the code now," said Evanton. "You want your mother to have to see your battered body? To have to bury her son? What's the code?"

Iksan dropped his head. His mother. What was she going to have to go through because of him?

"You can go to hell," he said slowly, looking back into Evanton's eyes.

"Put the gun down!" shouted a voice.

Evanton's attention was briefly drawn to a team of uniformed police officers who'd reached the harbour. He brandished his gun. He knew what they thought of him now, one of their own. There was no way they'd ever show him any mercy. He took aim, and fired again.

Inside the truck cabin, the sound of gunshots made Donna's eyes flicker. She coughed, spitting a mouthful of blood. Each shallow breath she managed to take made her ribs burn with pain. She couldn't lift her head. Her consciousness drifted in and out of a black fog, but little by little the fog began to shift. She couldn't understand where she was. What was happening to her?

Danny looked up from his position on the road. His head was pounding, and for a split second he thought he'd been having a nightmare. But up ahead, he saw the wall of people, swarming back and forth, pushing and shouting.

Slowly, he stood up and stumbled towards the scene. Above the heads of the crowd, he could see two men standing on top of the truck, one of them wearing a gas mask. The one who'd killed the two police officers on the road into the town. He watched a small group of men attempting to charge at the truck, and saw the first one drop dead before hearing the crack of the bullet. He saw a group of police officers approach the truck. Then the man in the gas mask levelled his gun towards the police officers, and Danny heard another shot.

He stopped in his tracks. He knew he needed to get out of here. Now. A rush of adrenaline prepared him to run faster than he'd ever run in his life. But as he turned, he heard a voice wildly calling for help. It seemed to be coming from beyond the harbour wall, and was failing to attract anyone else's attention. Danny ran towards the voice, skirting around the truck and keeping out of view of the gunman.

When he reached the wall, he looked over and was astonished to see a police officer clinging to the drop above the water.

"Help!"

"Here," called Danny. He lay flat on the path and reached down towards the stranded officer. He yelped as the officer grabbed his arm and felt himself being pulled towards the edge of the wall. But before he could react further, the officer managed to grip the top of the wall with his other hand, relieving Danny of some of the weight. Together they heaved the shaken officer up onto the path.

"Oh God," gasped Aiden Moore. "Thank you." He took several gulps of air. "What's going on up there?"

They were crouched next to one of the truck's huge wheels, the only two people on this side of it.

"The truck rammed into a whole lot of people," said Danny. "I followed it into town. The driver shot two police officers, about two miles back. And Donna . . . Donna's in the front cabin. I think she's dead."

"Donna? Oh God," said Aiden, trying to clear his spinning head and sitting up beside Danny. "Are there police or Army round there?"

"Five or six police round the other side," said Danny. "He shot at them, but I don't know if anyone got hit. He's wearing a gas mask. What the hell is he doing?"

"Try to calm down," said Aiden. "I'm going to make my way round there." He pointed to a front wheel. "Stay behind me. If the gunman looks in our direction, tell me immediately. I'm going to try and get a look inside the cabin."

Danny nodded his understanding, and scrambled on all fours after Aiden.

The shot from Evanton's gun fired wide and hit stonework beyond the group of police officers. They tightened their circle around him, holding steady. Evanton looked about, frantically seeking an escape. The whir of an approaching helicopter made him look up.

Lindsey Forsyth, appearing directly above the scene in the media helicopter, caught Evanton's wild stare.

"These are astonishing scenes," she reported, aware that the world's eyes would be pinned to their screens and millions would be listening to every word of her commentary. "The man, believed to be Jonas Evanton, a serving officer with Tayside Police, seems to be surrounded now. I can see what appears to be an unarmed civilian climbing onto the truck roof behind Evanton."

Aiden and Danny reached the cabin door, but Danny couldn't bear to look. That bastard had killed Donna. In a rage-filled surge of adrenalin, Danny clambered up onto the truck roof and almost collided with Iksan, who stared back in astonishment. Evanton's foot slid, and he almost fell as he spun round to see who had appeared at his back. He opened his mouth in surprise; it was Danny Quinn. A cacophony of angry and worried voices shouted at Danny to get back down. Camera phones caught his every move. Danny ignored them and advanced on Evanton. Evanton lashed out with the gun and struck him on the side of the head, but the blow failed to meet its target with any force, and Danny kicked out at Evanton's ankle. Evanton lost his balance and fell to his knees, losing hold of the gun. Iksan took his chance, and leaped from the truck roof.

Donna saw the gun fall past the open door of the truck, and heard it clatter onto the ground outside. She became aware of the sounds of men fighting somewhere above her head and the thrashing of helicopter blades not far above. With a sweat forming across her forehead, she heaved herself across the truck floor towards the opened door. She squinted painfully outside. The sunlight dazzled her after the dimness of the cabin. But she opened her mouth to breathe in the fresh air in quick, painful gasps. When she managed to open her eyes, she saw Iksan lying next to the truck wheel, whimpering in pain and clutching his shin, but she was unable to muster a response. Then Aiden Moore was there in front of her. Was she hallucinating now?

Aiden touched her head tenderly, then put a finger to his lips. "Shush," he whispered, "it's going to be okay. I'm going to get you help."

Evanton waited on his knees, not moving a muscle, as Danny advanced on him, fists balled in front of him.

Pathetic, thought Evanton. He could see that Iksan was in trouble, writhing on the ground below. It was a possible escape route, and Danny Quinn was going to help him get away.

Emboldened by Evanton's lack of movement, Danny drew close and held back his fist to deliver a blow. But as soon as his arm was raised, Evanton leaped up and grasped his head in an arm-lock, and twisted his neck. He tossed Danny's body over the front of the truck into the ring of police officers to create as much disturbance as possible. Then he slid down the side of the truck to get away.

Donna saw the shoes appear from above the rim of the truck door. Expensive shoes. A hate-filled rage engulfed her, and she thrust her arm out of the door. Her hand stretched out desperately grasping at the air. She gave her all and grabbed at Evanton's ankle.

"What the fuck?" she heard him shout out.

257

He lost his balance, and Donna saw him fall and land next to Iksan. She heard him grunt as the air was forced from his lungs by the impact.

Evanton squinted up, and saw Donna leaning from the truck cabin, lying flat out on the floor, with her bloodied arm dangling out of the door.

"Bitch!" he mouthed, and he drew his finger across his throat. But it was too late for Evanton. With a roar, Aiden Moore flew at him with a force that knocked him onto his stomach, with his face pressed into the dirt as he was handcuffed.

Danny landed heavily on the group of police officers, and felt a sickening crunch in his ankle. His neck felt as though it was on fire, but he couldn't believe he'd survived. As soon as he'd landed, all but one of the police officers had scrambled from the melee and run around to the truck cabin. The remaining officer sat next to Danny, loudly cursing and holding what looked like a broken nose.

"It's over! It's all over!" Danny heard shouted from the cabin side. Then he heard another voice frantically calling his name. It was Sally. Leaning up onto one elbow, he searched her out. There, across the northern edge of the harbour where the road joined the shingle beach, he saw her. She was running towards him.

An unnatural hush fell on the groups of people huddled around the harbour and across the main street. With the truck engine still rumbling and the media helicopter beating above their heads, they tried to take in the scene of carnage that they'd been caught up in. Disbelief and shock rooted them to where they stood. Then the wail of sirens filled the air as the first of the ambulance crews began to arrive. All around people slumped to the ground. It really was over.

Two police officers hauled Evanton to his feet. He spat into the face of one of his captors.

"You're a dead man, Evanton," growled one of the officers with a leer. "You've no idea what's waiting for *you* on the inside."

Two officers and a paramedic hauled Iksan to his feet. The youth dropped his head miserably as he was led away, hopping, in cuffs.

Evanton was marched past the truck cabin towards a waiting police van. As he went by, his eyes briefly met Donna's. PC Aiden

Moore was standing with his arm protectively around her.

She lay still, watching Evanton, and saw the fury and hatred that was packed into his stare. But he wasn't going to have the last unspoken word, she decided.

That was her prerogative.

Controlling her breathing against the pain, Donna lifted a shaky hand, and raised her middle finger at him.

Chapter Sixty-one

Acting Chief Superintendent Angus Ross placed the paperwork on the table before he sat down. The chair scraping on weathered concrete made him wince. All the time, he found it impossible to avoid the eyes. The cold grey eyes held his gaze captive from the moment he stepped into the interview room. Prison garb did nothing to diminish Evanton's ability to control the room. Two prison guards stood behind him, both shifting uneasily from one foot to the other while they watched Ross take his seat.

"Belmarsh far away enough for you?" said Ross, tapping the paperwork with a finger.

A smirk strained at the corner of Evanton's mouth. His features were unblemished, and a hint of a flush to his skin made him look healthy; nothing to show for the previous week's events at Arbroath harbour, and certainly nothing to suggest that solitary confinement was disagreeing with him. Ross had to press a fist into his gut to slow the rising knot there, a movement that didn't go unnoticed by Evanton.

"It's a small price to pay for the information I'm going to give you," said Evanton.

"Oh, don't dress this up as if you're doing us a favour," snapped Ross. "You're a murdering bastard. Two of our own!"

Evanton didn't flinch. The smirk remained firmly in place. "Temper, temper."

Ross took a deep breath, and tore his eyes from Evanton. The interview room was small. No windows, claustrophobic. From all accounts, Evanton would begin to feel uneasy in here. Small spaces freaked him out, Ross had learned. It was always handy to have nuggets like this.

"You could touch both walls in here," he remarked. "And here you are, stuck in a cramped space with all of us. Difference is, we . . . " he indicated the prison guards, "can walk out of here into the sunshine, go for a burger, whatever. You're going to be stuck in a tiny space like this for the rest of your miserable life. It might not be in here, where the cons know you and can't wait to get their own back on you, but you're kidding yourself if you think it's going to be any more luxurious in Belmarsh."

"Shut up."

"Your life is going to be spent locked up in a tiny cell, no windows, no fresh air . . . "

"Shut the fuck up!" Evanton sprang to his feet. The prison guards were on him in an instant, and Ross turned away, studying the door behind him. When he turned back, Evanton was once more in his seat, his hair ruffled, a cut below his eye. The smirk gone.

"You give us the information we want," said Ross, "and we'll offer you a transfer to a prison where you're anonymous. Now, talk. Who is bringing the MIC into the country?"

Evanton spat onto the floor. "You're looking for Abram Kozel."

"Kozel? Do you think I was born yesterday?"

"Kozel is alive and well," said Evanton. "The petrochemical sting in Aberdeen was a front. The whole thing was rigged up by Kozel's men to stage his death, to stop us looking for him."

"So, where do you fit in with Kozel's gang?"

"He knew I kept order at the port."

"Order?"

"I had my own method of policing," said Evanton.

"So I heard," said Ross.

"One that worked," said Evanton, leaning forward and jabbing a finger towards Ross. "You're not dealing with guys who care if they've broken the rules. You've got to show them who's boss. They respected me, and I stopped the gang warfare that would have ruined the city."

"Oh, don't give me the big hero thing," said Ross. "You were a thug and you were on the take. Tell me about Kozel. Where does he fit into all of this?"

Evanton frowned and stared up at the ceiling. "Kozel has a stake in a company called DeeChem in Russia, one of those set-ups that's supposed to make us think free enterprise is encouraged and flourishing there. DeeChem produces various chemicals and Kozel spotted a chance to undercut the competition Russian-style. DeeChem got the contracts – big ones – but unfortunately, they were left with MIC as an undeclared by-product that they needed to dispose of."

"Why didn't they just get rid of it in Russia?" asked Ross. "It's not a third world country. They've got lab facilities."

"They've got paperwork, too."

"So Kozel brought it here to avoid the paper trail in Russia?"

"He relies on a certain amount of *laissez faire* in his operations."

"And he just happened to come across you?" said Ross. "You're telling me it's a complete coincidence that you ended up with the MIC?"

"What are you getting at?"

"I know you were in Bhopal," said Ross. "I've had a long chat with Mo Skinner."

Evanton leaned back in his chair and raised his eyes to the ceiling. "Mo Skinner."

"You travelled together when you were younger?" Ross asked rhetorically. Evanton remained silent, and Ross caught the faraway look in his eyes. "My God, you've still got feelings for her, haven't you?"

"Leave Mo out of this, none of this has anything to do with Bhopal."

"Oh, doesn't it? According to her, you changed after the disaster. Became obsessed by it."

"Look, when I heard what Kozel was shipping, I was interested, I'll admit," said Evanton. "You don't leave behind an experience like Bhopal easily."

"And Hunter?" asked Ross.

"He owed me one," said Evanton. "A big one. So I figured he could pay his debt by making the MIC disappear."

"He had a whole chemistry department at his disposal," said Ross. "Why didn't he neutralise the MIC chemically?"

"Same reason Kozel didn't want it dealt with at a Russian lab," said Evanton. "Anyway, once Hunter took delivery, I wasn't much interested in what he did with it, as long as Kozel paid up."

"But why did Hunter take it to his own quarry?" asked Ross. "I mean, he wasn't a stupid man."

"No," said Evanton, "but he was lazy, and he thought he was above the law. Money does that to some people."

"So we go after Kozel."

Evanton chuckled. "Watch how you do that, Ross. I wasn't the only cop in Kozel's pocket. You might want to keep the details of our little chat off of the email system."

Ross felt his face grow pale.

"But let's see," said Evanton, leaning towards Ross again. "I'd be a dead man if Kozel found out I'd blown his cover. Who knows, once I'm safely tucked up in Belmarsh, maybe we can reach another agreement. Kozel for my freedom under witness protection."

"Oh, for God's sake," Ross spluttered.

"Take it or leave it," said Evanton. "Get me to Belmarsh, and we'll talk further. Until then, I'm saying nothing." He folded his arms.

"The transport's arranged," said Ross. "You'll be heading out tonight."

He couldn't bear to look at Evanton another second longer. He stood up and marched out of the room, barely acknowledging the guards posted outside the door. The prison might not be taking any chances with Evanton, thought Ross, but he couldn't say the same for his own top brass were they to be offered the prospect of Kozel.

Chapter Sixty-two

Donna and Libby arrived early. It was a perfect spring day, bright and cold. The burst of green from new leaves caught Libby's eye, and she found herself scarcely able to contemplate the events of the past two weeks. But something in the change in the air marked, for her, a new beginning, a fresh start, and she smiled back at Donna.

The old church wasn't particularly wheelchair friendly, and Libby hadn't fancied the thought of steering Donna through what was predicted to be quite a crowd. And she'd judged wisely. The media facility at the church entrance was packed and buzzing already, with two media teams already interviewing Bob and Mo Skinner. This was one church service that the whole country wanted to watch. After all, they had followed on their TV sets and twenty-four hours news feeds the terrible events of the evacuation, and now they wanted to weep with those who'd survived the horrors. Because it could have been them. It was all too close to home, wherever in the country they were.

Donna's legs were still badly bruised and the cuts were swathed in thick bandages. Her head was cocooned in a large woolly hat, and she had insisted on being wrapped in a tartan blanket so as to appear to be a *wee old biddy*.

Lindsey Forsyth was busy testing her sound equipment, when she became aware of the tartan blanket beside her.

"Donna!" she said, throwing her arms wide but letting them drop again at the sight of the bandages. "It's so good to see you here."

"You too," said Donna. "You did a great job that day."

Lindsey looked at the floor. "Thank you," she said. "But it was nothing compared to what you did."

Libby wheeled Donna on into the church.

By the time they approached the rear pews, there were some two hundred people seated before them. Libby looked upwards towards the high arched stonework, and saw TV cameras rigged up on the balcony that encircled the church's upper tier. The echoing voices of the technical crew reverberated around the huge building, until the strident first notes sounded from the enormous pipe organ and the church was filled with the comforting, muted keys of vaguely familiar hymns.

"In here?" Libby suggested, pausing beside an empty centre aisle row.

Donna nodded her head, and prepared herself for a shift out of the wheelchair. Two weeks on from her ordeal at Evanton's hands, and her physical injuries were still very much evident. One eye remained encircled in a grey-blue bruise. In her lighter moments, she amused herself by telling starers that it was a tattoo. In her darker ones, she stared into the mirror, wondering if she would ever be the same again. Her right arm was held in a sling, and the two bandaged legs meant she would be reliant on the wheelchair for the next three weeks.

Libby hunched down to let Donna place her good arm over her shoulders, and together they got her onto a seat. Donna had insisted on sitting within the main body of the congregation, rather than at the very front where there was more space for the wheelchair, having had enough of all the attention she'd received during the last fortnight.

Libby could read the discomfort on Donna's face as they moved her onto the pew, but she knew better than to attempt to change her mind about where to sit. No matter what toll it would take on her, Libby realized, Donna was going to attend this memorial service. And she wanted to do it with minimum fuss or recognition.

Two heads from further up the church turned, Natesh and Emma, and flashed smiles at Donna and Libby. Behind Emma's back, Natesh silently mouthed the words, *She's lovely*.

"Guess that's Nancy been dumped," Donna whispered to Libby.

They chatted quietly between themselves while groups and couples and individuals streamed into the church, and the old building filled to what appeared to be beyond capacity. Only the seats reserved for the yet to arrive police officers remained empty. The organ music hardly covered the growing chatter of voices that gave the old building life, and Libby could tell by Donna's sharp observations and witty remarks about the diverse characters around them that it was lifting her spirits to be part of it all, albeit she would never admit that.

The organ held a long note, calling their attention, and then ended its turn with a flourish. Onto the pulpit came the Reverend Norman Quinn to lead this next stage in the healing process for those who had been affected by the events of the past two weeks. He looked small up there, Libby thought. So much smaller than the figure he'd cut throughout her life. Since the day of the evacuation, he had phoned her every evening, and had begun to ask after Donna. It was a start, Libby thought. That new start ushered in by the fresh spring air.

As the congregation quietened down, muted whispers and sniffles of emotion could be heard from all around.

"Welcome to today's memorial service," said Norman Quinn. All eyes in the congregation were on him, and now his smallness had turned into something else. A quiet strength. The arms that were going to carry them all through this next hour. The speaker of the words they would all take comfort from. His calm, reassuring tones guided them through a scripture reading, through a brief prayer of thanks for those who were here today and of support for those who were grieving their loved ones, and then into the first strains of Amazing Grace.

During the hymn, Libby held on tight to Donna's hand. She'd come face to face with the very real possibility of Donna being dead, and there was no disguising how she'd felt the moment she'd seen her lying battered and bruised, but alive, at the hospital. She had no intention of ever letting her go again. And, to her enormous relief, Donna seemed to be learning to become more open about what was going on inside that head of hers. She'd even agreed to have a full discussion with Ross about her bipolar disorder. No doubt about it, there was a long recovery ahead, emotionally and physically. But Libby was going to be there to help with Donna's new journey.

She came out of her brief reverie when she began to see heads turn towards the back door of the church. She strained to see what everyone was looking at, and there, marching three abreast behind the Assistant Chief Constable into the main hall of the church, came a uniformed unit from Tayside Police. At a gesture from the Reverend Quinn, the body of one hundred officers stopped abruptly beside Libby and Donna, and turned to face them. Then each officer raised their right hand to their cap and saluted Donna, before they turned forward again and continued on their march to the front of the church, where they took their seats next to the great and the good who were already there. As the officers settled into position, one of them turned to look back again at Donna. PC Aiden Moore caught her eye, and they nodded solemnly to one another. Then, when the congregation, as one, rose and applauded, Libby could see that Donna's eyes were damp as she held a tissue to her nose.

Four people had died when Evanton's articulated truck drove through the crowd at the harbour that day. Big Davie, who was a visiting supporter to the town and was one of the men who'd tried to rush at the truck when Evanton had pulled on the gas mask, had joined their number at the end of a bullet. The four year old boy at *The Bampot*, Bill Geddes, Gorak, Graeme Hunter, Dom Hilton and Ted Granger had also lost their lives to Evanton's plans. As had another driver when Evanton almost killed Natesh by sabotaging his car. Almost Bob Skinner and almost Chief Superintendent Lawson too. It was little short of a miracle that there hadn't been more.

The Reverend Quinn read out their names slowly, amidst much weeping in the congregation. At the sound of her colleagues' names Donna could hold it in no longer, and she let her tears fall freely, sobbing without shame or embarrassment for the friends she'd lost. Libby squeezed her hand, the only thing she could think of to help Donna without intruding on her thoughts. How she desperately wished she could take away that pain she knew Donna was feeling.

The organ sounded the end of the parting hymn, and the Reverend Quinn said the final prayer, before he stepped slowly to the rear door of the church to greet the congregation as they left in anguished silence.

Libby and Donna waited until the church was almost empty before they got themselves up and went to join the throng outside. As they exited the main door, Sally approached them, accompanied by a tall man.

"Libby, this is my father," she said. "Professor David Chisholm. You two have a lot in common." They were both smiling, and Libby was struck by the close resemblance between them.

Norman Quinn came towards them, his hands opening wide. Without saying anything, he embraced Libby in a hug, then leaned down and encircled Donna with his arms.

He paused, somewhat stuck for words, and his cheeks blushed.

"Burger at *The Bampot*?" Donna offered.

Norman nodded his head, relief evident in his eyes.

The only one not present today at the memorial service was Danny Quinn. He had other things to do. He had received overwhelming support following the revelation of his own ordeal in the wake of the poisoning at his restaurant, and now *The Bampot* was fully booked for the foreseeable future.

Standing in the privacy of the church's vestry, where he'd stolen in to answer his phone right as the service ended, Acting Chief Superintendent Angus Ross clutched at his chest and wheezed.

"Gone?" he said into the phone. "What do you mean, he's gone? Belmarsh is a fucking high security prison . . . "

The End

About the Author
Jackie McLean

Jackie lives in Glasgow and has a varied background, including being a government economist, a political lobbyist, and running a pet shop in Glasgow's Southside (ask her anything about pets). She currently works with East Ayrshire Council, where until recently her job involved frequent visits to Kilmarnock Prison.

Her first novel *Toxic* introduced DI Donna Davenport, and was shortlisted in the Yeovil Literary Prize. The sequel, *Shadows*, was published in October 2017. Run is the third in this series.

Jackie has appeared at crime writing festivals Newcastle Noir, Crime at the Castle and Literally @ Newbattle, and regularly appears at Noir at the Bar events (including Edinburgh, Newcastle, Dundee and Dunfermline). She also forms part of the Dangerous Dames and Murder & Mayhem along with a number of other crime writers, and has appeared at events in libraries and bookstores across Scotland as part of these. She is also a Bloody Sotland 2019 Crime in the Spotlight author.

Jackie has run the writing group at Waterstones Braehead, and has also run creative writing sessions with the men in Kilmarnock Prison.

Jackie can be found online at:
https://jackiemcleanauthor.com
Twitter : @JackieJamxx
Facebook: www.facebook.com/WriterJackie/

Also from ThunderPoint
Shadows
Jackie McLean

ISBN: 978-1-910946-29-9 (Kindle)
ISBN: 978-1-910946-28-2 (Paperback)

When DI Donna Davenport is called out to investigate a body washed up on Arbroath beach, it looks like a routine murder inquiry. But then the enquiry takes on a more sinister form.

There are similarities with a previous murder, and now a woman connected to them both has also gone missing. For Donna, this is becoming personal, and with the added pressure of feeling watched at every turn, she is convinced that Jonas Evanton has returned to seek his revenge on her for his downfall.

Fearing they may be looking for a serial killer, Donna and her new team are taken in a horrifying and unexpected direction. Because it's not a serial killer - it's worse.

Moving from Dundee to the south coast of Turkey and the Syrian border, this is a fast paced novel about those who live their lives in the shadows, and those who exploit them.

"With sensitivity and honesty, Jackie has written a thriller that will shock and grip the reader in equal measure."

Run
Jackie McLean

ISBN: 978-1-910946-64-0 (Paperback)
ISBN: 978-1-910946-65-7 (Kindle)

RUN THE GAUNTLET

DI Donna Davenport and her team are under pressure.

With the hunt on for the country's most notorious cop killer, and an ongoing complex international investigation, the murder of a local thug during a football match is the last thing the police need.

But as more incidents overload the police, and fear brings vigilante mobs onto the streets, suspicion grows that the mayhem is being orchestrated.

CUT AND RUN

One man can make it stop. With the city heading towards chaos and disaster Donna prepares to abandon caution and the rules, even if it means she is ostracised by her own team.

The Peat Dead
Allan Martin

Shortlisted for the 2019 Bloody Scotland McIlvanney Debut Scottish Crime Prize.

ISBN: 978-1-910946-55-8 (Kindle)
ISBN: 978-1-910946-54-1 (Paperback)

On the Scottish Hebridean Island of Islay, five corpses are dug up by a peat-cutter. All of them have been shot in the back of the head, execution style.

Sent across from the mainland to investigate, Inspector Angus Blue and his team slowly piece together the little evidence they have, and discover the men were killed on a wartime base, over 70 years ago.

But there are still secrets worth protecting, and even killing for. Who can Inspector Blue trust?

"A mystery so redolent of its island setting that you practically smell the peat and whisky on the pages." – Douglas Skelton"

This atmospheric crime novel set on Islay gripped me from the start. A book that shows decades-old crimes cast long shadows." – Sarah Ward

In The Shadow Of The Hill
Helen Forbes

ISBN: 978-0-9929768-1-1 (eBook)
ISBN: 978-0-9929768-0-4 (Paperback)

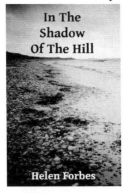

An elderly woman is found battered to death in the common stairwell of an Inverness block of flats.

Detective Sergeant Joe Galbraith starts what seems like one more depressing investigation of the untimely death of a poor unfortunate who was in the wrong place, at the wrong time.

As the investigation spreads across Scotland it reaches into a past that Joe has tried to forget, and takes him back to the Hebridean island of Harris, where he spent his childhood.

Among the mountains and the stunning landscape of religiously conservative Harris, in the shadow of Ceapabhal, long buried events and a tragic story are slowly uncovered, and the investigation takes on an altogether more sinister aspect.

In The Shadow Of The Hill skilfully captures the intricacies and malevolence of the underbelly of Highland and Island life, bringing tragedy and vengeance to the magical beauty of the Outer Hebrides.

'…our first real home-grown sample of modern Highland noir' – Roger Hutchinson; West Highland Free Press

Madness Lies
Helen Forbes

ISBN: 9781910946312 (Kindle)
ISBN: 9781910946305 (Paperback)

When an Inverness Councillor is murdered in broad daylight in the middle of town, Detective Sergeant Joe Galbraith sees a familiar figure running from the scene.

According to everyone who knows him, the Councillor had no enemies, but someone clearly wanted him dead.

The victim's high profile means the police want a quick resolution to the case, but no one seems to know anything. Or if they do, they're not prepared to say.

This second novel of Highland Noir from Helen Forbes continues the series with a crime thriller that moves between Inverness, North Uist and London, reaching a terrifying denouement at the notorious Black Rock Gorge.

"You would expect Helen Forbes to write well of an exile's experience of Sollas, Vallay and west side of North Uist, and she does. She evokes the machair, the changing sky and sea, the flowers, birds and waving grass, the dunes, the people and above all the peace." – Roger Hutchinson, West Highland Free Press

The Deaths on the Black Rock
BRM Stewart

ISBN: 978-1-910946-47-3 (Kindle)
ISBN: 978-1-910946-46-6 (Paperback)

It's been a year since Rima Khalaf died in a fall from the Black Rock, deemed to be a tragic accident by the police.

But her grieving parents are dissatisfied with the police in-vestigation, so DS Amanda Pitt is sent north from Glasgow to the small town of Clachdubh to re-examine the case.

Despite the suspicions of the distraught parents, all the cir-cumstances seem to confirm Rima's death was indeed a tragic accident, until another woman is also found dead in the town.

Frustrated by the lack of any real evidence, DS Pitt pushes the limits of legality in her quest for the truth.

Stewart writes with a gritty intensity that places the reader in intimate contact with the darker side of society, in a way that forces you to empathise with the uncomfortable idea that sometimes the end justifies the means for those who are supposed to uphold the law.

The False Men
Mhairead MacLeod

ISBN: 978-1-910946-27-5 (eBook)
ISBN: 978-1-910946-25-1 (Paperback)

North Uist, Outer Hebrides, 1848.

Jess MacKay has led a privileged life as the daughter of a local landowner, sheltered from the harsher aspects of life. Courted by the eligible Patrick Cooper, the Laird's new commissioner, Jess's future is mapped out, until Lachlan Macdonald arrives on North Uist, amid rumours of forced evictions on islands just to the south.

As the uncompromising brutality of the Clearances reaches the islands, and Jess sees her friends ripped from their homes, she must decide where her heart, and her loyalties, truly lie.

Set against the evocative backdrop of the Hebrides and inspired by a true story, *The False Men* is a compelling tale of love in a turbulent past that resonates with the upheavals of the modern world.

'...an engaging tale of powerlessness, love and disillusionment in the context of the type of injustice that, sadly, continues to this day' – Anne Goodwin

Dead Cat Bounce
Kevin Scott

ISBN: 978-1-910946-17-6 (eBook)
ISBN: 978-1-910946-15-2 (Paperback)

"Well, either way, you'll have to speak to your brother today because...unless I get my money by tomorrow morning there's not going to be a funeral."

When your 11 year old brother has been tragically killed in a car accident, you might think that organising his funeral would take priority. But when Nicky's coffin, complete with Nicky's body, goes missing, deadbeat loser Matt has only 26 hours in which to find the £20,000 he owes a Glasgow gangster or explain to his grieving mother why there's not going to be a funeral.

Enter middle brother, Pete, successful City trader with an expensive wife, expensive children, and an expensive villa in Tuscany. Pete's watches cost £20,000, but he has his own problems, and Matt doesn't want his help anyway.

Seething with old resentments, the betrayals of the past and the double-dealings of the present, the two brothers must find a way to work together to retrieve Nicky's body, discovering along the way that they are not so different after all.

'Underplaying the comic potential to highlight the troubled relationship between the equally flawed brothers. It's one of those books that keep the reader hooked right to the end' – The Herald

277

The Wrong Box
Andrew C Ferguson

ISBN: 978-1-910946-14-5 (Paperback)
ISBN: 978-1-910946-16-9 (eBook)

All I know is, I'm in exile in Scotland, and there's a dead Scouser businessman in my bath. With his toe up the tap.

Meet Simon English, corporate lawyer, heavy drinker and Scotophobe, banished from London after being caught misbehaving with one of the young associates on the corporate desk. As if that wasn't bad enough, English finds himself acting for a spiralling money laundering racket that could put not just his career, but his life, on the line.

Enter Karen Clamp, an 18 stone, well-read wann be couturier from the Auchendrossan sink estate, with an encyclopedic knowledge of Council misdeeds and 19th century Scottish fiction. With no one to trust but each other, this mismatched pair must work together to investigate a series of apparently unrelated frauds and discover how everything connects to the mysterious Wrong Box.

Manically funny, *The Wrong Box* is a chaotic story of lust, money, power and greed, and the importance of being able to sew a really good hem.

'...the makings of a new Caledonian Comic Noir genre:
Rebus with jokes, Val McDiarmid with buddha belly laughs,
or Trainspotting for the professional classes'

The Bogeyman Chronicles
Craig Watson

ISBN: 978-1-910946-11-4 (eBook)
ISBN: 978-1-910946-10-7 (Paperback)

In 14th Century Scotland, amidst the wars of independence, hatred, murder and betrayal are commonplace. People are driven to extraordinary lengths to survive, whilst those with power exercise it with cruel pleasure.

Royal Prince Alexander Stewart, son of King Robert II and plagued by rumours of his illegitimacy, becomes infamous as the Wolf of Badenoch, while young Andrew Christie commits an unforgivable sin and lay Brother Brodie Affleck in the Restenneth Priory pieces together the mystery that links them all together.

From the horror of the times and the changing fortunes of the characters, the legend of the Bogeyman is born and Craig Watson cleverly weaves together the disparate lives of the characters into a compelling historical mystery that will keep you gripped throughout.

Over 80 years the lives of three men are inextricably entwined, and through their hatreds, murders and betrayals the legend of Christie Cleek, the bogeyman, is born.

'The Bogeyman Chronicles haunted our imagination long after we finished it' – iScot Magazine

The Birds That Never Flew
Margot McCuaig
Shortlisted Dundee International Book Prize 2012
Longlisted Polari First Book Prize 2014
ISBN: 978-0-9929768-5-9 (eBook)
ISBN: 978-0-9929768-4-2 (Paperback)

'Have you got a light hen? I'm totally gaspin.'

Battered and bruised, Elizabeth has taken her daughter and left her abusive husband Patrick. Again. In the bleak and impersonal Glasgow housing office Elizabeth meets the provocatively intriguing drug addict Sadie, who is desperate to get her own life back on track.

The two women forge a fierce and interdependent relationship as they try to rebuild their shattered lives, but despite their bold, and sometimes illegal attempts it seems impossible to escape from the abuse they have always known, and tragedy strikes.

More than a decade later Elizabeth has started to implement her perfect revenge – until a surreal Glaswegian Virgin Mary steps in with imperfect timing and a less than divine attitude to stick a spoke in the wheel of retribution.

Tragic, darkly funny and irreverent, *The Birds That Never Flew* ushers in a new and vibrant voice in Scottish literature.

'…dark, beautiful and moving, I wholeheartedly
recommend' scanoir.co.uk

Printed by Amazon Italia Logistica S.r.l.
Torrazza Piemonte (TO), Italy

10948121R00167